GLENWOOD SPRINGS

DENVER CEREAL, VOLUME NINETEEN

GLENWOOD SPRINGS

DENVER CEREAL, VOLUME NINETEEN

Claudia Hall Christian

Cook Street Publishing
Denver, CO

PUBLISHER'S NOTE:
This is a work of fiction. Names, characters, places and incidents either are
either the product of the author's imagination or are used fictitiously.

First edition © May 2019
Cook Street Publishing
ISNI: 0000 0004 1443 6403
PO Box 7247
Denver, CO 80207

WHAT'S HAPPENED SO FAR

Denver Cereal is an addicting, fun, sweet and crunchy serial fiction filled with the tension, drama, and love of urban life.

The best way to catch up is to read *Grand Junction, Denver Cereal* Volume 1-10 and *Fort Garland, Denver Cereal* V11-13. They are very affordable and available wherever eBooks are sold. You can also read *Denver Cereal* online at StoriesbyClaudia.com.

We used to write a section here that gave a synopsis of all of the previous books. Frankly, the synopsis' wasn't very good. More than anything, they deprived you of the chance to hang out in Denver Cereal for a while. We were only be spoiling your fun

You deserve a chance to read all the crazy twists and turns, mischief, and wild adventures of Denver Cereal. These aren't books to be accomplished or checked off a list. They are stories to be savored and enjoys.

Get to it.

We'll be here when you get back.

~~~~~~~~~~~~

Denver Cereal is provided free online due to the generous support of our patrons and you, the book buyer. This book was created because of your support.

THANK YOU TO YOU, AND ALL OF OUR PATRONS.

CHAPTER 516

IN LEADVILLE

Turning off the highway, Jacob glanced at Blane.

"So . . ." Jacob said.

"So?" Blane asked.

"Dr. Nelson Weeks?" Jacob asked.

Blane groaned. His eyes flicked to the back seat.

"You really think this is the time?" Blane asked.

"They're asleep," Jacob said.

Blane turned around to see that everyone else in the car was asleep. Ares had his head resting on his son's shoulder, and Perses had rested his head against the window. Katy and Paddie were sound asleep in the far back.

"So . . ." Jacob said.

"Oh, I don't know," Blane said.

Blane crossed his arms and lowered his head into the collar of his shirt. Jacob laughed. Blane scowled at Jacob.

"Oh, come on," Jacob said.

"He is nice," Blane said with a sigh. "He's incredibly kind. The kids love him."

"He's very hot," Jacob said.

Blane grunted.

"And?" Jacob asked.

"He listens to what I say and remembers it," Blane said. "I came home one day, and he was talking to Heather in the Castle kitchen. He didn't know I was there. He was respectful to her. He wasn't afraid of her in any way, not even a little. When I came in, he smiled when I said 'Hello' to Heather first."

"Didn't bother him," Jacob said.

"Not in the least," Blane said.

Jacob let the silence lag. When it seemed like Blane wasn't going to add anything, Jacob asked, "Are you attracted to him?"

Blane nodded. Embarrassed, Blane tucked his hands into his armpits and lowered his head. Jacob smiled at him.

"He's attracted to you?" Jacob asked.

Blane nodded. Jacob gave a slight nod to his response. Seeing Jacob's nod, Blane blushed even darker.

"You may as well tell me," Jacob said. "We're bringing this lot back to the Castle. Aden's going to want to know the details."

Blane groaned and looked up at the ceiling of the vehicle. Jacob laughed.

"You're not going to let this go, are you?" Blane asked.

"Would you?" Jacob asked.

Blane gave him a long look.

"My bestfriend and cousin might actually have found someone to love who will love him back and . . ." Jacob started.

"No one said anything about love," Blane said quickly, cutting Jacob off.

Jacob laughed so loudly that the Olympians awoke. Paddie and Katy roused.

"See what you've done?" Blane asked between clenched teeth.

"What is going on?" Asclepius asked.

"We are almost to the cemetery," Jacob said, still bright from his laughter. "We have maybe ten more minutes."

"No, I meant between you boys," Asclepius said. "What is funny? Do tell, so we can all laugh. You know, laughter is the best medicine."

"My *cousin* might be in love," Jacob said.

"Jacob!" Blane said.

"He has found a man to love who will love him in return?" Asclepius asked. "How wonderful!"

"That's not a problem for you?" Blane asked.

"Don't be absurd," Asclepius said. "One can only be what one is made to be."

"What does that mean?" Blane asked, his scowl in his voice.

"Some people are interested in everyone," Asclepius's eyes flicked to his father.

"He's talking about me," Ares said.

"Some people are interested only in the opposite gender," Asclepius said. "So far, that has been me. Perses?"

"I've loved only two females in my long life," Perses said. "I am the God of Destruction, not the God of Love."

Jacob glanced at Blane, and they both nodded.

"Only females?" The God of War asked.

"Only females," Perses said with a nod. "Why are we talking about this?"

"Young Blane here thought we might have some issue with his interest in men," Ares said.

"Why?" Perses asked.

"It's not considered 'normal,'" Blane said, angrily.

The Greek gods and Titan laughed loudly.

"That's the dumbest thing I've ever heard," Asclepius said.

"In my day," Ares piped up to say, "every once in a while, men who like men were forced to bed women to make heirs. A few complained about it, but truthfully, it wasn't a big deal. Often children were made by servants or other siblings. The point was to have the child. As long as they looked close enough to the parents, no one bothered to think about it. I have heard that *sci-ence . . .*" he emphasized the word, " . . . has made it so male unions can raise children."

"It is brilliant," Perses said.

"That's right," Ares said. "It was you who told me that."

"Your grandson," Perses said.

"His grandson?" Blane asked.

"You don't know?" Jacob asked.

"Know what?" Blane shook his head.

"Meet your grandfather-in-law," Jacob said.

"You're the lad married to my Hedone?" Ares asked. "I knew I liked you."

"Even if I like men?" Blane asked.

"Hedone has children," Ares shrugged.

"She's had my sons," Blane said.

"Yes, that's right," Ares said. "That is the science that Perses was telling me about."

Blane turned around to look at the god. Ares nodded. When Blane's eyes flicked to Perses, the Titan shrugged.

"Why would we care?" Asclepius asked.

Blane looked at the God for a moment and then turned back to Jacob. They heard Perses tell Asclepius about the trouble gays, lesbians, and others have. For a moment, the gods digested this information. They fell silent.

"That's the dumbest thing I've ever heard," Asclepius repeated.

They laughed.

"Have you had carnal relations with this lad?" Asclepius asked.

"Not yet," Blane spit out.

"Why not?" Perses and Asclepius asked in near unison.

"My point exactly," Jacob said.

They laughed again. Jacob looked at Katy and Paddie through the rearview mirror. By some miracle, the children were still sound asleep. After a moment, Ares leaned forward.

"I had this wonderful affair with a man," Ares said.

For the rest of their ride to the cemetery, Ares regaled them with stories from his romance with a strapping warrior. Jacob was just parking the car when Ares finished his story. Jacob looked at Blane, and Blane just shook his head.

"See?" Jacob grinned.

"Shut up," Blane said.

Jacob laughed. They helped Asclepius, Ares, and Perses out of the SUV. They woke up Katy and Paddie. Each of them took a child as they got out of the SUV. Carrying a sleepy Paddie, Jacob gestured toward where he knew the vent to the Fire of Hell was located. The group started walking. Wide awake, Katy peppered Blane with questions.

"What do you think about having new brothers?" Katy asked brightly.

"Okay, I guess," Blane said. "I don't think it has anything to do with me."

"I *like* having brothers," Katy said, as if that was the point of her asking the question. "I *know* you will, too."

Katy kissed Blane's cheek and he set her down.

"Hold onto Blane's hand, Katy," Jacob said. "We don't know what we're dealing with here."

"Everything is okay, Daddy," Katy said. "I promise."

Jacob stopped walking.

"You'll hold Blane's hand anyway," Jacob said.

"Of course," Katy said.

Katy shot him an "I'm a good girl" grin. Jacob gave a rueful shake of his head and began walking again. Blane grabbed onto Katy's hand.

"I'm not a baby," Katy said under her breath when her father was out of hearing range.

"I know you're not a baby," Jacob yelled back to her.

Katy stopped and put her hands on her hips.

"He just wants to make sure you're safe," Blane said.

"But I . . ." Katy said.

"He was nearly killed," Blane said. "At this exact spot, due to an issue that's not resolved. Is it so unreasonable for him to be a little over-careful?"

Katy looked up into her Uncle Blane's face. Seeing his kind sincerity, she nodded in agreement. She held out her hand. As quickly as it had come up, her irritation had passed. They skipped until they caught up with Jacob, just as he was putting Paddie down.

Looking up, Jacob stopped walking. His hand went to his chest. He bent over, trying to catch his breath. Blane let go of Katy and went to Jacob.

"What is it?" Asclepius asked. "What has happened?"

The God of Medicine went to Jacob.

"I'm okay," Jacob said. "I'm okay. I just . . ."

"Panic," Asclepius said. "It's understandable."

"I didn't think that I'd . . ." Jacob said.

"You almost died, son," Ares said. "Not many know what that's like."

Ares and Perses looked at Jacob with understanding and knowing. Jacob gave them a quick nod.

"I'll hold your hand, Daddy," Katy said.

Jacob looked down at this girl, his daughter. She was outrageously brave. She gave her a soft smile and held out his hand.

"Jake?" Sam Lipson's voice came from behind monuments a few feet from them. "I think I just saw Jake!"

Jacob, Blane, Ares, Asclepius, and Perses, with Katy and Paddie, continued forward to the vent for the Fire of Hell. Now on their feet, it was clear that Delphie, Maresol, the three boys who might be Blane's brothers, and Sam had sat around this vent for the last few days.

A well of emotion rose in Jacob. These humans had sat here the entire time he and Abi had fought the soul stealer and when he'd rescued Ember, the fourth fairy queen. They'd believed in him throughout the entire thing. He wanted to weep and laugh at the same time.

His father grabbed his shoulder and pulled him into him. Jacob tried to come up with words, but nothing came. He held his father tight. Sam patted Jacob's back before letting him go.

"Let me take a look at you," Sam said.

Jacob stood before his father. Sam looked at his son as if he were seeing him for the first time.

"You're a little taller," Sam said, shrugging. "Otherwise, well done, Asclepius."

Asclepius blushed and was appropriately humble as he edged his way toward Delphie. When Jacob looked up, there was a great deal of general chaos. The youngest of the three young men had jumped into Blane's arms while the other brothers were loudly welcoming Blane. Ares was laughing at the boys' exuberance while Perses was suspiciously looking around the cemetery.

Through it all, Maresol sat meditating. Her head was shaking back and forth. Jacob went to Maresol's side.

"What is it?" Jacob asked.

"They are coming out," Maresol said.

Everyone stopped moving. Perses took two quick steps to Maresol's side.

"Who?" Perses asked, grabbing her shoulder to support her.

"The fairies and Abi," Maresol said.

Maresol pointed to the vent hole for the Fire of Hell. The group became very silent. Blane set down the youngest brother. They turned en masse to look at the vent hole in the middle of the circle. As they watched, the ground began to vibrate. Dirt and rocks began to slide into the vent hole.

"Move back!" Ares yelled.

Jacob lifted Maresol to her feet. Their eyes on the hole, everyone jogged back a few feet. They fell silent. The air filled with the sounds of nature — the wind in the trees, and birds chirping, in addition to — the tinny sound of the dirt slipping through the hole and landing on the rock below. They watched with equal doses of excitement and horror.

Abi's head slowly appeared as she rose out of the vent. Her shoulders and her waist were above the dirt when Asclepius and Perses dropped to their knees.

Ares, the God of War, squealed with delight. He did a fast pass at kneeling and then ran to Abi.

"Mother!" Ares said.

He twirled Abi around and then crushed her in a tight hug. His sheer delight was infectious. Perses and Asclepius rose to standing and went to say hello. Ares set Abi down and turned to see that they were looking at him.

"You told me about some 'Abi,'" Ares said. "I didn't realize that you meant the mother of us all! Where is . . .?"

He said an unpronounceable name.

"He was just at my house," Ares said.

"They know him by Gilfand," Abi said, breaking off from saying hello to Asclepius and Perses. "He went to work out a few things out while I am here."

Abi grinned at Jacob. "You look well."

Jacob felt the urge to drop to his knees, as well. Abi held out her arm and hugged him tight. She kissed Jacob's cheek.

"Sam!" Abi said. Sam and Abi hugged.

"You did some great work, Abi . . . mother, uh," Sam said.

"Just Abi," she corrected. "It was Jacob who did the hard work. Without him, and all of you, we would have been lost."

Abi looked around until she saw Maresol. She walked to Maresol. Before Maresol could say anything, Abi kissed the woman and hugged her tight.

"Thank you," Abi said. "I could feel your humanity. Your dedication truly helped."

Abi and Delphie hugged. They whispered something back and forth before they separated.

"Now, introduce me," Abi said to Jacob.

"Where are the fairy queens?" Jacob asked, wincing as if he was expecting to be hit.

"I sent them somewhere to reconnect," Abi said. "We won't see them for a while."

Abi laughed at the looks of relief on everyone's faces.

"Don't look too relieved," Abi said. "We will need to reorient the entire fairy world before they get back. There's bound to be some pushback by people who'd rather the fairies were four warring tribes."

"But you will," Delphie said, with a nod. "You will."

"Introduce me to these lovely young men," Abi said. She put her arm over Blane's shoulders and said, "Blane?"

"I don't know their names," Blane said. "Jake told me that we share a biological parent."

Abi nodded to the young men.

"Heather said that you found them?" Blane asked.

"I did," Abi said. "But I don't know their names, either."

"I'm Gregg," the eldest brother said. "Two 'g's if you're spelling it."

Gregg pushed the middle brother forward.

"Gary," the middle brother said. He gestured to his younger brother. "This is George."

"Lipson?" Blane asked.

The boys shook their heads. With their shake of head, Blane noticed that they looked quite a bit like Jacob. Their skin was darker, but closer to what Blane looked like when he had been in the sun. Their eyes were darker, but the youngest eyes were hazel. In fact, they looked quite a bit like what his son, Wyn, would look like when he grows up. Any of these boys could pass as his sons.

"We have our mom's name," Gregg said with a nod. "Luciano."

The boys nodded.

"How . . .?" Blane gestured to himself and the boys.

"Mom used a sperm donor," Gregg said.

"She just knew who it was," Gary added.

"Oh," Blane said. "Why would she . . .?"

"She doesn't like men," Gary said. "Plus, she interned at Cañon City when your dad was there."

Blane raised his eyebrows and then scowled. Blane had always been ashamed about his criminal father. Why would this woman choose to have his father's sons?

"Why . . .?" Blane started.

Sam came up behind him. He looked at Blane.

"Did you meet each other?" Sam asked.

"Gregg," Blane said, pointing to the eldest and then his brothers. "Gary and George."

"Nice to meet you," Sam shook each of their hands in turn. "I'm Sam Lipson."

The boys looked at each other and grinned.

"Gregg looked up the name 'Lipson,' and you came up," George said.

"We figured that we were from pretty good stock if you were our dad," Gregg said.

"As long as you don't drink," Sam said with a laugh.

The boys shook their head.

"We are really against that stuff," Gregg said. "Pot too. We know that we have a genetic tendency toward, it so we're careful."

The boys nodded.

"I'll tell you what," Sam said. "When we're done here, I'll show you around where I grew up."

"I haven't had that tour," Jacob said with a laugh.

"We'll all go," Blane said.

Sam nodded at Blane. They stood around smiling at each other for a moment.

"What's happening there?" the youngest brother, George, asked, pointing to Delphie and Asclepius.

The God of Medicine was weeping into his hands, while Delphie was comforting him by patting his shoulder.

Scowling, Jacob looked around. Perses was still watching their perimeter. Abi was standing next to his father, Sam. Ares was looking inside the hole that had been the vent to the Fire of Hell. Maresol was talking to Katy and Paddie.

Something was going on. Jacob looked at Abi.

"I am aware," Abi said to Jacob.

She turned and walked to Paddie. Abi put her hand on Paddie's shoulder and bent over to speak into his face. The boy's head bounced in a nod. Paddie turned toward the group. Katy moved to his side.

With a learned flourish, Paddie took out the Sword of Truth.

Katy dropped back into a fighting stance. Paddie set the tip of the sword into the earth. He held the sword perpendicular to the ground. He held his other hand next to the blade and looked at Abi.

Abi gave a slight nod and put a hand on Paddie's shoulder as well as one on Katy's shoulder.

Paddie ran his thumb and index finger along the steel blade. The sword made a slight humming sound, which grew in pitch. The humans' hands grabbed at their ears. They bent over in pain. The Greek gods were knocked off their feet. Delphie's eyes went to the sky while her hands covered her ears. Only Perses, Abi, and the children she was touching did not react.

"Wait for it," Perses yelled.

Paddie stroked the blade again, causing every human to groan.

"Wait for it," Perses yelled over the sound.

"One more time," Abi yelled to Paddie.

Nodding, Paddie stroked the blade one last time. The dark clouds appeared in the sunny sky. The wind picked up the dust of the cemetery. Soon they were belted by tiny rocks. Lightning began to crackle from cloud to cloud.

"It's Thor!" George yelled. "Thor's coming!"

"No, son," Ares, the God of War, yelled. "This is something evil."

There was a loud clap of thunder, and Ares' clothes transformed into his war clothing. He was wearing a tight metal armor and a metal helmet. His hand held a sword of power.

"He's coming," Abi said in a soft voice.

"Get down!" Jacob yelled and dropped to his belly. The humans followed his actions. "Cover your heads!"

Perses pulled out a broad sword. The air crackled as he unveiled another sword of power. Perses slapped his free hand against the hilt of its blade, and it began to vibrate. Perses' sword joined the hum of the Sword of Truth.

A monster-sized human form appeared. Delphie screamed in horror. Noting her horror, Asclepius pushed her behind him as he rose to his feet.

The man who'd won Delphie in a card game when she was a child. The man who'd held her hostage, raped, and beaten her, used her to make money until Delphie was rescued by Celia Marlowe and her father. The man whose returned had triggered Delphie's stroke. The man who'd died through Jill's efficient use of a hockey stick.

Levi Johannsen had returned.

CHAPTER 517

THE FINAL END OF LEVI JOHANNSEN

He was enormous in size. His menacing form towered over them. Perses and Ares ran toward the creature while Sam screamed for the humans to stay down.

As if to smash a bug, Levi's hand moved toward Blane and his new found brothers.

"Enough!" Abi screamed.

The wind stopped blowing.

The clouds stopped swirling overhead.

The earth became eerily still. No bird dared to sing.

Perses and Ares spun around to look at Abi.

Abi pointed to this incarnation of Levi Johannsen.

"Cover your faces!" Perses yelled. "Do it now!"

"All the way on the ground!" Ares screamed.

Jacob grabbed Katy and Paddie and pushed them to the ground under him. Asclepius pushed Delphie onto her stomach. Blane moved to his belly, and his new brothers followed his lead. Sam pulled Maresol down.

The world was eerily quiet. The humans were on the ground. Abi, Ares, Asclepius, and Perses remained standing.

Levi Johanssen sniggered at Abi.

"You dare to get in my way?" Levi asked.

"Shit!" Ares said. He dropped to his knee. He pointed to his son, "Drop!"

Asclepius dropped to his knee.

"Cover your eyes, son," Ares said.

"Be still!" Abi said in a soft voice.

Her finger twitched, and the creature no longer had a mouth.

"I'm tired," Abi said in such a soft voice that it was as if she were speaking to herself. "I'm bone weary. I want to see my children and rest my head on my beloved's chest. I can smell my favorite cookies! They are being baked — right this moment — just for me! By my friend, Sandy. I want a bath and a long drink of cool, clean water."

Abi sighed.

"But instead, I'm dealing with you," Abi said.

Her voice echoed with her exhaustion. She held out her hand toward Jacob.

"Jacob," Abi said. "I need you to hold me down."

"It's the only way to ensure the humans remain intact." In the silence, Asclepius's soft voice carried to Jacob.

Jacob jumped to his feet. He grabbed Abi's hand.

Abi raised her free hand to shoulder height. She cupped her hand and then flattened it quickly. This incarnation of Levi Johanssen blew to pieces with a soft "*pfft*" of an explosion. The carnage would have blown over them, but Perses held his sword over his head. The Titan held tight to the sword's hilt with both hands. The sword emanated a powerful force field that shielded them from the blast.

Still, the force of the blast made Perses stumble back. The air filled with the sound of pieces of flesh pinging off the force field. The pieces of the creature exploded with little "*pops*." The pinging and popping continued until the entire being was nothing more than a cloud of dust.

Abi turned her hand so that her palm faced down.

The dust dropped to the ground.

All that remained of Levi Johannsen was a grey, transparent wisp of smoke that hung over the destruction of his remains.

"Delphie," Abi said. She nodded to Maresol. "Let her up."

Asclepius hopped to his feet. He went to help Delphie up. The God of Medicine and Delphie walked to where Abi stood.

After she spoke, Abi clutched onto Jacob's shoulders.

"Say what you need," Abi said to Delphie, from Jacob's arms. "Where I am sending him, you will never see him again — not in this lifetime, not ever. It's more likely that the sun will burn out long before his soul can reunite."

Delphie nodded that she understood.

She walked to where Perses stood with his sword overhead. She touched Perses arm, and he lowered his sword.

"Paddie?" Abi said. "We need the sword to ensure that he can make no incantations."

"Stay down," Ares commanded the child.

Ares grabbed the Sword of Truth. Ares anchored the tip into the ground and held onto the hilt. Paddie stroked the blade until it hummed.

"Go ahead," Abi said.

Delphie's mind flooded with all the ways that Levi Johannsen had hurt her. She remembered what it was like to be his slave. She remembered Celia's father as he died fighting Levi Johanssen. She wanted to scream in rage at him. She wanted to go through each and every incident where he'd injured her. She wanted to express what it was like to grow up as his slave. She thought of how he'd returned, and she'd nearly died. At the edge of their group, near a tree, was her best friend Celia Marlowe's ghost.

Celia Marlowe, her best friend, was there for the sole purpose of supporting Delphie.

Just like her friend had always been there.

At this moment, Delphie only felt one thing.

Delphie nodded to the ghost of Celia Marlowe, and Celia smiled.

Delphie turned to the soul of Levi Johannsen.

"I am over you," Delphie said. "It's not up to me to forgive you. It's up to me to get over you. And, I assure you, I *am* over you."

Delphie took a breath.

"I don't feel sorry for you," Delphie said. "I'm not angry with you. I'm not even angry with me about you. It's very simply *done*."

Delphie nodded her thanks to Abi. Turning, she walked back to where Sam was lying. Delphie dropped to her knees, and Sam pulled her down.

Abi let go of Jacob. She gave him a soft smile.

"I will need you to hold me down," Abi said. "I'm too exhausted to do this and protect the humans."

Rather than speak, Jacob simply nodded. Jacob grabbed hold of her shoulder so that Abi could put her hands out in front of her.

Abi made a fist with both hands. She held them out in front of her, in the direction of Levi Johannsen's spirit.

"Be gone," Abi said in a soft, barely audible voice.

She wrenched her fists apart. The soul of Levi Johannsen blew into pieces. Tiny pieces of energy flew out from where he'd been. As with his physical form, the tiniest pieces disintegrated until there were only atoms of what had been his spirit.

Abi held up her hand. A breeze of the world gathered up the bits of soul and flesh. There was a light swirl as dust, leaves, and pieces of grass joined the detritus of this once-man. The swirl rose high over their heads. When it was almost out of sight, there was a *pop!* The bits of soul, flesh, dirt, and dust were scattered to the winds of the world.

The only sound that remained was the vibration of the Sword of Truth.

"Paddie," Abi said.

Paddie put his finger on the blade to stop it from vibrating.

"You can let go," Abi said in a soft voice to Jacob.

He let go, but no one dared to move. Abi sighed.

"Let's go home," Abi said.

With her words, the humans began to cheer. Blane's new brothers hooted with exuberance. The gods helped the humans to their feet and dusted off their clothing.

Fin appeared by Abi's side. She grinned at him.

"I take it you've saved the world," Fin said, with an artificially bored tone. "Again."

Abi laughed.

"Did you kill our children as you were asked to?" Abi asked.

"I couldn't do it." Fin shook his head. "I simply couldn't. I didn't try to kill you either."

"I am not going to thank you for that," Abi said.

Fin grabbed Abi and held her tight. Abi shrugged him off.

"Why are you here?" Abi asked in pretend irritation, continuing the game they'd always played.

"Sandy is making cookies, and she will not give me any," Fin said, in an exaggerated whine. "They are the cookies that you used to make when I was a child. She said that you had given her the recipe. She had to convert it to modern ingredients. And I helped her do it! But she . . ."

Abi leaned her head back and laughed. Fin gave her a soft, love-filled smile. He grabbed her tight, and they disappeared.

"I think that's our cue," Sam said. "Anyone who wants to see Leadville with me, I'll take a car."

Blane and his newfound brothers started in Sam's direction.

"Delphie?" Sam asked. He held out his hand for her. "Would you like to help with the tour?"

"You know what?" Delphie grinned and dusted off her skirt. "I'd like that very much."

"I'll pack up the house," Jacob said with a nod.

Sam nodded to him.

"I'll go with you, Jacob," Maresol said. "I have O'Malley's truck. We'll fit."

Jacob nodded. He picked up Katy and held a hand out for Paddie. The boy put away his sword and took Jacob's hand. They started off toward the house leaving the Gods and Titan to figure out what was next for themselves.

"Daddy?" Katy asked.

"Yes?" Jacob looked down at the girl in his arms.

"I think I want to be Abi when I grow up," Katy said.

"Me, too," Jacob said.

Maresol nodded in agreement. Katy and Paddie giggled.

The adventure of the Fires of Hell over, they went their separate ways.

~~~~~~~~~

Wednesday late afternoon — 4:15 p.m.
Watercourse Restaurant
Denver, Colorado

Tanesha pressed her napkin to her lips. Instinctively, she glanced across the street to Sandy's apartment. Even though her friend no longer lived there, just seeing the building, where they'd had so much fun, gave her courage.

"What?" Tanesha said in a loud whisper.

Jeraine looked at her and blinked.

"What do you mean, 'What'?" Jeraine asked.

"I'm sorry," Tanesha said with a sniff. She let her long-standing anger at this man push down the panic in her pounding heart. "What is confusing about my question?"

"Oh," Jeraine said. "No."

He read the betrayal on her face and shook his head.

"No, no," Jeraine said. "I was just wondering what part of what I said was confusing."

Tanesha took a few moments to breathe. In couple's therapy, she'd learned that her rage terrified Jeraine. He panicked the moment it came up. And nothing good came from that. If she was going to stay married . . .

She checked her heart and saw that she still *did* want to stay married to this man.

She cleared her throat and took a drink of water. If she was going to stay married to this man, she needed to calm down, or, as the therapist said, "Act. Don't react."

The waiter appeared at that moment and cleared their salad plates. They were eating at a gourmet vegan restaurant. They had both decided to go vegetarian while they lived at the Castle. Because of a variety of food allergies, health concerns, and Honey's Crohn's disease, everyone at the Castle ate vegetarian food — supplemented with regular intervals of meat from the barbeque.

The waiter placed their plates in front of them. Tanesha was eating her favorite food — a stir-fry of sweet potatoes, tofu, and marinated portabella mushrooms. Jeraine got something that looked like country-fried steak but was vegan. For a moment, they simply ate.

Never one to run from a conflict, Tanesha set her fork down.

"I wasn't sure what you said back there," Tanesha said.

Jeraine looked up at her. His mouth was full of food, and, for a moment, he just chewed.

"I was offered a residency in Las Vegas," Jeraine said.

Tanesha felt her panic rise again. She put her hand on her heart and tried to breathe.

"*Wherever love is present, fear is a stranger,*" she whispered to herself her favorite quote from angel expert, Kyle Gray. She let out a breath and spoke again.

"You're moving to Las Vegas?" Tanesha managed a whisper.

"Oh," Jeraine said. He chuckled. "That's what you panicked over?"

He laughed out loud. She scowled.

Maybe she didn't want to stay married to this man.

Catching her look, he flushed and swallowed hard.

"Okay. I'm sorry," Jeraine said. "You're right. That wasn't funny. It's just that I thought you . . . and . . . .."

To buy time, he stuck a fork load of food into his mouth. Shaking her head, Tanesha took another bite of food. Blissed out by her food, she *almost* forgot he was there.

"A residency is where I'd work for the casino," Jeraine said. "I would have a permanent show there. Their scout came to see us this last tour and liked the work we did together. I would work the weekends in Vegas. People would come to see me. No more crazy world travel."

"But you'd move to Vegas?" Tanesha said the words with slow, heartbreaking emphasis.

"Not a chance," Jeraine said.

Tanesha sucked in a breath.

"It's not safe for me to live in Vegas," Jeraine said. "Too many drugs. Too much temptation. Plus, I'd rather be here — with you and Jabari."

Stunned, Tanesha simply blinked at him. He nodded.

"I can come home every night," Jeraine said. "It'll be late, but I will be here during some of the day."

Tanesha tried not to breathe.

"I talked to O'Malley," Jeraine said. "When he's in New York, he hires a plane. Well, I guess you know that, because you've taken it there. I guess I have, too. He keeps it so it's available for him to go home at any time. Ava can go there. There's no hassle or waiting. They use it more than you'd think."

Tanesha nodded. She knew that Ava flew there when she had breaks from cases and was off for a few days. O'Malley came home when he could. Jeraine continued.

"Anyway, Jammy thinks we can get the casino to pay for the plane. It's about an hour there and an hour home. Most professionals commute longer than that. Just a part of modern life."

Tanesha nodded. In the past, she would have pointed out that he would have to take a half hour to get to the airport. So it was going to be more like three or four hours of commuting, not just two hours. She took a bite of food to keep from scratching at his enthusiasm.

"Because I know so many people in the industry," Jeraine continued, "I can invite people to join me in Vegas. Jammy put some feelers out for me. Most people have said that they would love to come for a weekend or whatever we can set up."

Jeraine set his fork down.

"That would be some weekdays in the summer, but I figured we could match it to your schedule," Jeraine said. "And Jabari just loves the Marlowe School."

Jeraine nodded.

"The money is good," Jeraine said. "And I'd get a percentage of the other acts that were playing through me."

Waiting for her to respond, Jeraine's head bounced up and down in an odd nod.

"What do you think?" Jeraine asked.

She opened her mouth to respond, but he cut her off.

"Oh, I'm the first African-American to *ever* be asked to do this. Those old, mobbed-up white guys didn't want us there. So this would be progress," Jeraine said with a nod. As an aside, he added, "O'Malley said that he would come and that he's ask his friends. So it's not just hip-hop and the R&B crowd. He thought maybe the movie studios would let him present the new soundtracks there, you know, under me. That would be a big deal. Jammy said he thought that I could host my own jazz festival, you know, like we talked about when we were kids."

Jeraine beamed. Tanesha smiled at his smile.

"Oh, O'Malley's friend . . . the drummer?" Jeraine asked.

"Malik?" Tanesha asked.

"He might join my band," Jeraine said. "His lady friend is looking to get out of New York City with her grandkids and daughter. Bad blood there. Some asshole ex-husband or something like that. They can get a house in Vegas. Plus, he's a good drummer and great people."

Jeraine shrugged.

"But you'd be home? Here? In Denver?" Tanesha asked.

Jeraine nodded.

"And you'll give me space to do my schoolwork and stuff?" Tanesha asked. "Even if you're home?"

"It's going to be a lot of work to put the whole thing together," Jeraine said. "I told Jammy that I wanted to try it for a weekend — you know, to see if *we* liked it."

Luckily, Tanesha had not been chewing, because she was so shocked that her mouth fell open.

"*We* — you know, like *you and me* . . . and Jabari and Blane and Heather and all of them," Jeraine said.

He gave her a big smile with his dazzling white teeth.

"It could go for years," Jabari said. "You could finish school and go to your fellowship and stuff, and maybe we could have another child and everything. I'll just be working the weekends like a regular Joe."

"A regular Joe?" Tanesha asked.

Jeraine beamed at her again. They fell silent. They both focused on finishing their meals.

"What about the tour?" Tanesha asked as the waiter took their plates away. "You were going to leave a week after I go back to school."

"That's the question," Jeraine said. "I was going to leave to set up the tour, hire musicians, stuff like that. If I have a residency, then I'd go to Vegas and set up a band. It's kind of the same thing, but this would be permanent and not roving. You'd be surprised. There's lots of real, quality musicians who are sick of traveling, sober, and still want to play."

The waiter set down a piece of dark chocolate cake, two forks, and napkins. He asked if they needed anything else, and Jeraine ordered a pot of green tea.

"I think of my dad," Jeraine said. "He would have kept playing if he could have figured out how to do it and stay sober and raise a family. I mean, Mom did some touring . . ."

"She doesn't have his demons," Tanesha said. "What about drugs? Or the temptation of it?"

"I'll insist on sober people — musicians *and* helpers," Jeraine said. "You'd be surprised how many music professionals our age are tired of the drugs and 'the life.'"

"Have you talked to your dad?" Tanesha asked.

"No." Jeraine vigorously shook his head. "I wanted to tell you first. Get your take on it. I talked to O'Malley only because Jammy told me to talk it through with him. He has a lot of experience staying sober in this field. I guess you know that."

Tanesha held her fork over the chocolate cake.

"What do you think?" Jeraine said.

Tanesha's fork skewered a peace of heaven in the form of cake. She put it in her mouth and let the taste linger. She shook her head.

"It's not as good as yours," Tanesha said.

"Of course, it's not," Jeraine said with a chuckle. "But is it better than *Blane*'s chocolate cake? That's the question that matters."

"Blane's cake is better than yours," Tanesha said with a wide smile.

Jeraine pretended to be offended by what he knew was the truth. Tanesha waited for a moment.

"This Vegas thing *sounds* good," Tanesha said.

"Too good to be true?" Jeraine asked.

"Other stars have done it," Tanesha said with a shrug. "You have a lot of breadth. You can do weeks of jazz with or without O'Malley and your father. You can do weeks of rap or R&B or hip-hop or . . ."

Tanesha shrugged.

"It sounds kind of perfect for you," Tanesha said.

"But just for me," Jeraine said.

Tanesha sighed. Over her own resistance to this man, she nodded her head.

"For us, too," Tanesha said.

"But?" Jeraine asked.

"We've heard a lot of promises in our lives," Tanesha said. "Let's let the ink dry and the work start. You may hate it."

Tanesha sighed.

"But then again, you might just love it," Tanesha said, despite her own terror of him relapsing.

Rather than respond, Jeraine just grinned at her.

CHAPTER 518

Wednesday late-afternoon — 4:15 p.m.

With Sam Lipson at the wheel of the SUV, he drove them straight to a diner just outside of town, where he fed the boys plate after plate of food while Delphie drank tea. When they were full and fed, they took turns in the bathroom before heading out into Leadville.

Delphie took the passenger seat, and Sam the driver's seat. In the way of brothers, the boys pressed themselves into the middle seat. Blane took the far back seat, where he could spread out. Sam waited until they were buckled in before starting on Sam's historic tour of Lipson. They were just heading toward Leadville when the youngest brother, George, leaned forward.

"Can I ask you something?" George asked.

"Sure," Sam said.

"That lady — you know, the one who came out of the hole we were watching?" George asked.

"Abi?" Delphie asked.

"Is she . . ." the boy leaned forward and said the last word in almost a whisper, "*human*?"

"No," Sam said with a shake of his head.

"No?" George asked. "What does that mean?"

"There are a lot of creatures who look like human beings but are not," Sam said. "It's weird to me. Sometimes, it kind of freaks me out. But we've met all kinds of people in the last few years."

"Where?" the eldest brother, Gregg, asked at the same time the middle brother, Gary, said, "Why?"

"Jacob and I went to the Isle of Man," Sam said.

"That's really where it started," Delphie said. "Meeting the fairies."

Sam glanced at her and smiled.

"What do you mean, 'fairies'?" Gary asked.

His brothers looked at him and nodded at his question.

"Fairies," Sam said. "At least that's what they call themselves."

"They were talking about the fairy queens," Gary said.

"According to Abi, there were four fairy queens who arrived on this planet," Delphie said. "Two were taken care of, and two were not. Much of what happened in the last few days was about the fairy queens."

"The war?" Gary asked.

"The fairy queens were going to go to war," Sam said. "They share the planet with us. When they go to war, they mess up our world."

"A lot of people have died when the fairies have gone to war," Delphie said.

"Entire civilizations," Sam said.

The boys fell silent for a while.

"But that's over?" George asked.

"No war?" Gary asked.

"No war," Sam said.

"Due in no short part to your hard work," Delphie said with a nod.

"What did 'Abi' *do* to that guy?" Gary asked.

"She obliterated his body and soul," Sam said, evenly.

The boys gave dramatic shivers.

"It made me feel weird," George said. "Scared and angry and just wow! All at the same time."

"Creepy," Gregg said.

"I was like . . ." Gary opened his mouth in a horrified, shocked look.

"I was, too," Sam said.

Delphie nodded in agreement. They fell into a thick silence. Blane tapped the top of the middle bench.

"It's certainly something we'll never see again," Blane said. "Being around Abi is really great. She's amazingly kind. I really like her. Jake does, too. Her partner, Fin, is just a good guy. Weird, but good."

"That's the guy who showed up?" George asked. "We know about black people because we watch television."

Gregg, the eldest brother, punched George in the shoulder.

"Don't be a racist," Gregg said.

"I've never seen a black person in person!" George said.

"He's not a person, *dumb ass*," Gregg said. "He's a *fairy*."

"They just said that," Gary said in a low tone.

"Plus, you don't say 'black,'" Gregg said. "They're African Americans."

"Fin's neither an African, nor an American," Blane said, mildly. "He was born on the Isle of Man."

"Like the Bee Gees?" Gary asked.

"The Bee Gees are white, *dumb ass*," George said.

"Most fairies have dark skin," Sam said. "At least the ones I've seen."

"They are an ancient people," Delphie said. "Outside of the babies born this year, the youngest among them is many hundreds of years old."

"The Isle of Man was populated in 6500 BC by people out of Africa," Blane said. "Fand, Fin's mother, was there long before then. Her beloved, Manannán, landed there sometime around in the early CE."

"Current Era," Gregg whispered, and his brothers nodded.

"We looked up his myth," Blane said. "He's in a poem from the year 1500 CE. But by the 1500s, Manannán was less a man and more of a god-like creature. The fairies created a fog that kept invaders out of most of the island. According to Jake, he was kind of like the mayor of a small colony on the Isle of Man. Queen Fand met him when he moved there."

"Fin?" George asked.

"His father, Manannán," Blane said.

"Fin must be really old," George said. "Do you ask him about it?"

"He's spent most of his life on the Isle of Man," Blane said. "They have an entire area there. He'd never even thought of leaving until Jake and Sam went there. He really knows about what was going on only in his little world. Kind of like you guys and Leadville."

He put his hand on the boy's shoulders and they smiled.

"I've been home taking care of the kids," Blane said. "We had some fairies visit from other Queendoms. I was fascinated at how distinct they were from each other. I mean they are *fairies*, right? That should make them kind of the same. They are not. Most fairies don't ever leave their Queendoms. There's only a few of them who are outside of their small, controlled world. Fin and Abi live with us with their kids."

Blane shrugged.

"Fin's not really so different from you," Blane said. "But one thing — he doesn't see you as 'white' or him as 'black.' That's a modern distinction, something created in America."

"Gregg's told us all about it," George said. "He wants to be a civil rights lawyer."

"I'm going to be a civil rights lawyer," Gregg said. "Help people who are hurt by the system."

"Good for you!" Delphie said, even though she knew his path would be much less straightforward than that. "You're really going to make a difference in this world."

They cheered for Gregg and his ambition.

"So," Blane said. "Fin, Abi . . . The stuff that happens around them is definitely different. But they are good folks. Our kids love their Zoe and Zaidy. Even though they are different from us — look different from us and have amazing powers — their hearts are beautiful. After you get your mind around all of this, you'll like them."

If only to say that they were willing to like them, the boys nodded.

"We cannot forget that Abi saved our lives," Delphie said.

"Levi Johannsen would have killed us," Sam added.

"He's tried to kill me any number of times," Delphie said with a nod. "He was planning on killing our bodies, at the very least."

"Capturing our souls," Sam said.

"'Capturing our souls'?" George asked in an excited voice. "Really?"

Blane nodded.

"Is it a problem that Fin and Abi have black skin?" Blane asked.

"Not for me," George said. "I just have never met anyone like that."

"He appeared and disappeared out of nowhere," Gary said.

"He didn't care if we saw him," Gregg said. "Like we didn't matter at all."

"My guess is that there's not much you could do to hurt him," Blane said. "He's powerful."

They fell silent for a while. George turned around to look at Blane.

"Do you think he'd show me how to do that?" George asked. "You know — appear and disappear."

"Where would you go?" Gregg said, punching George again.

"Hey!" Blane put up his hand to block Gregg's punch.

He shook his head at Gregg, and Gregg shook his head that Blane wouldn't understand.

"Fin might take you with him," Delphie said. "But the skill is really a fairy skill. It's something they can do that we can't."

The boys looked at Delphie with awe.

"He's taken Blane places," Delphie said.

"I throw up every single time," Blane said. "It is not pretty. I'd rather not go by fairy. The little kids, Katy and Paddie, had a terrible fever after going with them."

"It's not natural for us," Sam said. "We humans were born of the earth. We don't do great when we travel away from it."

When no one responded, Sam added, "At least that's what I think."

"Where's Abi from?" George asked.

No one responded. The silence lagged.

"I don't think anyone knows," Delphie said. "She doesn't. Like most of us, she found herself exactly where she was created."

"She's from the earth," Sam said. He glanced at Delphie, who nodded. "That's a lot of stuff about race and people and fairies. Makes our tour of Leadville kind of boring. Are you still up for it?"

"I am," Gregg said.

"I want to see where you grew up," George said.

"Hey look — there's mom," Gary said.

They looked out the window to see a woman wearing medical scrubs coming out of the supermarket on the edge of town.

"I thought you said she was working until six," Gary asked Gregg.

"That's what's on her schedule for this week," Gregg said.

Gregg took out his cellphone and looked at it. The screen was dark. He tried to turn it on, but it sparked and started to smoke.

"My phone's dead," Gregg said.

"That's probably why she's not at work," Gary said. His voice rose in panic. "She's looking for us!"

"*Dumb ass*," George said.

"It's not my fault that the phone broke!" Gregg said.

"Can we stop, Mr. Lipson?" Gary said. "Please."

"I really want to see my mom," George said in a low, whiney voice.

"Of course," Sam said.

Sam pulled into the supermarket parking. With George shouting directions, he pointed them down the aisle, where their mom was loading the back of her van. Sam waited for a car to pull out next to their mom's van. He pulled in to the spot next to him. The boys were clearly well trained, as they didn't move until the car had come to a full stop. As soon as Sam put the SUV into park, the boys spilled out of the SUV.

Grinning at the boys, Sam turned to Delphie.

"Let's give them a moment," Sam said.

Nodding, she smiled and looked out the window. Blane moved forward to the middle bench in the SUV.

"Sam," Delphie said.

She put her hand on his shoulder and pointed to the boys' mother.

"Oh," Sam said.

"What is it?" Blane asked.

"I'm sorry, Blane," Sam said. "The boys aren't your siblings."

"They aren't?" Blane asked.

"They are mine," Sam said.

"To be fair, we should ask," Delphie said, kindly.

Sam turned to look at her.

"Did you know?" Sam asked.

"I had no idea they even existed until Abi asked me to find someone like you," Delphie said. "I'm sorry. I can't see you, your family, and your life any more than I can see mine. I just care too much."

Sam gave her a nod.

"What do you mean that they are your siblings?" Blane asked.

"That woman?" Sam pointed to the boys' mother. "She took care of my father in the last years of his life. She was his caregiver."

"She's coming this way," Delphie said, as she opened her car door.

Sam got out of the driver's side and walked to the end of the SUV. He and the boys' mother hugged. Delphie came down her side of the car. The boys' mother seemed surprised to see Delphie. They hugged.

Blane had this odd sensation. He wasn't exactly disappointed, yet still he felt a little let down. Most of his life, he'd been alone. When he was in foster care, he'd comfort himself with the idea that somewhere he had a real family — brothers, sisters, and a loving mother and father.

He didn't have any of that. He'd never have any of that.

Blane sighed. He hadn't realized how much that dream still lingered inside him.

In a breath, he was overcome with gratitude for Sam and Jacob and Heather and his children and, particularly, Celia Marlowe. If she hadn't rescued him — made sure that he knew he belonged with them — he might not be here to be disappointed now. They might not be his biological mother, father, and siblings, but they were better than that. They chose him.

"Why didn't you tell me?" Sam asked.

The emotion in Sam's voice shook Blane from his thoughts. Blane jumped out of the SUV. He reached the end of the SUV, where they were talking before anyone said anything else. Blane put his arm around Sam's shoulder.

"This is Blane," Sam said. "He's my brother's child and my son."

Blane blushed at the introduction. He looked at Sam, his father by choice. The woman looked Blane up and down. Blane felt like he was being searched head to toe.

"I apologize," the woman said with a grin. "You look so much like Gregg, I thought maybe you . . ."

Blane shook his head.

"Sam's father had always said that your brothers had killed all of his children," the woman said, leaning toward Sam.

"He was rescued by a goddess," Sam said.

"Of course, he was," the woman grinned at Blane. "You must be very special."

Blane's eyebrows moved up and down as he attempted to work out why the woman had said that he was special.

"Goddess," the woman said.

"Oh," Blane said. "It's an expression. We all love the goddess Hedone."

"Isn't she a half-god?" the woman asked. "Her mother is human."

Blane blinked at her for a moment before turning to Sam. Blane gave him an "Are you okay?" look. Sam nodded.

"This is Ginger," Sam said. "We hired her to take care of my father when he was in his last years. She knows the family secrets."

"He was a real asshole," Ginger said with a smile.

"Worse than that," Sam said with a laugh. "Did he . . .He didn't assault you or . . .?"

"No," Ginger smiled at Sam. "I wanted a child. I met you and saw how great you were — You, Celia, Delphie, your kids. It's pretty creepy to think about now, but I had a big crush on Valerie. Your dad said that his sons had all died or were assholes, like you, Sam."

Sam nodded in agreement.

"Sounds like him," Delphie said.

"He wanted more kids. To leave a legacy. I thought, 'Why not? If the kids are anything like Sam, I'll be the luckiest mom in the world.'" Ginger smiled. "I was pregnant with Gregg when he died. Your dad insisted on donating so that 'we' could have more kids."

Ginger gave Sam a big smile and then sighed.

"You're right," Ginger said. "I should have told you. But I didn't want you to think that I wanted anything from you or from the estate. I just wanted the boys. That's all."

"He left you money," Sam said.

"I used it for medical school," Ginger said with a smile. "Gregg and Gary were just babies. We went to medical school together. I finished school and came back to start a small clinic here. Had George."

Ginger looked at Blane again.

"I didn't know about you," Ginger said. "It will be nice to catch up."

"Mr. Lipson was going to give us a tour of Leadville." George popped up from behind his mom's car.

Ginger put her hand on his messy brown hair. The boy was holding a popsicle, and his mouth was rimmed red from eating it. Ginger wiped at his mouth with her thumb.

"Well, by all means, don't let me intrude," Ginger said. "I got nervous when I couldn't contact Gregg. I knew he was doing something out at the cemetery."

Ginger looked at Sam and then at Delphie.

"Were you able to save the planet?" Ginger said with a little sarcasm.

"Actually we were," Delphie said with a smile. "Your boys really helped."

Ginger assessed Delphie for a long moment before smiling. She nodded.

"Good," Ginger said. She smiled at them. "Don't let me get in the way."

"Why don't we help you get these groceries home?" Sam asked. "We can do the tour when you're settled."

"You know," Ginger said with a smile. "I'd very much like to do the tour. Everything I know about you came through your dad. It wasn't very positive or helpful. It would be good to connect the dots."

Sam nodded.

"Boys?" Sam asked.

He worked with the boys to put the reusable bags full of groceries into the van. For a moment, Delphie and Ginger stood watching them.

"You don't remember me," Ginger said.

"I do," Delphie said. "I was always so grateful that you could help. We didn't want Sam's father to be without care. He had no friends, no living relatives. It was clear that we couldn't give it because . . . well, you knew the man. You were a godsend. Celia thought so, as well."

"Celia was very kind," Ginger said.

Delphie took a step forward, but Ginger put a hand on her arm. Delphie turned to look at the woman.

"You told me," Ginger said, and then swallowed hard. "You said, 'Don't hesitate. You'll make the right choice. You'll be just fine. You really should go for it.' Just out of the blue. You and Celia were leaving. I was showing you out. I don't think you'd said anything to me the entire visit. Then you were leaving, and you piped up."

"I'm so sorry, Ginger," Delphie said. "It sounds really startling. I wish I could tell you what I meant, but I rarely remember what I say to people."

Delphie leaned in.

"I'm kind of an asshole sometimes," Delphie said.

Ginger burst out laughing and then shook her head.

"No," Ginger said. "I went back in, and the old codger brought up having kids. I took your advice. I didn't hesitate. It was good, too, because he wouldn't have been able to . . . you know — donate — even two days later. The boys wouldn't be here if you hadn't said that. And, I went on to be the doctor I wanted to be."

Delphie gave Ginger a big smile.

"Whenever I felt down or afraid or like I couldn't do it, I hear your voice saying, 'You really should just go for it.' And I do," Ginger said, her eyes filling with tears. "Thank you for . . . being with me all this time."

Delphie hugged Ginger. When they pulled away, Delphie gave Ginger a soft look.

"Do you mind if I'm an asshole again?" Delphie asked.

"What is it?" Ginger asked. Nervous, Ginger put her hand to her chest, "What?"

"You'll meet exactly the right person in the next day or so," Delphie said. "It will seem like a complete accident, but in time, you'll find that it's the result of lots of years of happy accidents. You'll be with her, and she with you, until the end."

Ginger hugged Delphie.

"MOM!" the boys yelled from the van.

Ginger pointed to the van, and Delphie nodded. Wiping her eyes, Ginger went to the van.

"See you at your house!" Delphie said.

Ginger turned and nodded. Gregg and George got into the van with their mother while Gary got back into the SUV. Sam followed Ginger until they reached her home. Gary raced to join his brothers to carry in the groceries.

CHAPTER 519

HOME AGAIN, HOME AGAIN

Wednesday night — 9:15 p.m.

They had just wrapped up dinner when Sam arrived home with Ginger and her sons. There was a quick shuffle and, much to the visiting fairies' delight, the table filled with food again. As soon as it was determined that the children weren't going to school tomorrow, the kids and adults stayed up late talking and eating in the now-full dining room.

Jill, Aden, and Honey had to be up early, so they were the first to leave for bed. Otherwise, everyone else was still up.

Abi, Asclepius, and Fin were deep in conversation on one end of the table. Ares was talking to Nelson Weeks next to them. Heather, Sandy, Tanesha, and Yvonne were deep in conversation about Jeraine's new opportunity. Rodney and Jeraine were talking quietly in a corner of the room. Ginger's boys, Gregg, Gary, and George were taking everything in from their position at a corner of the table. The visiting fairies were happily eating everything in sight. Ginger and Sam were catching up.

Edie had returned in a foul mood. It seemed that the fairy armies were selfish jerks. Knowing what it was like to deal with selfish fairies, Jill sent Edie to her home on the Isle of Man to rest and recover. Edie swore she'd be back in the morning to help with the children. Sandy pressed a tin of cookies into Edie's arms, Jill called Edie's boyfriend, and the fairy disappeared.

The older kids were talking and laughing by themselves. Charlie had his arm around Tink, while Noelle and Teddy's heads were pressed together. Valerie's daughter, Jackie, was sitting on Tink's lap, listening and watching everything that was going on. Nash and Ivy were working through something on his laptop.

Jacob sat apart in a quiet corner of the room. The babies were asleep in the play pen next to where Jacob was sitting. Katy had been exhausted but hadn't wanted to miss out. She was sound asleep on his lap. Mack had finally fallen asleep where he was standing. Blane had picked him up and sat down next to Jacob. After a few minutes, Nelson Weeks came to sit next to Blane.

"That guy," Nelson said.

"Ares?" Jacob asked, raising his eyebrows.

Nelson nodded.

"I can't tell if he wants to fuck me or eat me," Nelson said.

"Probably both," Jacob said.

"Seriously?" He looked at Blane and then at Jacob.

"Probably," Blane said.

"God?" Nelson asked.

"Heather's grandfather," Blane said.

"But he's the god Ares, right?" Nelson asked.

Jacob and Blane nodded. Nelson gave a short shake of his head.

"Is something wrong?" Jacob asked.

"I have this desire to say something like, 'How many gods are there?' but I know there are . . ."

"Thousands," Blane said.

"Thousands," Nelson said. "And they just . . . show up?"

"Perses is Jill's father," Jacob said. "He's not around a lot, but he does stop by."

"Ares is new," Blane said. "He held a conference about this fairy war. Heather went to defend the human interests. Every war is run through the committee in Olympia. 'You can't have a good war without their approval.' Or so Heather has said."

"What's a 'good war'?" Nelson asked.

"There's a question," Jacob said with a nod.

"I've never met him," Blane said. "Ares. I met him today."

"We've met Heather's father," Jacob said with a sneer.

Nelson looked at Jacob and then at Blane.

"I take it that didn't go well," Nelson said.

Jacob opened his mouth to say something about Eros, the shade he created to curse them, and everything Heather's father had put them through. Instead, he just shrugged. Nelson nodded.

"Family," Nelson said. "No matter how great they are, they still suck sometimes."

"True," Jacob said.

"So if he's family, should I . . .?" Nelson started.

"No," Jacob and Blane said in near-unison.

They laughed. Across the room, Jabari climbed up onto Tanesha's lap.

"Boundaries," Blane said. "It's what keeps everyone happy and makes everything work."

"Mr. Weeks?" Maggie, Honey's daughter, came over from where the kids were playing.

"Yes, dear," Nelson said.

"Can I sleep on your lap for a while?" Maggie asked. "I'm really missing my daddy tonight."

"Where's your daddy?" Nelson asked.

"Af-rik-a," Maggie said.

Nelson leaned down and picked up Maggie. She situated herself so that her chest was against Nelson. With a sigh, the tiny red-haired girl fell asleep. Overwhelmed, Nelson looked up at the ceiling. Blane put his hand on Nelson's shoulder.

"What is it?" Blane asked.

"Just great," Nelson said. He gestured to the child in his lap. "My family kicked me out, a long, long time ago. I thought I'd never . . ."

Nelson looked at Blane and smiled.

"Thank you," Nelson said.

"Wait until it's diaper time," Jacob said, gesturing to the babies next to him.

"So what?" Nelson asked, with a shrug.

"Good attitude," Blane said.

Blane and Jacob looked at each other before saying, "Newbie."

The men laughed. Their laughter brought Rodney over to them. They watched Jeraine pluck Jabari off Tanesha's lap. Rodney got a chair for his son-in-law, and they sat down next to Jacob. Jabari settled in and was soon asleep.

"I wondered if we could talk," Rodney said to Jacob.

Jacob, Blane, and Nelson turned to look at Rodney. Embarrassed by the sudden attention, Rodney looked down.

"This is Rodney," Jacob said to Nelson. "He's Tanesha's father. He runs a large site for Lipson Construction."

"That's the construction company you own," Nelson said.

"A little less than half," Jacob said.

"We like to focus on the fact that the employees are slowly buying the company," Blane said.

Nelson nodded. He held out a hand to Rodney. They shook hands.

"I think you've met Jeraine," Jacob said to Nelson.

"At the Church," Nelson said of the time they were trying to catch drug dealers at the dance club, The Church.

Jeraine raised a hand in "Hello" to Nelson, and Nelson nodded.

"What's up?" Jacob asked.

"Tanesha said you own a lot of apartment complexes," Rodney said.

"A few," Jacob said, evenly.

"A few?" Blane asked, shaking his head. He looked over at Rodney. "He owns enough to make any man crazy."

"There was a time in Denver where a lot of 'smart people' were getting out of affordable housing," Jacob said. "I bought apartment buildings so people like our employees would have a safe, clean place to live."

"Preach it," Blane said with a laugh.

Smiling, Jacob continued, "It seemed dumb to me that we needed all of these people to work our sites and they couldn't find housing."

Rodney nodded. Nervous, Rodney scratched at his neck, just under his chin.

"Listen," Jacob said, reading Rodney's gesture. "Do you need a place to live? We certainly still have space here. Every apartment has a guest bedroom, and . . ."

"No, no," Rodney said with a laugh. "Everything's fine with me and Yvonne."

Rodney put his hand on his heart in reference to Yvonne. He sighed.

"Honey was telling me about the place you helped her and her husband put together," Rodney said.

"That place has really come together nicely." Jacob nodded. "It's a miracle, really. We're putting one together south of here, near Craig Hospital. We haven't even finished that one and they've asked us to make another — for families of their injured patients."

Jacob shook his head.

"Crazy," Jacob said. "The demand is crazy."

"I see," Rodney asked. He nodded his head for a moment.

Seeming to have heard his answer, Rodney fell silent.

"He wants to make a place like the one you made for Honey and MJ," Jeraine said.

"He does?" Jacob asked.

Blane turned to look at them. Seeing he had both Blane and Jacob's attention, Jeraine continued.

"He wants to make one for the men coming out of prison," Jeraine said. "You know, they are letting out all of these dudes caught on weed charges. Since weed is legal and all."

Jacob looked at Rodney. Jacob had worked with Rodney for a long time. He'd seen Rodney look just like he looked right now — as if he wanted to melt into the floor with shame. Jeraine pressed on.

"Some of these dudes went in when they were kids," Jeraine said. "They've got no skills and sometimes no education. They are poor, come from poor families, were in gangs, or went to gangs for protection in prison."

"These boys have struggled with every pestilence known to man," Rodney said.

"Just men?" Jacob asked.

"Women, too," Rodney said with a nod. "But the men . . . they . . ."

Rodney flushed with overwhelm. Jacob glanced at Jeraine.

"He wants to start with the men," Jeraine said. "Men only — at first — and then maybe families. But for now, he wants to help them when they get out of prison, get them ready for the world — you know, life skills and some *legal* way to make money."

"Education," Rodney managed to say.

"Is there state money for it?" Jacob asked.

"I can pay," Rodney said.

"No matter how much money you have, we'd run right through it in no time," Jacob said. "We'd need something to sustain it."

"I don't know," Rodney said. "I just don't know."

Jacob put his hand on Rodney's shoulder. Rodney looked up at him.

"It sounds like a good idea," Jacob said. "Let's see if we can work up the numbers. Figure out how it might work."

"I told him that I'd have a concert to raise money," Jeraine said. "I know a bunch of guys who would pitch in."

"Would you be willing to put up the plans on the Internet so other people could do it?" Jacob asked. "Or are we forming a national corporation?"

"No corporation," Rodney barked. "That'd just be another kind of private prison."

"Or a plantation," Jeraine said.

Jeraine and Rodney nodded.

"Okay, then let's be sure to document every step so people can follow behind us," Jacob said.

"How do we do that?" Rodney sounded miserable.

"I'll start a blog," Blane said. "That's what we did with Honey and MJ's project. I wrote updates every week or so. We published the plans when we were done."

"You'd do that for me?" Rodney asked.

"In a heartbeat," Blane said. "Anything. I think it's a great idea."

"I do, too," Nelson said.

Surprised, Rodney looked at Nelson and then at Blane. Blane nodded. Rodney looked at Jacob.

"We just need to figure out how to make it work," Jacob said. "That's all."

"You probably don't want to give up those apartments," Rodney said. "They must be gold mines now."

"Let's figure out if we want to," Jacob said. "We might be better off buying another property and build to fit. It's hard to imagine, but there are still buildings to be had. Let's take a look at the whole thing. See what we can figure out."

"When?" Rodney asked.

"Jill has her finals tomorrow," Jacob said. "I need to be here for the kids and pick up any slack."

"I have work." Rodney looked at his watch and swallowed hard.

"Friday? Saturday?" Jacob said with a shrug. "We'll get it going."

Rodney nodded and stood up. He'd walked across the room before turning and walking back.

"Thank you," Rodney said. "I'm sorry that I . . ."

"Don't be sorry," Jacob said with a grin. "It really is a great idea. If we do a good job making it happen, the idea could spread across the country. Re-adopt these men and women into our country. But we have to do it right, first."

Rodney gave Jacob a stiff nod and went to get Yvonne. Their departure encouraged everyone to head up to bed. Since Tink was sleeping in Honey's guest bedroom, she took Maggie from Nelson and went to bed. Nelson, Blane, and Jacob made quick work of the diaper changes. They were almost done when Jeraine appeared with Jabari.

"Jabari wants to be with Mack, Rachel Ann, and Jackie," Jeraine said.

Jabari's sleep-filled eyes blinked at Jacob, Blane, and Nelson.

"Need a diaper change?" Jacob asked.

"No, he's good," Jeraine said.

"I'll take him," Blane said.

They began carrying the infants and toddlers up to the loft nursery. When they'd finished, Jeraine left with a wave, and Jacob nodded to Nelson and Blane leaving them to figure out what was next for them.

Jill turned over when Jacob got to bed.

"How was second dinner?" Jill asked.

"Good," Jacob said. "Rodney wants to . . ."

He stopped talking when he noticed that Jill was asleep. He took a quick shower and went to bed. For the first time in what felt like years, he lay down in his own bed and fell sound asleep.

~~~~~~~~~

Undisclosed location

Mari was not the most powerful child of Queen Fand. She was definitely the cleverest and certainly the most stubborn of Queen Fand's children. Mari worked for less than a day before she found the trail of her mother. She bounced around the world until she zeroed in on her mother and the other fairy queens.

She arrived inside a gorgeous crystal cave deep inside the earth. The air was moist but not too humid. Somehow, the crystals reflected the light of the stars. For a moment, Mari stood where she'd landed. She breathed in the warm, moist air.

She almost chickened out. Gathering her courage, she set off across the cavern to where the fairy queens were lounging beside a warm salt bath.

"Mother," Mari said, as she approached.

Queen Fand looked up at her.

"Before you say anything, I want you to know that I am aware that you planned to have me killed in the last war," Mari said. "While I understand that I am not in the line of succession, I deeply resent you throwing me away like garbage. I have spent my *entire life* in the service of your every whim."

Mari felt such a rush of betrayal that she had to swallow hard to keep speaking. Queen Fand scowled and opened her mouth.

"You have no right to dispose of me," Mari said. "I am your *child*, your *flesh and blood,* who has worked her entire life to do your will and bidding."

Mari panted with rage. Queen Fand gave her a blank look.

"I am here to tell you that I have had enough," Mari said. "You wish me dead; I am dead to you."

"But . . ." Queen Fand said.

"Don't tell me that there is no longer any war," Mari said. "How long will it be before you decide you need another war?"

When Queen Fand didn't respond, Mari snorted.

"I figured as much," Mari said.

Without saying another word, Mari turned in place and stalked away from the group of fairy queens. She disappeared from where she started.

"Any idea who that might be?" Queen Shanti said.

"None whatsoever," Queen Fand said.

The fairy queen sisters giggled with laughter.

"She did seem very upset," Queen Fand said.

Queen Fand looked toward where Mari had disappeared. Shrugging, she got up and went into the salt bath.

~~~~~~~~

Wednesday night — 9:45 p.m.

"Well . . ." Nelson said.

Blane looked at Nelson for a long moment. He opened his mouth to say something.

"I should probably go," Nelson said. "I've got work tomorrow."

Blane closed his mouth and gave Nelson a nod.

"I'll walk you home," Blane said.

Nelson grinned at the idea that Blane was going to walk him to his house across the street and four houses away. Blane shrugged. Rather than object, Nelson put on his jacket, and they left through the side door. Blane was closing the outside gate when Nelson turned to him.

"Why do you think this is so hard for us?" Nelson asked.

Blane squinted at Nelson.

"I mean, I can tell that you like me," Nelson said. "And I really like you. I don't know why . . ."

"I don't know," Blane said.

Blane opened his mouth to say what he thought, but Nelson continued talking.

"I mean," Nelson said. "I remember when you were with Enrique. You were so free, so . . .easy. Nothing seemed to bother you. You kissed people when they came into the house. You were ready for a hug or a back rub. I . . . I mean, you didn't have sex with any one of us, except maybe Enrique, but you were so open, available. Now, it's like there's this wall between us."

Nelson glanced at Blane.

"Sorry to just vomit words," Nelson said. "I've just . . . It's just . . ."

Nelson scowled.

"I've wanted to say something for a long time," Nelson said. "I don't want to lose this, lose you, but I don't know how to scale the wall!"

"I don't know how to, either," Blane said with a sigh.

Blane jammed his hands into his pockets. They started walking. They passed Nelson's house, turning up 16th Avenue toward City Park. Blane stopped walking at the crosswalk on 17th Avenue.

"Do you mind walking for a bit?" Blane asked.

Nelson pointed back to his house and then at where they were. Blane grinned. When the light turned, they walked across the street. They were well into the park when Blane spoke.

"You mentioned Enrique," Blane said.

Nelson nodded.

"I . . . That whole thing . . ." Blane sighed. "You know, he came to the hospital and harassed Heather when I was in the ER. He told them that he was my *true* partner, and Heather was . . ."

"Heather couldn't have possibly cared about that," Nelson said.

"Oh, she wasn't upset," Blane said. "He just made everything so damned hard. It's like . . . I mean . . ."

Blane swallowed hard.

"Enrique destroyed my life," Blane said. "Destroyed me. He would have killed me if it weren't for Jake. Well, Delphie, too. As it was, he took away my home, my possessions, my livelihood, all of my friends, and . . . even my own sense of who I was. Then I finally build my life back, have a real home and children and everything, and he's there telling everyone that what I want was him."

Chapter 520

HAVE COURAGE

"You're afraid of losing Heather," Nelson said.

"No," Blane said, and then shrugged. "I mean, sure. I'm afraid of losing Heather, but I don't think I'd ever lose her over this."

"How would you lose her?" Nelson asked. He quickly added, "Just out of curiosity. You know — what's the lay of the land?"

Blane nodded and fell silent.

"If I betrayed her," Blane said. "Or betrayed our children or our life. If I was anything but myself and . . . So no, she wouldn't end things over being with you, even if you join our family. If I lie to her about it or you or . . . Anyway, I can't lie anymore because everyone I'm around just knows anyway."

"Really?" Nelson asked.

"Really," Blane said. "You can see that they know."

He sighed.

"It's hard to be human around so many super-humans," Blane said, and then nodded. "It forces me to try to be a better person."

Blane stopped walking to look at Nelson.

"Heather likes you," Blane said. "Even the girlfriends like you. That's like a badge of honor or a gold star from the heavens."

"Good to know," Nelson said with a grin.

"You mentioned before, when I was . . ." Blane said. "I remember that feeling of freedom, that easy safety of 'How bad could it be?' But I was naïve. I'd come out of Hell in the foster system. I thought nothing could hurt me. I was care-*less*. I wasn't care-*full* with myself, my health, my heart, my life — and I lost it all, every bit of it. I will never do that again."

"You don't want to risk being hurt." Nelson nodded.

"No," Blane said, shaking his head. "I'm going to get hurt. I could get hurt walking across the street. I could fall down on our walk or fail at my acupuncture practice or . . . Hurt is a natural part of life. I just . . ."

Nelson stopped walking to look at Blane.

"I think it *matters* to me — you and me," Blane said. "I'm surprised, but it matters to me a lot. *You* matter to me a lot. I don't want to start because . . ."

"What if I fuck it up?" Nelson asked.

Blane shook his head.

"That's what I think," Nelson said. "After all of this time, I finally have a chance at a real dream, *my* real dream, and I . . ."

"I'm your dream?" Blane asked. Shocked, he gawked at Nelson.

Nelson looked at Blane. Even in the dark of the night, Blane saw the embarrassment on his face. Nelson had said a lot more than he'd intended to. Nelson gave Blane a quick nod and turned to walk again.

They walked in silence as they made a loop around the park. When they were back to the entrance, Blane stopped walking.

"I think you're right," Blane said. "It's hard because we care too much, because I really care about you, about this. It's not fun and games. It's real. It's life."

Looking relieved, Nelson nodded.

They walked out of the park. Nelson said his goodbyes and went into his house. Blane let himself into the Castle. When he got to their apartment, Heather was asleep with Wyn on the bed. Blane smiled at them for a moment. He turned to go to the bathroom when Heather sat up in bed.

"Just go," Heather said. "We'll be here when you get back."

"I . . ." Blane said.

"Have courage, my love," Heather said. "You are so focused on what you might lose that you forget what you might gain. This is your *life* — your short *human* life. Why not make it magnificent? We'll be here either way. We'd just like you to have all that life can offer."

Blane turned to look at her. After a moment, he nodded and left the Castle.

~~~~~~~~~

Thursday morning — 7:05 a.m.

Paris, France

"What did she say?" Sissy asked.

Mari had appeared out of nowhere just as Sissy's alarm went off. Sissy was now putting her to use by having Mari brush Sissy's hair. It was a struggle only because Mari was attempting to do Sissy's hair without using magic. Every time Mari had put up Sissy's hair with magic, Sissy wasn't able to take it down at night. They were sitting on Sissy's bed, looking at each other through the mirror on the wall.

"That's just it," Mari said. "She didn't say anything."

"Nothing?" Sissy asked.

Mari nodded into the mirror, and Sissy looked surprised.

"And you were sassy and everything?" Sissy asked.

"Very disrespectful," Mari said, nodding.

"And she didn't respond?" Sissy asked.

Mari shook her head.

"Wow," Sissy said. "And you said everything we practiced."

"Every word," Mari said.

"Pshew," Sissy said with a gust of air.

"I know," Mari said. "I thought she'd be furious . . ."

"How dare you!" Sissy said in an almost perfect imitation of Mari's mother, Queen Fand.

"Exactly," Mari said. "I don't want to say this because I can't believe it's true . . ."

"What?" Sissy asked.

"I don't think she knew who I was," Mari said.

Sissy didn't respond. She could feel in her gut the truth of what Mari had said. Her heart didn't want it to be true. She couldn't think of anything to say.

"Yeah," Mari said. "That's the truth, isn't it?"

"Seems like," Sissy said. She opened her mouth to say something consoling but Mari was positively beaming. "What?"

"It's the best news I've heard in a long time," Mari said. "I can live *my* life, my own life. My life."

Mari giggled.

"Aren't you upset?" Sissy asked.

"I know," Mari said with a nod. "I should be. I really should be. But right this moment, I just feel relief. Like, *'Ahhh'*. I can just *live* for a while."

Frustrated with Sissy's hair, Mari dropped the brush and snapped her fingers. Sissy's hair was up in a beautiful knot with a shimmering bow.

"Pretty," Sissy said, looking side to side at her hair. "What will I do tonight?"

"Pull on the bow," Mari said. "It just occurred to me that I could give you a way to take your hair out."

Sissy grinned at her smart friend.

"I think I might get upset," Mari said. "Someday. Maybe. Don't you think someday . . . ?"

"You don't *have* to be upset about it," Sissy said.

Mari nodded.

"It's okay if you're not upset," Sissy said. "But you might be tomorrow. Or maybe next week."

"For now?" Mari asked. "I'm just going to enjoy it."

Mari kissed Sissy's cheek and disappeared. Chuckling at her friend, Sissy quickly put on her leotard. She checked herself in the mirror before heading downstairs for another day.

~~~~~~~~~
Thursday early morning — 5:05 a.m.

Aden came down the stairs, turned at the main Castle living room, and went into the kitchen where he saw Blane making breakfast. He stopped short. As if he were shocked, he put his hand on his heart.

"Very funny," Blane said. "It's my turn to make breakfast. Jeraine and I are competing for best breakfast. He won last week, but *this* is muffin week."

Grinning at himself, Aden took a travel mug down from the cabinet and went to fill it with coffee. Blane took a carton of half-and-half from the refrigerator.

"No dairy," Aden said.

"Sorry, I forgot about your delicate system," Blane said, while swiping his hand in front of his nose as if something smelled bad.

Aden snorted and got the soy milk out of the refrigerator. He poured some in his travel mug and screwed on the top. He gave Blane a long look.

"So?" Aden asked.

"So?" Blane asked. Intentionally avoiding Aden's question, Blane gestured to the oven, "I have three kinds of muffins — sweet for the fairy kind."

"Are the envoys still here?" Aden asked.

"We're going to have to use a flamethrower to get them out of here," Blane said.

"Or just stop feeding them," Aden said.

Blane nodded. He began adding ingredients to the bowl he was stirring with a wooden spoon.

"Blueberry, easily digestible fiber, no sugar, no-gluten — for Honey and the perpetually dieting," Blane said.

Aden stuck his finger in the batter and then put it in his mouth.

"That's surprisingly good," Aden said.

"Surprisingly?" Blane said.

Aden grinned and gestured to the full, unbaked muffin tins.

"Keto," Blane said. "High protein. Oat fiber. Charlie and Nash are trying to 'bulk up,' whatever that means. Delphie's eating them for her blood sugar."

Blane shrugged.

"Bacon, sausage — for cavemen like you," Blane grinned. He gestured to where a pan of bacon awaited. Aden picked up a piece. "Tofu scramble with marinated portobellos and sweet potato."

"Tanesha's favorite," Aden said. "Slick. Get back at your competition by making his wife's favorite."

Blane gave Aden an evil grin.

"Steamed vegetables for my lovely wife, who is still breast feeding," Blane said. "And your,s who is not breast feeding but likes vegetables anyway."

"Noelle eats them, too," Aden said.

"Tink, too," Blane said.

"Takes all kinds," Aden chuckled and finished his bacon.

"So," Aden said. "I saw you leave." When Blane didn't respond, he added, "Last night."

Blane shook his head as he stirred the muffin batter in the bowl in front of him.

"I went for a walk with Nelson," Blane said. "I dropped him off and came back to the Castle."

"Nelson was not with you when I saw you leave," Aden said.

"Stalking much?" Blane asked, with an exaggerated aggression.

"You *want* to tell me," Aden said. "You *need* to tell me."

"Hey, give the man a break," Jacob said, coming down the long stairs.

"What are you doing awake, slacker?" Aden asked.

"I'm on toddler duty," Jacob said. "Or did you not notice that Rachel Ann, your own flesh and blood, was missing?"

"That's how I witnessed . . .," Aden said, with a wave of his hand to Blane. "I brought Rachel Ann to *your* loft!"

Aden gave Jacob a frustrated look. Jacob laughed.

"You *want* to tell us," Jacob said. "You *need* to tell us."

Blane leaned his head back to implore the heavens.

"Hey." Jacob tapped Blane's chest. "We're right here."

Aden and Blane laughed.

"So . . .," Jacob said.

"I came home to check on Heather," Blane said. "She said that she was okay, so I went for a friendly visit with our neighbor."

Blane nodded. The timer rang, and he took a pair of muffin tins out of the oven. After setting them down in front of Jacob, he stuck the next pair of muffin tins into the oven. Jacob started taking the muffins out of the tins and placing them on a cooling rack.

"And?" Aden asked.

"It was nice," Blane said.

"Nice?" Aden asked.

Blane shot him another falsely aggressive look. Aden grinned.

"All of the equipment worked," Blane said, evenly. He paused for a moment before adding, "Well. All parties were satisfied. I think . . . Pretty sure."

"After all this time, we wondered if the equipment worked," Jacob said.

"No you didn't," Blane said.

"We might have," Aden said.

Blane laughed.

"Did you stay?" Jacob asked.

Blane shook his head.

"I felt weird," Blane said. "You know, he hasn't had anyone over — ever — and I just kind of showed up. Plus, I wanted to be back for Wyn's feeding. Heather's been in Olympia for this fairy-war crap. Sometimes, Wyn takes it out on her when she gets back."

"Was it a problem that you left?" Aden asked.

"He has court this morning," Blane said with a shake of his head.

They fell silent while Blane checked the cooling muffins' temperature. Jacob grabbed a large serving plate from the cabinet, and Blane started setting them on the plate. When the plate was full, Jacob took it to the Castle kitchen table.

"Are you and Nelson . . . 'on'?" Aden asked.

Blane nodded. Aden and Jacob didn't respond, so Blane looked up. Jacob was wiping tears from the corner of his eyes, and Aden was looking at the ground.

"What's this?" Blane asked.

"Just happy for you," Aden said.

Aden patted Blane's shoulder. Aden grabbed another piece of bacon and picked up a muffin from the plate on the table. Liking the idea that he was depriving the fairies, he picked up another muffin and left for work. Jacob hugged Blane tight, kissed his cheek, and went to get Maggie. When Jacob came back through the kitchen with a very sleepy Maggie, Blane was standing next to another tray of cooling muffins.

"Thanks," Blane said.

"For what?" Jacob asked.

He stopped walking to look at Blane.

"For caring," Blane said. "For having courage for me even when I didn't have any for myself."

"I love you, bro," Jacob said. "I want you to have a full, happy life."

Blane nodded. Jacob opened his mouth to say something else.

"Get the fuck out of here before they start shooting the 'Day of our Pathetic Life' in our kitchen," Blane said.

"Don't say bad words," Maggie admonished in a sleep filled voice.

"Sorry," Blane mouthed.

Jacob shrugged. He blew Blane a kiss and headed up stairs with Maggie.

~~~~~~~~

Thursday early morning — 6:05 a.m.

"What does that mean?" Nash asked.

He was speaking with Nadia via an Internet Video Chat. He hadn't realized how his question sounded until he saw her wince.

"Sorry," Nash said. "There's just so much buildup with this thing. I thought we'd were leaving in a few days."

"I guess that's the question," Nadia said.

"What's the question?" Nash asked.

"Is it safe for you to go?" Nadia asked.

Nash opened his mouth to protest, but Nadia pressed on.

"Before you say it, I know that you are not a child," Nadia said. She gave a heavy, resigned sigh. "You must understand that *you* are precious to *me*."

"I am?" Nash asked.

Nadia rolled her eyes at him and continued.

"By being precious to me, your life is no longer anonymous," Nadia said. "You are connected to me and the money my parents made. You are *vulnerable* because I *care* about you."

"It's never seemed to stop Ivan," Nash said.

"Ivan was in a *gulag*," Nadia said. "There's very little that freaks him out. Until he and Sissy sorted their lives out, I'm not sure he really wanted to live."

She gave Nash an "Is that what you want?" look. Nash acquiesced.

"I am sorry, Nash," Nadia said. "You, me, your family — we may need to all sit this one out."

"But . . ." Nash said.

Nadia shook her head.

"That doesn't mean we cannot go into the mine," Nadia said.

"How?" Nash asked.

"We hire people to do it," Nadia said. "They are not at risk because they are overpriced employees. They have the experience to get in and out without being noticed."

"But who would do that?" Nash asked.

"Military contractors," Nadia said with a nod. "Ten years ago, the Fey Team was for hire for this kind of thing."

"Alex and Raz?" Nash asked.

"Alex and her team, before Raz," Nadia said. "That's how Seth was able to free Ivan. You know them, and they know this project. Maybe you should ask."

"They are in Africa," Nash said.

"One of the team will call your house tonight," Nadia said. "Right?"

Nash nodded.

"There's your chance," Nadia said. "Anyone paying any attention will think that a father is checking in with his child. It's a good cover."

Seeing Nash's miserable look, Nadia softened.

"You will just have to be satisfied by setting this thing up," Nadia said.

"It doesn't seem like enough," Nash said.

"There are adults, making *a lot* of money — right now — who couldn't have done what you and Teddy have done," Nadia said. "It's an entire career."

"Don't be so quick to rush out ahead," Nash said, almost under his breath. His eyes flicked to Nadia, "It's something Colin always says. 'Don't be so quick to rush out ahead. There are people who thrive on being there first. There's no award for dying first.' That's what he says."

"He's right," Nadia said. "The people we remember from history weren't the ones who rushed in."

"Fools," Nash said.

"Yes, 'Fools rush in,'" Nadia said. "Listen, I know that you need to get to school, and I should get to the hospital for rounds. Just think about what we talked about."

"We'll talk tonight?" Nash asked.

"Of course," Nadia said with a smile.

"I'll talk to Honey," Nash said.

Nash raised his hand in a wave, and Nadia clicked off.

"Well, that sucks," Teddy said from behind Nash.

Nash nodded.

"I wonder if we can go to Paris instead," Teddy said. "You know, see Sissy."

"Good thinking," Nash said with a smile.

"Let's wait for it all to play out, and we'll see," Teddy said.

Their alarm went off. Sandy banged on the door to their room.

"School!" Sandy said at the door before moving on to Noelle's room.

Having already showered, Nash nodded to Teddy and started getting dressed.

~~~~~~~~~

Thursday morning — 8:05 a.m.

Ava O'Malley stood behind Nelson Weeks in the security line to get into the Alfred A. Arraj United States Courthouse. The team had met at eight outside the building. They were now working their way into the Courthouse. They were giving testimony in a criminal case this morning and were due in court at nine.

"So . . ." Ava said. She touched Nelson's wet hair. "Late night?"

"I noticed that, too!" Leslie McClintock, a fellow lab member, said.

"Leave him alone," Fran Dekay said from the back.

Nelson made it through the scanner and was picking up his laptop and backpack. As if he were trying to get away, Nelson rushed off down the hall. Ava caught up with him quickly. She grabbed his arm.

"Stop!" Leslie yelled to them.

Laughing, he stopped and waited for Leslie and Fran.

"I may as well tell you," Nelson said. "Last night, I . . ."

Having their attention, Nelson blushed and stopped talking.

"Oh, Nelson," Leslie said. She hugged Nelson tight. "I'm so glad."

"I want details!" Ava said with a laugh.

"Sexual harassment?" Fran asked Ava.

Ava laughed. They turned to Nelson.

"He's everything," Nelson said. "The whole package —smart and kind and he really listens. I mean. . . I got home late. I saw that they were up, so I went over. Heather always says that if the lights are on, I should just come over. So I did. They were starting a second dinner because Sam just arrived with some kids who are his siblings or something like that. He just met them. I ate this amazing food — some competition between Blane and that singer, Jeraine? I got cuddled by a tiny, little red-haired girl who was missing her 'Daddy.' I changed a bunch of diapers. I went for a walk with Blane around City Park in the dark, where we really talked about our *feelings* and history of knowing each other. He found out that he was my dream person, and I . . ."

"And?" Fran asked.

"He came over afterwards," Nelson said.

"And?" Fran asked.

"It was nice. Good. Great. Fun," Nelson said. "He is so hot . . . so hot."

"Yes, he is," Ava said.

"*Prosecutor*," Leslie said in a terse whisper. She gestured to the Prosecutor and her team.

The Prosecutor saw Ava and her team and stopped short. Ava's team had spent the last week working with this Prosecutor to make sure the case was ready for trial.

"So . . ." the Prosecutor said.

Expecting her to ask about the case, they turned to look at her.

"Blane?" the Prosecutor asked.

Nelson nodded his head.

"Yes!" the Prosecutor said, with a pump of her fist.

The Prosecutor wiggled her eyebrows and walked down the hall toward the court room. She got to the door, and she turned.

"Are you coming?" the Prosecutor asked.

Aware of her choice of words, she laughed and went inside. Leslie and Fran started down the hall. Ava put her arm over Nelson's shoulders.

"I feel like I'm vibrating," Nelson said in a low tone. "Was it like this for you?"

"With Seth?" Ava asked. She kissed Nelson on the cheek. "It still is. The man makes me weak in the knees."

They walked toward the courtroom. Ava opened the door, and Nelson started through.

"Blane is the whole package," Ava said, under her breath. "Very hot."

Nodding, he followed her into the courtroom.

CHAPTER 521

EVERY BEGINNING STARTS WITH . . .

Thursday night — 9:05 p.m.

Dr. Nelson Weeks got off the 15 bus and stepped out onto Colfax Boulevard. After a late night, he'd had a long, difficult day. He'd been on the witness stand all afternoon. They'd met with the prosecutor to go over his testimony. He was likely to be in the witness box for most of tomorrow. After meeting with the prosecutor, they'd met as a team at Ava's house.

This case would stand or fall based on their forensic work and their ability to explain complex science to a jury. They needed to be strategic. They ate amazing New Mexican food made by Maresol and talked shop. He'd walked to Colfax to clear his head. A short trip on the 15 Colfax bus took him to Race Street and Colfax Boulevard.

He made no attempt to kid himself.

He'd come this way so that he would have to pass the Castle before reaching his home. If the light was on, he was going inside.

And if the light wasn't on? What would he do then? Text Blane? Call? Drop by anyway?

Shaking his head at himself, he started down Race.

He stopped short just outside the Castle gate. From where he stood, the Castle and its wild inhabitants were awake. People were milling around in the back of the Castle driveway. He thought that this meant everyone was in back, but he wasn't sure.

He couldn't help but smile. He was about to put in the code that Jacob had given him when he saw Heather, carrying Wyn, walking toward him.

"How was today?" she asked as she let him inside.

"Okay," Nelson said. "Good. Hard. And . . ."

Nelson put her hand on Heather's arm.

"You know that Blane came to see me last night," Nelson said.

Nelson gave a serious nod to give context to his words. To his surprise, Heather grinned at him.

"Yes," Heather said. "And, was that okay?"

All at once, he felt a flush of surprise, relief, delight, and embarrassment. Nelson cleared his throat. Heather smiled.

"He makes me really happy," Nelson said softly.

"Good," Heather said. "That's really good."

Heather put her arm over his shoulder, and they walked toward the back.

"I'll take your jacket and get you some dessert," Heather said. "Would you like . . .?"

Heather gestured to Wyn.

"Love him," Nelson said.

Heather gave Wyn to Nelson. The baby grinned when he saw Nelson's face.

"How is he today?" Nelson asked.

"Oh, he's still mad at me," Heather said with a shrug. "But that's his right."

"That doesn't bother you?" Nelson asked.

"Oh," Heather said. "Depends on the moment. Sometimes, it really hurts. He's so different from his brother. Mack just takes everything as it comes."

Heather grinned.

"Wyn has a little Olympian god in him," Heather said.

Nelson laughed. She pointed to the back.

"Blane's in the back," Heather said. "Honey's husband is home from a long trip. He's in the military. We never know when he's leaving or coming home."

"Honey?" Nelson asked. His brows dropped in confusion.

"That's right. You haven't really met Honey, have you?" Heather asked. "She's Jake's sister. You've seen her. She's in a wheelchair?"

"I don't think so," Nelson said. "I mean, maybe we've met. We've been in the same places at the same time, but . . ."

"You've been pretty focused on Blane," Heather said. Nelson blushed. "As it should be."

Heather shrugged.

"You sat with her daughter Maggie last night," Heather said.

"She's adorable," Nelson said.

"Maggie?" Heather asked. "She really is a special child. You made a big impression on her."

"I did?" Nelson asked.

"She's been telling everyone that she met a handsome prince last night," Heather said.

Nelson grinned and stood up a little straighter.

"Head on back," Heather said. "I'll drop your jacket and grab you some dessert. We're hiding some of it from the fairies."

Heather winked, and Nelson grinned.

"Beer?" Nelson asked.

"In back," Heather said.

She started toward the Castle side door. When he didn't move, she waved him toward the back. He watched Heather until she reached the door.

"Go!" Heather said.

Smiling at her, he looked down at the bundle in his arms. Wyn was looking up at him. In that moment, Nelson felt as if the baby could see everything good and anything bad inside of him. Nelson smiled at the baby, and the baby touched his face.

"More than a *little* Olympian god," Nelson said as he started toward the back.

Blane was standing so that Nelson could see the side of his face. As he approached, Blane turned to look at him. Blane smiled that heart-pounding smile, and Nelson stopped walking. Blane took one step and kissed him on the lips.

Right there!

In front of everyone!

Terrified of public affection, Nelson broke off the kiss to look around.

No one even bothered to look at them. Jacob had been standing next to Blane. He stepped forward to shake Nelson's hand and welcome him into the little gathering. A tall, muscular guy who Blane introduced as "Aden" also shook Nelson's hand. Blane put his arm around Nelson.

"Hey, M.J.!" Blane said.

Blane reached out to touch Honey's husband M.J. Scully's shoulder. M.J. turned to look at Blane.

"I want to meet . . ." Blane started.

Nelson gasped and recoiled, breaking away from Blane.

M.J. jerked backward so fast that he tripped and fell.

Nelson pressed Wyn into Blane's arms. His heart was pounding in his ears, Nelson spun around and ran down the driveway. He'd just reached the gate when Jacob caught up with him.

Jacob put his hand on Nelson's arm.

"Stop!" Jacob commanded.

The pounding in his ears was so loud that Nelson could barely hear Jacob. He bent over to keep from throwing up. There were footsteps in their direction. Aden arrived, as did Blane.

"Please . . ." M.J. said from ten feet away. "Don't go."

There was a whirring as Honey came up behind him.

"What is . . .?" Honey asked.

Nelson stood up to look at her.

"Oh, my God," Honey said as she exhaled.

"What is going on?" Blane demanded of Nelson.

When Nelson couldn't respond, Blane turned to M.J. and Honey. Neither of them would meet Blane's eyes. Sam Lipson stepped in front of Nelson.

"Looks like we need to sit down and sort this out," Sam said.

"Really, I've had a long day, and . . ." Nelson started.

"You want me to believe that you'll sleep tonight, son," Sam said.

Nelson glanced at Blane and then back at Sam.

"Really, it's okay," Nelson said.

"It's not okay," M.J. said.

Without turning to M.J., Sam nodded his head.

"Come inside," Sam said. "We'll sit down like adults and work this out."

Gently pushing, Sam got M.J. and Honey moving toward the Castle. Used to doing whatever Sam asked, Blane started toward the Castle as well. Nelson didn't move from where he was standing. Jacob stood with him.

"Whatever it is," Jacob said in a low tone, "you can be sure that my dad can help sort this out."

Nelson looked up at Jacob.

"He has a lot of experience with this kind of thing," Jacob said.

Nelson looked at Jacob. Before he said another word, Nelson threw up into the little patch of grass in front of the house.

"Good thing the photographers aren't here," Nelson said, wiping his mouth with the sleeve of his shirt.

Jacob laughed. Nelson looked up at Jacob.

"I love my sister," Jacob said. "I fucking hate those photographers."

Nelson smiled.

"What do you have to lose?" Jacob asked.

"I should clean up." Nelson looked down at the pile of chewed New Mexican food.

"I'll get it. You don't know where a hose is or the hose bibb," Jacob said.

"Are you sure?" Nelson asked.

"Of course," Jacob said. "You'd be surprised how much vomit happens in my life."

"Really?" Nelson asked.

Jacob grinned in response. He gestured to Jeraine. "Hey, Jeraine!"

Jeraine looked out at the street to see which adoring fan was hailing him. Laughing, Tanesha hit his chest with the back of her hand. Jeraine turned to her and scowled. She pointed to Jacob. Jacob waved Jeraine in his direction.

"Can you take Nelson inside?" Jacob asked.

"Of course," Jeraine said. "What's going on?"

"There's some issue between Nelson and M.J.," Jacob said. "Maybe Honey, too. Dad is going to do his thing with them."

Jeraine nodded.

"I thought you'd want to be there," Jacob said.

"You're right," Jeraine said. "Blane's friend is in trouble. I'm in it."

Surprised, Nelson just gawked at him.

"Aren't you usually a narcissistic asshole?" Nelson blurted out.

His words must have carried because Tanesha burst out laughing. She nodded to Nelson.

"You're in luck," Jeraine said.

"Why's that?" Nelson asked.

"Tonight's my night off from being a narcissistic asshole," Jeraine said. He put his arm around Nelson and maneuvered him toward the front door. "Come on. I'll show you a secret."

Jeraine walked Nelson up to the vine-heavy porch. He took out a key and opened the front door to the Castle.

"Most people don't know this door opens," Jeraine said.

He pushed the door open.

"How did you . . .?" Nelson asked.

"Jake," Jeraine said. "When I was having trouble with my brain, I used to come over here sometimes and sit on the porch with Delphie."

Jeraine gestured to a corner of the porch.

"It's an amazing, quiet, private place to think," Jeraine said. "It's cool in the summer and not too cold in the winter. Delphie's out here a lot — just sitting and drinking tea."

"Why don't they use the door?" Nelson asked as they went inside.

"It was broken for a long time," Jeraine said. "Then the paparazzi showed up. It's just a lot easier to come and go from the side."

Before Nelson knew it, he was walking down a hallway into the main Castle living room.

"This is an amazing house," Nelson said in a low voice.

"You don't know the half of it," Jeraine said.

Jeraine stopped walking, and Nelson stepped to his side. Honey was sitting near the armchair where M.J. was sitting. Honey's sole focus seemed to be the teacup in her hand. M.J. didn't look up. Sam stood up and gestured for Nelson to take the other couch.

"Are you staying?" Sam asked.

"I thought maybe my man Nelson, here, might need me," Jeraine said.

Blane came in carrying two mugs of tea. He gave one to Nelson and another to Jeraine. He turned around to find Fin standing in the doorway with another mug of tea. Fin gave Blane the mug of tea and went into the kitchen. Heather came in from the kitchen with a tin of cookies.

"Sandy's been baking," Heather said.

Sam snorted a laugh. Nelson shook his head that he didn't understand.

"The fairies love sweet things," Blane said. "Since they've been here, it's all we can do to keep up with their appetites."

"Blane, me," Jeraine said, "and Sandy have been baking up a storm. Even Miss T has made chocolate-chip cookies."

Jeraine nodded, as did Blane. Heather took an armchair. Jeraine and Blane took the couch. Sam gestured for Nelson to sit next to him. Nelson glanced at Blane. With Nelson's look, Jeraine got up and sat down next to Sam on the couch. Nelson sat next to Blane. They sat with their hands in their laps like schoolchildren.

For a moment, no one said anything.

"We don't know what's going on," Sam said.

No one said anything.

"Honey?" Sam asked. Honey was Sam's daughter by marriage. He had more sway over her, so he pressed. "What is this?"

She looked up at him and winced. He gave her a stern look, and she swallowed hard.

"Guy lived next door to M.J.'s mom's house," Honey started. She looked at Nelson, and said, "How are you, Guy?"

"Don't you mean 'Gay'?" Nelson spit out. "Or how about 'Gay Semen'?"

Honey gasped. Her eyes flicked to Blane and then back to Nelson. She swallowed hard.

"Oh, crap," Honey said.

M.J. looked up at Honey.

"He's 'Nelson,'" Honey said.

M.J. looked at Nelson. Rather than say anything, he dropped his head into his hands.

"What does 'Oh crap, he's Nelson' mean?" Jeraine asked. "I may be an asshole, but *that* does not sound good."

"We've just heard about Nelson," Honey said. "'Nelson the doctor.' 'Nelson, Blane's new hunky friend.' 'Nelson who works with Ava.' Our daughter is positively smitten with you. I was looking forward to thanking you for helping her last night and..."

Honey's voice faded out. Nelson did not respond.

"Who is 'Guy'?" Blane asked.

"It's his name," M.J. said through his hands. "My bitch of a mother used to call him '*Gay*,' if she wasn't calling him '*Little Faggot*' or '*Gay Boy*' or. . . that other thing that he said."

"'*Gay Semen*'?" Jeraine asked. "Seriously?"

M.J. nodded.

"She made his life a living hell," Honey said.

"I didn't even know that I was gay," Nelson said. "I hadn't even admitted it to myself. And *you* two . . . You cannot sit there now and pretend that it was only your *mother*."

M.J. sat up straight.

"No, you're right," M.J. said. "I made your life a living hell."

"Me, too," Honey said. "I did that."

Sam gave Honey an angry look. She wilted at his look.

"You told my father!" Nelson said.

"My mother did," M.J. said. "I was just there."

"He kicked me out of the house," Nelson said. "I had nowhere to go!"

"What did you do?" Blane asked.

Feeling the weight of everyone's stares, Nelson shook his head.

"I . . . I had nowhere to go!" Nelson said. "I was out there in the *snow* and . . ."

Nelson looked at M.J.

"You really don't know?" Nelson asked.

"No," M.J. said. "You just disappeared. I was too caught up in my own bullshit that I didn't even think to ask . . ."

"Your dad saved my life," Nelson said.

"Michael," M.J. said evenly.

"Of course, you hated him," Nelson said. "He was a decent human being. Disgusting, filthy creatures like you couldn't even begin to understand someone kind, like he was."

"I hated him," M.J. said. In his words, he seemed to accept that he deserved Nelson's rage. "And, you are correct. I didn't understand him. What did he do?"

"He found me sleeping in the space between the garages," Nelson said. "He set me up in a hotel. A nice place. Gave me money for food. Fought it out with my dad to get my clothing. He paid for everything until I graduated high school. I'd already been accepted into Georgetown, so I left when school finished. He paid for my bus ticket, talked to some friend of his, who rented me a place. I stayed there all the way through school. He even checked in on me whenever he was in Washington."

Nelson shook his head.

"He was really great, and you *hated* him," Nelson said. "Of course."

"I was wrong," M.J. said.

"Then, again, *I'm* really great," Nelson said. "And you despise me and all disgusting creatures like me. What is it you *always* say? 'Why don't you just kill yourself, faggot?'"

"I don't despise you . . ." M.J. started.

"I always swore that if I *ever* saw you again, I'd . . ." Nelson started.

Overwhelmed with emotion, Nelson shook his head and stood up.

"I'm going home," Nelson said and stalked toward the door.

Blane hopped to his feet. Chasing after Nelson, Blane said, "Wait."

Nelson just shook his head and kept walking. He walked past Jacob, who was spraying the front grass with water from a hose. Blane caught him at the gate.

"Don't call me," Nelson said. "Don't come over."

"But, I . . ." Blane started.

"I feel like garbage," Nelson said. "I haven't felt this low since I was a child. I didn't deserve it as a child, and I certainly don't deserve to feel that way *now*."

Nelson shook his head. Blane reached out to touch Nelson, but Nelson batted away his hand.

"Just leave me alone," Nelson said.

Nelson went through the gate and jogged to his house.

Blane stood at the gate and watched the street long after Nelson had disappeared into his house. Jacob kept his eye on Blane while he cleared off the grass.

"What do I do?" Blane said in a soft voice.

"Give it some time," Jacob said.

"Time?" Blane asked.

His hand went to his chest. He whipped around to look at Jacob.

"It's over, isn't it?" Blane asked.

"Only if you want it to be over," Jacob said.

"What the hell does that mean?" Blane asked. After a beat, he added, "What are you doing?"

"Nelson threw up," Jacob said. "I was cleaning it off."

"Oh," Blane said.

Jacob stopped spraying. Blane followed him to where he turned off the water and coiled up the hose.

"Too bad you don't know the Goddess of Love," Jacob said.

"What?" Blane asked.

"Seems like what's needed here is healing and love," Jacob said. "Maybe you should make an offering to the Goddess."

"Like what?" Blane asked.

"Put the babies down?" Jacob asked with a laugh.

"You think it would work?" Blane asked.

Jacob nodded.

"You think she'd do it?" Blane asked.

"You can ask," Jacob said.

Blane walked toward the side door of the Castle to go find Heather. He was almost to the door when Jacob said, "Remind her to bring an apple."

Blane gave him a strange look but nodded and went inside. Jill had passed out after her finals and was sleeping or resting upstairs. So, Jacob went around to the backyard. The party was clearly over. This conflict between M.J., Honey, and Nelson had put a damper on the gathering. Everyone was inside. Jacob picked up a couple pieces of trash and checked to see if there was any beer left in the keg. Finding the keg empty, he poured out the ice from the bucket the keg had been sitting in and set the keg on the deck. He was just turning off the lights when Hedone came out of the back of the Castle.

"Goddess," Jacob said.

He lowered his eyes. Through the French doors, he saw the fairies getting up from their knees, having bowed to Hedone. He started down, and she laughed

"Jacob Marlowe," Hedone said. "Don't kneel. Not you."

"Did you . . .?" Jacob asked.

Hedone held up two apples. Jacob smiled.

"Good luck," Jacob said under his breath.

"Luck?" Hedone asked.

Laughing, she disappeared around the house. He could hear her beautiful laughter long after he'd finished cleaning up and was upstairs, putting the toddlers to bed.

CHAPTER 522

. . . WITH A BIG MESS

Thursday night — 10:15 p.m.

Emotionally overloaded, M.J. and Honey watched in silence as Blane ran after Nelson. Jeraine shook his head.

"What the hell?" Jeraine asked. "I *know* you. If someone were to ask me if you could behave like this, I would have said . . ."

"No," Sam said, cutting Jeraine off. Surprised, Jeraine shut his mouth. "I have to tell you both that I am beyond disappointed. I am truly shocked. '*Gay Semen*'?"

"His name is, was, I guess, Guy Se-main-es," Honey said in an exaggerated English accent. "It's French. It sounds like 'G-ee Sea-men.' M.J.'s mother changed it to the more cruel version. We didn't make it up."

"That didn't stop us from using it," M.J. said.

M.J. stood up from his seat.

"This is important, M.J.," Sam said. "We are not finished here."

"Yes, I realized that," M.J. said. "But I need to check in. With work."

Honey looked up at him and winced.

"We need to work this out," Sam said. "Blane feels really strongly about Nelson. This is not something we're going to sweep under the rug. We need to . . ."

"I agree with you," M.J. said. "You have to understand. This situation? This thing right here? I am off the Fey team. Boom."

He started toward the door.

"I have your cell phone," Honey said. She held the phone out to him. "You gave it to me when we went outside."

"What do you mean, you're 'off the Fey team'?" Jeraine asked.

"I cannot have this kind of conflict in my life," M.J. said. "It puts me at risk. If I'm at risk, the whole team is at risk, and..."

No one said anything. M.J. looked up at the ceiling and tried to gather his words.

"I didn't put this on my list," M.J. said.

"Your list?" Sam asked.

"They make a list of potential life situations that could blow up," Honey said.

"After Guy left, I never thought about him again," M.J. said. "Not one thought until just now, when I was standing in the backyard."

"Alex isn't going to care about this!" Sam said.

"Alex isn't the head of the Fey team anymore," M.J. said. "I mean, she's still the leader. It's still her team, but the administrative head is a real stickler for the rules."

"Just call Margaret," Honey said, speaking of M.J.'s partner.

"I can't," M.J. said. "That's the thing. It has to be someone assigned by the team head. And we just got home, and . . ."

M.J. tried to breathe.

"Why are you freaking out?" Jeraine asked.

"You have no idea how many people are standing in line to be on the Fey team," M.J. said. "Thousands. Hundreds of thousands. The moment I step aside, there will be a hundred more qualified, younger, fitter guys or gals who are ready to step in. People without brain injuries. People who have all of their limbs and college degrees and . . ."

Jeraine stood up.

"This is something I know a lot about," Jeraine said. He gave M.J. a nod. "Do you wish to resolve this situation?"

"I do," M.J. said.

"For more than to keep your job?" Sam asked with an uncharacteristic edge to his voice.

"Yes, for more than my job," M.J. said. "I am a member of this household. If Guy is a friend of Blane's, then he will be a member of our family. I need to work this out for myself and for my family."

Jeraine opened his mouth to say something, but M.J. kept talking.

"I feel awful," M.J. said. "I saw his face, and bam! I was right back there. I . . . I feel a great weight over who I was and what I did. There's no excuse, none. Honey was just a little kid. She . . ."

"That's not really an excuse," Honey said.

M.J. shook his head and dialed the phone. He turned his back and walked toward a quiet area of the living room.

"His language is really good," Jeraine said in a soft voice as he sat back down.

"He's been working on it," Honey said. "Being on the Fey team has pushed him to be a better person overall. They've really helped him with his language and . . . well, really everything. He will be devastated if he loses this position."

"We will deal with his situation later," Sam said. "You are not off the hook, young lady."

Honey winced at the tone in his voice.

"I want to know why you did this thing and what you intend to do about it," Sam said. "This is an egregious act of violence against another person. I am deeply disappointed in you."

Honey opened her mouth to say something.

"This happened while you were living under *my* roof," Sam said. "That means that part of the responsibility is on me."

Blane walked into the Castle. Without saying a word to them, he went downstairs.

"I don't care what god or goddess or fairy or magical intervention we can call on to fix this, for us and for Nelson," Sam said. "I want to know what *you* are going to do, and I want to know it now. It's a miracle that that boy is still alive!"

Sam turned the full intensity of his dark look onto Honey. For a long moment, Honey didn't respond.

"I was nine when I met M.J.," Honey said with a nod. "Nine. M.J. was fifteen. Guy left between the time I met and M.J. went into the army . . . He left when he was seventeen, almost eighteen. So, maybe a year or so after I met M.J., Guy left. I didn't know that he'd been kicked out. I don't think that M.J. knew. Guy was older than us. I didn't know how much older, just older. I didn't really think about him leaving."

Honey nodded.

"I'd just started living with you around the time that Guy left," Honey said. "I think I said something to you or around you about Guy or someone else being gay. You were furious. You ranted about love and people being who they were. You took me to meet your friend Jerry."

"I remember that," Sam said with a nod.

"Honestly, I know that it sounds like an excuse, but I don't mean it as one," Honey said. "I literally *did not* know better. I hated everyone, anyone, especially myself. I didn't know what 'gay' really meant except that it was someone different. I knew that it was a put-down. I knew I was being mean, putting Guy down. I didn't really know what it meant to be gay or live gay or that people lived and loved and . . ."

Honey shook her head.

"I don't think I thought of Guy as human because I didn't think of anyone as human," Honey said. "I mean other than me and the pain I felt, day in and day out. I just hurt, all the time, on the inside. I was so angry. So angry. It's hard for me to even believe that I was so angry. But my sister . . ."

"Is that the 'step-whore'?" Jeraine asked.

Sam looked up, and Honey nodded. Jeraine made a face to indicate what he knew about the woman. Honey continued.

"The only way I knew how to get out of the pain inside was to put other people down, to make myself feel bigger by making other people smaller. But I only made myself feel smaller and smaller and smaller. That's all I knew."

Honey looked at Sam.

"Until I lived with you," Honey said.

Sam opened his mouth to speak. Hedone walked past them. In the kitchen, the fairies dropped to their knees as she walked past them to the backyard.

"I don't know what to do," Honey said. "I honestly don't."

Blane appeared in the living room.

"What the hell was that about?" Blane asked. He looked at Honey. "What kind of a monster are you?"

"I'm sorry, Blane," Honey said. "I truly am. If I had known . . ."

"Do you think that of me?" Blane asked. "All this time, and I . . ."

"No," Honey said, shaking her head. Her face was a mask of pain and sorrow. "No. I have been cruel in my past. I'm sure that I'm cruel now, sometimes. That's true. I try to do better, to be better. M.J., too."

Honey gestured to where M.J. was pacing and talking into his phone.

"What's wrong with him?" Blane asked.

"He could lose his position over this," Honey said.

"Oh," Blane said. He scowled. "Seriously?"

Honey nodded.

"He feels really bad, too," Honey said. "I can't speak for him, but I know that I didn't know any better. I simply did not. When I think about it now, I am deeply . . . humiliated."

Blane's eyes raked her face.

"I am sorry," Honey said.

Not sure what to say, Blane simply shook his head. He was heartbroken that Nelson had left and that it was his wonderful family who had been so ugly.

"I need to take care of the kids," Blane said.

With that, he turned and went toward the basement stairs. M.J. got off the phone. Honey looked up at him.

"They are sending someone to speak with me," M.J. said.

"What do we do?" Honey asked.

"We wait," M.J. said. Before Sam could say anything, M.J. added, "Sir, I want you to know how badly I feel about this. I can assure you that I am not the person I was when I made those statements. I am horrified to remember the pain I inflicted by my own ignorance. Regardless of what happens, I would like to talk this through with Nelson. I need to know and understand to the full extent what I did to him before I can truly understand what might make it better."

"Me, too," Honey said, meekly.

The stairs creaked, and they turned to see who was there. Sandy came down the staircase holding little Maggie's hand. When they reached the main Castle living room, Maggie let go of Sandy's hand and ran to her mother. Honey picked up her daughter and hugged her tight. Oblivious to the heavy emotion in the air, Maggie started talking in her characteristically chipper tone.

"Mommy?" Maggie asked. "Noelle is having a sleepover for just the girls. Katy's going to be there! The boys are in the loft, but Mommy — Noelle asked *me* to come, too!"

Maggie gave her mother a big grin.

"Me and Rachel Ann," Maggie said. "Even Jackie's coming! We're going to stay in Noelle's room. Tink is sleeping in Sissy's old bed, and Charlie made little beds for us little kids!"

"Noelle and Tink thought it would be fun to have the girls sleep together," Sandy said. "Heather's boys, Jabari, Jill's twins, Charlie, Nash, and Teddy are upstairs in the loft. Charlie, Nash, and Teddy wanted to talk to Jake about the trip to Poland and . . ."

"Are you okay with that?" Honey asked. "It sounds like a lot."

"Of course," Sandy said. "We're all up so late, we figured this might be a fun end."

"Daddy's home, so you can sleep with him!" Maggie said.

The little girl gave her mother a big smile as if she'd thought of a special treat for her mother. Maggie jumped off Honey's lap and ran to her father, M.J. He picked her up and hugged her tight. He blew raspberries on her stomach until she was breathless from giggling. He set her down.

"Is there any way we can help?" Honey asked.

"We'll be fine," Sandy said with a grin. "I wanted to check if Maggie had any dietary restrictions."

"She eats what I eat because it's easier to feed her what I'm eating," Honey said.

"Jackie can't drink milk or eat wheat," Sandy said.

"Oh?" Honey asked. "I didn't realize that."

"We'll be fine," Sandy said. "We were talking about doing some baking tonight — keep up with the fairies. We'll make sure to make something she can eat."

Sandy looked from face to face. She opened her mouth to ask what was going on, but Sam shook his head. She nodded.

"Let me know if I can help," Honey said.

"Feel free to send her home at any time," M.J. said.

"You, too," Sandy said looking at Honey.

She bent over and hugged Honey. Assuming that Honey was upset about something M.J. had done, Sandy scowled at him. M.J. put his hand on his chest and shook his head.

"Sure," Sandy said under her breath, which made M.J. laugh.

Sandy held her hand out to Maggie, but Maggie took off up the stairs.

"My cue," Sandy said.

She followed Maggie up the stairs.

"Daddy?" Jabari asked as he and Tanesha entered the room.

He squirmed from Tanesha's grasp and ran to his father. Not one to stand on ceremony, he climbed up onto Jeraine's lap. Unlike Maggie, he was acutely aware of the tension in the air. He settled in on Jeraine's lap.

"What's happened?" Jabari asked. "Who fucked up?"

"Jabari!" Tanesha said.

M.J. and Honey struggled to keep from laughing. Sam scowled.

"That's what happened — right?" Jabari said with a shrug. "So, did you screw around?"

He looked at his father and then at M.J. Shaking her head incredulously, Tanesha plucked Jabari up from Jeraine's lap.

"But, Mommy — they might need my help!" Jabari said as she carried him away. "Daaaddddy! You can come get me if you need help."

They waited until the boy was out of hearing range before everyone laughed.

"He has a lot of experience with this kind of thing," Jeraine said. "You know, from his mom's house."

"Daaaddddy!" Jabari yelled from upstairs. "You didn't say 'goood niiiiight.'"

"The boy has a set of lungs on him," Jeraine said. He got up and started toward the door. He stopped and turned back, "You know, Jabari's mom is really cruel. She says horrible things to people all the time. My therapist says it's because she feels like she's powerless. She doesn't remember what she says — to me, to Jabari, to Tanesha. We were supposed to switch to shared custody, but she went crazy on Jabari. Again. She doesn't feel bad about any of it. The fact that you feel badly means there's a chance we'll work this stuff out."

"I agree," Sam said.

Jeraine nodded and went into the kitchen to head up to the loft. They sat silently for a moment.

"I don't know what else to say; I . . ." M.J. said.

The gate alarm buzzed, and M.J. went to the closet, where the gate video feed was visible.

"I have to go," M.J. said.

"This isn't done until we make it right with Nelson," Sam said.

"Yes, sir," M.J. said. "I agree. Thank you for your patience with us."

"We'll make it right," Honey said to Sam. "I give you my word."

"Good," Sam said.

Honey rolled to where M.J. was putting on his jacket.

"Who is it?" Honey asked.

"One of my dad's old teammates," M.J. said. "Major Joseph Walter."

"Good," Honey said.

M.J. leaned down to hug Honey. They kissed, and he left the Castle. She watched him greet his father's teammate and his superior officer. They set off into the night. Honey sighed.

"What do I do?" Honey asked as she wheeled back to Sam.

"We have to set the intention that this will work out," Sam said. "If we give it time and energy, we'll get there."

Sam leaned down to kiss Honey's cheek. She watched him say 'Good night' to the fairies in the kitchen and head up the stairs to Delphie's apartment. Sighing to herself, she rolled back to her apartment. She filled her bathtub.

Only when she was in the warm water did she let go and weep.

~~~~~~~~~
Thursday night — 10:20 p.m.

Nelson had stepped inside the door to his apartment and stopped walking. He may or may not have locked the door.

In his exhausted state, his mind began to fall apart. He'd carefully constructed his entire life in order to specifically to avoid any thought about his childhood and this person who was at the very center of his pain. He felt like a nuclear bomb had gone off in his psyche. Standing in the entryway to his home, he could feel his life crumble around him.

There was something wrong with his eyes. He couldn't focus on the world around him. As if he were surrounded by a dark cloud, he only saw darkness.

He felt oddly blank.

A breeze came up from behind him. He didn't respond. He didn't care if some drug-crazed criminal broke into his house and killed him outright. At this moment, he was more dead than alive.

The wind seemed to blow him into his kitchen. The next thing he knew, he was eating the best apple he'd ever eaten. He knew it was an apple by the taste and texture.

He blinked. His eyes were starting to clear.

"This must be what magic feels like," he said out loud.

Then he did something he'd never done before — he ate the core of the apple. Another apple appeared in his hand. He found himself devouring the apple as if his life depended on it.

Only when he'd eaten the entire thing, core and all, was he able to take his first real breath since seeing M.J. again.

"Fuck," he said out loud.

His eyes cleared completely. He saw that what he'd taken for his kitchen was actually some other kitchen filled with a kind of golden light.

He closed and opened his eyes. Thinking it might help, he loosened his tie.

A blurry figure appeared before him. He felt such overwhelming joy in the presence of this creature that he fell to his knees.

And so Nelson Weeks began the second half of his life.

Before he was a forensic scientist with the Best Fucking Back Up Laboratory, before he was an emergency medicine doctor, before he was at the top of his fellowship, before he was the best person to ever go through his residency program, before he was *summa cum laude* in his medical school class at University of California, San Francisco, before he was *summa cum laude* at Georgetown University, before he'd graduated at the top of his class at East High School in Denver, when he was simple old Guy Semaines, he was a human child whose mother had died a horrible death and whose father had never recovered from it.

That human child met the Goddess of Love one night.

For a while, he hung in the in-between.

And, then, his life started again.

CHAPTER 523

... AND A DANCE WITH GHOSTS FROM THE PAST

Hedone found Nelson standing just inside the carriage house where he lived. He seemed to be in some kind of dissociative fugue. He didn't or possibly couldn't see her. She opened her hands and her arms, causing golden light to flood him. She let the light do its work. When he seemed to be waking, she put a golden apple in his hand.

As if he hadn't eaten in a year, he devoured the apple with giant bites. He ate the apple core and seeds. She put another apple in his hand. He ate that down.

His entire body shuddered. His eyes closed for a long moment. When he opened his eyes again, he was awake. Seeing her, he instinctively dropped to his knees.

Hedone wasn't sure what caused this reaction in others. The fairies had started doing this when she transformed into a full goddess. The longer she was the Goddess of Love, the more beings fell to their knees. Hedone was not comfortable with this kind of prostration.

She held out her hands and helped him up. They stood face to face.

He gasped.

"Hedone," Nelson said, recognizing her for the first time. "I didn't recognize you."

He started to drop to his knees again, but she held him up.

"Please don't," Hedone said.

"Is it possible to have another apple?" Nelson asked.

"Of course," Hedone said.

This time, Nelson seemed to savor every bite of this apple.

"This is the best apple I've ever eaten," Nelson said. He held the apple to his nose. "Just the smell is divine."

"Apples are my thing," Hedone said.

"Now that you're a goddess?" Nelson asked.

"Always," Hedone said. "It was a long time before apples were common fruit. Most of history, they were something people could only dream about. But then again, some apples are worth dreaming about."

"I will dream about this apple for as long as I live," Nelson said. "Have you ever thought about trying to grow them?"

"Of course," Hedone said. "There might be a tree behind the Castle — a gift in homage to the Oracle."

Nelson suddenly looked surprised. Hedone smiled.

"Am I still alive?" Nelson asked as he looked around. He was standing in a white-walled room with a beautiful blue sky above him. It seemed to be day light, but he was sure that was artificial.

"You're in the in-between," Hedone said.

"What is the in-between?" Nelson asked.

"The in-between is a place that humans fall into when they've been dislodged from their lives and aren't sure what will happen next," Hedone said. "Everyone sees it a little differently. Clearly, you see yourself in some kind of medical exam room."

"It does look like an ED exam room," Nelson said with a nod. Nelson pointed to the blue sky above. "I've never seen one like that, though."

"Fair enough. This is a place in the mind as much as it's a place in the world," Hedone said. "You may be here for hours or many days, even years."

"What ends the time in the in-between?" Nelson asked.

"You decide that you've had enough of life, or you commit to life again," Hedone said. "You've done this before."

"On the bus to Georgetown," Nelson said. "Yes. But then I had this great future ahead of me — college, medical school, being an ER doctor. It wasn't hard to commit to life then."

"And now?" Hedone asked.

"I . . ." Nelson started and then stopped. He nodded his head. "I have nothing to look forward to. I've blown it with Blane, and I've been sick, and my career is . . ."

He stopped talking and looked horrified.

"I have to be in court tomorrow morning," Nelson said. "I don't have time for this."

Hedone smiled.

"Why do you look so smirky?" Nelson asked.

"You have time *only* for this," Hedone said. She gave him a kind look.

"I need sleep," Nelson said. "I'm exhausted. I don't have time for an existential crisis!"

"You're in the middle of one, anyway," Hedone said.

Nelson scowled. Hedone lifted a shoulder.

"It's bent time," Hedone said. "I can put you back to where you were when you walked into your home. You can go to bed, and . . ."

"No," Nelson said, shaking his head. "If I go back, I'll go back to . . . the darkness."

Hedone nodded.

"Can you help?" Nelson asked.

"That's why I am here," Hedone said.

"What needs to happen?" Nelson asked.

"We need to look into the dark spot that has consumed your life," Hedone said.

"You mean that cretin M.J.," Nelson said with disgust in his voice.

"No," Hedone said. "He is merely a screen for the real darkness, your real pain."

"'A screen'?"

"Like a metaphor," Hedone said. "He did something awful that you remember. You then hang all of this emotion on it. Some of the emotion belongs to what M.J. did. But let's be honest . . ."

Nelson looked into her eyes.

"You felt this way long before you met M.J.," Hedone said.

Nelson opened his mouth to respond. Looking into the goddess's eyes, his excuses and defenses seemed like a waste of time. His head went up and down in a slight nod. She smiled at him.

"But . . ." Nelson said.

"It is frightening to look into the darkest places of your psyche," Hedone said. "Terrifying. At least it was for me."

Nelson didn't respond.

"I can allow you someone to go with you," Hedone said. "Someone to be your witness and help you when it's too hard."

"You'll be there," Nelson said.

"I will," Hedone said. "But I will need to be impartial. I cannot comfort you or help you in anyway. I cannot give you advice. If I do, we can get lost in the web of time."

Nelson squinted at her. She sighed.

"It's like the *Christmas Carol*," Hedone said.

"I love that play," Nelson said.

"You're in that play right now," Hedone said.

"Oh, I get it," Nelson said. "The ghosts can only show Scrooge things. They cannot advise about them. Some of them say some snide things, but . . ."

"Exactly," Hedone said. "You may want someone there to be on your side. To help you and only you."

Nelson nodded his head. He looked down at the ground.

"Can it be someone who is dead?" Nelson asked.

Assuming that Nelson was thinking of his mother, Hedone gave him a soft smile.

"I would like . . ." Nelson took a deep breath. "Jackson Theriot."

"Jax?" Hedone asked in surprise. "From the Fey Special Forces Team."

Nelson nodded.

"He was like a brother to me," Nelson said. "If you have sex with your brother, which only really happened a couple of times, but it felt weird because he really was like a brother to me. Plus, he got serious with Roger and . . . M.J.'s dad . . . You know Michael? He introduced us. Jax was there with me every step of the way when I was at Georgetown, and then he and Roger were there when I was in medical school and... I see Roger every year when . . ."

"October 8," Hedone said.

Nodding, Nelson began to cry.

"My name . . ." Nelson looked at Hedone. "Nelson. It means 'son of Neil.' It was Alex Hargreaves' idea because Jax's middle name was Neil. He was like my friend and brother and father, all rolled into one. When I got sick, Roger came to Denver take care of me because we promised to be each other's family since Jax was gone."

Nelson sniffed without making a dent into the snot and tears running down his face.

"Roger gave me . . ." Nelson held up his right middle finger where he always wore a gold band. "It was Jax's. He wore it every day. He was wearing it when he was killed. Roger got the wedding ring that I helped Jax get him, so he figured I deserved this one."

Nelson nodded.

"I . . . miss . . . him," Nelson said. "He would know just what to do with all of this. He'd love Blane and Heather and the kids and . . . Can you?"

"I can try," Hedone said.

Hedone nodded.

"Give me a minute," Hedone said.

Nelson stumbled to sit on a nearby stool. Bending forward, he cried into his hands. A minute — or, maybe, a couple of years — later, Nelson felt a hand on his back. Nelson looked up. Jackson Theriot was standing next to Nelson as real as life. Seeing his friend, Nelson stood up into Jax's arms. The men held each other tight for a long time while Hedone watched. Jax broke off first.

"What are you wearing?" Jax asked.

Jax was wearing jeans, a T-shirt, and a light-orange, zipped hooded sweater. He plucked at the inexpensive suit that Nelson was wearing. He pointed to Nelson's thick glasses and shook his head.

"Glasses? Again? Really?" Jax asked. "Those are your back-up glasses. Don't deny it."

Nelson shook his head.

"What happened to your hair?" Jax asked

Jax plucked at Nelson's glasses. Nelson opened his mouth to defend himself, but Jax continued.

"Did you buy this suit?" Jax asked Nelson.

"Yes, why?" Nelson asked defensively.

"No, you actually spent your hard-earned money on . . . this?" Jax asked.

Jax tipped his head to the side. Jackson pointed to Nelson's face. Nelson took out a handkerchief and wiped his face.

"You got that suit at Goodwill," Jax said. "Those shoes, too."

"Uh . . ." Nelson said and blushed.

The men laughed.

"Do you ever get laid?" Jax asked.

"No," Nelson said, laughing.

Turning to Hedone, Jax asked, "May I?"

"Be my guest," Hedone said.

Jax snapped his fingers. Nelson's glasses were gone, exposing his amber-colored eyes. His tightly shaven hair grew into dark, wavy curls that fell to his shoulders. The bad suit disappeared and was replaced by brown wool slacks and a pastel-green, fitted cotton dress shirt. Without his ill-fitting clothing, Nelson looked taller and fitter than he had before. Jax was nearly six feet. Nelson was just a smidge under that. Nelson's battered dress shoes became ankle boots. Jax leaned back to look at Nelson.

"One more thing," Jax said.

Jax snapped his fingers. Nelson's scraggly mustache and goatee disappeared, exposing Nelson's jutting jaw line. Jax nodded and looked at Hedone.

"Better?" Jax asked.

"Better," Hedone said. "He no longer hides his shine."

"I'm a serious scientist!" Nelson defended himself.

"Seriously ugly scientist," Jax said, quickly.

They laughed and embraced again.

"How long do I have?" Jax asked.

"We have permission for you to stay as long as Nelson needs you," Hedone said. "I have also received permission for some extra time so that you can see Roger and Alex."

"Like I have before?" Jax asked.

"In their dreams," Hedone nodded.

"Good," Jax said.

Jax was so fit and youthful that even Hedone smiled at him. Catching her smile, Jax grinned in return.

"We need to find the source of the black hole inside Nelson's psyche," Hedone said.

"Guy." When Jax said Nelson's birth name, it sounded like "Gee."

"I feel so much better now. Why . . .?" Nelson asked.

"Because this dream will end, and you will be stuck in the dark again," Jax said. His voice caught with emotion. "Don't waste your precious life in the dark. Let's get this done so you can live in the light."

"So says the soldier," Nelson mumbled.

"So says someone who died before he was able to live the life of his dreams," Jax said evenly.

Tears appeared in Nelson's eyes.

"Please," Jax said. "You have life — let's get this done so you can live it."

Jax grabbed Nelson, and the men hugged. Rather than wait, Hedone took them to where they needed to start from.

They were looking at a handsome young couple sitting with their heads pressed together on a bench seat of a high-speed train, at the back, near the baggage compartment. There was an empty bench seat across from them. The man and woman were both looking down at a strikingly beautiful seven-month-old baby who was sitting between them. Wide awake, the baby cooed, and his mother "Ahhed." The baby's eyes were amber. He had a small tuft of dark hair. Seeing his mother's face, the baby laughed.

"Il rit!" his father exclaimed that his son had laughed.

The father kissed the mother's face. They turned to look at their son again. The two were so transfixed that they barely noticed their surroundings.

"Wow," Nelson whispered. "My father looks so young."

"Is that your mother?" Jax asked.

"I don't know," Nelson said. He walked up to where she was sitting and leaned down to see her face. "I guess so. I've never seen her before."

"She is very beautiful," Hedone said. "So full of love. Life. She truly loves you."

"Sometimes, when I sleep, I have this feeling . . ." Nelson said. "I can hear her voice."

Nelson hummed a soft tune.

"*Dodo l'enfant do*," Jax said.

Nelson looked at Jax and then at Hedone.

"It's a French lullaby," Hedone said. "Very traditional."

Nelson's hand went to cover his mouth.

"She probably sang it to you," Jax said. "You've never seen her before?"

"Dad didn't keep photos of her," Nelson said. "He's such a bastard that he. . ."

Nelson looked up at Hedone and looked back at the couple in front of them.

"He's so young, so beautiful here," Nelson said. "Happy. I *think* that's him but I . . ."

The mother's head jerked up. Her nostrils flared as a man walked down the aisle. She squinted. By instinct, she turned, grabbed the child, and wrapped her body around him. Before the father could react, a bomb went off in the baggage compartment behind them. The man and the woman were blown forward into the empty chair in front of them. Somehow, the woman's body ended up between the man and the bomb. When they landed, the baby was tucked between the woman's abdomen and the man's abdomen.

The woman's head had been sliced in half by a piece of metal from the baggage compartment. Most of her body had been shredded by tiny pieces of the metal shrapnel. Only her belly and lap surrounding the baby remained intact. The father was knocked out cold from the shock. His legs and arms were broken.

Miraculously, the baby was uninjured. Startled by the bomb, the baby began to wail.

The scene changed back to the white medical exam room.

"Oh, my God," Nelson whispered. "Oh, my God."

Visibly shaken, Nelson dropped down on the low stool.

"March 29, 1982, on the *Capitale*," Jax said evenly.

"Carlos the Jackal," Nelson said. He glanced at Hedone. "I watched the hearings on French television the first year I was at Denver Health."

"Your father testified," Hedone said, evenly.

"He . . . What?" Nelson broke down.

Jax grabbed him. Nelson wept into Jax's arms. Jax looked at Hedone, and she nodded. They had time for Nelson to cry.

"I don't know why I'm crying," Nelson said. "I don't remember any of that. I never saw her, met her . . . It's him! I never saw him without a sneer on his face. He hated me. Always. Nothing I did was good enough for him. He . . ."

Nelson looked at Hedone.

"He is my dark space," Nelson said.

"One of them," Hedone said. "Let's take a look."

"Leave him with me," an elderly woman said.

She held her arms out to take the baby. The father jerked his wheelchair away from the woman. The infant was sound asleep on Nelson's father Pierre Semaine's lap. Pierre's legs and arms were in casts. His face was covered in scratches. His head was wrapped in gauze. His eyes were glassy, as if he were ill or in terrible pain.

"I will take care of my own child!" Nelson's father, Pierre Semaines, said to the elderly woman.

"You are a young man," the elderly woman said. "What will you do with a child?"

"I will love him," Pierre Semaines said.

The elderly woman clucked and shook her head.

"You cannot have him," Pierre Semaines said.

The elderly woman leaned over to look at the sleeping baby.

"He looks just like my daughter," the elderly woman said, in a soft voice.

"He is all I have of . . ." Pierre said. "I will do whatever it takes. Whatever it takes . . . He is my child. My blessing. He belongs with me."

Time seemed to pass at double speed. The young father and the infant stayed in the hospital. The child was cared for by the nurses and his father. Slowly, Pierre began to heal.

The elderly woman continued to pester Pierre for the child. Pierre remained firm.

"My child belongs with me," Pierre said.

As soon as Pierre was able to walk, he left the hospital with his child. He went straight to the airport, where he boarded a plane to Denver, Colorado where he'd found an entry-level engineer job at Martin Marietta.

They were back in the white exam room with the blue-sky ceiling. Nelson stumbled, and Jax caught him.

"I know that woman," Nelson said. "She . . ."

Nelson looked at Hedone.

"Is that possible?" Nelson asked.

"Of course," Hedone said.

"She came to the house," Nelson said. "Once, twice . . . She was there when . . ."

Nelson shook his head and covered his eyes. Jax looked at Hedone.

"His grandmother was at the house when Michael's wife informed his father that Guy was gay," Jax said. "It's a part of his story — this crazy old lady that started screeching in French at Guy and his father. She's a part of this story."

"Why?" Hedone asked.

"She went crazy," Nelson said. "She screeched at me in French. Hit me. Hard. Across the face and neck. Spit at me. Then she started hitting my father. My father was so angry, enraged. He went ballistic. At me. At M.J.'s mother. He kept saying . . ."

Nelson gasped. His fist went to his mouth and he bit his finger.

"What is it?" Hedone asked.

"He wasn't speaking to me," Nelson said. "I thought . . . I thought . . . Oh, God . . ."

Chapter 524

Dr. Nelson Weeks

"Shall we continue?" Hedone asked.

Dr. Nelson Weeks looked at the floor of the odd medical-exam room. After a moment, he glanced at Jackson "Jax" Theriot, who had come back from the grave to help him. Jax gave Nelson a cocky grin. Nelson looked at Hedone and nodded.

Ten-year-old Nelson was standing with his hands on his hips as he evaluated the creation in front of him. He and the next-door-neighbor boy, Junior, were making a snowman. The younger, red-haired boy was rolling the final ball of snow for the head. When he got close, Nelson bent down to help the boy lift the ball of snow.

The ball was too heavy. In a gale of laughter, the boys fell over into the snow. Junior's sister was sitting in the snow, making snowballs in preparation for their "epic" snowball fight.

They'd spent the last week working on snowmen in the morning and watching cartoons in the afternoon. Nelson was getting paid to watch Junior and his sister while their mom was on bed rest for another baby. Junior's father traveled for work, so they never knew when he'd be home. Nelson was on child duty, regardless. Right now, Nelson's father and Junior's father were drinking beer and watching the children from the porch of Nelson's house.

"Ut," Nelson's father, Pierre, said from the porch. "Attends une minute!"

Pierre yelled for the boys to wait. He ran to the boys. He made a show of struggling to lift the ball. Junior's father ran to aid Pierre. Laughing the entire time, the two men put the head on the snowman.

Junior's father pulled a carrot out of his pocket. Pierre took two pieces of coal out for the eyes of the snowman. Junior's father stuck the nose in the middle of the snowman's face. Pierre put the pieces of coal in the snowman for eyes. Excited, Nelson and Junior were jumping up and down. Pierre snatched Nelson's hat off his head and stuck it on the snowman.

Everyone laughed. Pierre put his arm over his son's shoulder, and they surveyed their work. There was a noise from inside the next-door-neighbor's house. Junior's mother came out to say something like "It's time."

The dance of labor had begun. Junior and his sister did their part by scooting over to Nelson's house. Pierre ushered the children inside the house for afternoon cartoons.

"Michael and your father were good friends," Jax said in an even voice. Nelson looked at Jax but didn't respond.

"Do you remember playing with M.J.?" Hedone asked.

"Sort of," Nelson said. "I remember that we were friends. I mean, we used to play together. I was his babysitter for . . . Gosh, a long time. He was a lot younger. I mean, at that age, even a couple of years feels like decades. "

"What happened?" Jax asked.

"He changed," Nelson said. His voice became hard. "Became the homophobic prick you know today."

"Let's take a look," Hedone said.

Nelson was fast asleep in his bedroom when the sound of glass shattering awakened him.

The next-door-neighbor lady was screaming and breaking things. Again.

As he did every time he woke this way, he went to his window and looked out through the curtains. They lived in small houses situated right next to each other. There wasn't any real sound insulation. He could tell before he opened the blinds that tonight was going to be a bad one.

He heard his father's door open. His father came up behind Nelson. He put his hand on his son's shoulder as they looked out Nelson's window at the little house next door.

"Wait here," Pierre said in French. "I will go take a look."

Pierre turned to go.

"Papa!" Nelson said.

Nelson pointed out the window. Junior, his sister, and the toddler boy were looking out at Nelson from the bathroom window on the second floor.

"Papa!" Nelson pleaded.

Pierre sighed. From where they stood, they could hear the mother banging on the bathroom door and screaming like a banshee.

"Put on your shoes," Pierre commanded in French.

Nelson pulled on his Converse All-Stars. For good measure, he pulled his bathrobe over his pajamas. Pierre took Nelson's hand, and they ran to stand under the bathroom window. Junior pushed up the double-hung window. For a moment, Junior's panicked eyes locked on Nelson's.

Nelson's life was mostly devoid of drama. They lived a sedate, structured life of intellectuals. Nelson did what was expected of him, and Pierre loved him. Nelson got up at the same time every day. He went to bed at the same time every day. They ate at "meal times" and had pizza every Friday.

Outside of Pierre's struggle with tobacco, their lives were free of conflict. Nelson had no experience with the kind of drama that had started to happen next door.

With Junior's look, Nelson felt flooded with Junior's desperation.

"Il est terrifie," Nelson told his father that Junior was terrified.

"Oui," Pierre nodded to Nelson. Looking up to the window, Pierre spoke in unaccented English to Junior, "Throw the baby, then your sister. You know how to climb down?"

Junior's head nodded.

"Do it now!" Pierre commanded.

Junior grabbed the toddler by the straps of his overalls. The baby hung in the air for a moment before dropping into Nelson's arms. Nelson set him down.

They heard wood splinter. Junior and his sister turned to look behind them.

"Now," Pierre commanded.

Junior pushed his sister out of the window. Always strong, Nelson easily caught the girl. Junior hurled himself out the window. He almost made it, but a large hand wrapped itself around his leg.

Shock and horror fixed on Junior's face. Nelson felt the full force of his friend's terror. The furious woman pulled her son back into the bathroom. They heard the boy scream with pain as the blows rained down on him.

"Go," Pierre said in French to Nelson. "Take them. I will deal with this."

"But, Papa!" Nelson said.

"Go to the basement," Pierre said. "Take the children. I will deal with this."

Nelson picked up the baby and grabbed onto the girl's arm.

"Guy?" Pierre called as they neared the house.

Nelson stopped and looked at his father.

"Tu es mon coeur," Pierre said, reminding his son of Pierre's love for him.

Nelson nodded and ran into the house with the children. As soon as they were in the still quiet of the basement, the baby began to wail. Only a few years older than the baby, the girl shuffled to take care of the baby.

"I will do it," Nelson said.

The girl looked at him in surprise. He realized that he must have mistakenly spoken in French. That hadn't happened in years. Embarrassed, he shrugged.

"It's okay," Nelson said in English. "I'll take care of him when you're settled."

He turned on the television and set it to the girl's favorite cartoons. When she was settled in cozy blankets, he took the baby to the bathroom and undressed him. The baby was filthy. It had been at least a day since anyone had changed his diaper. Nelson peeled off layer after filthy layer of clothing. Once out of his wet, smelly clothing, the baby stopped crying. Nelson bathed the baby in the sink. They didn't have diapers, so Nelson wrapped the child in towels and set him in the now-dry sink.

To be sure, he ushered the girl into the bathroom. She was filthy, too. He helped her out of her clothing. As she stepped into the shower, he saw that she was nearly a skeleton. While she showered, he warmed up towels in the dryer and found some of his old clothing for her to wear. He left the towels and the clothing on the toilet cover and took the baby out into the television room. When she came out, she was clean and starving.

He fed the children packets of oatmeal, beef jerky, and cocoa from their camping supplies. He was making more cocoa in the microwave when he heard his father's footsteps on the porch.

Nelson was frightened.

It wasn't like his father not to come to see him. They were a team, a pair. His father cared for Nelson more than anyone or anything in his life. Yet his father was lingering on the porch! Nelson couldn't shake the feeling that something was terribly wrong.

Why didn't his father come down to see him? To praise him for caring for these children? To help him with the baby?

Instead, his father paced back and forth on the front porch.

Nelson's chest clenched with fear. The girl's face reflected Nelson's fear. The baby began to whimper.

Something different, something bad, was going on.

Nelson didn't like it. Seeing the fear in the small children, Nelson did what his father did when Nelson was afraid. He put on a happy face. He finished making the cocoa and dug the last of the homemade strawberry ice cream from the freezer.

Nelson was handing the children their bowls of ice cream when they heard the front door burst open. Pierre's heavy footfall followed a set of lighter steps.

"Downstairs," Pierre said, in English. "Get cleaned up."

Nelson gasped when Junior said something nasty to Pierre.

"If you will not speak with the police, you will go downstairs with your brother and sister," Pierre said, in firm English.

"Fuck you," Junior said.

Nelson flushed bright red. The girl gasped.

Pierre's footfall came down the stairwell. He had Junior by the scruff of his shirt. Pierre may not be the tallest of men, but he was fit and very *strong. Pierre and Nelson worked out in the garage gym every single morning and evening. It was part of their routine and the only thing that kept his father's pain at bay.*

Junior was no match for Pierre.

They took the last few steps at a run. Pierre pushed Junior forward into the basement. Junior's face was a mask of fury. The boy was bruised and bleeding. He had a swelling knot on his head. His nose was broken. He had choke marks on his neck. He was limping. The boy's face was marked with shame and the fury brought by shame.

"I need to speak with the police," Pierre said, in French to Nelson. "Keep him here."

"I will do it, Papa," Nelson said.

"Good boy," Pierre said. Turning to Junior, Pierre said in English, "Get cleaned up."

Pierre slammed the downstairs basement door and locked the deadbolt with his key.

"The bathroom's right . . ." Nelson started.

"Get off me, faggot," Junior said.

Nelson reeled back. Junior sneered at Nelson and stalked to the bathroom.

They were back in the medical-exam room with a blue sky as the ceiling. Nelson didn't say anything. Jax looked at Hedone, and she gestured for him to wait.

"I've gone over that memory in therapy," Nelson said finally. "Over and over it. Again and again. EMDR, hypnosis, Cognitive Behavioral Therapy, 'The Work.' I know this memory, backwards and forwards."

"Why is this memory so important?" Hedone asked.

"It's the first time I heard the word," Nelson looked up at her, "applied to me, that is. The moment I heard it, I knew that it was true. Why did he say it?"

Nelson looked up at Jax. His words held emotion, but his face was clear.

"Why did he say it to *me*?" Nelson asked. "I was just trying to help. I was a child, too. Their family mess didn't have anything to do with me or my father. Until now, I never . . ."

"You never?" Jax asked.

"I never realized that he knew, too," Nelson said. "He knew that I was trying to help. He knew that the chaos and abuse which had become a part of his life was not a part of my life."

Nelson gave a quick nod.

"So it wasn't M.J.'s mother who mocked you for being gay," Hedone said mildly.

Nelson shook his head.

"She'd said it many times before," Nelson said. "She was a psycho. Why did I care? It just didn't . . . I just didn't . . . I mean, my father was right there and . . . But when M.J. said it, I knew it was true — and worse, so did he."

Nelson sighed.

"As an adult, a doctor, I can see that he was injured," Nelson said with a nod. "Beaten. Humiliated by his brutal mother. I have seen it in the ER before. Abused boys in early adolescence. The rage of shame pumps through them. They lash out at everyone, especially those who are trying to help."

"Sounds like you've learned things in therapy," Jax said.

Nelson grinned at him.

"Jax was the one who convinced me to go," Nelson said as he looked back at Hedone. "Do the work. So I did."

Jax put his hand around Nelson's shoulder for support. Nelson looked at Hedone.

"Is it possible that it never really had anything to do with me?" Nelson asked. "Things were falling apart more and more at M.J.'s house. We were there at least once a week. M.J.'s mother started calling me that horrible name to get back at us for witnessing her insanity, for helping the children, her children, in the middle of the night."

"You knew what she did to them," Jax said. "Her secret."

Nelson nodded.

"M.J., his little girlfriend," Nelson shook his head. "It's like I started to hold my breath the moment he said the word, 'faggot.' I'm not sure I've ever stopped."

Nelson let out a slow steady breath. After a moment, he shook his head.

"Could it be so simple?" Nelson asked.

"I don't know," Hedone said. "He is standing outside of your house, knocking on your front door. We could go ask him."

Hedone waved her hand over a framed picture. They were looking at Nelson's doorstep where M.J. and Joseph Walter were standing. Jax sucked in a breath at the sight of his former teammate.

"I can take you there if you're ready," Hedone said.

"Not yet," Jax said.

Hedone and M.J. looked at Jax.

"There is something that you need to know," Jax said. "You were to be told when you finished medical school, but . . ."

Jax sighed.

"We were killed," Jax said. "You had already changed your name so . . ."

"What is it?" Nelson asked.

"Can we go there?" Nelson asked Hedone.

"Of course," Hedone said.

"No," Pierre said to Michael, the next-door neighbor and Fey Special Forces Team Member. "I will not."

They were sitting on Pierre's front porch. Pierre was chain-smoking unfiltered cigarettes. They were speaking fast French.

"I promised Mabelle when she agreed to marry me and again when we learned that we would have a baby," Pierre said. "I will not let them have her or my son. I will not."

"But . . ." Michael started.

"That evil witch has found us now," Pierre said. "She will not give up."

"She's found you before," Michael said.

"Now she has something to exploit," Pierre said. "You don't understand."

"Explain it to me," Michael said.

"Guy is almost eighteen," Pierre said. "Once he turns eighteen, he will be subject to all kinds of pressure. Mabelle barely escaped from it with her sanity intact. They will only get more desperate, especially now that they know that he is a homosexual. They will use his nature to exploit him and . . ."

Pierre shook his head.

"I should have sent him away a year ago," Pierre said. "If I had any kind of courage, I would have done just that but . . . I love him too much. He looks so like my Mabelle. He is such a good and kind soul. I wanted him with me. Now . . ."

Pierre sighed, lit another cigarette, and wiped his face.

"Guy has done what I could not," Pierre said.

Michael nodded to Pierre.

"Where do you think he went?" Michael asked.

"In the small space between the garages," Pierre said. "It is his safe place. He found Yves . . ."

Seeing that Michael didn't seem to know who Yves was, Pierre added, "the cat."

"He found the cat there," Pierre said. "He will be there. Take him to a hotel. Some place nice. He has already been accepted to university. Send him away as soon as high school is over. Away from me. Away from this place. I will pay."

"I owe you so much," Michael said. "You've saved my children's lives over and over again."

Pierre took a deep drag on a cigarette and shook his head.

"If you can . . ." Pierre said.

"Yes?" Michael asked.

"Get him to change his name," Pierre said. "It may keep him safe."

Michael nodded to Pierre and got up. Pierre grabbed his arm.

"Please," Pierre said. "Please keep an eye on him. I need to know . . ."

Pierre's strong façade cracked. Tears began to well in his eyes.

"I need to know that he is alive and well," Pierre said. "He is . . . my heart."

Rather than force a proud man to weep, Michael nodded and got up. Michael sauntered to the back of the house. Pierre took another drag off his cigarette and went inside. Michael walked down the driveway with his arm around Guy Semaines.

While his father watched from the window of the front door, Guy Semaines walked off into the night. Pierre wiped his tear-wet face and retreated into the house.

They were back in the medical-exam room. Nelson was sitting on the stool and staring at the floor.

"How are you?" Jax asked. He put a hand on Nelson's shoulder.

"I was just wondering that myself," Nelson said. He smiled at his friend. "Tired, mostly."

"But about . . ." Jax started.

"I don't know why, but I am not surprised," Nelson said. "I think I always knew. It was just easier to hate him."

"Rather than hate yourself?" Hedone asked.

"Oh, no — I've done plenty of that," Nelson said.

Nelson looked at Jax for a long moment.

"Thank you," Nelson said.

"Mike just introduced us," Jax said. "He thought that I might be able to help you when you first came out. Talk to you. That's all. He didn't make us friends or lovers. You made us family."

Nelson's eyes scanned Jax's face.

"You are a lovely soul," Jax said.

Nelson stood, and the two men embraced.

CHAPTER 525

AN APOLOGY

Thursday night — 10:35 p.m.

Distracted, Dr. Nelson Weeks answered the knock at his door. He found M.J. and Joseph Walter standing on his front stoop.

"Nelson," Joseph said.

"Joey," Nelson said.

While M.J. gaped, Nelson and Joseph hugged.

"How are the kids?" Nelson asked. "Nancy? Is she still in remission?"

"Good, everyone's good," Joseph said. "I hear you're finally dating Blane."

Joseph grinned from ear to ear.

"How did you . . .?" Nelson asked. His mouth dropped open. "Blane is your acupuncturist. Helped Nancy with the cancer."

"You met him," Joseph said. "More than once."

"I did?" Nelson asked. He shook his head. He looked at the floor for a moment. "When you returned to Denver?"

Nelson shook his head.

"Wow," Nelson said. "I was so focused on . . . You know, the anniversary and all of that."

"We all miss Jax," Joseph said. He looked at M.J. "Nelson and Jax were close."

"Family," Nelson said, with a nod.

M.J. gave Nelson a solemn look.

"Listen, man, I . . ." M.J. started.

"I have something I need to do," Nelson cut M.J. off.

"What is it?" Joseph asked. "Maybe we can help."

"My dad's in the hospital," Nelson said.

"Pierre?" M.J. asked.

"I just really want to see him tonight," Nelson said. "I can't really explain it."

Nelson looked at Joseph and then at M.J.

"You don't happen to have a car, do you?" Nelson asked with a sly grin.

Joseph laughed.

"Why is that funny?" M.J. asked.

"Nelson never has a car," Joseph said. "He even talked Jax into being a non-driver. I had to drive them all over Washington."

"San Francisco," Nelson said.

"Can we talk on the way?" Joseph asked. "M.J. has a lot to say and . . ."

"*D'accord*," Nelson said. He wasn't sure why he said "Okay" in French. It's just what came out. He looked at M.J. and raised his eyebrows.

"I speak French and a few other languages now," M.J. said. "Bloody . . ."

"Foreigner!" Nelson and M.J. said their childhood battle cry in unison. They laughed.

"I'm so sorry," M.J. said. "I really . . ."

"If we can talk on the way," Nelson said. "I have to be in court first thing. So I'm kind of pressed for time."

M.J. nodded. They went out to the street. Joseph led them to an armored SUV. He got in the driver's seat.

"I'll take the back," Nelson said.

M.J. got in the passenger seat. Nelson's phone went off when he got in. He looked at the text and responded. They were on the way to the highway when Nelson looked up.

"How do you know where we are going?" Nelson asked.

"Pierre is a friend of the family," Joseph said. "He will be glad to see you."

Nelson gave Joseph a tight nod. M.J. turned around in the passenger seat.

"Listen, I . . ." M.J. started and stopped. He cleared his throat.

Nelson looked at M.J. Jax wouldn't let him go until he agreed to listen to M.J., to really listen. According to Jax, resentments have an addictive quality to them. In order to live fully and freely, we must be willing to let them go.

"Yes?" Nelson asked.

M.J. just looked at Nelson. Joseph caught Nelson's eye in the rearview mirror.

"M.J. has a TBI," Joseph said. "He's working on his language skills while under pressure."

Nelson gave Joseph a quick nod. His resentment right there, he wondered why M.J.'s brain injury had anything to do with him. Immediately, he could hear Jax coaching him — "Compassion, Nelson, compassion."

Joseph turned to M.J., "What is a full apology?"

"Say you are sorry, ask for what it was like for the other person, wait until they speak all of their pain, take responsibility, ask how you can make it better," M.J. said by rote. His eyes flicked to Nelson. "It's a part of team training."

"Okay?" Nelson asked, his resentment flaring.

"I guess I'm not sure where to start," M.J. said. "This is part of the problem. You were our friend, my friend, for most of my life — and then everything went to shit."

"I didn't have anything to do with that," Nelson said.

"I know," M.J. said. "I do know that. I just want . . ."

M.J. blew out a breath.

"I wanted you to know that I really cherished the time at your house," M.J. said. "Bonnie asked me about you recently."

"Bonnie?" Joseph asked.

"His sister," Nelson said. "Younger."

Joseph nodded.

"She loved going to your house," M.J. said. "It was so quiet, calm, ordered. Everything was in its place. You were always so kind to us."

"How is Bonnie?" Nelson asked. "Kenny?"

"Good," M.J. said. "Honey and I have supported them since . . . You probably don't know, but Mom took all of Dad's death benefits. Even ours. Kicked us out. And, anyway, Bonnie just finished college. Ted's starting."

M.J. nodded.

"They are good," M.J. said. "But that's not what we were talking about."

"No, it wasn't," Joseph said in a low, growl-like voice.

M.J. cleared his throat.

"I loved that," M.J. said. "Going to your house."

"Then why . . ." Nelson started.

"And I hated it," M.J. said, cutting Nelson off. "When Mom had just me, our house was like your house. Even with Bonnie, Mom was able to keep her shit together. But as soon as Kenny was born . . . Everything went to hell."

M.J. stopped talking.

"Your house was the same — day in and day out — quiet, clean, orderly," M.J. said. "Our house was falling apart. Literally. Things were falling apart. Mom made holes in the wall. She was just . . . crazy. Insane. Dad was gone all the time and . . ."

M.J. stopped talking and shook his head.

"This sounds very hard," Nelson said. No matter what Jax had said, he found himself unwilling to give in too soon. "But I don't know what it has to do with being so cruel to me. I was your friend. I went way out of my way to take care of you, to help, at every turn! And you . . ."

M.J. nodded.

"No, you're right," M.J. said. "And . . . I guess that's it. There are no reasons for me to have been so mean. It's just . . . That first time, you know . . ."

"When you called me a 'faggot'?" Nelson asked, his temper flaring.

"Right," M.J. said.

"What about it?" Nelson asked.

"It's the first time I saw even a dent in your happy-go-lucky calm," M.J. said. "I had all of this rage and emotion and pain and . . . You were just cool as a fish. It felt good to offload some of my pain onto you. To make it your fault. I . . .

"I am ashamed of myself," M.J. said. "But there it is. That's what I was doing."

M.J. swallowed hard and nodded. Joseph cleared his throat, and M.J. looked at him. Joseph gave him a "get on with it" nod.

"Oh, right," M.J. said. "What was my behavior like for you?"

"Awful," Nelson said. "Horrible."

"But I don't get that," M.J. said, defensively. "It was true!"

Joseph's big, beefy chest thumped M.J. in the chest. M.J. looked at Joseph.

"He's gay!" M.J. said.

"The word 'faggot' comes from the slang for a bundle of sticks or kindling. It is a reference to the burning of homosexuals," Nelson said, primly.

"Oh," M.J. said. He fell silent for a moment. He shook his head. "I really am an asshole."

"Yes, you are," Nelson said.

M.J. looked offended, but Joseph laughed. After a moment, M.J. smiled sheepishly.

"What happened to you?" M.J. asked. "I mean, you know, when everything came apart, and then you just disappeared. Your dad moved right after that."

Nelson wasn't sure how to respond. He knew that he should share how he felt, but he didn't feel safe enough to do that.

"Go ahead, Nelson," Joseph said. "M.J. will *listen* to what you have to say. I will, too."

"Oh, yeah," M.J. said. "I can do that."

Nelson sighed. He looked out the window, and, then, as if Jax was standing on his shoulder, he realized that he really didn't have anything to lose.

"Your mom had said it to me for a while," Nelson said. "So, I guess it wasn't that much of a surprise when you did. It's just that . . . I thought we were friends. I was out, in the cold, in the middle of the night. It wasn't easy to catch your brother and sister. I know my dad went over to get you. He called the cops and . . . I mean, what do you think would have happened to you if we hadn't been there? Did you ever think of that?"

"Can I say something?" M.J. asked Joseph.

"Go ahead," Joseph said.

"When I hear you say that, I realize that it never occurred to me that you wouldn't be there," M.J. said. "You were just . . . always there."

"I wasn't your family," Nelson said. "We were *neighbors*. You go down the street and see how many people would help you out. How many people helped you when we left?"

M.J. didn't respond.

"You should answer that," Joseph said.

"None. No one," M.J. said. "The new neighbor built a ten-foot-high cinderblock fence between the yards so they didn't have to deal with us."

He stopped talking.

"I guess I just figured that was your fault for leaving," M.J. said after a moment.

Nelson threw up his hands in frustration.

"I'm not saying it's rational," M.J. said.

"Well, there's something we agree on," Nelson said.

They fell silent for a while. Each focused on their own thoughts.

"You've asked me what it was like for me," Nelson said. "It was nice to have you, your sister, and your brother in my life. I didn't have siblings. Dad never married. He and I were close, but he worked a lot. I really enjoyed playing with you. Hanging out after school."

"Dad paid you," M.J. said.

"Not very much," Nelson said. "It would have been a lot more if you had a nanny or even a real babysitter. And I gave up every afternoon sometimes to be with you. It was a lot."

"What did you spend your money on?" M.J. asked.

"We built rockets," Nelson said.

"You really are a geek," M.J. said.

"Of the highest order," Nelson said. "But also, Pierre was an engineer on actual NASA projects. He always had cool stuff to add to the rockets. And they always worked."

"I'll tell you that you being so smart," M.J. said. "It made me want to be smart, do well in school and stuff. If I hadn't, I wouldn't have qualified for SF, uh, Special Forces. I know you and your dad had a big impact on Honey. You know, she's going to college and working full time."

"Why aren't you?" Nelson asked.

M.J. cleared his throat and didn't respond. Joseph shot him a side-eyed glance.

"If you join my family, you can help remind me," M.J. said. "Rejoin my family again, that is. Because you're really saying that we were family until I fucked it all up."

Nelson didn't respond for a moment.

"No, it was really just life," Nelson said. "I am gay. That would have always been something between us."

"Why?" M.J. asked.

"You were Catholic," Nelson said.

"Aren't you?" M.J. asked.

Nelson didn't answer. After a moment, he continued.

"It was really hard for me," Nelson said. "I lost you guys and then a few weeks later lost my dad. I thought it was because I was gay. I thought my father . . . Pierre . . . He . . ."

Nelson cleared his throat.

"I'm just coming to terms with the fact that there were other factors involved," Nelson said.

"You know about your dad? And Mike?" Joseph seemed surprised.

"Jax told me," Nelson said before realizing what he was saying. "And anyway, I would have left for college in a few weeks anyway."

M.J. didn't respond. Nelson sighed.

"I guess I'm learning that I was pretty lucky, after all," Nelson said. "I had friends and love. I went to college and med school. I mean, I always . . . this . . . *thing* was so painful that I . . ."

"I'm sorry," M.J. said. "I truly am. I know Honey. She was just doing what I was doing. She really didn't know any better. She moved in with Sam . . ."

"Sam Lipson?" Joseph asked.

M.J. nodded.

"Good man," Joseph said.

"He tried to get Honey and her sister to be better people," M.J. said. "Honey fought it tooth and nail. But it really sunk in. Her sister was too far gone."

"How did Honey end up in the wheelchair?" Nelson asked.

"Her sister stabbed her," M.J. said. "She nearly died. I nearly died. I . . ."

Emotional, M.J. cleared his throat.

"I was hit by an I.E.D. in Iraq," M.J. said. "I'm a medic, like Jax was."

Nelson shifted uncomfortably at this monster's mere mention of his Jax. Noticing his reaction, he tried to breathe out his emotion.

"I lost my leg, got a TBI," M.J. said. "I was pretty much an asshole until then. Well . . . You went to the anniversary, right?"

"The first party?" Nelson asked. "I was there, and every one since then."

"Me, too," M.J. said. He cleared his throat. "I didn't really know my dad. Not like you did. My dad just came and went. I thought he didn't really care about us kids. Like he wasn't affected by mom and didn't care what happened to us. I found out at the anniversary that he paid for you to help. He put mom in the mental hospital twice. He tried to get help for us. Your dad was in touch with him all the time. In fact, your dad is the one who told me. You didn't see him there?"

"No," Nelson said.

"Wow," M.J. said.

"Wow?" Nelson asked.

"It never occurred to me that you and your dad weren't still best friends," M.J. said. "I really envied that."

"I haven't seen him since that time." Nelson thought for a moment. "Almost twenty years."

Joseph looked at Nelson in the rearview mirror.

"Why go tonight?" Joseph asked as he pulled into the hospital parking lot.

"I learned some things tonight," Nelson said. "I can't explain it. I just really want to see him, need to see him."

"Will you forgive me?" M.J. asked as Nelson moved to get out of the SUV.

Nelson turned to look at him.

"I want to say 'Yes, of course,' but the truth is that I don't know," Nelson said. "I've been so angry for such a long time. And . . . tonight's been a lot. I think I need some time."

"Fair enough," M.J. said. "You'll let me know."

"I will," Nelson said. "Are you heading back to the Castle?"

"Eventually," M.J. said.

"Can you tell Blane that I'll call him?" Nelson asked. "Heather, too?"

Joseph cheered. Nelson shook his head and moved to get out.

"I'll do it," M.J. said.

Nelson wanted back inside the SUV the moment he closed the door. Nodding toward his own exhaustion, Nelson went to the information desk. With a little "I am his doctor" bluster, he managed to find out his father's room number. He took the elevator to the floor. He didn't bother to stop at the desk. He picked up Pierre's chart tucked onto the door of the hospital room.

"Hip replacement," Nelson said.

He snorted. Hedone could have told him it was something like this. The goddess had mildly said that his father was in the hospital right now. If he wished to see him, he'd need to go there.

"Dr. Weeks?" a nurse asked.

Nelson turned to look at her.

"It *is* you," the nurse said. "Your father has been bragging about you all night."

"He has?" Nelson asked.

"You testified in that big federal trial today?" the nurse asked. She turned over her watch to see the time. "They covered it on the news."

"I wanted to see my father," Nelson said.

The nurse looked at him and nodded.

"I know he'll be happy to see you," the nurse said.

"How is he?" Nelson asked.

"Great," the nurse said. "He's kind of a frequent flyer here. This is his fourth joint. I think he's hoping it will be his last. I guess he was in some kind of train accident?"

The image of the bomb going off on the train played through Nelson's mind.

"*The Capitale*," Nelson said with a nod.

"The new joints have brought him a lot of relief," the nurse said.

She opened the door. Nelson took a step inside the room. His father was sound asleep. Nelson took a chair near the bed and assessed his father. He could see a few gray hairs. According to Hedone, his father and mother had been very young when they had him. His father was now only in his mid-fifties. Pierre wore it well.

Nelson noticed his father still wore the wedding ring from his marriage to Nelson's mother. Nelson sighed and picked up his father's hand.

With sleep-filled eyes, Pierre turned to look at Nelson.

"*Mabelle*," Pierre said in French. Tears rolled down his cheeks. "You are so beautiful."

His father simply looked at him.

"I am so glad to see you, Mabelle," Pierre said. "Please. Don't waste your time with me, my darling. Watch over our boy."

"Papa, it's me," Nelson said. "Guy."

Pierre's eyes popped open. His eyes scanned Nelson's face. His hand reached out to stroke Nelson's face.

"I only found out tonight . . . what you did . . ." Nelson said. "Oh, Papa . . ."

Pierre stroked Nelson's head as Nelson cried into Pierre's hospital sheets.

"I knew it the moment I learned," Nelson said, tipping his head up to look at Pierre. "I knew that you had set the whole thing up. You paid for everything, took care of me — even though we were not . . ."

"Shh, shh," Pierre said. "You were safe. This is all I ever cared about."

"Oh, Papa," Nelson said. "I am so sorry."

Pierre made a gesture, and Nelson leaned over to hug his father. They held each other tight for a while. Pierre kissed Nelson's face and released him.

"Now," Pierre said. "Do tell me . . . What has happened to your beautiful hair? And those glasses?"

Nelson tipped his head back and laughed. Pierre grabbed his son's hand and kissed the back of it.

"You have the best laugh," Pierre said.

Nelson grinned at his father. Pierre's face broke open in a bright smile.

"If this is a dream, I am on some very good medications," Pierre said. "Now, tell me all about this trial. I have been watching in the papers and the news, but I want to hear it from you."

Nelson had never had anyone interested in his work. He blinked at Pierre. As he had when Nelson was a child, Pierre made a gesture with his hand to encourage Nelson to speak. So Nelson told him about the trial. Pierre asked piercing questions, which Nelson was able to answer. As time passed, Nelson noticed that his father was tiring. After a while, Pierre fell into a sound sleep.

Early the next morning, Pierre awoke alone. His heart broke. The dream he'd had last night had been so real that he'd hoped that maybe . . . The morning nurse came in to give him his meds. She was leaving when she stopped.

"Oh, I almost forgot," the morning nurse said. "There's a note here for you."

The morning nurse gave him the note and left the room. Thinking it was nothing, Pierre didn't bother to read the note. Instead, he closed his eyes to remember his beautiful dream. His beautiful son had come to see him. They had cried and hugged. He had fallen asleep knowing that his Guy was well.

The effeminate African American physical therapist shook him awake.

"Time to get moving!" the man said.

Not remembering the note, Pierre let the physical therapist help him up. They had started shuffling toward the bathroom when the piece of paper fluttered to the ground.

"Is this yours?" the physical therapist asked.

Pierre looked at the man.

"It says, 'Have court. I'll see you tonight. Love you, Dad. Guy'" The physical therapist said. "There's a phone number and it says . . . Hey, isn't that your son?"

Pierre grinned. It had not been a dream.

"Say, I've seen your son on television," the physical therapist said. "He is very attractive. Do you know if he's single?"

"I have heard that he's finally dating my acupuncturist," Pierre said. "He's very handsome. I've been trying to set them up for . . . a very long time."

"I love it when good-looking people get together," the physical therapist said.

Pierre smiled. They continued their way across the floor to the bathroom.

CHAPTER 526

WINGS OF CHANGE

Friday afternoon — 2:35 p.m.
Denver, Colorado

The sound of a child laughing and talking woke Pierre Semaines. He blinked.

He had no idea where he was.

He remembered getting on the shuttle to the extended-care facility where he would spend the next few weeks in rehabilitation from his hip surgery. That was the last thing he remembered.

He turned his head to look at the child.

A little girl with long, golden hair and dark eyes was having an animated conversation with . . .

Pierre looked and saw no one. He squinted to look at the child.

"Hello?" Pierre asked.

"Oh, hi," Katy Roper-Marlowe said. Turning back to the empty air, she said, "He's awake now."

Pierre looked at the empty air and the girl again.

"Would you mind . . ." Pierre started.

The little girl came to the edge of his bed. Her height was such that her eyes were barely able to peek over the high bed and covers. Pierre realized that she was older than he'd originally assumed. She was just small.

"Where am I?" Pierre asked.

"You're at O'Malley's house," Katy said with a big grin.

"Seth?" Pierre asked.

Nodding, Katy said, "He is my piano teacher, when he's in town. Mostly, I see his dad, Bernie. And I'm *not* being disrespectful. He *wants* to be called 'O'Malley' and Bernie *wants* to be called 'Bernie.'"

"Yes," Pierre grinned at the little girl. He wasn't sure why, but he innately liked her. "They are like that."

He raised an eyebrow at the girl. In his life experience, little girls knew everything that was going on.

"Any idea how I got here?" Pierre asked.

"Um," Katy scowled. "Do you know who Ava is?"

Pierre nodded.

"Uncle Nelson told Ava that you were in the hospital," Katy said. "Last night. Ava told Maresol . . ."

Pierre grinned. Hearing Maresol's name, he visibly relaxed.

" . . . this morning, which was a big mess because Maresol would have liked to know last night."

Pierre chuckled, as that *did* sound like Maresol.

"But don't worry. They're not in a big fight," Katy said. "Maresol is just like that."

"Yes, she is," Pierre said with a nod.

"Maresol told O'Malley that she was going to get you," Katy said. In an imitation of Maresol, she added, "I don't care what you say, old man. Pierre is staying with us and not at some random center."

Pierre laughed at Katy's impression.

"She really did say that," Katy said.

"I have no doubt that Maresol said those words just like that," Pierre said. "I do have one question."

"Okay," Katy said.

"How did you know that she said it?" Pierre asked.

"Oh," Katy said. "That's easy. The ghost told me."

"The what?" Pierre asked.

Katy pointed to where she'd been directing her conversation when he'd awakened. Katy leaned in.

"She says her name is 'Mabelle,'" Katy said.

Pierre choked. He coughed for a moment. Katy went to rub his back like her mommy did when Katy had a cough.

"Don't be upset," Katy said. "Ghosts lie. It's one of the reasons my dad hates them."

Pierre looked at the little girl and then the empty air. He then said the only thing he could think of.

"Your father hates ghosts?" Pierre asked.

"It's just his thing," Katy said. The little girl raised her shoulders in an exaggerated shrug. "That's why I came in here. My Daddy hates ghosts, so he'll send them on before they have a chance to . . ."

Katy leaned in and whispered, "Lie."

"I saw the ghost and came in to see if she was a good ghost or a bad ghost," Katy said.

Pierre simply looked at her. Nodding, Katy continued talking.

"My daddy and mommy are on a date," Katy said. "My daddy has been saving the world in a mine, and my mommy's been studying for finals at college. They wanted some time alone."

"Good for them," Pierre said.

"Daddy's going to come here to pick me up after their date," Katy said. "So I figured I should check before he sends her on."

Katy nodded. Pierre cleared his throat.

"I would very much like it if your father didn't 'send on' this ghost," Pierre said.

"Oh," Katy said. She blinked at him. "The ghost said it doesn't matter."

Pierre scowled. As if she were talking to a moron, the little girl sighed.

"Most ghosts are stuck here," Katy said.

"'Stuck here'?" Pierre asked. "As opposed to where?"

"The other side," Katy said with a shake of her head.

Pierre opened his mouth to ask a question, but he shook his head instead, "What?"

"Okay," Katy said. "This is how it works. People have souls."

She looked at Pierre, and he nodded.

"Sometimes, when people die, their soul gets stuck here," Katy said. "Usually it's because they die suddenly or they are control freaks or they want to tell someone something or stuff like that. The natural process is this — live, die, soul to the other side."

As if the child had made great sense, Katy nodded.

"And Mabelle?" Pierre asked.

"She said that she was from a long line of saints . . ." Katy said.

Pierre gawked at Katy.

" . . . she went to the other side and returned to the side of her beloved when he was in the hospital," Katy said. "In France. That's a place. My friend Sissy is there now. She looks like my Uncle Nelson."

"Your friend Sissy?" Pierre asked.

"The ghost," Katy said. "A lot."

Katy looked at the man and saw that he was kind of stunned.

"She said that she has been at your side ever since you were injured by the jackal," Katy said. "Whatever that is."

"It is a person," Pierre said. "Carlos the Jackal. He . . ."

He looked at the little girl for a moment. For some reason, he felt that she would understand what he would say. He found his voice.

"He was an angry man," Pierre said. "He blew up a train that my wife, our child, and I were riding. My wife, Mabelle, protected our child but was killed."

"That's what she said," Katy said. "Except she said he was a 'bad man.' We kind of argued because bad men are usually just men who have bad ideas. But she knew that I had seen true evil."

"You have?" Pierre asked.

Katy nodded. Pierre watched the girl while he tried to think through everything this child had said.

"Oh, she didn't say 'beloved,'" Katy said. "She's kind of irritated about it. She keeps saying, 'Tell him that he is my *amour sacré*.'"

Pierre gasped. Tears began to fall from his eyes.

"Don't be sad." Katy gave him a hug.

The child patted his back like her mother did when she cried. After a few moments, Pierre shifted, and she moved away. Katy gave him a pensive look.

"Your father?" Pierre found himself suddenly protective of his wife's spirit. "He will injure the ghost?"

"Oh, right. We were talking about Daddy sending her to the other side," Katy said with a nod.

Wiping his face, Pierre nodded.

"If she's already been to the other side, she'll just come right back," Katy said. "If he sends her, she'll be right back if she wants to, and she's kind of throwing a fit to say that she wants to be with you. Being with you is her soul's *amour sacré*.'"

Struck by the truth of what the child had said, Pierre couldn't think of anything to say. Katy nodded.

"And anyway, Daddy's pretty good at knowing ghosts who've already been on the other side," Katy said. She blinked at the man. "Do you want to talk to her?"

"Talk to her?" Pierre asked.

"She asked if you could use me to talk to her," Katy said. "Since you can't hear her."

"Uh . . ." Pierre scowled at the child. "She never spoke English."

"It's okay," Katy said. "Mind language is the same across all languages. I just said that other thing because she said you would know it was her."

The door opened, and a white-blond-haired boy ran into the room.

"There you are!" Paddie Hargreaves said to Katy. "I've been looking everywhere!"

"I had to talk to a ghost," Katy said. "This is Paddie. He takes piano lessons, too."

Pierre saw a spark of light on some metal at the boy's waist. He looked carefully and saw a thick metal sword tucked into a child's plastic scabbard. Pierre squinted at the boy and then the girl. The girl turned to look at the blank space.

"Uh, huh," Katy said and nodded. "Paddie has the Sword of Truth."

"He has what?" Pierre asked.

Not thinking, he swung his legs over the bed and then cried out in pain. Maresol ran into the room. She pushed the children out of the way and went to where Pierre was gulping air and sweating.

"Out!" Maresol said.

"But . . ." Katy said.

"Now!" Maresol said. Screaming, she said, "Seth O'Malley!"

His hair wet from the pool, Seth O'Malley poked his head into the room. He nodded to Pierre and lifted an eyebrow to Maresol.

"Take your students," Maresol ordered.

Seth raised both eyebrows at Katy, and she shrugged. He waved toward her, and Katy slunk out of the room. Paddie followed her close behind. Seth closed the door.

Maresol helped Pierre back into bed. She kissed his cheek.

"Stay there," Maresol said. "You need to rest. The doctor said that this hip was harder than the other. He had to break away much bone. It will just take more time to heal completely."

"Thank you," Pierre said.

He gave her a soft smile, which she returned. She smoothed his covers and filled his water cup from the pitcher on the table. She stood by him while he drank some water.

"The nurse will be here in an hour," Maresol said. "Blane will be here after she leaves. Please rest in the meantime. You need to heal completely."

Pierre nodded.

"I am sorry the children disturbed you," Maresol said.

"They were lovely," Pierre said.

"But?" Maresol asked.

"Do you think the child can see ghosts?" Pierre asked. "The girl? I know it's crazy, but she said that she saw Mabelle and mentioned that I was Mabelle's 'sacred love.'"

"The ceremony you went through," Maresol said.

Pierre nodded. Maresol looked at the wall while she decided what to say.

"As for the girl," Maresol said. She sucked in a breath and then let it out. "Yes. She has . . . powers. She is a special girl. Her mother is Seth's daughter Sandy's best friend, Jill. Katy's been around here most of her life. Her mother insists on treating her like a little girl, so that's what we do."

"She looks like a little girl," Pierre said. "With a powerful soul."

"Yes," Maresol said. "That is a good description."

"She said that the boy has the Sword of Truth." Pierre said.

Expecting Maresol to laugh, he looked at her. Maresol didn't respond. After a moment, she sighed.

"In any family, there are things that are hard to explain," Maresol said.

Trusting that Maresol would tell him when she could, he simply nodded to Maresol.

"My son knows that I am here?" Pierre asked. "I know that we've been separated, but now that I see him again, I do not want to be apart from him."

"He will be here tonight for dinner," Maresol said. "If Ava forgets to tell him, he will know tonight."

"Thank you," Pierre said. His face lit up with a smile. "I was looking forward to two weeks in the hospital. It is a great relief to me to be here. Thank you. I am most grateful."

Maresol kissed his cheek again and left the room.

For a long time, Pierre looked at the space the little girl had been talking to. Finally, he sighed.

"The quest continues," Pierre said. "Despite my best efforts, I am right in the middle of it. I am so glad that you are here with me."

He sighed and closed his eyes. After a few minutes, he was sound asleep. His dreams were filled with gallant knights of old.

~~~~~~~~~

Friday evening — 8:35 p.m.
Paris, France

After dinner, Sissy and her friend Amelia Hutchins had excused themselves from the table to go to the bathroom. They were eating at an upscale, exclusive Parisian restaurant. Amelia was allowed in only after she produced a clipping that announced her engagement to Frederec in *Le Parisien*. Sissy got in because, oddly enough, of her Internet exposure. The hostess knew that Sissy was going to school at *Opéra de Ballet* (Paris Opera School of Ballet.) They were eating dinner with Sissy's hosts — Benjamin and Claire — as well as Max Hargreaves.

Sissy was following Amelia out of the bathroom when Amelia stopped short. Sissy ran into her back.

"What's happened?" Sissy asked, recovering first.

Grinning, Amelia nodded toward the table. The waiter was setting another chair next to hers at the table. Sissy shrugged.

"No," Amelia said. "Look."

Sissy followed Amelia's finger to where a man was standing. Even with his back to them, Sissy knew exactly who it was. She squeezed by Amelia and ran to the table. Once there, her hand lingered over his back. Sissy was flooded with insecurity.

Ivan spun in place, and she was in his arms. Sissy cried and laughed and then cried again. It was five minutes — or, possibly, five days —

before she took her seat again. The entire restaurant had been cheering for them. When she sat down, she saw everyone's smiling and laughing faces. She leaned over to Ivan.

"How did you get in?" Sissy asked, quietly.

"I made the reservation," Ivan said.

A man came out from the back, and Ivan stood up. They hugged in greeting and then spoke quickly back and forth. When Ivan introduced a dazed Sissy, the man kissed her hand and welcomed her warmly. When all of the greetings were finished and another bottle of wine delivered, Ivan sat down next to Sissy. He held his hand out, and she grabbed onto it.

Chatting, everyone ate dessert while Ivan made his way through the dinner they had completed. The conversation lingered over coffee and aperitifs.

Sissy simply sat there holding Ivan's hand.

When they got up to leave, Sissy followed the Martins out. Ivan tugged on her hand, so she turned to look at him. In the light of her eyes, he was suddenly a loss for words.

Ivan shook his head. Sissy watched his face.

"I am here for a while," Ivan said. "If it is tolerable for you."

"When do you leave for Poland?" Sissy asked.

"We aren't going to Poland," Ivan said.

"But . . ." Sissy said.

"It was decided in the moment just before I walked into the restaurant," Ivan said. "You should hear from your brothers when you check your phone."

Realizing she wouldn't see her family, Sissy looked down. She was surprised at how sad and lonely she felt. Ivan touched her chin, and she looked up.

"There has been a serious threat," Ivan said. "Nadia has hired a team of professionals to go into the mine in secret."

Sissy numbly nodded. She turned to walk, but Ivan held her in place.

"I am here. In Paris," Ivan said. He took in her surprised face before continuing, "For as long as it is tolerable for you."

"'Tolerable'?" Sissy asked. "I . . ."

She hugged Ivan tight.

"Benjamin is an old friend," Ivan said. "He's arranged for me to move into an apartment that our friend Max owns in the Montmartre."

Sissy nodded.

"We have agreed that you will continue to live with Claire and Benjamin," Ivan said.

"But . . ." Sissy started.

He held up a hand, and she stopped talking.

"Please, let me finish," Ivan said. "I find myself exhausted. I . . ."

Ivan shook his head.

"It was Seth O'Malley who got this ball rolling," Ivan said. "He brought me proof that the man who chased me around the globe is no longer living."

"Wow," Sissy said.

"I am free, and I . . ." Ivan said. He touched his chest. " . . . weary. I have lived in Paris off and on in my life. Living here is always a joy. I need time to heal, to rest. You need the structure of a family to get to class and continue your studies."

"Will I see you?" Sissy asked.

"As much as you wish," Ivan laughed.

Sissy hugged him. When she let him go, she realized that their dinner companions had disappeared.

"Would you like to spend the weekend with me?" Ivan asked.

"I have a session in the morning tomorrow," Sissy said.

"We can go," Ivan said. "It would be a great joy for me to see you dance."

Sissy grinned.

"Come on," Ivan said. "The night is warm and lovely. Shall we walk?"

He tucked Sissy's hand into his arm, and they started toward his new apartment.

~~~~~~~~~

Friday afternoon — 2:35 p.m.
Denver, Colorado

Jill sat up on the side of the bed. She paused for a moment and moved across the bedroom toward the bathroom. Feeling Jacob's eyes, she grinned at him before going inside.

Her mind reviewed how they'd gotten here.

Jacob had insisted on spending the afternoon today for a "date." He told her about this great restaurant downtown. She'd been in the middle of some detail with the twins when she realized where they were.

Chuckling, Jacob had tucked her hand into his elbow, and they went into the five-star hotel in downtown Denver. She'd started toward the desk when Jacob held up a key card.

"This is where you went this morning?" Jill asked.

"One of the places," Jacob said.

Suddenly nervous, Jill watched the elevator click through the floors. When she looked at her husband, he simply smiled at her. They got off the elevator at the top floor.

"But . . ." Jill started ask about their tight finances.

"This is one of the projects I helped finance before I met you," Jacob said. "It took a while to get going and finally built, which is why it's not an item on our finances. It was finally built last year. The hotel opened a month or so ago. One of the stipulations in the loan was that we would get free visits as often as we'd like until the building is paid off, which will be ten, twenty, years from now."

"Downtown building projects?" Jill asked about a very large lump sum on their financial ledger.

"This is one of those projects," Jacob said. "There was a gorgeous home on this land. 1800s timber baron. I bought the home and the land when I first moved here to Denver. That's how I got connected here."

"Where is the house now?" Jill asked.

"I moved it to a big lot in the Montclair," Jacob said. "Sold it before . . . you know, the engagement party and everything."

She gave him a sly smile.

"Shall we go in?" Jacob asked.

"One more thing," Jill said.

CHAPTER 527

RESTORE OUR SPIRITS

He raised his eyebrows.

"Are they paying their loan back?" Jill asked.

"They just started." Jacob nodded. "This month."

"How many more of these projects are we involved in?" Jill asked.

"Eight," Jacob said. "They start paying when they are up and running."

"Some loan," Jill said.

Jacob smiled.

"How much a month are they paying?" Jill asked.

Jacob told her.

"Percentage rate?" Jill asked.

He told her. She sucked in a breath in surprise.

"The fees are loaded in the beginning so most of their monthly goes to pay off their debt," Jacob said.

"This is a part of that big mysterious debt?" Jill asked.

"It is," Jacob said.

Jill laughed.

"Why is that funny?" Jacob asked.

"I just . . ." Jill shrugged. He shook his head that he had no idea what she was saying. "I have worried, *a lot*, about that debt."

"Why?" Jacob asked. "I've told you that it would pay off. Didn't I say that it was investments?"

"Yeah, but . . ." Jill said.

She looked at him, and he laughed. She gave him a relieved smile.

"At least you're not offended," Jill said.

"Because you think I'm an idiot?" Jacob asked.

Jill opened her mouth in mock indignation. He laughed.

"I just . . ." Jill said. "You know, you hear about bachelors and their 'debts.'"

"Booze and broads?" Jacob asked with a saucy grin.

Jill laughed at herself. They started walking toward the room. Jill stopped short.

"Is that what Aden's debt is, too?" Jill asked.

"He's not involved in this project," Jacob said. "Like I said, I bought the property a long time ago."

"But this kind of thing," Jill said.

"Sure. Blane, too," Jacob said with a nod. "It's a great way to tuck money away when you have it. You never know when you won't have any money. These projects take a long time to start to pay off, but they usually pay off."

Jill was more relieved than she wanted him to know. She simply smiled.

"I'm glad you're okay with this," Jacob said.

"Why?" Jill asked.

"This is a good time to get involved in another," Jacob said. "Roll the money we make off this into another project."

Jill looked at him for a moment.

"We can talk about it later," Jacob said.

He winked at her, and, as always, her heart fluttered. Grinning, he nodded to the door.

She smiled.

He used a keycard to open the door. Jill was drawn into the room. A table was set with all of her favorite temperature independent foods. She grinned. The food could sit there until they were ready to eat. There was champagne in a bucket.

Then she noticed the view. She gasped and floated past the table to the view.

From this location, she could see the glistening water of the South Platte with the Rocky Mountains in the background. She wasn't sure why, but the amusement park and numerous condos and apartment buildings that line the South Platte weren't visible in this view.

"The hotel is angled on the lot over the park so we see the mountains and not the rest of the mess," Jacob said in answer to her question.

He slipped his hands around her waist. They stood watching the gorgeous view for a long moment.

"I have something for you," Jacob said.

He dropped a knuckle-sized blue rock in her hand.

"What is it?" Jill asked.

"Blue diamond," Jacob said. "You know, from the mine?"

Jill stared at the diamond in her hand. After a moment, she looked up at him.

"I thought we could get it cut and made into whatever you want," Jacob said. "It's big enough to make something for the kids, too, if you'd like."

"You just 'got' this from the mine?" Jill asked.

"Sort of," Jacob said, shifting uncomfortably. "Why?"

"I had the Marlowe diamond appraised," Jill said.

Jacob shrugged.

"It's worth a fortune," Jill said. She moved her hand up and down. "This thing, right here? It's three times the size of the Marlowe diamond. It's got to be worth . . . many millions or more!"

Jacob wasn't sure what to say. He just looked at her. After an uncomfortable moment, he said, "And?"

"You just found this?" Jill asked. "The reason the Marlowe diamond is worth so much money is because they are so rare. Are you saying we have an entire mine filled with these things?"

Jacob scratched his chin.

"Yes?" Jill asked.

"This is a lovely view, isn't it?" Jacob asked.

Jill laughed at him.

"I'm just saying . . ." Jill said.

Jacob kissed her and held her tight.

"I know that the last few years have been tough," Jacob said. "We gave up our financial security to secure Lipson's employees health insurance. There were times when money was really tight."

Not sure why, Jill felt a well of pain and sorrow rise inside her. Rather than let him see her pain, she pressed her face into his chest.

"We are in this together," Jacob said. "You are not alone in the middle of the sea of our financial life. It's not up to you alone to carry the load."

"I just . . ." Jill said.

He held on. She sighed and looked up at him.

"Do I still have to work?" Jill asked.

"I thought you wanted to work!" Jacob laughed. "'I am not a kept woman' and all of that."

"I do, but . . ." Jill said.

He looked at her.

"I miss the kids," Jill said finally.

"I know," Jacob said and hugged her again. After a moment, he pulled back to look at her. "Was this a bad idea?"

"I . . ." Jill shook her head. She put her hand over her heart. "I want to be here, but . . ."

"So much worry," Jacob said.

"Rage," Jill said. "Hopelessness. Not you — just everything."

"What if we try to set that aside for a few hours?" Jacob kissed her lips. "Restore our spirits before returning to the world."

Biting her lip, Jill nodded.

"I want that," Jill said.

"Would you like to eat?" Jacob asked.

She leaned back to look at him. Grinning, he led her to the bed.

Jill washed her hands and left the bathroom.

"Would you like to eat our lunch?" Jacob asked.

"I'm starving," Jill said.

Smiling, he got out of bed and pulled out a chair for her.

"I'm naked," Jill said. "So are you!"

"All the better," Jacob said. He nodded to the seat. "Shall we?"

Laughing at the impropriety, she sat down. He sat next to her. They ate their meal.

~~~~~~~~~

Friday evening — 5:35 p.m.

Pierre Semaines awoke to the sensation of the point of a sword pressing into his neck. Shocked, he opened his eyes. He looked at the sword and then at the man-like person who was holding it.

"That sword won't work on me," Pierre said, mildly.

"And why is that?" the man asked.

"That is the Sword of Death, is it not?" Pierre said.

"What if it is?" the man asked.

"Try it," Pierre said.

The man moved the blade away from Pierre's neck and slid it down Pierre's arm.

Nothing happened.

"As I said," Pierre said.

The man squinted at Pierre, and Pierre shrugged.

"Good genes," Pierre said. "Who might you be?"

"I am Perses," the man said.

"The Titan?" Pierre asked.

Perses didn't respond to such stupid questions. Instead, he looked at the sword.

"It's been a long time since I checked, but I thought that you were in Zimbabwe," Pierre said.

"Rhodesia," Perses said.

"Ah," Pierre said. "You were forced out of hiding by the revolution."

Perses glared at Pierre.

"I thought the Sword of Death was lost," Pierre said. "Were you looking for it in Zimbabwe?"

"'Looking for it'?" Perses asked, squinting at Pierre. "It was made for me. I've never lost possession of it."

"That makes more sense," Pierre said. "To what do I owe the pleasure?"

"You threatened my grandchild," Perses said.

"I what?" Pierre asked. He thought for a moment and then laughed. "The boy or the girl?"

"The girl," Perses said. "Katy. She is my youngest daughter's child."

"The mother who insists that Katy is a child?" Pierre laughed. "Now, that *does* make sense."

Perses raised the sword again and then thought better of it.

"She said that the boy is carrying the Sword of Truth," Pierre said. "How is that possible?"

"How is anything possible?" The man gave Pierre an impassive look.

Pierre scowled. The Titan could not kill him, but he was under no obligation to answer Pierre's questions.

"Fair enough," Pierre said finally. He let out a breath. "I was quite charmed by the girl. *And*, I did not threaten her, and you know it."

Perses scowled.

"Knowing about her is dangerous for her," Perses said. "I came to impress upon you the need to hold your tongue."

"You are telling me to keep the secret?" Pierre laughed.

Perses scowled. There was a knock on the door, and Nelson stuck his head into his father's room.

"Papa?" Nelson asked.

Pierre raised his eyebrows to Perses.

"My son," Pierre said.

"He can't see me," Perses said, under his breath.

"Mr. Roper, isn't it?" Nelson asked. Pierre gave Perses a hard look. "I didn't realize that you were here."

Perses glanced at Pierre, who simply smiled.

"Nelson!" Perses said. He stuck the sword into his belt, where it disappeared. "Lovely to see you."

"Did you come to show dad your sword?" Nelson asked. "You probably don't remember, but we talked about my dad's collection at one of those parties at the Castle."

"That's right," Perses said, chuckling. "You did tell me about your father's collection of swords. Remind me again — why do you collect swords?"

"Family heirlooms," Nelson said at the same time Pierre said, "Sacred duty."

Perses blinked at the men. He plastered what he called his "stupid human" smile on his face.

"I will leave you to it," Perses said, and left the room. "My granddaughter is having an impromptu piano recital."

Perses gestured outside the room.

"You are most welcome to come," Perses said.

With a nod to Pierre, Perses left the room.

"Papa," Nelson said. Falling into French, he continued, "How are you?"

"Good," Pierre replied in French. "Tell me about your day."

Nelson shook his head. They continued the conversation in French.

"I want to know about you," Nelson said. "What was that about with Mr. Roper? You know, I think he's Perses, the Titan God of Destruction."

"Oh, my dear boy," Pierre said. "We have plenty of time to talk swords, old gods, and other family issues. I would love to hear about you."

Nodding, Nelson sat down.

"Now, tell me everything about Blane," Pierre said. "Have you met the children? Heather? Have you kissed? Or . . .?"

"Papa, that's . . ." Nelson blushed. "You know that I'm gay?"

"Since you were a young child," Pierre said.

"And you don't have a problem with it?" Nelson asked.

"It's a family heirloom," Pierre said, repeating Nelson's words and adding a mimicking shrug.

Nelson opened his mouth to say something, but nothing came out. He shook his head.

"How do you know Blane?" Nelson asked.

"He's my acupuncturist," Pierre said.

"Of course, he is," Nelson said with a laugh.

~~~~~~~~~

Friday evening — 6:30 p.m.
Denver, Colorado

"Do stay for dinner," Maresol said as she led Jill and Jacob through the house. "I know the kids were looking forward to playing for you."

Jill and Jacob entered the newly remodeled kitchen and den.

"This is lovely," Jill said. She glanced at Jacob.

"It came out well," Jacob said, mildly.

"Seth wants to redo the upstairs," Maresol said. "We were hoping you would be able to help, Jill."

The need to remodel this area of Seth's home had come about the same time that Jill was having her twins. She wasn't able to help, and, of course, Maresol knew exactly what she wanted.

"Happy to help," Jill said.

"But why isn't the coffee pot bigger?" Seth repeated his oft-uttered complaint.

Maresol rolled her eyes, and Ava laughed from where she was sitting at the bar. Ava's lab members Leslie and Fran turned around from the seats at the bar to introduce themselves. Nelson came out of a room off the main den with his father.

"Nelson!" Jacob said.

He went to say "Hello" to Nelson. He stopped short and looked up.

"No, don't!" Pierre yelled.

Everyone turned to look at them.

"You realize there is a ghost here?" Jacob asked with a derisive sniff.

"Yes, yes. I just learned that," Pierre said. "Please."

"You should not waste your life with those who have none," Jacob said.

"She watches over me. Our son," Pierre said. "Please. I have just learned that she was there."

Jacob scowled.

"Your daughter told me about her," Pierre said.

"Papa?" Nelson asked. "What is going on?"

"It is against my better judgment but I will leave her," Jacob said.

"Thank you," Pierre said. He squinted at Jacob. "Has anyone ever told you that you look a lot like Blane Lipson?"

"He's my cousin," Jacob said. "I'm Jacob Marlowe. My father is Sam Lipson. Blane and I are very close. We have even traded places when necessary."

Pierre grinned at Jacob.

"I'm sorry," Jill said. "I'm Jill. My husband is usually not such an asshole. He hates ghosts."

"No, no," Pierre said. "I understand. We all have our things."

"Nelson," Jill said.

To Nelson's surprise, Jill hugged him. She kissed his cheek.

Jacob gave the ghost the evil eye. When the ghost laughed at him, Jacob realized that she looked nearly exactly like Nelson. When Jill released Nelson, Jacob shook his hand.

"Nelson," Jacob said. "I can't tell you how sorry we were about last night."

"Yes," Nelson said. "Me, too. And . . . overall, it was really good for me. I was able to work through things that I had shoved into a dark corner of my mind. I've reconnected with my father. I even had a chance to speak with M.J."

"Junior?" Pierre asked. "Is that so?"

"Yes," Nelson said. He smiled and nodded to Pierre before turning back to Jacob. "I feel foolish for having made such a scene."

"Oh, well," Jacob said with a shrug. "When you live with a lot of people, someone is always making a scene."

"Usually, it's Fin," Jill said with a laugh.

Nelson and Jacob laughed with her.

"Who is Fin?" Pierre asked.

"Prince Finegal of Queen Fand's realm," Nelson said.

"*Tu connaise les fée*?" Pierre's head jerked to look at his son. Switching to English, he managed to add, "You know that they cannot be trusted!"

"I have met them through your acupuncturist," Nelson said with a laugh.

Pierre blushed before quickly recovering himself.

"We were coming for the recital," Pierre said with a grin. "Your charming daughter came to invite me. I could not say 'No'."

Jacob put his hand on Pierre's arm.

"Can I help you inside?" Jacob asked.

Pierre shook his head.

"It's good for me to walk," Pierre said. "I don't need my son's assistance. I want to keep him close."

"Of course," Jacob said.

Jacob and Jill waited for them to take seats at the table. They sat down on the couch. Pierre leaned into Nelson.

"They have the smell of the first woman," Pierre said. "I have heard that she consorts with Prince Finegal."

Nelson laughed out loud. Colin and Julie Hargreaves came in the den. As they were greeting everyone, Pierre leaned over.

"Have you met this woman?" Pierre asked.

"Same place," Nelson nodded.

Nelson nodded. Pierre shook his head in disbelief. Nelson impulsively leaned over to kiss his father's cheek. Smiling from ear to ear, Pierre's hand covered the precious kiss. He put his arm around his son.

"You will love them," Nelson said.

Pierre silently hoped he was right. A young man with long sandy hair and green eyes rolled a baby grand piano into the room. Bernie, Seth's biological father, came in behind it. The two men set up the bench and the music.

"We are ready," Bernie said to the two little champions in the doorway.

Katy and Paddie shuffled out toward the piano. For a moment, they looked like they were going to melt into the floor. Bernie touched the children on the shoulder. Paddie recovered first.

"Come on, Katy," Paddie said.

He took her hand and helped her onto the piano bench. He sat down, next to her, to the right. Sam Lipson and Delphie scooted into the room, giving Pierre a chance to whisper to Nelson again.

"Can you see the Sword of Truth?" Pierre whispered to Nelson. "Metal? On the boy's belt?"

Nelson nodded.

"Good," Pierre said.

Katy stood up, and Paddie scooted to his left. Katy sat down in front of the upper keys, and Paddie was sitting in front of the lower register.

"Hello," Seth said. "This is Katy Marlowe and Paddie Hargreaves. They've taken piano lessons for the last year with my father, Bernie. When I'm in town, they play with me."

"They are really good, so we thought you'd like to hear them," Seth said.

Katy started playing the opening lines of the children's lullaby, *Lavender Blue*. After a moment, Paddie joined in the song in the lower register. The children played with clear precision. Paddie played the lower register and Katy played the upper. While neither of them seemed particularly gifted in the piano, they did a great job with the simple song.

Everyone cheered loudly. Bernie helped them up. As they'd practiced, Paddie bowed and Katy curtsied. The children were kissed and hugged until they were squirming. With Jacob carrying Katy, he and Jill followed Colin, Paddie, and Julie out the door.

"But . . ." Katy said when she was clicked into her car seat.

Jacob kissed her cheek and went to the driver's seat. With an eye on Colin, Jacob made sure he went a different way.

"Weren't we going to ice cream?" Katy asked. "You said if Paddie and I played, we'd go for special ice cream."

"Do you want to?" Jill asked.

"We thought maybe you'd like to go home and get some rest," Jacob said.

Katy scowled at her parents but didn't say anything else. She squealed with delight when Jacob pulled into the parking lot behind Colin.

"I'm really glad," Katy said.

"Did you think I'd back out on a promise?" Jacob asked.

"I was going to turn you into a frog!" Katy said.

Jacob laughed. Jill came to his side and slipped her hand into his. Katy ran ahead to catch up with Paddie.

"Do you think she can do that?" Jill asked.

"I don't really want to find out," Jacob said.

Jill smiled, and they walked toward the ice cream shop.

"What are we going to do when she turns thirteen?" Jacob asked.

Not knowing how to respond, Jill just laughed. Smiling at her, Jacob shook his head and followed her inside.

CHAPTER 528

ROAD TO WHERE?

Saturday morning — 8:15 a.m.
Denver, Colorado

"But we'll be there all week!" Nash complained.

"Yes. Imagine how horrible it would be to drill more than one well," Jacob said.

He pushed on the boy's head. Nash swatted at his hand. Nash and Charlie were helping Jacob sort through their camping gear from the storage room in the basement.

"It's not Paris," Charlie said, mildly.

"Yeah!" Nash said angrily. "It's not like we're going to Paris!"

"We're going to the Navajo reservation to help some good people get water," Jacob said. "But if you'd rather stay here and work on a Lipson crew, I'd totally understand."

Nash grumbled. He grabbed the heavy large tent and carried out of the basement.

"He's upset because he thought he was going to see Nadia this week," Charlie said.

"I probably should tell him that she's coming," Jacob said.

"She is?" Charlie asked.

"She offered to relieve a doctor at the clinic," Jacob said. "As you can imagine, he was delighted to have a few days off. Nelson thinks he can get away on Wednesday. Blane's bringing his needles. M.J. and Tanesha are going to help, too. I think Alex's husband is coming. Her nephew and niece. We hope to relieve some of the congestion in the clinic there. In fact, if you want to observe, it's a pretty good chance to see what every specialty does. I bet they could use your help, too. Tink's, too."

Nodding, Charlie grinned. He and Tink had just started working on their Certified Medical Assistant degree at night. They were already volunteering a few hours at the free clinic Tanesha was working at. Jacob pointed to a large cooler.

"Can you bring that up to the girlfriends?" Jacob said.

"'The girlfriends'?" Charlie asked with a laugh.

"Jill, Tanesha, Heather, your sister?" Jacob asked.

"I know who they are," Charlie said. "I just didn't know anyone called them that besides me."

Jacob grinned. Charlie picked up the cooler and started out of the room.

"They're going to ask you where the little ones are," Jacob said.

Charlie turned to look at him.

"Inside the cooler," Jacob said. "We have two more of the big ones."

Charlie nodded.

"Come back," Jacob said. "Don't let them send you somewhere else."

Teddy showed up at the door.

"How do the sleeping bags look?" Jacob said.

"Mrs. Valerie is washing a couple of them," Teddy said. "You know, we have a bunch of these at my Dad's house. Alex's, too."

"Your Dad's bringing what they have," Jacob said. "He and your siblings are coming for a few days. Your sister didn't tell you?"

"She's not talking to me," Teddy said with a shrug.

"Ah, yes," Jacob said. "I'm sure that will teach you a lesson."

Grinning, Teddy grabbed another armload of sleeping bags and carried them to the laundry room. Nash appeared in the doorway.

"Could I just go to Paris?" Nash asked. "Maybe New York?"

"What did your mom and dad say?" Jacob asked.

Nash slumped into himself.

"Nadia has arranged to be there with us," Jacob said. "She and the rest of the medical crew are taking over the clinic there to give the medical staff some relief."

"Oh," Nash said. He flushed red and looked down. When he looked up, he had tears in his eyes. "I don't know if I . . ."

Jacob hugged the boy.

"You'll be great," Jacob said. "We're going to go, dig a few wells for some nice people, camp out, eat some great food. We'll have a great time. You know Margaret Peaches, don't you?"

Nash nodded.

"She's already there," Jacob said. "She, Cian, and their daughter are there getting everything ready for us. We're going to stay on some of their land. Cian says it's like heaven on earth."

"But I don't know how to dig a well," Nash said.

"You know how to show up and work," Jacob said. "You'll learn the rest."

"Is my dad coming, too?" Nash asked.

"He's coming today to help us get set up," Jacob said. "He has to go back to work on Tuesday. If we're still working and happy next weekend, he'll come down on Saturday. You don't go back to school until Tuesday."

Nodding at the information, Nash darkened.

"These people don't have *water*," Jacob said. "Imagine what that would be like."

"Awful," Nash said. He wiped his nose with the back of his hand.

"We can go down there, bring some equipment, and remedy that situation," Jacob said. "If we're lucky, we'll dig a well a day. If not, we'll at least get water to Margaret's grandparents. And, we'll go back again when we can."

Nash looked up at Jacob.

"We're going to have a blast," Jacob said. "I promise."

Nash nodded. Jacob pointed to the five two-person tents hanging on hooks along the wall. Nash pulled the tents down and went upstairs.

Jacob watched Nash head out the door. Charlie appeared in the door.

"They want the other coolers," Charlie said.

Grinning, Jacob pointed him toward the other coolers. The boy picked up two coolers and started out of the room. Jacob called him back.

"Tell Abi that there's still an entire deer in the freezer," Jacob said.

Charlie shook his head.

"She's talking to the girlfriends about going hunting," Jacob said. "We can bring the deer. We have some fly-fishing planned, but no hunting on the reservation this time of year. Tell her all of that."

Charlie nodded and left.

"Jake!" Valerie's voice came to him in the storage room at the same time that Tink showed up.

"Any ideas?" Jacob asked Tink.

"She wants to talk to you," Tink said with a shrug. "She sent me here to bring you to her."

Seeing Teddy in the hallway, Jacob pointed Teddy into the storage room. He went to the laundry room.

"Yes?" Jacob asked.

Valerie was standing next to the two big washing machines. She had her son, Eddie, strapped onto her back in a baby backpack, and her daughter, Jackie, was sitting on the folding table. Tink came in behind Jacob. She was folding towels on the folding table in the corner.

"Jackie tells me that the kids have been sleeping together every night," Valerie said.

"Many of them," Jacob said. "Not all of them, of course."

"Should they sleep together on the trip?" Valerie asked.

Jacob squinted at her.

"How would I know?" Jacob asked, irritably.

Valerie grinned at him, and he smiled at her.

"What do you really want?" Jacob asked.

"I . . ." Valerie looked at him. "I was standing here telling Tink about the camping trips we took as kids and how I would get really scared but you were super fierce and protective and . . ."

"And?" Jacob asked.

"I realized I could call you in here," Valerie said. She shrugged. "I haven't been around in a long time."

Jacob went to his sister and kissed her cheek.

"Are we almost ready?" Valerie asked.

"Another hour," Jacob said. "If we don't go into major meltdown mode."

"Don't have a meltdown, Jacob," Valerie said, in a pleading voice. "Use your words."

He gave her an exasperated look and left the room. From the storage room, he could hear her yelling, "Use your words."

"What in the world?" Jeraine asked as he came out of the apartment they were staying in.

Jeraine was carrying two backpacks stuffed with gear and sleeping bags.

"She misses me," Jacob said.

"Do you need an extra sleeping bag?" Jeraine asked. "We have an extra bag and a one-man tent."

"If you can give it to Nash, that would be great," Jacob said.

"Sure thing," Jeraine said. "I'll drop these off and get what we have."

Jacob watched Jeraine head up the stairs and went back into the storage area. The teenagers had cleared out nearly all of their camping gear. He grinned.

They were going to have a great time.

~~~~~~~~~

Saturday morning — 10:15 a.m.

Blane kissed Heather's cheek, and she stroked his face.

"Drive safely," Heather said, softly.

"I will," Blane said. He couldn't keep himself from asking again. "You're sure this is okay?"

Blane was hot and tired. Angry with himself for even attempting to have a relationship with Nelson, he needed some time to think everything through. Also, he truly hated all of the chaos and drama involved in getting these family trips underway. These teenagers were getting on his last nerve. He dared not say anything or have Jacob laugh at him. Jacob and Aden loved the chaos. But Blane was ill suited to chaos and drama.

"Absolutely," Heather said. "You have a lot to think about. This is a long drive. The two things are a good fit. If you get tired of being alone, I can join you or any of..."

Heather gestured to the teenagers. Nash was pushing Charlie, and Charlie was laughing. Tink rolled her eyes at the boys. Noelle was obsessing about her paint in the back of Aden's SUV.

"Leave it!" Aden ordered.

"What if I need...?" Noelle asked for the hundredth time.

Katy and Paddie skipped past while Jacob struggled by carrying the twins in two car seats. Sandy dropped Maggie into Heather's arms before going to referee in the escalating fight between Noelle and her father. Honey wheeled out from the house. She zoomed to her van currently filled with coolers and full backpacks.

Jeraine was standing just outside the chaos looking stunned by the activity and noise.

"Man up, buttercup." M.J. shot Jeraine the dig Jeraine usually said to him.

M.J. bumped Jeraine's shoulder as he passed. M.J. was carrying a heavy duffle bag. He dropped it in the back of the SUV Blane was driving and turned again to Jeraine.

"Are you coming?" M.J. asked Jeraine.

This seemed to shake Jeraine out of his shock. He jogged to Honey's van.

"The usual chaos," Blane said.

"I'm sure we'll have enough of chaos this week." Heather raised her eyebrows at Blane.

He nodded.

"I don't want to . . ." Blane started.

"We'll be fine," Heather said. "If we're not, I'll use the walkie-talkie to let you know. Easy."

He leaned forward, and they hugged. Heather gave him a little wave and went to her Subaru, where Jill was in the driver's seat. Blane watched Heather greet Tanesha before the women got into the stationwagon. Tink stepped in after Tanesha. Carrying Rachel Ann, Sandy was the last to join them.

As the gear driver, Blane waited to leave until everyone was underway. Honey was the first person out of the parking lot. Jill followed in the Subaru. Noelle ran out from Aden's SUV. She ran around Mike as he came out of the Castle, carrying his children. Valerie was right behind Mike. Because Valerie had been gone, they were leisurely driving to New Mexico together as a family in her mother's old diesel Mercedes. Mike waved to Blane as they left the parking lot. Jacob, with Katy, Paddie, and a host of infants, followed Mike.

Noelle ran out of the Castle toward Blane's SUV. Blane hopped out of the driver's seat to grab another plastic storage container filled with pastels and colored pencils from Noelle. She followed him to the SUV to put her pad of paper inside. He put her colors and paper near the driver's seat so that nothing could happen to them.

"Come on!" Charlie yelled to Noelle.

She ran to Aden's SUV. There was much groaning, but she was soon seat-belted inside. Aden started out of the Castle parking lot. Blane checked the straps on the carrier on top of the SUV. He made sure the bicycles were locked into the rack on the roof. He did one last check around the vehicle before he got back into the driver's seat.

Nelson was sitting in the passenger's seat.

"What do you want?" Blane asked, irritably.

"I'm going with you," Nelson said.

"What about 'Don't call me'?" Blane asked. "I thought you didn't *ever* want to see me again."

Nelson looked at Blane for a moment.

"I'm not a fucking Greek god," Blane said. "I don't fucking innately understand your human frailties."

His rage rising, Blane pointed his index finger at Nelson.

"And this is not a game," Blane said. "I have young children who were wondering why Uncle Nelson stormed out of their lives. My life is not conducive to the push-pull of teenage girls."

Nelson watched Blane.

"Who the fuck do you think you are?" Blane asked. "Get the fuck out of the car!"

"No," Nelson said.

"Someone was mean to you. Big fucking deal!" Blane said. "*Years* ago. And you're out of here. It wasn't even me! I wasn't the one who was cruel to you. But I'm the one you never, ever want to see again! Me! Well, guess what? The feeling's mutual. Get the fuck out of the car!"

Nelson didn't move. Blane shook with fury. He opened his mouth to yell some more, but futility overwhelmed him. His rage drained out of him as hopelessness overwhelmed him.

"Go," Blane said.

Nelson didn't respond. Blane shook his head and grabbed the steering wheel to keep from falling over.

"Fine," Blane said through his teeth. "If you have something to say, say it, and be gone."

Nelson nodded.

"You have a right to be mad," Nelson said.

Blane snorted at Nelson.

"I have a right to need space," Nelson said. "To feel things strongly. To react! You know, I might be a scientist, but I am not an automaton."

"No one asked you to be an automaton," Blane said. "You don't need my permission to feel whatever the fuck you want to feel. You're allowed."

"Then why are you so angry?" Nelson asked.

Blane tried to take a few deep breaths to calm himself. Instead, he hit the wheel with his hand.

"You begged me to start this thing with you. For years. Since that night at the Church," Blane said. "'Come on, Blane.' 'Don't be afraid.' 'We can do this.' 'I love you, love Heather, love the kids.' 'We're good together, Blane.' 'We owe it to ourselves to at least try.' Or the kicker — 'What could possibly happen?'"

Blane glared at Nelson.

"Then something happens," Blane said. "And you're out. No conversation. No honoring of the commitment you *begged* for. Nothing. Just bam, you're gone. You don't ever want to see me again."

Blane leaned over Nelson and flicked open the lever on the passenger door. The passenger door swung open.

"I don't have time for liars," Blane said. "Now, please. You wanted out. You wanted no contact. Get out. Go live your life. Leave me the fuck alone!"

Nelson sighed. He shifted from looking at Blane to looking out of the windscreen. The sound of the traffic on Colfax Boulevard echoed through the vehicle. Nelson turned to Blane.

"You're right," Nelson said evenly. "I was exhausted, overwrought, completely out there on the skinny branches."

"Why?" Blane asked. "That's what I don't get. Why didn't you talk to me? *Trust* me to stand up for you, to want work it out?"

"Oh, I don't know," Nelson said. "I am a part of a federal case to take down a major crime family. I've been working on this project off and on for six months or more. I haven't had a lot of sleep because I've been in meetings; then . . ."

Nelson paused.

"Then?" Blane asked.

"Then my dream man comes over to my home and we were up. . . almost all night," Nelson said. "I . . . Anything I say will sound like an excuse. But I will tell you — this thing with Junior is a big fucking deal to me. It might not be severe, unadulterated trauma. That's true, but it changed my life. . ."

Nelson shook his head. Not able to meet Blane's eyes, Nelson stayed focused out the front windscreen.

"It's like one moment, I was one person," Nelson said. "The next moment, I was someone else, all because of something Junior said."

"Junior?" Blane asked.

"M.J." Nelson said. "Michael Scully, Junior. We used to call him 'Junior.'"

Blane shook his head and looked away.

"Why . . .?" Blane started.

"My soul was . . . broken," Nelson said. "I don't think I even realized it until . . ."

Nelson stopped talking. He turned to Blane.

"Until?" Blane asked.

"Hedone," Nelson said.

"Apples?" Blane asked.

"What is the deal with those apples?" Nelson asked.

"They are infused with love," Blane said. "They heal, on the inside."

"Amazing," Nelson said.

Not one to let things go, Blane scowled.

"So, that's it?" Blane asked. "You've had some apples and, like some reverse fucking Snow White, you're okay?"

"No," Nelson said. "No."

"Then what?" Blane asked.

Nelson didn't respond for a moment.

"I'm sorry," Nelson said. "When I think through what it must have been like for you, I . . ."

He sighed.

"I should not have run off," Nelson said. "I . . ."

Nelson gave a sad chuckle.

"I've learned that running away has caused most of my suffering," Nelson said.

"And that means?" Blane asked.

"I ran away when Michael's mother taunted me about being gay," Nelson said. "My dad and my grandmother were arguing. My grandmother hit me, and his mother was calling me a 'faggot,' and my father was screaming, and . . ."

Nelson sighed. Sorrow came off the young man in waves. He looked over at Blane.

"My father has always known that I was gay," Nelson said. "Said it was something that runs in our family."

"He doesn't have a problem with it?" Blane asked. "With you."

Nelson shook his head.

"He's been trying to set me up," Nelson said. Blane raised his eyebrows. "With you. He's one of your acupuncture clients. Said he's been trying to set us up for years."

"Your *father* sees me for acupuncture?" Blane asked. "You're sure?"

Nelson nodded.

"What is your father's name?" Blane asked.

CHAPTER 529

YOU'RE WHAT?

"Pierre Semaines," Nelson said.

"Fuck," Blane said. "Of course, he is. God. No wonder he was so weird today."

"Weird?" Nelson asked.

"'How are things going, Blane?'" Blane exaggerated Pierre's accent. "'I've heard you're doing really *well*.' 'Anything wonderful happening?'"

"He thinks you're a miracle worker," Nelson said.

Blane just shook his head.

"That man does *not* have a problem with gay people," Blane said. "Says his best friend growing up was gay. His father, too."

"Yes," Nelson said. "I learned that today."

Nelson gave a heavy sigh.

"So running away from him really screwed up my head," Nelson said. "Running away from you was dumb. I should have stayed."

"It's all right to leave a situation," Blane said. "You can leave a room without blowing up the entire fucking house."

Nelson sniffed and then cleared his throat.

"Yes, well," Nelson said. After a moment, he sighed, "I'm willing to learn."

Blane groaned and leaned his head against the head rest.

"My mother gave her life for me," Nelson said. "I can do this."

"My mother did as well," Blane said. "How does that relate to this?"

"Something we have in common," Nelson said.

The silence dragged. Nelson didn't get out of the vehicle, and Blane didn't know what else to say. Blane sighed.

"What the deal with all of the swords?" Blane asked.

"Swords?" Nelson asked.

"Your dad has an entire room of antique swords," Blane said.

"That's a long story," Nelson said. He pulled his seatbelt down and locked it in. "I can tell you on our drive."

Blane glared at Nelson for a long moment. Nelson responded by closing his door.

"It's a long drive," Nelson said. "We should go."

They sat in silence as the SUV became unbearably hot.

"I am ready when you are," Nelson said.

Shaking his head, Blane started the SUV. They rolled to the gate and waited for it to open. Before Blane could complain, Nelson leaned over and kissed Blane. Their faces were inches apart.

"I am sorry," Nelson said. "I was too caught up in myself to realize that I hurt you."

Blane snorted in agreement. Nelson leaned in to kiss Blane again but Blane pushed him away.

"Get off me," Blane said. "I'm not a 'kiss and make up' kind of person."

"Oh?" Nelson laughed. "What are you?"

"A grumbling, growling, bitter, resentful man until I figure out what *I* want to do," Blane said. "But it's up to me."

Blane drove through the security gate to the street.

"You'd better have packed some cash," Blane said.

"Why?" Nelson asked.

"It's a long drive," Blane said. "I'm not above kicking your ass out on the side of the road if you piss me off."

Blane put on his dark sunglasses. He looked at Nelson when they stopped at the stoplight on Colfax Boulevard.

"You shaved," Blane said.

"Yeah . . ." Nelson nodded.

"Contacts?" Blane asked.

Blushing, Nelson cleared his throat.

"I *do* have to wear glasses in the lab," Nelson said.

"Good thing you're not in the lab," Blane said mildly.

"That's what Fran said," Nelson said. He shook his head and put on his sunglasses. "Do you know Fran?"

"What do you think?" Blane asked.

"Fuck," Nelson said.

Blane grinned. They drove in silence from stoplight to stoplight as they made their way up Colfax Boulevard.

"You look good," Blane said.

Nelson flushed with sheer joy.

"Shut the fuck up," Blane grumbled.

"Put your safety belt on, bitter, resentful man," Nelson said.

Blane shot Nelson a dark look but did what he was told.

"So, swords?" Blane asked.

"Oh, what?" Nelson pretended to be surprised. "You hold the threat of being throwing out of the car over my head to get my family secrets out of me."

"I might slow down before I throw you out," Blane said.

Nelson swallowed hard and looked at Blane. With his sunglasses on and his focus on driving, Nelson couldn't tell if Blane was joking.

"Fine," Blane said. "I'll slow down before chucking you out of the car."

Nelson laughed. He was rewarded with a small smile from Blane.

"Swords," Blane ordered as he turned onto Colorado Boulevard.

"Yes, well," Nelson said.

Blane groaned. He pulled to stop at another stoplight and flicked open the locks on the vehicle. Nelson held onto the armrest. Blane laughed.

Nelson didn't say anything.

"Ah, fuck it," Blane said.

He pulled into a fast-food restaurant. He ordered for himself and then looked at Nelson.

"I never . . ." Nelson said.

"Bullshit," Blane said. "Just order."

While Blane rolled his eyes, Nelson gave a detailed, specific order and checked to make sure the person had it. They were on their way in no time. Blane mellowed out with some fat and sugar in his system.

Blane continued down Colorado Boulevard.

"Are we taking this to the 285?" Nelson asked.

"No," Blane said. "We're going to Moab and heading south."

"That's not the way to go!" Nelson protested.

Blane gave him an irritated look. He smiled.

"Just trying to make sure that we get there," Nelson said.

"How did you get in this car?" Blane asked. "I mean, how did you know we were going?"

"Oh," Nelson said. "Jake told me. After the piano recital while we were all standing around. I didn't think I could go until Wednesday, but I talked to Ava and . . . Here I am. I have to check in on Sunday night, but I can probably stay all week."

Nelson shrugged.

"If they need me, they'll call me," Nelson said.

"Where did Jake tell you we were going?" Blane asked.

"Navajo Nation," Nelson said. "Nadia Kerminoff called and asked if I could help her out at the clinic. I guess they transitioned from a rural clinic to a hospital at the end of last year. They've been really overrun. We're going to relieve the emergency docs and anyone else who needs help."

Blane didn't respond as he transitioned onto I-70.

"I was surprised when she called," Nelson said.

"Why?" Blane asked.

"I've known Nadia for a long time," Nelson said.

"Oh, yeah?" Blane asked. "Where'd you meet?"

"We have the same specialty and are about the same age," Nelson said. "She applied for the same residencies and fellowships. I saw her at so many sites that we started planning to go on the same days."

Nelson paused for a moment.

"She's a really great person," Nelson said. "I was surprised that she was connected to you and all of this."

"Do you know who Ivan is?" Blane asked.

Nelson grunted and nodded.

"He taught Sissy ballet," Blane said. "Sissy is Sandy's sister."

"Aren't they dating?" Nelson asked. "Sissy and Ivan, I mean, not Sandy."

Blane nodded.

"We don't talk about it because she's so much younger than he is," Blane said. "How do you know about it?"

"Nadia sent me Sissy's file after she was shot," Nelson said. "Gunshots are kind of my thing. Nadia wanted to know what I thought the girl's chances were."

"And?" Blane asked.

"I'm glad she's all right," Nelson said. "Those shots were brutal, designed to kill her. And if she survived? They should have stopped her from ever dancing again. If I didn't know better, I'd say that she had some kind of magical intervention."

Blane kept a kind of stony silence. Nelson looked at him for a moment before continuing.

"Nadia's in a weird relationship with one of the kids that lives at Jake's house," Nelson said.

"Nash," Nelson and Blane said at the same time.

"You know about that?" Blane asked.

Nelson sighed and looked away. After a while, he turned back to Blane.

"Anyway, you're going the wrong way," Nelson said. "I looked it up this morning."

"You looked up how to get to Kayenta, Arizona, this morning?" Blane asked.

"Oh," Nelson said. "No. Just to the Navajo Nation."

"We're meeting everyone at one of the hotels there," Blane said. "Tomorrow, we'll make trips out to the site to see if we can stay there or if we'd rather stay in the hotel."

Nelson put the coordinates into his phone. After a few minutes, he nodded.

"Guess what?" Nelson asked.

"I'm right?" Blane asked.

Nelson laughed. Blane grinned.

"Here's a question," Nelson said.

"Don't hold back on my account," Blane said.

"Why are we going to the Navajo Nation in the middle of the summer?" Nelson asked.

"For the last year or so, there's been a plan to go to Poland to investigate a salt mine," Blane said.

"Wieliczka?" Nelson asked.

"No," Blane said. He opened his mouth to continue, but Nelson interrupted.

"Bochnia?" Nelson asked.

"Not that one, either," Blane said.

He waited a few moments to see if Nelson had something else to say.

"Okay, I'll bite," Nelson said. "Where?"

Blane grinned.

"It's a spot between those two mines," Blane said. "Private land."

"Mysterious," Nelson said. "How did this get on the plan?"

"Sandy has a little project of buying old artifacts from people," Blane said. "She has some money that she's had since she was a child. For lack of a better word, she's 'laundering' it through artifacts. Because she is Seth's daughter, and so Bernie's granddaughter, she has access to truly rare items from Holocaust survivors and their children. These elderly people or their children need cash to enjoy their last years. She can provide that."

"What does she do with the artifacts?" Nelson asked.

"She's found things that are on the register," Blane said. "She's returned what she can but, in some rare cases, the register was wrong. The object was in the possession of a family, just not the family members that reported it missing."

"The artifacts would be worth a small fortune," Nelson said.

Blane looked at Nelson.

"Sandy can prove provenance," Nelson said. "That's like the golden egg."

"She tries to get them into museums, when she can," Blane said.

Nelson nodded and looked out the window.

"Did Paddie get his sword from Sandy?" Nelson asked to the glass.

"The Sword of Truth was given to Paddie by Maughold when he and Katy were kidnapped on the Isle of Man," Blane said evenly.

Nelson didn't respond. Blane blinked. It was a weird enough statement that most normal people would, at the very least, ask him to repeat it. Blane's eyes flicked to Nelson, but Nelson was looking out the passenger window.

"Anyway, the trip was canceled because it's too dangerous for the children to go," Blane said. "Rather than have them all at home driving everyone crazy, Jake thought we could go dig some wells."

"With teenagers?" Nelson asked.

"They're really great kids," Blane said. "You'll see. They will jump right in and get to work. The little ones will do what they can. It's just how it works in this family."

"Good to know," Nelson said. "So, we're going to Kayenta?"

"We're supposed to go straight through," Blane said. "Jake and Aden have the kids. The girlfriends are in Heather's car. I think Rachel and Maggie are in with them."

"I saw them leave," Nelson said.

"The way Jake figures it, the kids are going to want their moms," Blane said. "The moms are going to decide that the men are doing it wrong. The teenagers are going to fight. The little kids will have some unfixable need."

"Like boredom?" Nelson asked.

Blane glanced at him.

"I was surprised that Jake didn't have videos playing for the kids," Nelson said.

"Jake doesn't believe in that kind of thing," Blane said. "He thinks kids get enough TV time."

"Hence the switching cars," Nelson said.

"Exactly," Blane said. "Anyway, we have bets on what the cars will look like by the time they get to Kayenta."

Nelson grinned.

"You want to listen to music?" Nelson asked.

"I want to know about the swords," Blane said. "Why did you ask about Paddie and his sword? Do you know who Maughold is? I didn't when it first happened."

"Oh," Nelson said.

Nelson didn't say anything for a good fifteen minutes. Blane cleared his throat and glanced at Nelson.

"Oh, sorry," Nelson said. "You don't happen to speak French, do you?"

"High school," Blane said. "My Spanish is solid. Some Russian, just from knowing Ivan. But my French is vague."

"We'll have to work on that," Nelson said.

"Why?" Blane asked.

"Because this story is a story of France, if not *the* story of France," Nelson said.

"And we live in the United States?" Blane shook his head.

"I am the culmination of this story," Nelson said. "I didn't tell you before because I . . . But now . . . Are you angry?"

"Why don't you just tell me? We'll see what we need to sort out," Blane said. He surprised himself at how much he sounded like Jacob. "Go on."

~~~~~~~~
Saturday morning — 10:25 a.m.

Pierre Semaines awoke to the sound of a man's laughter. The man standing next to his bed clearly thought that something was hilarious. He looked past the laughing man to see Perses, the Titan God of Destruction. Pierre leaned against his elbow to push himself up.

"What is funny?" Pierre asked.

"He speaks *French*," the man said, as he pointed to Pierre. "That wasn't a clue?"

"I thought they were all dead," Perses said. "Kill off by the jealous French king."

The man spun in place and leaned over Pierre.

"What is it?" the man demanded. His tone was hostile, laced with disdain. "How did you survive?"

Pierre blinked at the man and then shot a look at Perses. The man near him had shoulder length sandy-colored hair. His eyes were blue and his nose long. Pierre took a deep breath through his nose.

"You smell Greek," Pierre said with equal disdain. "Minor god? Bastard child?"

The man lunged toward Pierre. Perses jumped between the man and Pierre. He held the man back from the bed.

"Do not antagonize him," Perses said when the man was under control.

"Why not?" Pierre asked.

"He is your in-law," Perses said.

"I should have eaten your son when I had the chance," the man said.

For the first time in a long time, Pierre felt a sliver of real fear. This man was threatening to eat his precious boy. And Pierre was too sick to stop him.

Perses turned to the man and growled in an ancient version of language: "Be silent."

The man stopped moving. He looked at Perses and then at Pierre.

"Perses is correct," the man said. "My granddaughter is married to your son's love interest. We are family or will be soon enough."

Pierre was still trying to work out who this man was and what he was talking about.

"Introduce yourself," Perses commanded the man as if he were a petulant child.

"I am Ares, God of War," the man said. "And you?"

"Pierre Semaines," Pierre said. "Engineer. American. French national."

"Already he lies," Ares said.

"He would like you to reveal your titles," Perses said. "I asked him here to see if he knew what or who you were. He says that you look like a Templar."

Pierre gave a sincere nod and moved to get up.

"Could you help me up?" Pierre asked. "I'm okay in bed and good on my feet. It's the transition that's hard."

Perses held out his forearm. Pierre pulled himself up to sitting. He rotated his legs around to the edge of the bed. With Perses' help, he stood. Pierre held his hand out to a walking stick in the corner of the room. Ares gave Pierre the walking stick.

Pierre pulled at the ornate top of the walking stick and a long, thin sword appeared. He held it to his forehead.

"I am of the Order of Solomon's Temple," Pierre said.

In a swift, practiced movement, he moved the sword from his forehead to his side.

"You *are* a Templar," Perses said, a sucking in a breath.

When no challenge came, Pierre slid the sword back into the walking stick.

"My family," Pierre said. "It is our sacred duty to protect . . ."

"You are a long way from Temple Mound," Ares said, wryly.

"Yes," Pierre said simply.

"How did you survive?" Perses asked.

"We hid," Pierre said. "But you are correct. Most of our order were killed or forced to join other orders. Many were murdered outright for their land or possessions."

"But not you," Ares said. "How strange."

"My ancestors were weapons makers, as am I. They were the order's weapons masters," Pierre said. "We kept the weapons. At home. In France. No one realized that we were there. When the order was outlawed, we continued about our business. Everyone needs a weapon or two. You don't kill the weapons makers."

"And the boy?" Perses asked.

"May I ask something first?" Pierre asked.

After time to think it through, Perses gave a nod.

"Which grandchild of the god Ares is my son involved with?" Pierre asked.

Perses' gave Pierre a wide grin. Ares laughed. Pierre raised his eyebrows.

"Hedone goes by the modern name 'Heather,'" Perses said, evenly.

Pierre was so startled that his hand went to his heart. Perses helped him to sit on the bed. Pierre stared off into space.

"She is one of my daughter's best-friends," Perses said. "So we are also related, as it were."

"H . . .h . . .how?" Pierre asked.

"Her mother, Psyche, was horribly abused by Aphrodite," Ares said. "So Psyche took their child and hid her through time. Hedone was human enough to pass as a human child. Every time Hedone was twenty or so, Psyche would return her to ten years old, the age the child was when Aphrodite released her mother. They would move to the next age. They did this. . . thousands of times."

"But she is older than twenty now," Pierre said. "I have met her. She's 26 or maybe 28 years old."

"Hedone convinced her mother that they were well hidden in the modern world," Ares said. "Her grandmother adores Hedone, so she was able to convince her grandmother to leave Psyche alone."

"Psyche and Eros have reunited in the last few years," Perses said. "They are on a permanent break, somewhere out of time."

"My son has given his commission to his daughter," Ares said. "Hedone is now the Goddess of Love, like her Grandmother."

Ares nodded to Perses.

"He got the ball rolling," Ares said. "Of course, it was a great relief to everyone involved."

"Why?" Pierre asked.

"My son lost his mind looking for his beloved," Ares said. "He needs a long break."

Pierre fell silent. After a moment, he looked at Ares.

"The child?" Pierre asked. "Hedone? She was born before . . ."

"Yes," Ares said at the same time Perses said, "Of course. You cannot lie with a young woman and not have a child."

"Your son?" Perses asked. "Who or what is he?"

"It's a long story," Pierre said.

"We have time," Ares said. "But tell me first, weapons master, do you have the Sword of the Sacred Flame?"

"The Sword of the Moon?" Pierre asked. "That was given to Walter Raleigh by his Queen and lost in the Americas. I've traced it to something called the Lost Colony of Roanoke. It's believed that the sword was lost with them."

"But you don't believe that," Ares said.

"I don't," Pierre said. "I believe it's in a private collection. I haven't been able to get in to see the collection. Yet."

"Maybe we can help," Perses said.

"Maybe you can," Pierre said. "I have the Sword of the Sun."

"The Sword of the Sacred Fire," Ares said.

"It is a beautiful weapon," Pierre said. "Gorgeous. Would you mind me asking? Where did the boy get the Sword of Truth?"

"Maughold," Perses said.

"Maughold?" Pierre asked. "What?"

The men laughed.

"Why is that funny?" Pierre asked.

"You really should spend some time with your acupuncturist," Perses said.

"It's his family," Ares said. "There's an odd mixture of folks living at that Castle."

The men looked at each other and laughed.

"What?" Pierre asked.

Chapter 530

All In

Saturday afternoon — 4:45 p.m.
Paris, France,

"See you Monday," Sissy's friend, Brigitte, said in thickly accented English.

Brigitte had been the most advanced student in their class before Sissy arrived. Since then, Sissy had gradually taken Brigitte's place. Sissy's down-to-earth nature and her genuine friendliness caused Brigitte's resentment to fade away. They were friends, which was a blessing to them both. Sissy had been helping Brigitte with her English, and Brigitte helped Sissy with her French.

"*Au revoir*, Ivan!" Brigitte said with a little wave. She blew him a kiss.

Ivan scowled at the impropriety but Sissy laughed. Sissy tucked her hand into the crook of Ivan's arm, and they walked out of the *Opéra National de Paris*, where Sissy was going to ballet school

"She should not be so forward on your partner," Ivan said with a sniff. Sissy kissed his cheek.

"You must assert yourself or be overlooked," Ivan said.

"By whom?" Sissy asked. "Will I be overlooked by you?"

Flustered, Ivan looked down. As they walked, he couldn't help but pull her closer.

"You danced beautifully today," Ivan said. "I can see the results of your hard work here. You are more even, side to side, not favoring the side you were shot. You are stronger, more confident, and yet . . . light on your feet. You took my breath away."

Sissy smiled, and he kissed her nose.

"I forget how good you are," Sissy said.

"I am an old man," Ivan said.

"I have seen lots of men dance since I've been here," Sissy said. "Ben and Claire take me to watch ballet every Saturday and sometimes on Sunday. Here in Paris. We've been in London a few times as well. There really aren't men who dance like you."

"Of course, we are best together," Ivan said, with a hint of pride.

"I'm kind of old news, but you!" Sissy gave him a bright smile. "You had everyone mesmerized."

It was such a Sissy thing to say that he couldn't help but smile.

"It felt so good to dance with you again," Sissy said in a soft, secret way.

Flushed with delight, his face nearly broke with his smile. Sissy gave him a bright smile and continued on.

"I have other ways of asserting myself," Sissy said. "I've done really well by being friendly and open. Brigitte and Bastien have stood up for me more than once when I've forgotten a word or been less than Parisian. I am their friend. My classmates introduce me as 'Sissy' and not '*l'Américain*' as they did at first."

"That is only because they expect that you will benefit them in some way," Ivan said. "You must always be aware of this give and take. If you get out of balance, either way, it can affect your career forever."

Sissy smiled. They continued to walk.

"Why do you smile?" Ivan asked.

"Because not so long ago, the only thing I could *expect* was another argument with my mother," Sissy said. "Or possibly that Charlie would die on the streets. Or another battle with eating. My expectation was that I would never, ever get out of the clutches of that awful eating disorder. Sandy was gone. You were in New York. Then there were the months of pain and recovery from being shot. My terror of losing you to injury or infirmity or death, I expected . . ."

She cleared her throat rather than complete the sentence.

"The mere fact that these French people *expect* something from me other than dysfunction and imminent death?" Sissy asked.

Sissy kissed his cheek again.

"It's nothing short of miraculous," Sissy said.

Flushing, Ivan cleared his throat and looked down. After a moment, he glanced at her, and she smiled.

"We are living a miracle," Ivan said, softly. "This is true."

"Shall we take the subway?" Sissy asked.

"I'd rather walk," Ivan said. "If it's not too much for you, my love. You have had a long week of dance."

"Can we walk along the river?" Sissy asked. "That is my favorite."

"Of course," Ivan said.

They turned onto the path along the Seine. The smell of the river was heavy on this warm summer day, but neither of them minded it. The dank air and the thick smell of the slow-moving river were all just a part of this experience.

"How has my dancing changed?" Sissy asked.

"Oh . . ." Ivan said. "Your body is stronger, leaner. We would expect that, as you are growing into a woman. You . . ."

Ivan smiled softly.

"You look like a prima ballerina," Ivan said. "There aren't words to describe it. You are beginning to possess a sense of the dance and yourself that translates into power. You have been competent at the skills for a long time, but now you are using the skills to create something more vivid, more emotional. This school has been a very good choice, much better than if you'd stayed in New York."

Sissy nodded. They walked along in silence.

"How do I seem to you?" Ivan asked. His heart clenched with his fear. "Like an old man?"

Sissy grinned. He looked at her and shrugged.

"I feel like an old man," Ivan said.

"You are just tired," Sissy said. "Letting go of all that you've been through, leaving your home, being in a new place . . . It's like releasing an entire life. Exhausting. You will recover."

"How is it that you are so sure?" Ivan asked.

"I know you," Sissy said. She gave him a soft smile and continued, "Let's see . . . How do you seem to me?"

Sissy sighed and searched for words.

"Stunningly handsome, deeply . . ." Sissy's words faltered. "I . . ."

Embarrassed at her own feelings, she looked down. They walked for a bit as Sissy searched for words.

"You are the best dancer I've ever seen, even now, when we are both older," Sissy said. He gave her a fond look. "But to me, you look like my heart and soul. My very breath. I am so proud to see you dance and not surprised at all that they were begging for more."

Sissy looked at him for a long moment.

"I am very glad that you are here," Sissy said. "I'm afraid of what will happen when you leave again."

"What will happen?" Ivan asked.

"I will be very sad," Sissy said.

At her sweet words, Ivan's hand covered her hand on his elbow. For the rest of their journey to the apartment where Ivan was staying, they lightly held onto each other in a silent acknowledgement of the miracle that was their life.

~~~~~~~~~

Saturday morning — 10:45 a.m.
Denver, Colorado

Yawning as she moved, the fairy envoy from Queen Áthas' Queendom came out of a downstairs bedroom. She arrived at the kitchen table at the same time as the envoy from Queen Shanti sat down. Queen Fand's envoy was standing in front of the large pantry next to the refrigerator.

Edie was drinking a cup of coffee and leaning against the kitchen counter.

"There is nothing here!" Queen Fand's envoy said. Her voice was laced with horror.

"Surely, there is *something* yummy," Queen Áthas' envoy said.

"I'm sorry," Edie said. "The humans left."

"All of them?" Queen Fand's envoy asked.

"All of them," Edie said.

"'Left'?" the envoy from Queen Shanti said, her voice rising in hysteria. "What do you mean they 'left'?"

"Where did they go?" Queen Áthas' envoy asked.

"But there is nothing for us to eat!" Queen Fand's envoy said.

"Coffee," Edie said.

"Where are the cakes? Cookies?" Queen Áthas' envoy asked.

"They took them with them," Edie said, mildly.

"Where did they go?" Queen Áthas' envoy asked.

"We'll just have to go with them," Queen Fand's envoy said. The other fairy queen envoys nodded.

"Where is Fin?" Queen Shanti's envoy asked. "Surely, he will work this out for us."

"Fin has returned home to the Isle of Man," Edie said. "His school starts again next week. He wanted to check in with the Queendom before he becomes focused on his school work."

"Abi?" Queen Áthas' envoy asked. "Where is Abi?"

"Where she always is: wherever she wants to be," Edie said. "My guess is that she is with Fin. As you can imagine, there's a lot of work to do since the queens are on retreat."

None of the envoys dared to utter a word.

"You mean they left us?" Queen Áthas' envoy whispered.

"They left," Edie said. "I believe they told you they were leaving."

"Yes, but . . ." Queen Áthas' envoy said.

"We didn't think they'd take all of the food!" Queen Fand's envoy said.

"But where did they go?" Queen Shanti's envoy asked.

"The humans?" Edie asked.

"Of course, the humans," Queen Áthas's envoy said. "If you are hiding them, Edie, so help me . . ."

Edie gave Queen Áthas' envoy a hard, threatening look and said, "Don't ever threaten me."

"She's not threatening you, dear," Queen Fand's envoy said. "She's merely wondering where we might catch up with the humans, our hosts and friends."

"As you said, they did tell us they were leaving," Queen Shanti's envoy said. "We were just confused as to what that might mean."

"Now . . ." Queen Fand's envoy said. "Where did they go?"

"They have gone to the desert to help some people dig water wells," Edie said.

"Using magic," Queen Áthas' envoy said.

"Using equipment and shovels," Edie said. She took a drink of her coffee as the envoys watched her intensely. "No magic."

The envoys gasped in unison.

"You know as well as I do that water wells drawn with magic don't run for very long," Edie said.

"Yes, but . . ." Queen Shanti's envoy said. She looked at the other two envoys in desperation.

"When are they coming back?" Queen Áthas' envoy whined.

"Ten days," Edie said. "Maybe longer."

The envoys gave each other a panicked look.

"I made this coffee," Edie said. "You are welcome to a cup."

Without ceremony, Queen Áthas' envoy disappeared from where she was standing. Queen Shanti's followed a moment later.

"Are you coming home, Princess Edith?" Queen Fand's envoy asked. "If Fin is needed, I'm sure there's a lot for you to do."

"I'm going with the humans," Edie said. "I've agreed to help with the children."

"In the desert?" Queen Fand's envoy asked. "Work with your hands?"

Edie gave her a slight nod. Queen Fand's envoy gasped in horror.

"I get so much out of living here that it's important to me to help out when and where I can," Edie said, working to keep the judgment out of her voice. "The children need me. That is enough for me."

Queen Fand's envoy gave Edie a long look. Edie blinked, and her mother's envoy disappeared. Laughing to herself, Edie drank her coffee. It really was awful.

"Are they gone?" Abi asked as she came out from their apartment.

"Finally," Edie said.

"Good work," Abi said with a grin. "I will say that they wore out their welcome."

"At the very least," Edie said.

Abi clapped her hands.

"What was that?" Edie asked.

"They must be invited back," Abi said.

"But I can . . ." Edie said. "Fin?"

"You are family, as is Fin," Abi said. "Jacob and Delphie have said that family never needs an invitation in this household."

Edie rushed to Abi and hugged her tight. Abi kissed Edie's cheek.

"Are you heading to the Isle of Man?" Edie asked.

"For all of that drama?" Abi asked. "Not a chance. Fin can handle all of that by himself. I sent the girls with him to give him something to do."

Edie grinned at the idea of Fin taking care of the children. Of course, in reality, Fin would find some relative of his father's, and she would care for the children.

"I notice that you aren't heading home to your mother's Queendom," Abi said, mildly

Edie grinned.

"I am going to see this Navajo Nation," Abi said. "I've not been there in a long, long time. Gilfand will likely join us."

Edie nodded.

"Come with me?" Abi asked.

"Right behind you," Edie said. "I need to check the house. I promised Jacob that I would."

"Your gear is in Blane's SUV," Abi said. "The house is clear. They are going to be driving for a good ten hours."

Abi smiled an invitation that made Edie scowl.

"What did you have in mind?" Edie asked.

"Let's have some fun," Abi said.

"What were you thinking?" Edie asked. Her eyebrows furrowed with concern.

"Did you know that little Ares is here in Denver?" Abi asked.

"I've seen him a few times," Edie said. "He says he's 'investigating modern life.' Why?"

"That means that his home in Olympia is Ares-free," Abi said.

"And?" Edie asked.

"He has wonderful servants," Abi said. "The best masseuse I've ever had the pleasure of meeting. An amazing chef and a wine cellar full of the best vintages."

"Will they let us in?" Edie asked.

"They are bored out of their minds," Abi said. "Ares won't let them go home because he might *need* them. They will be glad we are there."

"Are you sure?" Edie asked.

"I just came from there," Abi said. "We can enjoy a little break and return to the family ready for action."

With Edie's smile, the fairy and Abi disappeared.

The Castle seemed to sigh. For the first time in a very long time, the house was devoid of humans, fairies, dogs, a god in the shape of a cat, a bunny, gods, and other creatures.

Abi appeared again.

"Rest for now, noble home," Abi said. "We shall return soon enough."

Abi blew a kiss to the house itself and disappeared.

Safe from intruders, the Castle would enjoy a little break from the noise and mess of its inhabitants.

~~~~~~~~

Saturday mid-day — 11:35 a.m.
Somewhere on the I-70

"A Templar?" Blane asked.

Nelson was taking a drink of his soda, so he just made an agreeing sound.

"What does that even mean?" Blane asked.

"What do you mean?" Nelson asked.

Blane shot Nelson an irritated look, and Nelson smiled.

"Irritated," Blane pointed at himself. "With you."

"With me?" Nelson asked as if surprised.

Blane scowled.

"Start at the beginning," Blane commanded, as if he were talking to a child.

"Beginning?" Nelson asked. "You mean like 1100 CE?"

"For you," Blane said.

"Oh, that's easy," Nelson said. "Both of my parents are descendants."

They drove in silence for a while. Blane waited for Nelson to explain.

"Why is this so hard?" Blane asked.

"Well, it's a secret," Nelson said. Continuing in French, he added, "Something you never speak about to those outside the order."

"And that means?" Blane asked.

Nelson turned to look at Blane. After a moment, he turned to look out the wind screen again.

"It means that I would really be going all in," Nelson said.

Blane laughed.

"Why is that funny?" Nelson asked.

"Tell me," Blane said. "How are you not already all in? You met a goddess!"

Nelson turned back to look at Blane. After a few miles in silence, Blane sighed.

"Just tell me about your parents," Blane said. "Where did they meet?"

"Oh, okay," Nelson said. "That's easy."

When Nelson didn't say anything for a while, Blane slowed down to pull off the highway at Kipling Boulevard.

"What are you doing?" Nelson asked.

"Letting you out," Blane said.

"Wha . . .?" Nelson started.

"You're clearly not ready to be honest," Blane said. "You are not ready to be 'all in.' You have to be all in. That was our agreement. You're not there yet."

Blane pulled over to a sidewalk.

"Out," Blane said. "Keep your secrets. Keep your silence, your aloneness. You know where to find me when you decide to uphold your end of a relationship."

Nelson didn't move. They sat in silence for more than five minutes.

"Out," Blane said. "I am as sick as my secrets. With you in my life, everything is some fetid secret. I cannot have that in my sincere, *sober* life."

Nelson gasped a breath. Blane turned to look at him.

"What is going on with you?" Blane asked.

"I feel like I'm being cut in two," Nelson said.

Blane groaned and leaned his head against the headrest. They sat in the SUV. The air conditioning blew cold air. The car vibrated slightly as it idled. But neither man said a word.

"I want to," Nelson said, finally. "And you're right. I need to be honest. No secrets. You've said that from the beginning. 'You're as sick as your secrets.'"

"Why is this such a big deal?" Blane asked. "You're talking about things that happened more than 900 years ago."

"You are such an American," Nelson said.

"You're right," Blane said. "I was born and raised here. What does that have to do with anything?"

"900 years ago is today," Nelson said. "Today is 900 years ago. It is how life works."

"I have only this life," Blane said. "Only this moment in time. Even the next moment is a gift. 900 years ago, a bunch of men had a moment in time. They used it as they chose. It's not their time to choose what *we* do with *our* time. It is up to us."

Blane turned to look at Nelson and found that he was weeping. Blane put his hand on Nelson's shoulder. Nelson turned to look at Blane.

"You're right," Nelson said, in a flood of tears, words, and snot. "I find myself not ready to tell you about . . . everything. Me. I'm not ready and . . . I feel like if I leave this car, you, I will be split in two. I will never survive it. I can't live without you. I cannot speak the truth. You cannot live with secrets, and my entire life is secrets. Everything about me is secrets. I love you and give away my truth. I love my truth and destroy any chance of us. I am being torn in two."

Nelson dared to look Blane in the eyes. Blane's eyes reflected a brotherly concern and worry for Nelson, but not a reaction to Nelson's expression of love. Shocked, Nelson took a steadying breath and then another. A thought occurred to him.

"I said all of that in French?" Nelson asked.

"You did," Blane said. "French and snot."

Despite his tears, Nelson chuckled. Blane leaned over to open the glove compartment. He took out a container of tissues and put them in Nelson's lap. Nelson mopped up his tears.

"I met Heather on this trip to Maine," Blane said. He started down the street. "We used to go every summer. I think Jake still owns the house, well, more like an inn. Anyway, we got everyone together and headed out. It was just the adults, and Katy. It was before all the kids. Even Delphie went, which was a big deal because Delphie hates to fly — well, *hated to fly*; she's better now."

Blane made a U-turn and started back toward the highway.

"I met Heather there at this place by the lake in Maine," Blane said. "We hit it off right away. Not like lovers, but like best friends. She'd been a med tech for people with Hep C so she knew about the treatment. I wanted to get Interferon treatment from the Hep C I caught from Enrique. I was just healthy enough to try it."

Nelson didn't respond, so Blane kept talking.

CHAPTER 531

ABOUT YOUR FATHER

"We were heading back when she admitted that she was homeless and pregnant," Blane said. "She wasn't even talking to me. She was talking to Jill. Well, you've met the girlfriends. She told them, and I just said, 'You can live with me.' I don't know why I said it. Honestly, no idea. It just came out of me."

Blane took the on ramp to the highway.

"Of course, she thought I was joking," Blane said. "She'd been betrayed enough to know that people say things that they don't mean. She gave me every opportunity to turn back, but I knew I was doing the right thing. She came to live at my house. I don't know why, but I insisted that we own the house together. I even bought her the diamond ring she wears. We got married at *my* insistence. Seriously. It was weird, but everything was just so honest and true."

"She is a goddess," Nelson said.

"No, it wasn't that," Blane said. "It was me. I wanted to do it, more than anything else I had ever wanted. When she moved in, she hadn't even been in Olympia for . . . a thousand human years or more. I was in the middle of the Interferon treatment for Hep C, sick as a dog. She was about six months pregnant. I didn't think I would survive. That's when she told me about her mother and father."

"What did she say?" Nelson asked.

"She told me that her mother was hiding from her father," Blane said. "Her mother had been brutally abused by her grandmother. Of course, Heather's grandmother adored Heather, which made everything more painful and complicated. I said something like, 'Sounds like Hedone.' And she said, 'Yes. That's me.' I'm pretty sure she thought that I wouldn't remember. I was that sick."

Nelson grunted.

"The next day, I asked her about it," Blane said. "She wasn't working, and I was off work for this treatment. I had her give me acupuncture just to keep me alive. So . . ."

Blane fell silent. They drove for a while before Blane sighed.

"She finally told me all of it," Blane said. "Of course, it was literally thousands of years of living, but we had time. Weeks passed. We agreed to ask her grandmother to come to see her, you know, before the baby — Mack — was born."

"Aphrodite," Nelson said.

"Her," Blane said. "When Heather's grandmother saw that I knew, she told Hedone that it was time for her to shed her secrets. They made this agreement that Hedone would be honest about who she was, and Aphrodite would no longer chase Psyche, Heather's mother."

Blane glanced at Nelson.

"Honesty," Blane said. "It wasn't easy, but it set Hedone free."

Blane felt Nelson's eyes on his face.

"Your soul longs to be free, Nelson," Blane said. "You deserve to set this burden down."

Nelson didn't respond. After a moment, he cleared his throat.

"You're right," Nelson said. "I will tell you. Everything."

"We'll see what happens next," Blane said. "There's water in a bottle under your seat. Take a drink."

Spent from his strong emotions, Nelson took a long drink. He held the water bottle out to Blane, but Blane gestured to his soda. Nelson finished the bottle and stuck it next to the two others under his seat.

"Start at the beginning," Blane said and immediately added, "For you. The beginning for you."

Nelson thought for a moment.

"Tell me about Pierre," Blane said. "What is his family like?"

"I've never met them," Nelson said. "That's a part of all of this. I've never met any of them, except my mother's grandmother. My father said that she is no longer living."

"I see," Blane said. "No wonder you don't know how to tell all of this."

"Why?" Nelson asked.

"It's not formulated into a story yet," Blane said. "That's how it was for Heather, too. I was like that before Celia got me, well, and AA. Why don't I ask you questions? That might get you started."

Nelson nodded.

"How is Pierre's family connected to the Templars?" Blane asked.

"My father's family were the Templars' Weapons Masters," Nelson said. "You see, most of the Templars were killed outright for their land. There was this idea that the Templars had a lot of gold. Once they were no longer in power, people came for their gold or what they thought was their gold. Well, maybe it's really what was gold at that time — land, homes, possessions."

"But not your father's family?" Blane asked.

"No one knew they were involved," Nelson said. "My father says that no one really cared. Their skill was unique and necessary, so no one really cared. 'If they had sold weapons to the Templars, who could blame them? The Templars had cash, so why not?' That kind of thing."

"Did the Templars have a lot of gold?" Blane asked. "Have a lot of gold?"

"That's the question," Nelson said. "I don't know. I don't think my father knows, either."

Nelson looked out at the scenery passing outside. They'd left the Denver suburbs and were now traveling up into the mountains.

"But . . ." Nelson said. He took a breath and let it out. "The money, the gold — that's a part of all of this, too."

"How so?" Blane asked.

Nelson shook his head.

"Too much?" Blane asked.

Nelson nodded.

"Let's go back to the story," Blane said. "Your father's family were weapons makers. Blacksmiths?"

"Yes," Nelson said. "Smithies."

"Can your father make a sword?" Blane asked.

"Yes," Nelson said. "I can as well."

"Really?" Blane said.

"I've made a few," Nelson nodded. "I have one that I made in college. I think my father has the others."

Nelson looked at Blane.

"I gave one to Enrique," Nelson said.

"That's where that came from," Blane said with a slow shake of his head. "What did he do to deserve such a gift?"

"He paid me," Nelson said. "I needed the money. It's not a very good sword. It's not sharp, nor will it hold a sharp edge. It's just a standard broad sword. He wanted it for the Gay Renaissance Fair or something like that."

"I remember," Blane said.

"I don't know if he still has it," Nelson said.

"He doesn't," Blane said. He looked at Nelson. "Jake took it. It's at the Castle. You are welcome to it."

"Really?" Nelson asked. "Technically, I'm not supposed to make weapons for 'fun.' I just needed the cash."

"You are welcome to it," Blane said.

"How did Jake get it?" Nelson asked.

"Jake went to talk to Enrique about getting my stuff back," Blane said. "I'm not exactly sure what went down, but Jake came home with the sword."

"And not your stuff?" Nelson asked.

"Nope," Blane said. "Enrique had a party and burned it all."

"Everything?" Nelson asked.

"Everything," Blane said. "But get this — Enrique is still pissed about Jake taking the sword."

"'Still pissed'?" Nelson asked. "You've seen him?"

"He has this idea that I can't live without him," Blane said. "He came to the hospital when I was in isolation for a month. That's the last time I saw him."

Nelson scowled at Blane.

"I had him removed by security," Blane said. He snorted a laugh. "That was the final straw. That is, until he wants something else."

"'Wants'? From you?" Nelson asked.

Blane nodded.

"What did he want the last time?" Nelson asked.

"He's infected," Blane said. "He wants to do the procedure I went through."

Blane glanced at Nelson. He watched the muscle in Nelson's jaw work.

"Are you jealous?" Blane asked with a laugh.

"Angry," Nelson said. "He is such an asshole. How could you . . .?"

"Good question. But not one that's really relevant," Blane cut Nelson off. "He's my past. Jake, Delphie, Heather, our children, and maybe even you are my present."

Nelson scowled but nodded.

"You were telling me about Pierre," Blane said. "Your family are weapons makers."

Nelson glanced at Blane before continuing.

"Pierre will tell you that he is a weapons maker now," Nelson said. "His father, my grandfather, worked on nuclear weapons. His father told him that he needed to work on modern weapons. It was his duty to keep the family current. So that's what he does for a living."

"Your grandfather is gone?" Blane asked.

"Yes," Nelson said. "Cancer from the radiation. My father's mother is gone as well. He has three sisters. One of them is a blacksmith."

"Can women be involved in this Templar thing?" Blane asked.

"Sort of," Nelson said. "I mean, I don't really know because I've been hidden away from all of it, but according to Dad, girls have a role to play."

"Breeding sons?" Blane asked.

Nelson laughed and nodded.

"I haven't met my aunt, you know, the blacksmith," Nelson said. "But according to Dad, she's pretty tough. My guess is that she's involved in the order."

"'The order'?" Blane asked.

"Order of Solomon's Temple," Nelson said. "That's what the Templars are, officially. But again, my family are weapons makers. Or my father's family. We made the Sword of Truth."

"Oh, yeah?" Blane asked.

"It was said to have been commissioned by Ares, the God of War," Nelson said. "I asked him about it, you know, at dinner, but . . ."

Nelson smiled.

"What?" Blane asked.

"He seemed more interested in eating me," Nelson said. "And not in a fun way."

Blane laughed.

"But yeah, my father's family made all of the weapons of acclaim," Nelson said. "The sword that Perses wields, you know Jill's father?"

"I know Jill's father is Perses the God of Destruction," Blane said.

"He carries the Sword of Death," Nelson said. "It's said to be lethal to any creature who even looks upon it."

"But not the maker?" Blane asked.

"Well, that's the thing," Nelson said. "My father says that my ancestor was asked to make a weapon for an ancient god. My ancestor refused, saying that the god would just kill him when it was made. Why bother? They haggled for a very long time. Years. Finally, the god agreed to give him protection from any of the weapons he made. That's passed down in the bloodline."

"Any idea what ancient god that might be?" Blane asked.

"Chronos?" Nelson shrugged. "Have you met him?"

"Not yet," Blane said, with a laugh.

"We're not sure he's still among us," Nelson said.

"We?" Blane asked.

"The Templars," Nelson said. "When they went to Jerusalem, they discovered that the Gods walked among us. They found the three fairy Queendoms . . ."

"Four," Blane said.

"Four?" Nelson asked.

"It's complicated," Blane said. "Go on."

"Well, that's just it," Nelson said. "It seems that this ancient and secret knowledge all lives at the Castle."

Blane smiled.

"We should ask Abi," Blane said. "About Perses' sword, that is."

"Abi? The partner of that fairy prince? Uh, Prince Finegal?" Nelson asked. He blinked a few times before saying, "Wait — you're not saying that she really is the first woman?"

"She and Gilfand are the first," Blane said. "That's just a fact."

Nelson shivered.

"What happened?" Blane asked.

"Just frightening," Nelson said. "She was joking with me about . . . and she's . . . Do you think she knew what I am?"

"Probably," Blane said.

They fell silent. They continued on the I-70 past lush pine-tree forests.

"Maybe I should ask *her* about you," Blane said.

Nelson laughed.

"Okay, how did it work?" Blane asked.

"What?" Nelson asked.

"We're talking about your father's life," Blane said. "How was he brought into the order?"

"Oh," Nelson said. "It's a family thing. In the 20th century, you're not brought into the order. You're born there."

"Both of your grandparents?" Blane asked.

"Of course," Nelson said. "The blacksmith thing is passed from father to son. My father says it was just something that went on at home. But the order . . ."

Nelson took a breath, and his hand went to his chest.

"Easy," Blane said. "We're just talking about things that happened a long time ago."

Nelson took a few more deep breaths to calm himself.

"No one will hear you," Blane said. "You're just talking to me."

"How can you be sure?" Nelson said. "Gods, goddesses, and . . ."

"Because I am charmed," Blane said. "I am the consort of a goddess. No being can fuck with me. It comes with the territory. I wouldn't be surprised if you carry the same charm."

"Really?" Nelson asked.

"How many apples did you eat?" Blane asked.

"Three," Nelson said.

"Maybe," Blane said. "But back to your story — you were just here with me talking about your father's childhood. I love your father. So what's the problem?"

Nelson nodded. He took a breath and started again.

"When he was four or five, the children of his age were taken into a kind of after-school program," Nelson said. "Children from other families left in the order, that is."

"Like J-school for Jewish kids," Blane said.

"Yeah, that's it," Nelson said. "He said that there were five or six of them. Four girls and two boys. So six, I guess. My mother was one of the girls. His best friend was the other boy."

"His gay best friend?" Blane asked.

"Right," Nelson said. "That's a part of this story, my story."

"Do you know who the other people in the class were?" Blane asked.

"One is high up in the French government," Nelson said. "I don't know what. When I was a child, my father used to watch French television. He would point to her and say that she was a friend in the order. She is his age. One is married to the head of a national party. She's younger than my father."

"So the Templars are everywhere," Blane said.

"Basically," Nelson said. "It's a very small order. There aren't that many families left and over time, people die off."

Blane didn't say anything, and Nelson fell silent.

"We were talking about your father," Blane said.

"Yes," Nelson said. "My father and mother met when they were young children. He used to say, '*Le moment où nos yeux se sont recontrés mon âme fut complète.*' That's something like, 'My soul was complete the moment we saw each other' or something like that. The connection between them was immediate. Even their Templar teachers noticed it right away."

"It sounds like a good thing," Blane said.

"No," Nelson said. "Someone from my mother's family could not be in a relationship with a blacksmith. No. No way. It was not something that could happen."

"Why?" Blane asked.

"My mother . . ." Nelson sighed. "Her birth, the birth of her parents and back to the 1100s — it was all planned."

"Yuck," Blane said.

"You are an American," Nelson said with a smile.

"We've been all through that," Blane said. "So who is your mother? Who was her family?"

"That's the question, isn't it?" Nelson asked.

They drove in silence. Blane glanced at the clock; six minutes had passed. He scowled.

"You are sincerely the most annoying man," Blane said.

"How so?" Nelson said.

"Who was your mother?" Blane asked.

"Oh, sorry," Nelson said. "I was just thinking about her. She died when I was ten months old. I've never seen even a picture of her. She is . . . was . . ."

"Why no pictures?" Blane asked.

"I thought it was because my father was cruel," Nelson said. "He told me yesterday that he was protecting me. If anyone knew that she was my mother . . ."

"Goes back to . . ." Blane started.

"Yes, who was my mother?" Nelson asked. He turned to look at Blane. "What do you know about the Knights Templar?"

"Nothing," Blane said. "Uh, they are French? Indiana Jones? Three Musketeers?"

"*Le Trois Mousquetaires* was set in the 1600s," Nelson said. "You're five hundred years too late."

"What do *you* know about them, Nelson?" Blane asked in a mock interviewer voice.

Nelson laughed.

"A lot," Nelson said. He nodded. "Basically, after the First Crusade, a lot of European Christians were traveling from Europe to the 'Holy Land,' Jerusalem basically. We have this idea that they traveled on horseback from Europe."

"Suffering for their pilgrimage," Blane said.

"Exactly," Nelson said. "Mostly, they traveled on boats. They landed at Jaffa, just south of modern day Tel Aviv. These tours were mostly for wealthy people, but a few poor pilgrims came along. It was . . . uh . . . for lack of a better word, *stylish* to go to Jerusalem.

"The first years, it was a safe journey. But soon it became dangerous for Christian travelers," Nelson said. "At first, the Knights Templar were there to protect these travelers. They took up residence in the King's home at the Temple of the Mount. The Temple of the Mount was built on the site of Temple of Solomon. Thus the name '*The Poor*

Fellow-Soldiers of Christ and the Temple of Solomon' shortened to the 'Order of Solomon's Temple.' That's their actual name."

"'Their'?"

"Well, *ours*, but I'm not really . . ." Nelson looked at Blane and saw that Blane was scowling. "No, really — my father kept me away from all of this. I only know the stories."

"And have had the training," Blane said.

"Whatever," Nelson said. "You asked about my father."

"Yes, do continue," Blane said.

"The Templars needed weapons, so they went to my father's family," Nelson said. "As I said, they'd been making weapons since . . . a long time, so it was a no-brainer to make the family the weapons masters."

"What did your father's family get for their work?" Blane asked.

"Commissions, certainly," Nelson said.

"This is zealot work," Blane pressed.

"Sure," Nelson said. "They found a way to fight for Christ, to be soldiers for Christ. But for me? For my father? It's just family stuff."

Blane nodded.

"One of the founders of the order was a man named Andre de Montbard," Nelson said. "It's a little complicated, but he was born in 1097, and Bernard of Clairvaux — you know, Saint Bernard — was born in 1090."

"Okay?" Blane asked.

"You don't recognize the name 'Saint Bernard'?" Nelson asked.

"No," Blane said. "Should I?"

"If you knew anything about the Templars, you would," Nelson said.

"What do I need to know?" Blane laughed. "I have you!"

Nelson grinned. He reached over and took Blane's hand. They smiled at each other.

"So, Andre?" Blane asked to encourage Nelson to speak.

Nelson swallowed hard, nodded, and began to tell his story.

Chapter 532

"Andre is Bernard's uncle," Nelson said. "Well, technically, step-uncle. They were nearly the same age, so they grew up together."

"So a founder of the Templars is the uncle of a powerful servant of Rome," Blane said. "They are childhood friends and playmates."

"Exactly," Nelson said with a grin. "That's right."

"What did I say?" Blane asked.

"Oh," Nelson said with a chuckle. "I thought . . . never mind. So Rome was actually a world power — a country with the pope as the leader of this world power. Bernard of Clairvaux was an abbot and Benedictine. My father says that he had tremendous charisma and quickly grew to being very powerful in the church. He had the ear of the pope."

"His younger uncle was in Jerusalem saving rich pilgrims," Blane said.

"Exactly," Nelson said. "This is kind of important. Bernard believed that anyone could be saved by Christ with the intercession of the Virgin Mother. He believed that the holy should live like Christ. That was a big change in the entire philosophy of Christianity — at that time, the religion-state. The pope was swayed by Bernard, and thus all of Christianity changed. Today, these ideas are taught as Christianity, but before Bernard? They did not exist in the canon."

"It seems kind of convenient," Blane said.

"Oh?" Nelson asked.

"Well, sure," Blane said. "Bernard and his brother...

"Uncle," Nelson said.

"Right," Blane said. "Bernard and his uncle, or possibly just the uncle, are in the business of protecting wealthy people on their way to the Holy Land. So you change the entire religion to say that any person can become saved if they have intercession of the Virgin Mary. You have Andre to facilitate the intercession and his uncle to pocket the proceeds."

"I never connected those two things," Nelson said. "Huh. I'm sure you're right. Of course, people flocked to Bernard. He put through the idea that the Templars must live like Christ . . ."

"Or what *they decided* Christ lived like," Blane said, wryly.

"Well, exactly," Nelson said. "And that's why I am such a secret."

"What does that mean?" Blane asked.

"Do you mind if we stop?" Nelson asked. "There's a gas station up ahead. I just need to pee."

"Sure," Blane said. "We should fill up before the desert. But you have to promise — you'll finish this, right?"

"I will," Nelson said. "No secrets."

"No secrets," Blane said. "Do I need to guard you?"

"No," Nelson said with a laugh. "No one knows that I am here. If they find out?"

Nelson shook his head.

"Maybe," Nelson said.

Blane scowled but pulled off the highway. They pulled into a gas station. Blane filled the tank of the SUV, and Nelson went inside. When the gas tank was full, Blane drove the SUV and parked in a spot in front of the small gas-station store. He went inside and used the restroom. When he came out, Nelson was buying Reece's Peanut Butter cups and more soda for both of them. Laughing, Blane grabbed some bags of chips and tossed them onto the counter.

"Road-trip food," Nelson said.

Nelson paid for the food, and they returned to the SUV. Blane got into the driver's seat.

"Before we go," Nelson said. He leaned over and kissed Blane's lips. When Blane didn't push him away, Nelson smiled. "Thank you."

"For what?" Blane asked.

"For making me tell you all of this," Nelson said. "You were right. I need to tell it. I need to make it into *my* story and not just something that happened."

"It seems like it is your story," Blane said.

"Yeah," Nelson said. "I do feel better. You were right."

Nelson filled their cups with the soda and opened the bags of chips. He gave Blane a water bottle, and Blane drank it down.

"Ready?" Blane asked.

"To go?" Nelson asked. "Sure."

"To tell me what this is about," Blane said.

"Oh. I thought I *was* doing that," Nelson said.

"I've heard a lot about an ancient order," Blane said. "After hearing about it, I can't imagine why there are so many gay people in your family when the order made up of men who spurned the company of women to live in each other's company."

Nelson grinned.

"Funny, eh?" Nelson asked. "Did you look it up?"

"You stopped talking at the 'live like Christ' part," Blane said. "I wondered what that was, so I looked it up before I went in."

Nelson grinned.

"What?" Blane asked.

"You were paying attention," Nelson said.

Blane groaned and imploringly looked at the ceiling of the car. Nelson laughed.

"Come on," Nelson said. "You drive; I'll talk."

Blane started the car. They got back on the I-70 near Grand Junction and headed out across the Utah desert.

"So . . ." Blane said, glancing at Nelson.

Nelson was sound asleep. His head was against the headrest. His eyes were closed and his breathing deep. Blane groaned. He raised his hand to shake Nelson awake but then thought better of it.

Nelson was exhausted. He looked almost angelic in his sleep. Blane grinned at the beautiful man.

Blane took out his wireless headset and connected it to his phone. He, Jacob, and Aden were listening to Homer's *Odyssey* for this trip. He hadn't started. He turned on the audiobook program and started the book.

Traveling with a sleeping angel at his side, Blane listened to the ancient story as he moved on the I-70 across the gorgeous Utah desert.

~~~~~~~~

Saturday morning — 2:20 p.m.
Gas station outside of Grand Junction, Colorado

Jacob pulled into the gas station just as Heather's Subaru was making its way to the entrance. The women waved at him and Jeraine as they continued out of the gas station and back onto the highway.

So far, the trip had been uneventful. The babies and toddlers had played with each other for a while. They'd stopped once to change a couple of diapers, but the children fell asleep around Dillon Lake. They were now sound asleep. Jacob pulled the large SUV to the pumps to fill up and got out.

By agreement, Jeraine hopped out of the passenger seat and headed into the small gas-station store. Jacob put the nozzle into the gas tank and went to look inside.

The children were still asleep.

Honey's van pulled in to the pump next to his. M.J. got out to pump the gas. Honey swung easily out of the driver's seat into her wheelchair. She rolled into the gas station.

"How's it going?" M.J. asked, gesturing to the children.

"So far, so good," Jacob said.

M.J. nodded.

"Drug 'em?" M.J. asked.

Jacob shook his head.

"Just tired, I think," Jacob said. "We've had a lot going on. I think they're catching up on sleep."

"You are a lucky man," M.J. said. "We heard from Maggie from the girlfriends' car. She wants to switch at the next stop."

Jacob nodded.

"Mostly, I think, she misses Jackie and Mack," M.J. said. "With Rachel Ann, they're kind of a team."

"Mack's with Tink in Aden's SUV," Jacob said. "Jackie's with Valerie."

He nodded his head, and Mike pulled into the gas station. As Mike moved to the pump across from M.J., Aden pulled into the gas station. Jacob pointed to Aden, and Aden rolled his eyes. They could hear the teens and tweens arguing as Aden drove to a pump away from the babies. The moment Aden's SUV stopped moving, the noisy children swarmed out of the car and into the store.

The adults gaped at them. Jacob checked the babies.

They were still sleeping.

Jacob's gas nozzle popped, indicating that his tank was full. He got the receipt and put the nozzle back onto the gas pump. When he got into the SUV, he saw Jeraine trailing two young girls as he came out of the gas-station store. Jacob caught his eye and pointed to the girls. Jeraine spun around to greet his fans. Jacob waited while Jeraine spoke with the girls. Jacob parked in a parking spot in front of the store. In a few minutes, Jeraine pointed to the SUV and got into the passenger seat.

The babies and toddlers were still asleep.

Jacob got out of the SUV and went inside. He used the restroom and came out. He was on snack detail, so he picked up a couple bags of chips and some Reese's Peanut Butter Cups. They had coolers full of sandwiches, breast milk, and healthy snacks for the kids. This was for himself and Jeraine.

"Hey, you were just here," the man behind the counter said. "What'd you do with that beautiful guy?"

"What beautiful guy?" Jacob asked.

"The last time you were here, you were with this guy who looked like a model," the man behind the counter said. "Hey, I'm not gay, but that man was too good looking for this store."

Blane and Nelson must have come through the store ahead of them. Jacob grinned.

"What'd you do with him?" the man asked.

"It wasn't me," Jacob said.

"You say that, but . . ." the man said. He gestured behind him. "I got you on tape. So if you killed that guy, I'll . . ."

"You saw my cousin," Jacob said. "He and I look a lot alike, especially lately."

Jacob felt someone close to him and looked to see Valerie. She was laughing.

"Did you kill him?" Valerie asked.

"Very funny," Jacob said to Valerie. "We're traveling to Kayenta. He and Nelson went ahead of us with the supplies."

The man looked at Valerie and coughed.

"You're Valerie Lipson," the man said. "I just saw Jeraine and . . ."

"He's driving with me," Jacob said. "His wife, Miss T? She was just here."

The man blinked at Jacob and turned back to Valerie.

"You're Valerie Lipson," the man repeated.

Valerie put her arm around Jacob's shoulders.

"This is my brother," Valerie said. "He isn't lying. He and our cousin are nearly twins. I mean, they work at it, you know, but they look a lot alike. Nelson is our new friend. He is pretty, isn't he?"

The man gave a slight nod. Overwhelmed by Valerie's presence, the man started checking out Jacob's snacks. Mike came into the story carrying Eddie.

"Where's Jackie?" Valerie asked, her voice rising in panic.

"With Honey," Mike said.

Valerie took Eddie from Mike and carried the baby into the bathroom. With Valerie gone, the man behind the counter seemed to regain his equilibrium. Jacob paid for his snacks.

"That's really your sister?" the man asked. "What's that like?"

"Do you have a sister?" Jacob asked.

"Two," the man said.

"It's like having a sister," Jacob said.

"But . . ." the man started.

Jacob nodded.

"And Jeraine?" the man asked. "He's a huge star."

"His wife is one of my wife's best friends," Jacob said. "You must have seen them as they came through."

"Four women, two kids?" the man asked.

"That's them," Jacob said. "Jeraine's a friend. He's off tour for now, so he's just hanging out. We're going to drill some wells on the Navajo reservation."

The man nodded, and Jacob left the store. He held the door for Aden and Aden went inside. Jacob went to the SUV.

The children were still asleep.

He grinned at Jeraine and started the SUV.

Heather's son Wyn began to whimper. Jacob's son, Bladen, started wailing. Bladen's twin, Tanner, joined in the call. Sitting behind Jeraine, Jabari began to kick Jeraine's seat. In less time than it took to take a breath, every child in the enormous SUV was screaming at the top of his or her lungs.

Jeraine threw himself at the coolers to look for breast milk for the babies.

"Bye, bye, brother," Valerie said as she walked by.

She gave him a little wave and went to the Bronco. Mike gave Jacob a "need help" look.

Confident that he was fine, Jacob waved him on. The Bronco pulled out of the parking lot.

The noise in the SUV was deafening as each child screamed at the top of his or her lungs. Katy ran out of Aden's car and threw herself at her father. With Katy latched around his legs, Jacob tried to get to the snacks for the infants.

"Looks really hard," Aden's voice came above the din.

With a nod, Aden walked to his SUV. He counted the teenagers.

"Can you take Katy and Mack?" Aden asked.

"Sure," Jacob yelled. His head inside a cooler, he was not sure what he'd agreed to. "In a minute."

Mack appeared in front of him.

"Mr. Jacob?" Mack asked, tugging on Jacob's arm. "Mr. Jacob? Mr. Jacob?"

Jacob glanced down at Mack.

"Can I go with you?" Mack asked. "I miss Jabari and . . ."

Mack's big eyes filled with tears, and, in no time flat, Mack was screaming.

"Jake!" Jeraine yelled over the din.

Jacob looked up at him. Jeraine had a crazy smile on his face.

"We've got this?" Jeraine asked.

"Without a doubt," Jacob said with a laugh. "Just do what's next, one thing at a time."

"Got it," Jeraine said. "Just like being on tour."

Jacob laughed. Jeraine popped out of the passenger seat and jogged into the store with three bottles of breast milk for Bladen, Tanner, and Wyn.

"Jabari," Jacob yelled. "Do you need the bathroom?"

Jabari nodded.

"When your dad gets back, we'll head in," Jacob said.

"I can take them," Honey said. "Valerie wanted to know if you could take Jackie. She wants to be with Jabari and Mack."

"Sure," Jacob said. "Jackie? Do you need to go potty?"

Jackie's head went up and down.

"I'll take them," Honey said. "You sure you're all right?"

"You bet," Jacob said.

Katy refused to leave her father, so Honey left with Jabari, Mack, and Jackie. He knew better than to change diapers before the babies ate. Until the breast milk returned from being warmed up, there wasn't anything Jacob could do. The babies would just have to scream for a while. He knelt down to Katy.

"What's going on?" Jacob asked.

Katy threw her arms around Jacob and held on tight.

"Did you have a vision?" Jacob asked.

He felt more than saw Katy's nod.

"What happened?" Jacob asked. He leaned back to look at her face. "What did you see?"

Katy looked up at her father.

"Do you know where Mommy is?" Katy asked.

"She is with her girlfriends," Jacob said.

"I really want my mommy," Katy said.

Before Jacob could say anything else, Katy began to wail. To his knowledge, Katy had not been this upset in years. But here she was crying and screaming. He did the only thing he could do — hold her tight.

"That guy sure has a way with kids," a man said as he left the store.

His friend sniggered.

Jacob scowled at them but kept himself from doing something satisfying like blowing their tires out.

"Children have feelings," M.J. said as he left the store. "Maybe you should get in touch with yours."

The men whipped around to look at M.J. He gave them a gleeful "Go ahead, mess with me" look. They went back to their car.

"Faggots," one of the men said as they got in the car.

Never one to back down easily, M.J. leaned over and kissed Jacob on the mouth. Jacob laughed.

"Get a room," Jeraine said as he jogged back with the breast milk. "Where's Jabari?

"Inside," Jacob said.

"I'll set up the diaper station," M.J. said.

Jeraine climbed into the SUV and passed out the bottles of breast milk. They were finally not crying when Honey returned.

"How can I help?" Honey asked.

"I think we're okay," Jacob said.

"We waited because we knew you'd need help," Honey said. "We told Aden and Val that we would help. That's why they left. Let us help. We have seats if the toddlers want to go with us. Otherwise, we're happy to help."

"It's also nice to get some time alone with your husband after he's been gone," Jacob said, mildly.

Honey squeezed Jacob's hand.

"Why don't I help get the toddlers lunch?" Honey asked. "You can spend some time with Katy."

A police cruiser pulled in next to the SUV, and two uniformed police stepped out.

"This your SUV?" the uniformed police asked.

"Sure," Jacob said. Katy refused to budge from her grasp on his legs. "What's up?"

"We heard that some kids were being abused," the uniformed police officer said.

"The changing station is set up," M.J. said. "Bladen's done with his milk."

Jacob nodded. M.J. moved to take Bladen from his car seat.

"Stop," the uniformed police officer said.

"Why?" M.J. asked.

Jeraine stuck his head out from the SUV. He had Wyn on his lap.

"Are these all your kids?" the uniformed police officer asked.

"They are a mixture of our kids," M.J. said. "Those two are Jake's."

"My daddy is Jeraine!" Jabari said.

"This is our friend's infant," Jeraine said. "Wyn."

The baby burped in response to his name.

"He's my brother," Mack said.

"Our family is traveling together," Jacob said. "There are five cars — two SUVs, a station wagon, an old Bronco, my sister's van, and another SUV with gear. So, three SUVs. This is the biggest."

"With all of these kids?" the uniformed officer asked.

"The women wanted some time to themselves," Jacob said. "They are traveling ahead. My cousin and his friend are taking our gear. This is my brother-in-law M.J. He's in the military and has been out of the country for more than a month. He's driving in my sister, Honey's van. They wanted some time alone as well. We're taking the kids."

Jacob gestured to Honey.

"Afghanistan," the uniformed officer said.

"Africa," M.J. said. "U.S. Marine."

"Oo-rah," the uniformed officer's partner said.

"You know who Jeraine is," Jacob said. "My other sister, Valerie Lipson, and her husband are driving with their infant in the Bronco. That's her toddler right there."

Jackie gave the officers an uncomfortable wave.

"If you wait about six hours, you'll catch up with my father, his girlfriend, her niece, and her friend," Jacob said. "They had something they had to take care of before they came on the trip. But . . ."

"Stop," the uniformed officer said. "I get it. We just had a report and wanted to check it out. We take child welfare very seriously."

"That's a good thing. Glad you checked," Jacob said. "We're not great at it, but we're doing our best. Right, Jeraine?"

Jeraine waved a juice box at them.

"M.J.?" Jacob asked.

Rather than respond, he climbed into the SUV to get Bladen.

"Are you going to shoot us?" Jabari asked.

The uniformed officers laughed. Jeraine grabbed Jabari and pulled him away from the officers.

"How about if we get you some ice cream?" the uniformed officer asked.

"We *love* ice cream," Mack said.

"Consider it done," the uniformed officer said as they went inside.

CHAPTER 533

Saturday morning — 3:15 p.m.
Moab, Utah

Blane pulled the SUV into the gas station on Main Street. Moab was busy with summer visitors. Even though he had a third of a tank of gas, this was the gas stop on the trip. He didn't dare run out.

"Okay," Blane said. "Time to wake up. This is our last stop before we . . ."

Nelson stirred but didn't wake up. Blane put his hand on Nelson's leg. He felt heat through Nelson's jeans. Blane turned to look at Nelson.

Nelson's forehead glistened with sweat. Blane put the back of his hand on the back of Nelson's forehead.

"Shit," Blane said. "You stupid, stupid, asshole."

Rage and impotence flushed through Blane. Nelson's AIDS had flared up. Even though it had been less than a year since he had the virus, his mind went completely blank on what to do to help Nelson.

Someone behind Blane honked their horn. Blane waved his hand. He jumped out and started the pump to fill up the tank. He opened the back door of the SUV to grab a water bottle from the stash in the back. He dug around the SUV until he found the paper bag filled with Nash and Charlie's electrolyte drink powders. He fixed a bottle and returned to the driver's seat. He shook Nelson.

"Wake up," Blane said.

Nelson groaned. Blane pinched Nelson's collar bone. Nelson's eyes opened.

"You're having a flare-up," Blane said, his face inches from Nelson's. "Drink this."

Nelson waved his hand in front of his face, but Blane insisted.

"I'll leave you alone if you drink this," Blane said.

Nelson shook his head.

"Drink this, and I'll leave you alone," Blane said.

Nelson opened his eyes. His eyes were glassy with fever.

"Blane!" Nelson said with a smile.

"Do something for me?" Blane asked in his most seductive voice.

"Anything," Nelson said. His face was as open as a young child. "I love you."

Blane gave him a saucy grin.

"Drink this for me?" Blane asked.

Nelson took the bottle. He drank the electrolyte water down.

"Where are your meds?" Blane asked.

"In my bag," Nelson said.

Nelson's head dropped back to the headrest. He gestured behind him. Nelson fell asleep again.

The gasoline pump gave a low "*thunk*" to indicate that the tank was full. Blane got out of the SUV. He took care of the gasoline pump and drove to a parking spot in the shade. This gas station was not as well set up as the last place they'd stopped. People, children, dogs, and all kinds of vehicles swarmed all over the small area. As soon as the SUV was parked, Blane threw himself into the back. He found Nelson's large backpack on top of the rest of the junk.

He glanced at Nelson and winced.

Nelson would be furious if Blane invaded Nelson's privacy in any way. Blane was weighing the conflict when Nelson coughed.

Nelson's lungs were thick with mucus, indicating that Nelson had been sick for a while.

"You stupid fuck," Blane said under his breath.

Blane pushed on the backpack until he heard the telltale sound of medication bottles. There were three unopened white bags from the chain pharmacy. Blane opened the first and saw an antibacterial inhaler for the treatment of AIDS-related lung disease. The next bag had a prescription for antibiotics. The third bag had two different bottles of antiviral medications. The prescriptions had been filled last night.

Nelson had not taken his meds this morning or last night.

There was no way around it.

Blane was going to have to get him to take these meds. Blane grabbed another plastic bottle with water. He doctored it with the electrolyte mixture and went to the driver's seat again.

"Wake up," Blane demanded.

Nelson opened his eyes.

"Blane!" Nelson said, as if he hadn't just seen him. "What are you doing here?"

Nelson sat up. He looked out the windscreen and then back at Blane.

"Where are we?" Nelson asked.

"Moab," Blane said. Pressing forward, he said, "You're in the middle of an AIDS flare."

"Oh, yeah," Nelson said. "I know. Sucks."

"Then why did you . . .?" Blane started, but Nelson was asleep.

Blane sighed. Clearly, Mack and Wyn were not the only children under his care.

"Wake up!" Blane bullied.

Nelson opened his eyes. His face flushed with joy. Before he could utter a word, Blane stuck the antipneumocystic inhaler into Nelson's mouth.

"Breathe in," Blane ordered.

Nelson took the inhaler from Blane. He used it twice.

"Now this," Blane said.

He gave Nelson enormous-sized antibiotics and a couple of acetaminophen for his fever. Nelson drank them down with the electrolyte water in the plastic bottle.

"And these," Blane said.

He gave Nelson his antivirals.

"I took those this morning," Nelson said, pushing Blane's hand away.

"You have to double up when you're in a flare," Blane said.

"Says who?" Nelson asked.

"Says me," Blane said, rather than argue.

Nelson glared at Blane but took the meds.

"Thank you," Blane said. "Do you need the toilet?"

Nelson nodded. Nelson squinted and looked confused.

"Where are we?" Nelson asked.

"Moab," Blane said. "Come on, now."

Blane hopped out of the SUV and went around to the passenger side. By the time he got there, Nelson was asleep again. Blane grabbed a pack of baby wipes from the glove compartment before he dragged Nelson out of the SUV. They went into the gas station. By some miracle, there were large clean toilets. Blane had to hold Nelson up in line.

"Hey, no funny business," said a jovial, middle-aged, pot-bellied man as Blane started toward the handicapped toilet.

"He's sick," Blane said.

The man looked at Blane for a long moment. One of the nice things about swapping places with Jacob was that Blane knew how to play a convincing heterosexual man. Blane gave the man his most Jacob nod.

"Let me help you," the middle-aged man said.

He took the other side of Nelson. Between the two of them, they negotiated Nelson's pants down and got him onto the toilet. The men looked at each other with vague relief when Nelson used the toilet. Nelson's immune response caused a flush of diarrhea.

"You need help cleaning up?" the middle-aged man asked.

"I have two boys," Blane said in his imitation of Jacob. "This shouldn't be harder."

"I can hold him upright," the man said.

"That would be great." Blane gave the man a very Jacob nod.

They rescued Nelson from the toilet. Blane cleaned up Nelson's diarrhea and put his pants back on while the man held him up.

"You're Blane, right?" the man asked. "Blane Lipson."

Blane looked at the man.

"Mitt," the man said. "David Mitchell. Everyone calls me 'Mitt.' We've talked on the phone."

Blane blinked at the man and his familiar name. He had no idea why he knew that name.

"You're on your way to Kayenta, right?" Mitt said.

Blane nodded.

"I'm your big-equipment broker," Mitt said.

Blane laughed. Nelson slipped a bit, but Mitt held him tight.

"Go wash up," Mitt said.

Blane went to wash his hands and forearms.

"Where's Heather?" Mitt asked.

"The girlfriends wanted to drive together," Blane said.

"She knows about . . ." Mitt nodded toward Nelson.

"Of course she does," Blane said, irritably. "Nelson is her friend, too."

"No offense meant," Mitt said. "Just trying to get the lay of the land."

Blane looked at the man through the mirror. Mitt smiled, and Blane nodded.

"I brought the family," Mitt said. "I figure we could all use some time helping other people. Plus, those kids will drive us crazy if they're home all week."

Blane made sure he was clean before taking Nelson from Mitt. For good measure, Mitt used the sink to wash up.

"Do you have leads on what we need?" Blane asked.

"I have the list you sent me," Mitt said. "The real question is whether you want to buy or rent."

"Rent," Blane said.

"Right," Mitt said. "That's what you said, but Sam called. He wants to buy the equipment and set up a team."

Blane grimaced. Mitt laughed at Blane's grimace.

"A lot of work for you," Mitt said.

Blane nodded.

"Doesn't matter to me," Mitt said.

"Whatever Sam Lipson wants . . ." Blane started.

"Sam Lipson gets," Mitt finished with Blane. "Isn't that the way of things?"

Blane nodded. Mitt gestured to Nelson.

"What's wrong with him?"

"He hasn't slept in the last few weeks," Blane said. "Flared up his infection."

"New boyfriend?" Mitt asked with a knowing chuckle.

"Big court case," Blane said. "He's a forensic analyst for the Denver Crime Lab."

"Ah," Mitt said. "Court case. Yep. That would do it."

He winked at Blane, and Blane shook his head.

"Hey, I hope it works out for you," Mitt said. "You deserve it."

Blane wasn't sure why, but the kind, supportive words from this man in the middle of a public bathroom made Blane tear up. Blane nodded.

"Come on," Mitt said. "Let's get him back in the car."

Mitt took one side of Nelson, and Blane took the other. They got Nelson back to the car.

"Come, meet the family," Mitt said.

Blane rolled down the window for Nelson and went to meet Mitt's two daughters and wife. They chatted excitedly about going to the Navajo reservation. Blane smiled and nodded.

"I need to get back," Blane said, gesturing to the SUV.

"His friend is sick," Mitt said. "Here's my cell. If you need help, just call us."

"I'll see you in Kayenta?" Blane asked.

"We got one of those air places in Mexican Hat," Mitt said.

"It's an authentic hogan," Mitt's younger daughter said.

"We won't be far," Mitt said. "The big breakfast meeting is tomorrow morning?"

Blane nodded. Mitt leaned in.

"My eldest has a crush on Aden's kid," Mitt said.

"Nash?" Blane asked.

"No accounting for taste," Mitt nodded.

Blane smiled.

"You know, he's got a girlfriend," Blane said.

"Good-looking kid like that? He's probably got a harem," Mitt said with a wave of his hand. "Doesn't stop the heart from wanting."

Blane grinned. Mitt slapped him on the back, and Blane started back to the SUV.

"Hey, Blane!" Mitt said.

Blane turned to look at the man.

"Great imitation of Jake," Mitt said.

Blane laughed. Shaking his head, he went back to the SUV. As soon as the door to the SUV closed, Blane was once again overwhelmed.

He was all alone in the middle of nowhere with an increasingly ill man.

If he didn't stem this flare-up, Nelson could easily die on the ride between here and Kayenta. Blane looked at Nelson.

"Why didn't you take care of yourself?" Blane asked in a low voice. "You need to sleep — not to be on some cross-country journey to 'Nowhere,' Arizona."

Nelson's eyes fluttered.

"I love you," Nelson said, softly. "Had to try."

Scowling, Blane shook his head.

"Totally worth it," Nelson said.

Blane closed his eyes and wondered what he should do.

Take Nelson to the hospital?

Was there a hospital in Moab, Utah?

Blane looked around.

"Think, think, think," he muttered to himself.

He thought about calling Ava or one of his other co-workers and then instantly rejected it. They would feel disloyal to Nelson if they told Blane anything.

He shook his head and took a drink of watery soda.

Out of nowhere, he remembered the acupuncture treatment that had helped him the most when he was sick. It felt like a life-time since he'd been this sick, but the truth of the matter was that Blane was often a lot sicker than Nelson was now. Blane sighed. He looked at Nelson. He could do most of the treatment right here in the SUV.

He also remembered that Nelson was close with Roger Whitaker. Blane knew Roger through Alex Hargreaves. Whenever Roger was in town, Roger stopped in for an acupuncture treatment from Blane. Blane thought for a moment. He looked down at his phone. He had bars. With a silent thank-you to Lipson Construction, who still paid for his phone, he connected his headset to his phone and dialed Roger.

"Blane!" Roger said.

"Oh, good," Blane said, not bothering to keep the relief from his voice. Roger was a world-famous psychiatrist. "You answered."

"Just between things," Roger said. "Plus, I was hoping I'd hear from you."

"Oh, yeah?" Blane asked.

He started the car to turn on the air conditioning. Nelson moaned but didn't wake up.

"I've heard that you might be dating someone new," Roger said.

"News travels," Blane laughed.

"He loves you," Roger said. "So, be nice."

"Always," Blane said.

"Now, you didn't call me to hear me threaten you over *my* little brother," Roger said.

Even with Roger's southern accent, the threat in his words came through loud and clear. Blane grinned but didn't respond.

"What's happened?" Roger asked.

"We're heading to the Navajo Reservation . . ." Blane wondered if they'd ever get there.

"Water wells," Roger said. "I told him to just show up. Did you work it out? Did you work it out?"

"Sort of," Blane said.

"What does that mean?" Roger asked.

"He fell asleep in the middle of our conversation," Blane said. "Now he seems to be in the middle of a fairly severe AIDS flare."

Roger took a quick intake of breath.

"His lungs are filling," Blane said. "He's got meds for pneumocystis and . . ."

Roger didn't say anything to interrupt, so Blane continued.

"He's burning up," Blane said.

"How can I help?" Roger asked.

In the background, Blane heard someone speak in the background on Roger's end.

"I need a moment," Roger said. Returning to Blane, he said, "Sorry, I'm due for television."

"When we talked about his health, he told me that he had low-virus, high T-cell," Blane said. "Now he's really sick."

"I see," Roger said. "You know this happens."

"Not like this," Blane said.

"True," Roger said.

"This seems to have come out of nowhere," Blane said. "What's going on?"

"He didn't lie," Roger said. "He has almost no virus. His T-cells are freakishly resilient."

"Pneumocystis?" Blane asked.

"He has some lung problems," Roger said. "Dating back to when he was a kid."

Blane made an acknowledging noise. In Chinese medicine, unresolved grief settled in the lungs. Roger continued.

"How he hasn't scarred his lungs is anyone's guess," Roger said. "You'd have to ask Pierre. I think he got sick with some lung ailment as a child and simply hasn't recovered."

Blane got out of the SUV to dig out his acupuncture needles from the mess in the far back.

"He's really sick?" Roger asked.

"I'm not sure he'll make it to our destination," Blane said.

Roger sucked in a breath. Blane found the duffle bag Heather had packed his acupuncture needles in. He grabbed a box of needles and an applicator.

"Does he use oxygen?" Blane asked.

"No," Roger said. "Not usually. He's very strong."

"Mmm," Blane said mildly.

"Yes," Roger said. "He is sick now. But you'll see. He will rebound. It was like that after he was infected. It's freaky."

"Okay," Blane said. "Anything else? History wise?"

"Why?" Roger asked.

"I'm going to treat him here," Blane said.

"Good thinking," Roger said. The line was silent for a moment. "Let's see . . ."

After a moment, Roger added, "No. I think that's it."

"Allergies?" Blane asked.

"None," Roger said. "Or none that I know of."

"Okay," Blane said. "By the way . . ."

"Yes?" Roger asked.

"Who is his mother?" Blane asked.

"Why, she was the only heir of Saint Bernard," Roger said. "You know, the chaste monk? Guess he wasn't as chaste as people thought."

"The Templar?" Blane asked.

"Exactly," Roger said. "It's a big secret. His mother was basically held hostage by her family. They've managed the mating since the time of Bernard, himself, but the line was frightfully barren and filled with females. Nelson is the first male since Bernard. Supposedly looks like Bernard."

"How did they get away?" Blane asked.

"I'm not sure," Roger said. "I doubt Nelson knows. I will tell you that Carlos the Jackal has never claimed the bombing of the train. In fact, he is sure that he did not do it."

"There's a possibility that the bomb was to kill . . ." Blane started.

"Pierre, his wife," Roger said. "Their child, our Nelson, was a big secret. No one knew that he existed until his mother was killed."

"Why?" Blane asked.

"He's the first male heir since Bernard," Roger said. "Child of the lowly weapon's master. There's quite a bit of mystery around what it means to be the male descendent of Saint Bernard. He doesn't know what it means, just that his father has hid him because he was the heir."

"And we think that means. . ." Blane said.

"Jax looked into it," Roger said, interrupting. "The legend says that there's a fortune waiting, uh, gold from heaven, I think, for the legitimate *male* heir of Bernard. Maybe. No one knows for sure — that's the problem."

"Only if he survives," Blane said.

"Pierre swore he would protect Nelson *from* the Templars," Roger said.

"Good to know," Blane said. "Listen, I should go. See what I can do."

"Good luck," Roger said, and hung up the phone.

A second later, the phone rang again.

"You will let me know," Roger said without greeting.

"Of course," Blane said.

Blane pocketed the cell phone. Taking a breath, he got back into the driver's seat of the SUV. Nelson looked even sicker.

"Hang in there," Blane said to himself.

He thought for a moment. He lifted Nelson's right wrist to take a pulse. He lifted Nelson's left wrist. After a moment of panic, he got to work.

Having never given acupuncture to Nelson, he had to start slow. He put in an acupuncture needle and then tested Nelson's pulse. He put in another and checked Nelson's pulse again.

To his surprise, Nelson seemed to respond right away.

"Maybe there's hope," Blane said.

He quickly set a few acupuncture needles. There was nothing to do now but wait. Nodding to himself, Blane put the SUV into reverse and left the gas station.

If all went well, Nelson would be well enough to get himself into the hotel. If not, Blane would take him to the hospital in Kayenta.

The next three hours would determine what happened next.

CHAPTER 534

FINALLY KAYENTA

Blane got back on the US-191 S, returned to listening to *The Odyssey*, and started on the last leg of the journey toward Kayenta. A half hour later, and every half hour afterwards, Blane stopped on the side of the road to change Nelson's acupuncture needles. At one stop, about an hour outside of Kayenta, Nelson coughed up a fist full of moisture. Blane caught it in a towel. He forced Nelson to drink another water bottle and take his lung treatment. They continued to Kayenta.

Blane was just pulling into the motel when Nelson awoke.

"We're here," Blane said, softly.

"I was hoping we'd . . ." Nelson gave him a feverish look. "I'll have to give you a raincheck."

Blane grinned.

"I feel like crap," Nelson said. He shifted to sitting more upright. "Did I sleep the whole way? God, you must be pissed for me not telling you about my mom."

"You don't remember?" Blane asked.

"What?" Nelson asked.

"You're in the middle of an AIDS flare," Blane said. He pulled the last acupuncture needles out of Nelson's chest.

"I am?" Nelson asked.

Blane nodded.

"I thought you were going to die," Blane said.

Nelson just looked at Blane.

"I feel like death warmed over," Nelson said, finally.

"You should," Blane said.

Blane's phone rang. Blane looked down at it.

"It's Roger," Blane said.

"Roger who?" Nelson asked.

"Roger Whitaker," Blane said. "I called him to find out what was going on with you."

"Oh," Nelson said.

Blane held the phone out. Nelson took the call. Blane waited for a moment to see if Nelson needed him. Nelson didn't give Blane even a look. Shaking his head, Blane grabbed his messenger bag and went into check everyone in to the hotel.

"How are you?" the desk clerk asked.

"Good," Blane said.

"You look like you're thinking deep thoughts," the desk clerk said.

"Yeah, I guess," Blane said.

"Care to share?" the desk clerk asked.

"Ever notice how fragile life is?" Blane asked. "It's here one moment and gone. You just never know when that might be. Today? Tomorrow? This moment. It's just . . ."

"It's the big mystery," the desk clerk nodded.

Blane gave an agreeing nod.

"Anyway, I need to check in," Blane said.

With a glance to the SUV outside, Blane took out his notebook computer, and the clerk worked the computer in front of him. Feeling someone near him, Blane looked up to see Cian Kelly. Cian was Alex Hargreaves' husband's brother. Cian grabbed Blane and hugged him tight. He was married to Margaret Peaches, whose grandparents were due to be the first recipients of a new water well.

Like a drowning man, Blane hung on to Cian. No stranger to overwhelm, Cian stayed steady until Blane was ready to let go.

"I've taken care of this," Cian said, in his Northern Irish accent. "Based on your list. Everyone is checked in. We've even checked the rooms to make sure that they are right."

Blane almost collapsed with relief. Cian grabbed his arm.

"Steady on," Cian said.

Blane nodded.

"I need help . . ." Blane gestured to the SUV.

Through the pane of glass, Blane saw Gando Peaches, Margaret Peaches' uncle, walking toward the hotel with his arm around Nelson.

"Roger called Alex," Cian said. "She called me. We tried to get yo, but you must have been out of service. So we called your misses. The ladies are coming straight here to help."

Blane nodded. He should have expected the information to spread through the Hargreaves household and into his own. The idea that he hadn't been alone all of this time made him tear up.

"Now, none of that. Ganny's taking over for a bit while you rest," Cian said. "Why don't I take you to your room? You can rest up. Ganny and I will unpack and greet the bloody horde as they come in."

"'Bloody horde'?" the clerk behind the counter asked.

"Turn of phrase," Cian said with a grin. He turned to Blane, "Come on, now. You've been through hell. Ganny will get Nelson cleaned up and in bed. You can check on him after you've rested and eaten something."

Blane nodded. He followed Cian down a hallway to a room. Opening the door, he saw that there were two queen-sized beds and a crib. It was exactly what they needed. The adjoining door was open, where he could see another queen-sized bed.

"This is what you wanted?" Cian asked.

Gando gave them a nod and closed the adjoining door.

Blane wasn't sure whether to weep with relief, laugh, or simply fall over. Grinning, Cian pushed Blane backward.

"Rest up," Cian said. "This week is going to be full of all kinds of drama. We'll need you at your best."

Blane nodded. Without saying goodbye, Cian walked out of the room. Blane stared at the door for a moment before going into the bathroom. He felt like he was covered with vomit, shit, sweat, and whatever else. He stripped off his clothing and got into the shower.

A few minutes later, he heard the water turn on next door. Gando was helping Nelson with a bath. Blane was so relieved that his knees buckled. He forced himself to shower. When he got out, his dirty clothing was gone, and his bag was sitting on the table. He changed into a clean pair of boxer briefs and lay down.

He was sound asleep in minutes. The next thing he knew, two hours had passed, and Wyn was sitting on his chest.

"Wha . . .?" Blane asked.

Heather leaned down to kiss his cheek.

"I'll get up," Blane said.

"If you feel up to it," Heather said. "Nelson is asleep. Nadia's taken a look at him. He seemed to be out of the woods — thanks to you. He just needs sleep now."

"I . . ." Blane said. He took her hand and squeezed it.

"What was that?" Heather asked.

"I'm grateful for our life," Blane said. "That's all. Thank you."

She leaned down to kiss him again.

"I want to hear about every detail, but for now, I need to go find Mack," Heather said. "Can you keep an eye on Wyn? He needs some sleep, too."

"Of course," Blane said.

Blane shifted the child to the center of the queen-sized bed. Fully intending to get up, he rolled onto his side. Wyn blinked at Blane and then closed his eyes. They joked about Wyn being a little "Olympian God," but he was a really mellow baby. Blane watched the baby sleep for longer than he would care to admit, before getting up to unpack their belongings.

~~~~~~~~

Sunday morning — 4:10 a.m.
Kayenta, Arizona

Nelson woke with a start.

Where was he?

He was lying naked in a queen-sized bed. The sheets were hotel clean. The room smelled like a motel. The light was dim.

He rolled onto his side.

The clock said that it was 4:10 a.m.

That wasn't a big surprise. He woke up at 4:10 a.m. every morning. Usually, he got up, started coffee, and went for a run. He was home by 5 a.m. He grabbed a cup of coffee and went to his basement, where he lifted weights from 5 a.m. to 6 a.m. every single day. He was in the shower by 6:10 a.m. Breakfast at 7 a.m. and on the 15 Colfax bus by 7:30 a.m.

His life had structure. His life had order.

This morning, he felt sick. His chest was constricted, and he had a pounding headache. He was also starving.

He sat up on the bed. He reached for the light and noticed a stack of clothing on the bedside table. A note was sitting on top of the clothing.

"You're in Kayenta, Arizona," the note said. "You had an AIDS flare. Take your meds. Drink some water. Come see us. We're next door. Put something on because the boys are with us. House rule is at least underwear at all times."

There was a little smiley face.

The handwriting looked familiar, but, at this moment, he couldn't place it.

Who was "we"?

Who were the boys?

Why was he in Kayenta, Arizona?

He took a breath. His lungs seized in spasm. He could believe that he was having an AIDS flare. He grabbed his lung treatment and took a deep breath. He did it twice. Turning the device over, he saw that more than twenty of his treatments had been used.

He blinked.

Had someone used his nebulizer? Didn't he just get this prescription filled?

Why was he in Kayenta, Arizona?

He pulled on the boxer briefs. For good measure, he put on the pajama bottoms. He looked at them.

These were his pajama bottoms.

The whole thing was unsettling. He had no idea what was going on. In spite of himself, he checked to make sure that he had both of his kidneys. After laughing at himself, his worry returned.

How could he have been sick and not remember any of it?

Scowling, he went to use the bathroom. There was a note on the mirror written in fuchsia lipstick.

"Don't freak out."

That handwriting he knew. He and Nadia Keminoff used to leave messages for each other on the bathroom mirrors of the hotel rooms they shared when they were interviewing for positions at hospitals or fellowships or residencies. They told each other: "Don't freak out" or "You've got this."

Her color was this fuchsia. His was a classic deep red.

Nadia must be here. Somewhere.

Was she "we"?

Nadia and Ivan.

No. Something about that wasn't right. Nadia and . . .?

Nelson was sure that, if his head ever stopped pounding, he could figure it all out. He took some acetaminophen and drank down a plastic bottle of water sitting next to his medicine kit.

He stumbled back to the bed and sat down. He was about to get in it when he saw the note again.

Who was "we"?

Careful not to make any noise, he got up. He saw that the adjoining door was ajar. Not sure what he'd find, he moved the door and peered inside.

The smell hit him first — baby lotion.

He blinked and saw . . . Blane. Heather. Mack. Wyn. All in one queen bed. Asleep. Blane's arm was around Heather, and her head was on his shoulder. Wyn was in some kind of bed-extender thing next to Heather. Mack was asleep in the space between his parents' feet.

Nelson stepped back.

The "we" was *Blane* and his family.

He retreated to his room and sat down on the bed again. He dropped his head into his hands and tried to figure out what was going on.

He fell asleep, or at least he thought he fell asleep.

Nelson woke when a small hand touched his arm. Still sitting on the side of the bed, he looked up.

Mack was standing in front of him. The boy's enormous blue eyes blinked at Nelson. The child's black hair was sleep-messy. He was wearing a grey shirt with a yellow backhoe on the front. His pajama legs had various road equipment printed on them.

Nelson closed his eyes.

When he opened his eyes, Mack held out a green apple to him. The apple glowed with light and love. Before he knew it, Nelson had grabbed the apple from the child.

Nelson ate the apple in four bites.

Mack turned his hand over, and another apple appeared. The child held it out to Nelson.

Nelson took the apple at ate it more slowly. Six bites. Nelson's empty stomach seized. He bent over with pain. When he sat up again, the child was still standing in front of him.

Mack held out his hand to Nelson. Instinctively, Nelson took the child's hand.

The child led Nelson into the room where *Blane* and *his* family were sleeping.

Nelson stopped short.

This was Blane's family.

It had nothing to do with him.

Mack's hand tugged at him. Nelson looked down at the child. Mack gave him a broad smile.

Mack nodded to the bed. Nelson stepped into the room.

One step. Another step. The smell of baby lotion and soap filled the air. He took another step.

The child pushed back the covers on the second queen-sized bed. Mack gestured to the bed. Nelson got into the bed. Mack climbed in on the other side of the bed. The child burrowed down in the covers. Nelson rolled onto his side, his back toward Blane and his family. The child took Nelson's arm and put it over himself.

"Sleep," Mack whispered.

Beyond all reason, Nelson fell into a sound sleep, cuddling the small child. As Nelson slept, he remembered everything from his night with Hedone, reuniting with his father, his courage to get into the SUV with Blane, every moment of sick, and Blane's care for him.

He argued with himself in some crazy dream that included Jax. He didn't want a family. People were dangerous. He would get hurt. His heart would break, and he . . .

Jax's voice echoed in his ears: "What is this aloneness that you cling to so tightly?"

Nelson roused from his sleep. He opened his eyes and saw the sweet face of Mack. Heather had told him that Mack cared about people. Mack cared about the connections between people — not love, really, but something like love. Connection. This small child had reached into his aloneness and dragged him out.

"Nothing," Nelson whispered. "It's nothing at all."

"Fear and stupidity," Jax's voice said in his mind. "Fear and stupidity, that's what it is."

Wordlessly agreeing, the dream faded away, and Nelson slept. For the first time, likely ever, Nelson felt like he was home.

"Hey."

Nelson felt a hand on his shoulder. He woke up with a start.

"Sorry to wake you."

He rolled over to see Heather. His hand went to his mouth.

"Oh, my God," Nelson said. "I have pneumocystis!"

"I know," Heather said.

"It's contagious," Nelson said. "And Mack . . ."

He held out his hand to the place the child had slept, but the child was no longer there. Heather grinned at him. Nelson sat up.

"We're vaccinated," Heather said.

"Oh," Nelson said.

"Blane was sick for a long time," Heather said with a nod. "He's vaccinated as well."

"Right." Nelson nodded. "What's going . . .?"

"Blane, Jake, Sam, Honey, and a bunch of other people are out at the site," Heather said. "You know, Margaret's grandparents' home."

"Right," Nelson said. "Water well."

"They left about five-thirty," Heather said. "Did you see them?"

Nelson shook his head and rubbed his eyes.

"Just Mack," Nelson said. "He . . ."

Nelson blinked at his own memory.

"He gave me apples?" Nelson asked. "Your apples?"

Heather nodded.

"He made them appear." Nelson turned over his hand like Mack had. "Just, *bang*."

"About that," Heather said.

"Yeah?" Nelson asked.

"Don't tell Blane," Heather said. "He doesn't know about our Mack."

"He doesn't?" Nelson asked. "He told me that Mack was magical when it came to connection. He . . . Mack . . ."

Nelson shrugged.

"I think he knows," Nelson said.

"Yes, but we're pretending that he doesn't." Heather smiled.

"Fair enough." Nelson nodded as if she'd given him an order.

Heather grinned.

"How are you feeling?" Heather asked.

"Better," Nelson said. "Good."

"I'm glad to hear it," Heather said. "Nadia's been looking for you."

"Oh?" Nelson asked.

"There's a three-day-old gunshot wound she wants you to consult on," Heather said.

"What about my pneumocystis?" Nelson asked.

"She knows that you've been ill," Heather said with a roll of her eyes. Without waiting, she continued her report, "We've used both showers. Jill's in yours right now. Edie took Mack and the other kids to the pool. Wyn's . . . with Jabari, I think. Valerie took the toddlers. She hasn't spent a lot of time with Wyn, so she wanted to have him this morning."

Heather shrugged.

"I was sent to ask you this question," Heather said.

"What's that?" Nelson asked.

He suddenly realized that he wasn't wearing a T-shirt. He checked and was relieved to see that he was wearing his pajama bottoms and boxer briefs. He looked up at Heather.

"You're immune to magic?" Heather asked.

"Right," Nelson said. "My family line takes on the properties of the weapons it creates. Except the nuclear ones, that is."

Heather nodded and opened her mouth to speak.

"Well, and the rockets my father makes," Nelson said. "Just the magical ones. I think. I am not really sure. I was supposed to read some chronicles or get some kind of arduous training, but I was in hiding."

Nelson lifted a shoulder in a shrug.

"Good. I mean about being immune to magic," Heather said. "Jill is wondering if you might be able to help with her twins."

"Pneumocystis?" Nelson asked.

"Vaccination?" Heather asked. "We're not morons. You cannot imagine how many children I've seen killed by diseases that are now preventable. Millions."

"I bet that's true," Nelson said. "What help does Jill need with her twins?"

"They are feeling . . . *rebellious*, I guess, is the right word," Heather said. "They are mad that they aren't at home. Edie was gone for a while, and they are mad at her. They are babies. Twins."

Heather opened her mouth, took a breath, and then closed it.

"They're not jerks, really," Heather said. "They are sweet, smart boys, twins, with psychokinetic powers."

"But boys none-the-less?" Nelson asked.

Heather nodded.

"How can I help?" Nelson asked.

"She can't get their diapers changed. Katy's threatened to burn them, so she's with Jake," Heather said. "There's been some difficulty this morning."

"I can see why Jill's showering off by herself," Nelson said.

"Exactly," Heather said.

"You can't do it?" Nelson asked.

"This is a human body," Heather said. "Not immune to magic. And anyway, Hedone is a goddess. Goddesses are not immune to magic."

"Good to know," Nelson said. "Where are these twins?"

"On the other bed," Heather said. She pointed to the queen-sized bed next to them.

Nelson looked to see two adorable boys with black curly hair and hazel-blue eyes. They were wearing matching blue jumpsuit, which made them look like they were ready for business. The boys gave him a disarming smile and started jumping on the bed.

"They look like Blane," Nelson said.

"Yes, well . . ." Heather said.

"Adorable monsters?" Nelson asked.

Heather laughed.

"I created a bubble around them so they can't get out or hear us," Heather said. "They don't like it, but they know they are out-powered by . . ."

Heather cleared her throat.

"Hedone?" Nelson offered.

"Sure," Heather said. "Listen. I'd understand if you don't want to do it. They can be a bit . . ."

"I've got it," Nelson said.

"You know how to change diapers?" Heather asked.

"I've changed quite a few in my life," Nelson said. "Where's Tink?"

"With Charlie," Heather said with a shrug. "He's eighteen now and . . . Well, they've been together for years and years. This trip, we decided to give them their own room. We figured it was better than fighting to keep them apart. Of course, all of the teenagers are in their room now, so it's not like a romantic hideaway."

"I think it's the battle with street kids," Nelson said. "In some ways, they have experienced so much that they are not children."

"But in other ways, they are infants," Heather said. "Exactly. We'll see how it goes. My guess is that she'll go back and forth."

Nodding, Nelson jumped up out of bed. He went into the bathroom to scrub his hands and forearms. He went to the other room and grabbed a bandanna from his backpack. He tied the bandana over his mouth and nose. The children might be immunized but it was still best to reduce the amount of pneumocystis he transmitted. When he returned, he stripped off his pajama bottoms.

"Why?" Heather asked.

"I am immune," Nelson said. "My pajamas are not. I brought only the one set. It's my understanding that we're a clothed family."

Smiling and nodding, Heather said, "Ready?"

Nelson nodded and moved to the bed.

"I'll be here if you need me," Heather said, pointing to the other room.

He watched her leave.

"All right, lads," Nelson said. "I'm Uncle Nelson, and we're going to get these diapers changed."

Once near the bed, he added, "Maybe a bath, too."

CHAPTER 535

AT THE POOL

Sunday mid-day — 10:13 a.m.
Kayenta, Arizona, at the hotel on the Navajo Reservation

Nelson was lying on a chaise lounge under a large umbrella by the hotel's large pool. Nadia was listening to music on headphones and reading a book on a chaise lounge on his left. The chaise next to him was empty. His chest still congested, he was taking a day of rest before he joined whatever mayhem he chose. He and Nadia had been making plans to work in the health clinic, but nothing had come together yet.

Right now, he was enjoying the sauna-like heat and watching this new "family" interact. In the pool, the younger children were laughing and playing with each other and their mothers in the shallow end. The teenagers talked among themselves at the deep end.

Feeling movement, he looked up to see a bear of a man walk toward him. The man was about his height, solid, thick muscle under a thick coat of dark brown hair. He had more than a few significant, life threatening scars under all of that hair. He was wearing a pair of tight, designer sunning white trunks that left little to the imagination. The man gave him a strong, direct look before sitting down.

"I hear you're thinking about getting involved with Blane," the man said in a hostile tone. "Joining the family."

Nelson pulled off his sunglasses to look at the man. The man's eyes were hidden under a pair of dark sunglasses. Nelson slid his sunglasses back on.

"What's it to you, little Titan-ling?" Nelson asked with a sniff.

The man sat up and leaned forward.

"What?" the man asked.

"You are clearly Perses' son. Outside of the hair, you look just like him," Nelson said. He reached out and touched the man's forehead. "Not quite in your powers yet, are you?"

"My what?" the man asked.

"Hey, Mike," Tanesha said as she hustled in their direction. She looked at Nelson and said, "His bark is worse than his bite."

"Mike?" Nelson asked.

"This is Mike Roper," Tanesha said. "Jill's eldest brother. He's a painter. You've probably seen his work at the Denver Art Museum?"

As if he were thinking about it, Nelson gave a vague nod.

"Meet Nelson Weeks," Tanesha said. In a soft voice, she said, "Templar."

Mike blinked and then blinked again. He lay back on the chaise lounge. Tanesha touched Nelson's shoulder in silent support and continued to the snack bar. Nelson rested his head back on the lounge.

"What did you mean?" Mike asked in fluent French.

Nelson sat up on the lounge and looked at Mike.

"U.S. Army," Mike said, pointing to his chest. "Vet."

Nelson nodded.

"Perses was always one of the most powerful Titans," Nelson said, in French. He raised his eyebrows to see if Mike understood. Mike gave him a quick nod. "Perses would have been killed, like so many of them, but he went into hiding in Rhodesia. He had a large patch of land, a plantation, really."

"Slaves?" Mike asked, continuing in French.

"Not that I know of," Nelson said. "Having met your father, I doubt he would tolerate owning human beings. It surprises me that he tolerates humans at all."

Mike snorted.

"Why did he go into hiding?" Mike asked.

"No one knows," Nelson said, lying back. "His daughter is Hecate."

Nelson raised his eyebrows at Mike, but Mike shook his head.

"Hecate is the mother of witchcraft," Nelson said. "Very strong. There are a lot of stories about her power. She . . . Well, anyway, it's the Order's guess that she foresaw the coming purge and told her parents to go into hiding. They survived."

"His wife?" Mike asked.

"Boy, you really don't like him," Nelson said.

"Don't know him," Mike said. "We grew up with a step-father because Perses was . . ."

"Held captive — that's right," Nelson said. "I'd forgotten."

"Who's his wife?" Mike asked.

"He was married to his cousin, Asteria," Nelson said. "It wasn't a love match, but one ordained by his father. There weren't a lot of people around and few Titans. Their unions and breeding were controlled by their families."

"What's she?" Mike asked. "This Asteria."

"She's also a Titan," Nelson said. "Her powers aren't well known, but the Order says she's a shape shifter. She's said to have prophetic dreams, so it could have been her who gave the warning as well. You could ask Hedone about her. Hedone and Hecate know each other well, so it's likely that she knows Asteria."

Mike grunted.

"Why did you say that I have powers?" Mike asked.

"You're a half-ling, like Hedone was, correct?" Nelson asked.

"My mother is human, if that's what you're asking," Mike said. "From a line of healers. Her family is from Russia. Have you met Otis?"

Nelson shook his head.

"He's my grandfather, mother's father," Mike said. "He's traveling the world with his girlfriend, Princess Mari of Queen Fand's realm."

"Prince Finegal's sister?" Nelson said.

Mike nodded.

"Met her?" Mike asked.

Nelson shook his head.

"Things to look forward to," Mike said. Abruptly he said, "What powers will I get?"

"No way to know," Nelson said. "But yes, you and your siblings will grow into some power — each unique and suited to you individually. It's possible that one or two of you won't have powers, but unlikely. Are all five of you Perses' children?"

"Only three," Mike said.

"Three Titan-lings," Nelson said with a little awe in his voice.

"And?" Mike asked.

"It's very rare, that's all," Nelson said. "I doubt any Titan has had even one child since . . . Well, long before we were born."

Mike scowled but didn't say anything.

"How did you know? About me, I mean."

"I've met your father, and you look like him. That's a no-brainer," Nelson said. "As for the powers, it's age, mostly. You're in your mid-thirties?"

Mike grunted in agreement.

"That's around the time you should start getting your powers," Nelson said with a shrug. "I don't think anyone's seen it happen, so it will be interesting to see you get yours."

Mike shook his head and scowled.

"You live at the Castle?" Nelson asked.

"I'm married to Jake's sister, Valerie," Mike said. "I'm also a good *friend* of Blane's. I was there when Enrique . . ."

"So was I," Nelson said.

Not sure of what would happen next, he sat up.

"That's where I remember you from," Mike said with a sneer. "Enrique's group."

Nelson nodded.

"You hurt Blane, and I'll . . ." Mike said, sitting up.

Nelson raised his hands as if Mike had a gun. Nelson turned to look at Mike.

"I have loved him a long time," Nelson said evenly. "He is just getting to know me, but I . . ."

Nelson's hand went to his chest. He gave Mike a nod and lay back down.

"You know love, Mike Roper," Nelson said. "I see it on you."

Mike grunted.

"You know then that I would never risk injuring the creature that owns my own heart," Nelson said.

Mike scowled.

"What about Enrique?" Mike asked.

"I was new to town," Nelson said. "Broke. Enrique paid me to smith a few objects for him. I needed the money."

Nelson shrugged.

"You don't need money now?" Mike asked.

Nelson shook his head.

"Enrique was gay royalty," Nelson said. "Blane was the prince at his side. I fell in love with the prince. That is why I was there."

"And when it all went to shit?" Mike asked. "I saw you at the *burning* party."

"I was there when Enrique burned Blane's possessions," Nelson said, stiffly.

Mike didn't respond.

"And?" Mike asked.

"And what?" Nelson asked.

"Why were you there?" Mike asked.

Nelson sighed.

"I'm not sure," Nelson said. "I . . . Maybe I hoped that Blane would show up to defend himself or . . . I don't know."

"When was the last time you . . ." Mike asked.

"Around that time," Nelson said. "My life took off in a different direction. I was sick for a year or so and then started working at the Denver Crime Lab."

"Ava," Mike nodded.

"Right," Nelson said. "I haven't seen Enrique for . . . years. I will tell you, Enrique always knew how I felt about Blane. Thought it was funny."

"What do you think he will do when he finds out that you've joined their family, *our* family?" Mike asked.

"Have I joined their family?" Nelson asked.

"Looks like it to me," Mike said.

Emotion rushing through him, Nelson looked away. After a moment, he sighed.

"I don't really care," Nelson said with a shrug.

"Hey!" a young girl's voice interrupted them.

They turned to see Noelle run up to Mike. Noelle was wearing a pair of overalls splattered with paint and a bandanna over her hair.

"Don't run," Mike said, pointing to the pool.

"We're late!" Noelle said. "Margaret's grandfather is waiting for us, and you're here chatting with Nelson! What are you wearing?"

Mike looked down at the trunks.

"You need to get dressed!" Noelle said.

Mike raised his eyebrows at Noelle and then turned to Nelson.

"Duty calls," Mike said.

Mike nodded to Nelson and left. Nadia pulled off her headset to look at Nelson. Nelson shrugged, and she smiled. She reached over to squeeze his hand before putting her ear bud headset back in. Unsure of what had just happened, Nelson lay back to rest for a while.

~~~~~~~~~~

Sunday mid-day — 12:14 p.m.
Kayenta, Arizona, at the hotel on the Navajo Reservation

"Sandwiches," Jeraine said, gesturing to the tray he was carrying from the hotel kitchen.

They were setting up lunch in one of the group rooms.

"Great," Heather said. "I thought we might eat and see if we can get the kids to nap."

"Jabari's been sitting with Miss T for a while," Jeraine said. "Worn out."

"Mack, too," Heather said. She pointed to where Mack was sitting with Nelson. "He won't come in. Doesn't want to miss anything."

Jeraine nodded.

"It's so exciting to be in the pool," Jeraine said. "I didn't know Jabari could swim!"

"He's our little fish," Heather said with a grin. "He took lessons last spring with the other kids. He took right to it. I think he'll be our swimmer."

Heather shrugged.

"Where was I?" Jeraine asked with a laugh.

"I know, right?" Heather grinned. "I feel like that."

"Life," Jeraine said.

Heather looked at him. Jeraine was looking down while he put cut carrots out into a bowl. She had the feeling that he wanted to talk to her about something. He looked up at her.

"You okay with this Nelson?" Jeraine asked.

"Are you?" she asked.

Heather turned the question on him rather than answer. She'd known him almost his entire life. He could be very vague when he had something important to talk about.

"He seems nice enough," Jeraine said. "This Templar stuff is weird. And he's sick."

Jeraine shrugged.

"The dude is gorgeous," Jeraine said with a laugh. "With those glasses and that beard, he just looked like some geek. Here he is and . . . wow."

"I know — it's a complete transformation," Heather said.

Jeraine nodded.

"I wanted to talk to you about something," Jeraine said.

Heather sighed with relief. Her wait might be over.

"You remember La Tonya?" Jeraine asked.

"Your sister?" Heather asked. "Sure."

"You probably remember how she married that perfect guy," Jeraine said. "Not a stupid addict asshole like me. Perfect. She went to med school and graduated in the top percentile of her class and stuff. Had perfect babies. Waited to get work so that she could be with them until they went to school."

Heather nodded.

"Her guy . . ." Jeraine swallowed and looked around to see if they were alone. "Turns out he wasn't so perfect."

"What happened?" Heather asked.

"He . . . well . . ." Jeraine looked up at her. "It's kind of a secret because it just happened. . . Like just now, while we were sitting at the pool."

"What happened?" Heather asked.

"He was arrested for embezzling money from his work," Jeraine said. "Remember how they had that nice house and . . ."

Heather watched Jeraine struggle with his words.

"I was the asshole," Jeraine said, with his hand on his chest. "That's my family role. I'm the asshole; she's the perfect princess. I was the jerk who couldn't keep his life together. But he . . . "

Jeraine shook his head and looked away. When he looked back, his eyes burned with indignation.

"Everything was a lie. He . . . My sister is . . . They have two kids, and she's pregnant and . . ."

"What's happened?" Heather asked.

"They picked him up from his work. Yesterday. Saturday," Jeraine said. "So like an hour ago, La Tonya was dropping the kids at summer school. The Sheriffs were there when she got home. She can't go inside. They told her that the house had been bought with some loan from some hostile government."

"He was a spy?" Heather asked.

"Banker, spy, backer of terrorism, money launderer," Jeraine said with a shake of his head. "We don't really know."

"Sounds bad," Heather said.

"No notice. They've lost everything they have," Jeraine said. "She . . . um . . . doesn't want mom or dad to know. I called Seth, you know, to see if he could help, but it turns out that the guy her husband was involved with was the same guy that . . . that . . ."

Jeraine swallowed hard.

"That stuff with Ivan in Russia?" Jeraine asked. "Otis? You know the guy who just died? La Tonya's husband was one of his bankers."

"Oh, wow," Heather said.

"Yeah," Jeraine said. "She called because, um, well . . . She doesn't have anyone else. Like no one. I don't think she would have called me either, but they . . . I mean, La Tonya's never asked me for anything. Not one thing. Ever. But she . . ."

"What can we do?" Heather asked.

"She and the kids need a place to stay while they sort this out," Jeraine said. "I know that we said we'd put our house — you know the yellow house? — on the market on Monday, but I wondered . . ."

"What does Tanesha say?" Heather asked. "It's really her house."

"Oh, Miss T," Jeraine said. "She's wiring La Tonya some money right now. Hiring lawyers. You know, taking care of everything. Miss T called her mom to go be with La Tonya. I guess, Yvonne's on her way."

Jeraine looked up at Heather.

"They took her car," Jeraine said. "While she was in it! She drove up, and they made her get out. Frisked her head to toe and . . ."

Jeraine swallowed hard.

"Took her watch, wedding ring, necklace, phone, purse . . ." Jeraine said. "They took her shoes. They wanted her clothing, but . . . She's supposed to turn in her clothing when she has a chance to change. She said they're trying to 'break' him, you know, her husband."

"Sounds awful," Heather said with a smile.

"Miss T said that you and Blane would have to agree, but I know that you put money into the house. Time," Jeraine said. "It didn't feel right not to ask you . . . I know Blane's working, but I figured that he wouldn't mind if you . . ."

Jeraine stopped talking and looked down.

"Ask me what?" Heather asked.

"Would it be okay if La Tonya and her kids lived at our little yellow house?"

"Of course," Heather said. "Should we send you back to help? Edie's here. She could . . ."

"No," Jeraine said with a shake of his head. "I will only make her crazy. She and I . . . you know."

"She *did* call you," Heather said.

"No. Did I say she called me?" Jeraine asked with a shake of his head. "Sorry. She didn't call me. One of the Sheriffs called Miss T. He's someone Miss T knows from some of the nonsense you guys have been through. I called La Tonya after I found out. The Sheriff answered because, you know, they were taking her phone and . . ."

Jeraine shook his head.

"No, she doesn't need me," Jeraine said. "She does need a place to live until she can sort this stuff out."

"She had no idea?" Heather asked.

"Not a clue," Jeraine said. He shook his head. "No one did. I guess it was some kind of international banking thing. They swooped in out of nowhere to make sure he didn't destroy anything."

He took a breath and let it out.

"You okay to let her use our beds and stuff?" Jeraine asked.

"Of course," Heather said. "Whatever she needs."

"She doesn't even have any clothes!" Jeraine said, his voice rising. "She . . . When I talked to her, she was just sobbing. I've . . ."

Jeraine looked up at Heather and shook his head.

"Never seen her cry," Jeraine said. "She was always been . . .just . . . perfect."

Jeraine shrugged.

"I wondered if . . ." Jeraine said. "Um . . ."

"You want me to see if I can help?" Heather asked.

"I'm afraid she'll kill herself," Jeraine said. "She's been depressed. This pregnancy has been really hard. Mom's been with her almost every day."

"Sure," Heather said. "But you should know that I've never liked her husband. I'm not going to 'fix' that marriage."

Jeraine gave her a nod.

"Help my sister, and it will make up for you never helping me," Jeraine said, in an attempted joke.

"Why do you think I haven't helped you?" Heather asked.

For the first time in this conversation, Jeraine looked Heather in the face.

"I just figured that . . ." Jeraine started.

"Tanesha asked me not to 'fix it' — your marriage, you, that is," Heather said. "When you left and all of that. She said that you needed to grow on your own. She would never trust it if you didn't do that work yourself. So you're right — I didn't fix it."

"But you helped me?" Jeraine asked.

"You're alive," Heather said. "Ever wonder how that's possible?"

Jeraine threw his arms around Heather. She hugged him while he cried for his sister and then for himself. Heather held onto him until he was more stable.

"The guys are back," Heather said softly.

Jeraine pulled back from hugging her. They heard the noise and general chaos created by the Lipson Construction men returning for lunch.

"I should tell Blane," Heather said. "But I'm sure he'll be as concerned about her as I am."

"I'll go tell Miss T," Jeraine said.

"If you need to go back . . ." Heather said.

"Thanks," Jeraine said.

With that, he turned on his heel and walked out of the room.

Chapter 536

Ober Welp'd

Sunday afternoon — 4:14 p.m.
Kayenta, Arizona, at the hotel on the Navajo Reservation

"Hey," Nadia said to Sandy, as she walked out onto the patio by the pool.

"Hey," Sandy said.

With Rachel Ann in her arms, Sandy was standing in the shade near the swimming pool. Rachel's face was bright red, her eyes wet with tears, and her fists were clenched.

"She okay?" Nadia asked.

"We got a little angry and sad this afternoon," Sandy said.

"Oberwhelp'd," Rachel Ann said.

"Overwhelmed," Sandy said with a nod. "Too much fun. Too much sun."

Grinning, Nadia had to look away to keep from laughing from the sheer sweetness of the little girl.

"We're having a little break," Sandy said. She kissed Rachel Ann's hair. "How was your run?"

"Great," Nadia said. "I . . ."

Sandy turned to look at Nadia.

"You know, when I'm at home, I think — 'What the hell am I doing with . . .'" Nadia's voice trailed off. "Well, you know."

"With Nash," Sandy said. She nodded. "I *do* know."

"Then we get together," Nadia said. "Just for a run after he got back from the site. And . . . I *feel* . . . in ways I cannot even begin to explain. I want more and more — time, conversation, laughter . . . It's intoxicating and terrifying but mostly. . ."

Nadia looked at Sandy for a moment.

"Oberwhelping," Nadia said with a grin.

Sandy smiled.

"He's really great," Nadia said, with a nod. "I feel whole when he's around."

"I think he'd say the same thing," Sandy said. "You saw the girls?"

Three teenaged girls were waiting for Nash to return to the hotel. He had a bevy of female attention the moment he stepped into the hotel.

"I *did* see the girls," Nadia said with a nod.

Sandy chuckled while Nadia blushed.

"I mean, I saw them and was like: 'He should be with kids his own age,'" Nadia said. "I don't want to ever stand in the way of something he wants or needs. Ever."

She sighed.

"God, I sound like Ivan. He used to say that all the time about Sissy." Imitating Ivan's accent, Nadia added, "She should grow at her own pace, not be saddled with old man."

She uncomfortably looked around.

"You know, Nash has something to say about what he wants," Sandy said.

Looking uncomfortable, Nadia looked out across the patio, where two brand-new propane barbecues sat. Nelson was drinking a beer and talking to Tres Sierra while he worked one of the grills. The other grill was run by Gando Peaches.

"Who's that?" Nadia asked. "The tall guy talking to Nelson."

"Tres Sierra," Sandy said. "He works at Lipson Construction as their CFO."

"Hot guy," Nadia said. "Kinda young to be a CFO."

"He's good at it," Sandy said.

"Is he here for . . .?" Nadia let her words hang in the air as Heather walked over to the men. Tres and Heather's heads pressed together as they spoke for a few minutes. Tres kissed her cheek, and she smiled.

"Heather and Tres?" Nadia asked.

"Maybe," Sandy said. "They're trying things out this week."

Nadia gave Sandy a long look and then looked back.

"Nelson knows," Sandy said. "If that's what you're thinking. He's a part of the 'trying it out.'"

"He should be happy about that," Nadia said. She put her hand over her mouth. "Sorry — that sounded shitty. I didn't mean to be an ass. I just..."

Nadia turned to look at Sandy.

"I'm caught up in my own judgments of myself," Nadia said.

"The entire situation is new," Sandy said. "For everyone. Just because we keep our judgments to ourselves doesn't mean we don't have them."

Sandy sighed and looked at Nadia.

"I've been friends with Heather since we were ten years old," Sandy said. "She is the nicest, most grounded person I've ever known. When I've needed someone, she's been there — no matter what time of day or night or even what I needed. She's been there for me when ... Well, when I couldn't be there for me. All of the rest of this stuff?"

Sandy shrugged.

"The only thing that really matters to me is my friend's happiness," Sandy said. "At the end of my life, I hope I can say that I participated in helping her live a happy life. Because she's done that for me."

Sandy nodded.

"That's where I try to stay," Sandy said. "In my mind and heart."

"Good thinking," Nadia said with a nod.

"Sometimes, I. . . stray," Sandy leaned into Nadia. "I'm mean, how many smoking-hot men do you need?"

Nadia burst out laughing. At the same time, a cluster of men standing at the other end of the pool started yelling at each other. Squinting at the pack, Nadia picked out Blane, Jacob, Aden, Sam, and a group of other men she didn't know.

"What's that?" Sandy asked.

"Jake's dad wants to start a business here," Sandy said.

"So?" Nadia asked.

"Lipson construction is owned by the employees now," Sandy said. "Or half owned. Sam can't just decide to take a business risk on the company dime."

Nadia nodded.

"He wants to do it on his own, but 'on his own' means Jake and Blane," Sandy said. "Five years ago? Six? That would have been easy to do. But Jake and Blane have young families and other things to do.

Blane's Chinese medicine practice has really exploded. He's busy. Jake's just getting his feet under him from everything that's happened. They can't drop everything to keep a business running five hundred miles away."

They watched the men argue for a moment.

"I think Sam misses it," Sandy said. "Wants things to be the way they were. Things just aren't that way anymore."

Nadia looked at Sandy and nodded.

"They love Sam so much that it just kills them to say 'no' to him," Sandy said. She looked at Nadia. "Heavy talk for an afternoon. Sorry."

Sandy shrugged.

"Truthfully, this kind of arguing is fun for them," Sandy said. "It's uncomfortable for me. I kind of panic when the voices get loud, but it's the way they communicate."

"'They'?" Nadia asked.

"At least Sam, Jake, and Blane," Sandy said. "Aden says it's uncomfortable for him, but you'll notice that he's not backing down."

Nadia nodded.

"Give them a minute — they'll be laughing again," Sandy said.

Blane said something, and Sam laughed. The men laughed.

"I understand this," Nadia said. "My dad was eighty when my mom took over. He'd show up every once and a while and expect everything to be exactly like it was when he was there. Things change. It's painful for everyone because you don't want the person — my Dad, Sam — to feel old or useless; they just don't fit in their old role. Sam has to find a new role for himself."

"That's a good way to think about it," Sandy said.

"Who's that guy?" Charlie asked as he walked out of the hotel.

Nadia's business manager, Ian, hugged Nelson tight. When they separated, Ian put his arm around Nelson's shoulders and kissed Nelson's cheek.

"Whoa," Charlie said. "You think they're going to . . ."

Charlie looked at Sandy and then noticed Nadia. Charlie blushed.

"If you're asking if Ian and Nelson are going to 'get it on' tonight," Nadia said, "I sincerely doubt it, but you could ask them. You interested in joining them?"

"Me?" Charlie asked. Shaking his head, he added, "No."

"Then why do you care?" Nadia asked.

"Hey, I didn't mean anything," Charlie said. "I just know that gay guys . . ."

"Not all gay men are sexually promiscuous. Not all gay men have a sexual addiction," Nadia said. "Not Nelson, for sure. He's very prim. When Ian was younger, he was pretty . . . busy. I mean, look at the man. But now, he and his husband are about to have their second child. I doubt he'd risk it."

"I didn't realize that Ian was married," Sandy said.

"As soon as it was legal," Nadia said. "They'd already adopted their daughter, Madison, from the Ukraine — you know, where Ian and my mother are from. Jeff, that's Ian's husband, is here with their daughter, Madison. Have you met them?"

Sandy and Charlie shook their heads.

"They're probably resting," Nadia said. "I'll ask Ian. Jeff works in films. He wanted to meet Valerie to ask her if she'd work on his film."

Nadia wiggled her eyebrows.

"Exciting," Nadia said. "Do you think Blane would want to take on Nelson, Ian, Jeff?"

"Not at all," Charlie said. "That's not what I was saying . . ."

He blushed.

"Little homophobia coming out?" Nadia asked.

"Probably," Charlie said. "Sorry."

"Judgments," Nadia said. "We were just talking about it. We all have them."

"They catch us off guard," Sandy said. "Blane hasn't been with anyone since Enrique. So I don't think any of us know what's going to happen — with Blane and Nelson or Heather and Tres."

Sandy nodded.

"It's all new," Sandy said. "Everything is new, for all of us."

"I'm really sorry," Charlie said to Nadia. "I didn't mean to be prejudiced. I don't have any problem with . . . well, anyone. When I was on the street, I had all kinds of friends. The gay kids stayed with us for protection. Tink would find the girls in bad situations. We don't have a problem with how or who people love."

Nadia smiled to him.

"It's not you," Nadia said. "It's easier to point out your edges than have to deal with my own."

Nadia shrugged.

"That's the truth of it," Nadia said. "Can you tell Nash that I went to take a nap?"

"Are you going to take a nap?" Sandy asked.

"No, I just . . ." Nadia said. "I was going to go for a swim, but . . ."

Nadia gestured to the pool. Nash's admirers were hanging out in the deep end. One thing was for sure — the girls did not like Nadia.

"Charlie, why don't you show Nadia the spa?" Sandy asked. She nodded to Nadia. "Sam bought out the spa for the week. As long as they have time, we can use it. I happen to know that they are free. Jill was scheduled in a couple of minutes, but she is . . . well, oberwhelp'd herself. Go. Get a massage. If you want to, you can tip them."

Nadia opened her mouth to protest, and then she shook her head at herself.

"Lead on," Nadia said to Charlie.

Charlie held out his elbow. Nadia hooked her hand, and they went to the spa room. Sandy looked down at Rachel Ann. The child was sound asleep. Smiling at her little girl, she set Rachel Ann on her chaise lounge and sat down next to her. Jacob walked by.

"How's the war?" Sandy asked.

"About the same," Jacob said with a laugh. "Dad always gets what he wants. It's hard for us to remember — but that's the truth. The crazy thing is that he's always right."

Jacob shrugged.

"We just have to figure out how to match his idea with something livable for us," Jacob said.

Sandy nodded.

"We'll get there," Jacob said. "Do you happen to know where Jill is?"

"She went to your room," Sandy said.

Jacob nodded and took a step toward the hotel.

"Jake?" Sandy asked.

Jacob turned to look at her.

"She's not in a great place," Sandy said.

"It's Katy," Jacob said. "Katy's been out of her mind lately."

Sandy tilted her head to the side.

"Oh, I see. You're saying that Katy's off because Jill's not in a good place," Jacob said. "Good to know. Thanks."

Sandy smiled at him.

"I'll do what I can," Jacob said. "Wish me luck."

"Good luck," Sandy said.

Jacob grinned at Sandy, and she smiled. She'd just packed up all of the toys, sunscreen, water bottles, books, towels, and general "stuff" left by two teenagers, herself, and Rachel Ann. Aden came up. He picked up her full bag.

"How is she?" Aden asked.

"She got oberwelp'd," Sandy said with a smile. "She just needs a little sleep."

Aden grinned at Sandy. He bent down and picked up their daughter.

"Where are the kids?" Aden asked.

"I think they're in the room," Sandy said. "It's been a big day of sun and friends."

Sandy and Aden started into the hotel. They walked past Abi and her twins on their way to the barbecue. She waved, and they continued down the hotel hallway.

"How was Noelle's time with Margaret's grandfather?" Aden asked.

"Good, I think," Sandy said. "She's . . . Well . . ."

"Oberwelp'd?" Aden asked.

"Exactly," Sandy said. "Nash came in from his run with Nadia and then had time to have a little meltdown. In private. Nadia doesn't know."

"Should I . . .?" Aden pointed toward the room where Charlie and Tink were staying.

"No, he's in the room. The lights are off, and the a/c is going full blast," Sandy said. "They're where they need to be. Luckily, Charlie was there to help when Nash lost it. Nash's resting now."

"What's going on with Nash?" Aden asked.

Sandy's eyes flicked to Aden. He raised his eyebrows, and she nodded.

"The deadly disease of oberwelp'd has taken down another Norsen," Aden said.

Sandy chuckled. Wanda and Ivy came rushing down the hallway past them.

"Wanda looks . . ." Aden stopped talking.

Sandy looked at him.

"Can I say that she looks great?" Aden asked. "Is that bad? Inappropriate?"

"She does look great," Sandy said. "Happy."

Her eyes flicked to him.

"Right," Aden said. "Happy. Erik's here, but Edith is on bed rest."

"Twins on the way," Sandy said.

"You think we should have another?" Aden asked and looked at her.

Sandy held her hand up, palm facing him.

"Oberwelping?" Aden asked.

Sandy laughed. They stopped at their door.

"Ready for some teen angst?" Sandy asked.

"You mean we can't just go next door to our quiet, lovely, tatty hotel room and lock the adjoining door?" Aden asked.

Sandy shook her head.

"Lead on, brave woman," Aden said. "Lead on."

~~~~~~~~~

Sunday afternoon — 4:44 p.m.
Kayenta, Arizona, at the hotel on the Navajo Reservation

Wanting to give Jill a heads up, Jacob tapped on the room door before going inside. He stuck his head inside the room and looked.

Jill and Katy were lying on the king-sized bed together. Both of his girls were crying their eyes out. Oblivious to the world, the twins were in their crib along the wall.

He felt like he'd been stabbed. There was nothing that felt more like a failure than when Jill or Katy cried. Here they were *both* crying. Never one to back away from a fight, Jacob stepped into the room.

Jill looked up at him. Her sad eyes tore at his heart. As he approached the bed, Katy looked up at him.

"'s all my fault," Katy said.

Rather than respond, he got on the bed with them. He reached out to Jill and Katy. They clung to him while they both sobbed.

"I'm a bad girl," Katy said. "I'm a bad girl."

"No, no," Jill said. "No."

He squeezed them to him. After a few long minutes, Jill and Katy's sobs slowed to simple tears.

"What's going on?" Jacob asked in a soft voice that he hoped was kind.

"'s all my fault," Katy repeated. "I'm a bad girl."

"No, no — you're not," Jill said.

Their tears started to fall again. Always ready to solve problems, Jacob knew enough to be patient. He waited until their tears slowed again.

"Jill?" Jacob asked.

Jill looked up at him.

"Would you mind if we found out why Katy is upset?" Jacob asked.

Jill opened her mouth to say something. She paused for a brief moment before shaking her head.

"Katy, you've been really upset," Jacob said. "You've had bad dreams and visions. I've been up with you almost every night this week. I know Jill has been too. When I've asked what's going on, you won't tell me. I know that Delphie has talked to you a couple of times, but you won't tell her, either. Now, you and your mommy are really upset. I can't help you if I don't know what's going on."

Katy leaned up to look at him. Her big, sad eyes gutted him, but he vowed to stay strong. He needed to get her to tell him what was going on.

"Will you please tell me?" Jacob asked.

Katy blinked. Her impossibly long eyelashes pushed her tears from her eyes. Tears ran down her face.

"You asked me to be your daddy," Jacob said. "When we got married, I asked you to be my Katy. Part of being your daddy means that I have to talk to you. Part of you being my Katy means that you have to talk to me. We have to talk to each other."

With his words, he heard an echo of his father from years ago.

"I . . . um . . ." Katy started.

"What have you seen in your visions?" Jacob asked.

"No one loves me," Katy said.

Jill gasped and moved to respond. Jacob squeezed Jill's shoulder. She looked at him.

"You've had a vision where no one loves you," Jacob said.

Chapter 537

Katy nodded.

"I was really bratty," Katy said. "Mean. Snappy. Knows everything. And then no one loved me anymore. Paddy found new friends, and Mommy had new babies, and you found a new girl to be daddy to, and I was just . . . Katy, just Katy. Everybody hates Katy."

Katy began to sob. To keep from responding, Jill had to bite her lips so hard that she tasted blood.

"Everybody loves the boys 'cuz they're boys and cute, and I'm just stupid Katy," the girl said. "No one even introduced themselves to me on my birthday."

Jill scowled. Katy had told her that it was too babyish to be introduced on birthdays. Jill had missed their usual little ceremony.

"They just ignored me," Katy said. "Just forgot all about me."

"I will never forget you," Jacob said.

"You will, too," Katy said. "Everybody will, and I'll be all alone, by myself, alone, forever."

When Katy tucked her head against him, Jacob squinted.

"How old were you in your vision?" Jacob asked.

"I don't know," Katy said.

"Tell me a little bit more about this vision," Jacob said. "It sounds really scary. Do you think you can? Takes a lot of courage to do that. Are you brave enough?"

"I can do it, Daddy," Katy said. "I'm brave enough."

Jacob felt Jill relax against him. There was something in all of this that Jill needed. He only hoped that when Katy was done, he would be able to help Jill.

"Where were you in this vision?" Jacob asked.

"I don't know. I've never been before," Katy said. "There were big buildings and yellow leaves on the ground."

"So it's fall," Jacob said. "What were the buildings like? Were they like houses or like . . ."

"Not houses or apartments," Katy said. "Like buildings. They were kind of white colored. One looks old, like it's stone and . . ."

"Are there cars there?" Jacob asked. "Roads? Streets?"

"It's a road," Katy said. "We're walking on the sidewalk, but there aren't any parked cars."

Jacob opened his mouth to say something, but Katy cut him off.

"There are lots of people," Katy said.

"People?" Jacob asked. "Old people like me or maybe young people like you?"

"Like Charlie's age," Katy said. "Big-kids kind of people."

"Ah," Jacob said.

"I felt really scared and alone," Katy said. "Because nobody loves me anymore. Why else would I be so scared and so alone? And I didn't I know anyone there."

"It sounds really hard," Jacob said. "Where was Mommy?"

"In Denver," Katy said.

"So you weren't in Denver?" Jacob asked.

Katy shook her head.

"Where was I?" Jacob asked.

"With Mommy," Katy said. The girl took a breath, and words flew out of her. "Then I remembered that I've been really grumpy lately and snappy and bossy and . . . And I've seen that people are sick of it. But I can't stop myself. I just get sick of everything. Mad at stupid people and stupid stuff. No one wants to be friends with someone like that."

"Did Paddie say that?" Jacob asked.

Katy shook her head.

"Hmm," Jacob said. "So you had a vision and then had bad dreams about the vision."

Katy nodded.

"Okay," Jacob said. "What stupid people and stupid stuff are you mad at?"

"That stupid politics and that guy who yelled at Mommy and that lady at the grocery store and. . ." Katy looked at her daddy. "I don't know. Everybody seems mad now. Mommy and me — we don't go places because there's always some old guy yelling at us. I want to zap them because girls aren't stupid like they say, but Mommy says I shouldn't."

"Is there a particular old guy who's been yelling at you?" Jacob asked.

"That guy who lives next to Uncle Nelson," Katy said. "He told Mommy that he was going to burn that . . . I don't know the word, but Mommy said it was a bad word I should never say. It meant somebody like Uncle Blane. And I told him that he was being mean. He told me and Mommy to shut the f . . . — you know that word — up. That he didn't need some *stupid* woman and her brat telling him not to do what God told everyone to do. So I asked him 'Which God?'"

"Good question," Jacob said.

"And I didn't ask to be snappy or anything just because Auntie Heather's grandfather has been visiting, and he's the God Ares, and if he's the one who told the old man, well, anything, then he was probably joking. But the man got really mad and chased us. I wanted to sic Buster on him, because Buster would bite him, but Mommy said we were safe behind the fence."

"Whoa — he chased you back to the Castle?" Jacob asked. "When did this happen?"

"When you were in the mine," Jill said.

"You mean Mr. Matchel?" Jacob asked with a wince.

Jill nodded.

"We shovel his walks," Jacob said in a low voice. "Blane's mowed his lawn all summer."

Jill nodded. Jacob raised his eyebrows and shook his head.

"I will talk to him," Jacob said.

"Don't," Jill said. "He's just another angry man. There's a million of them out there ready to abuse you."

Jacob scowled.

"The man in the market told Mommy that it was good that she had boys and not stupid, worthless girls," Katy said. "He said the boys were ten times more valuable than the girls."

"So you zapped him?" Jacob asked.

Katy gave a little knowing laugh.

"Jacob!" Jill said, horrified.

"You didn't, did you?" Jacob asked.

"Mommy told me not to," Katy said. "But I really wanted to show him what girls can do. Doesn't he know that girls run the world? We only let boys think they do."

"He's probably still convinced that boys run the world," Jacob said.

"Well, he is wrong," Katy said.

Katy smiled with certainty. Seeing Katy brighten a little bit, Jacob decided to ask about the vision that had scared Katy.

"How old are you in your vision?" Jacob asked.

"I don't know," Katy said. She thought for a moment. "I'm as old as the other kids."

"Before you just answer, think about it," Jacob said.

"Okay, Daddy," Katy said.

"Close your eyes, and let your vision get really big," Jacob said. "Let it fill you up. Nod your head when you're done."

Katy closed her eyes. After a moment, she nodded.

"Where's Paddie?" Jacob asked.

Katy's right hand reached out as if to hold someone's hand.

"He's right there," Jacob said.

Katy nodded.

"What does it say on the building in front of you?" Jacob asked.

"It's too far to see," Katy said.

"If you knew what it said, what would it say?" Jacob asked.

Her eyes still closed, Katy fell silent for a long moment.

"What are you doing?" Jacob asked.

"Asking Paddie," Katy said. After a moment, Katy said, "Paddie says that we are going to class. He says that I'm in the building on the right, and he's in the building on the left."

"Can you see the name of the buildings?" Jacob asked.

"Um, just the one on the left," Katy said. "Where Paddie's going."

"What does it say?" Jacob asked.

"'Campbell Hall,'" Katy said.

"Okay," Jacob said. "How do you feel now?"

"Kind of scared," Katy said.

"Why, do you think?" Jacob asked.

"I think I have a test," Katy said. Her eyes popped open. "I'm in college!"

Jacob smiled. Jill cheered.

"Nothing to be sad about there," Jacob said.

"*You're* not there," Katy said.

Her happiness evaporated. She scowled.

"We will miss you so much," Jill said. "So, so much."

"You won't want us around by then," Jacob said. "You'll be like — 'I'm grown up now.'"

"Like Nash is?" Katy asked.

Jacob nodded.

"It will be good for you to get out into the world on your own," Jill said.

"*You* never did that," Katy said to her mother.

"I had *you*," Jill said. "Why would I want to go anywhere else? You probably won't have a baby right away. You certainly won't be as poor as we were. Remember how poor we were?"

Jill reached out to tickle Katy, and the girl laughed.

"You will have different choices than I did," Jill said. "You will find different answers; you will find your own answers to your own questions. It sounds like you'll go away to college, and Paddie will go with you. That will be great."

Rather than respond, Katy hugged Jill.

"But not for a long, long while," Jacob said.

"I'm sorry I've been so snappy," Katy said. "I don't want to be. I just feel mad at everything."

"I understand," Jacob said. "I know Mommy does, too. We want to make a difference, make things better, and we can't change these angry people."

Jacob lifted a shoulder in a shrug.

"That's just a fact," Jacob said.

"What do we do?" Jill asked softly. Katy looked over at him.

"Are we doing everything we can do?" Jacob asked. "Talking to our political representatives? Be kind to our friends? Being aware of what's going on? Are we doing what we can to make the world a better place? You and Katy have done a lot of this kind of thing."

"We always have," Jill said with a nod. "Mom grew up in Russia when it was communist. She always said that democracy was a gift that needed regular tending. We've participated in political campaigns since we were little. Katy's been in marches since she was a baby."

Katy's dark eyes watched her mother. When Jacob looked at her, the little girl nodded.

"Then we've done what we can," Jacob said. "Feeling hopeless is just letting the situation infect our energy. We have to shift our focus onto what's within our control."

"Like what?" Jill asked.

"We can be kind to each other," Jacob said. "We can make it our number-one job to make sure the people we love know that we care. We can talk to each other, listen to each other, be there for each other. We can focus on our work and school."

"That doesn't work!" Katy said. "How does that change everything?"

"It doesn't give us control over everything," Jacob said. "That's true, but it does give us control over *ourselves*."

Jill and Katy seemed to be thinking about what he was saying, so he continued.

"Mostly, we need to protect our energy from these angry people," Jacob said. "Our angry neighbor infected you with his anger, Katy. Then you got angry, and people were angry with you! That doesn't work. You've been spreading his anger all over the place!"

Katy's eyebrows furrowed. Jill stroked her child's back.

"Let him keep his anger," Jacob said. "We can just be who we are and how we feel."

"But I was mad that he was mean!" Katy said. "To me! To Mommy! He wouldn't listen, and I was . . ."

Katy made a kind of growling sound.

"So you were snappy to me?" Jacob asked. "How does that get back at him? How does that hurt him?"

Katy shook her head at her father. He smiled.

"I've done it, too," Jacob said. "Far, far too much of my life has been spent stuck in impotence."

"What's that?" Katy asked.

"Being stuck and feeling like there's nothing I can do about it," Jacob said. "I have everything I want right here, in this room."

Katy looked up at him. He nodded.

"I want to spend my life focusing on *my* family," Jacob said. "Not some angry guy I barely know. He doesn't matter to me. You. Your mommy. Your brothers. You matter to me, more than anything in this whole world."

Katy looked away from him.

"You're not mad?" Katy asked.

"I'm not," Jacob said. He looked at Jill. "Are you?"

"Oh . . ." Jill sighed. "I'd like *my* non-snappy Katy back."

Katy looked at her mother for a moment.

"Okay," Katy said. "I'm going to try not to be snappy anymore. But sometimes . . ."

Holding her hand about five inches apart, Katy made lightning bolts fly from one palm to the other. Jacob laughed.

"Don't I know it," Jacob said.

"Why can't I?" Katy's voice rose with frustration.

The twins roused at their sister's rebel call. Jacob held his finger in front of his mouth to quiet her. She scowled.

"Why can't I?" Katy whispered.

"Because we're nice people," Jacob said. "We only use our power only to defend good."

Blue lightning bolts still shooting out of her palms, Katy shook her head.

"Mostly, we don't want to be like them," Jacob said. "Let's leave the anger to them. We can be happy over here."

Katy nodded. She looked at her hands for a minute.

"Pretty," Jill said.

Katy grinned at her mother. For the moment, Katy's storm was over. The girl dropped her hands.

"You want to lie down for a nap?" Jill asked. "Or is that too babyish? I bet you would feel better if you slept for a while."

"Everyone else is resting," Jacob said. "We're going to have a big barbecue dinner, so it's probably best to rest."

Katy nodded. Jill started to get up, but Jacob beat her to it. He got up and helped Katy get comfortable on her cot. Katy picked up her chapter book, *A Wrinkle in Time*. Jacob tucked her covers up around her. As soon as he turned his back, Katy had kicked the covers off.

Smiling at Katy, he went back to sit on the side of the bed where Jill lay. They sat like that, lost in their own thoughts, until Katy was sound asleep. Jacob reached out to touch her face.

"Can I mansplain anything for *you*?" Jacob asked in a low voice.

Jill treated him to a broad grin.

"I can't tell if you're tired from caring for everyone or . . ." Jacob started.

"No," Jill said. "I want to be with Katy and the boys. With school and Edie's help, I feel like I don't get enough time with them."

"But?" Jacob asked.

She looked at him for a long time before shaking her head.

"I don't *feel* depressed," Jill said. "I've been depressed before. That's definitely not how I feel. I mean, I ask myself — do I want to stay in school? Yes. Am I upset with you? No. I mean, I've gone through every single thing in my life, and . . . I love it all. Our home, my car, our children . . . I feel . . ."

"I wonder if you've given too much," Jacob said.

Her eyes flicked to look at him.

"I don't really know how your skills work, but it makes sense to me that if you give out more than you're getting back, you might get worn out," Jacob said.

"I don't know," Jill said.

Jacob nodded.

"How can I help?" Jacob asked.

"Oh," Jill said. "I don't know. I guess . . ."

She fell silent and looked off into space.

"I guess, just be patient with me," Jill said. "I don't really know what's going on with me or what I need. When I do know, I'll tell you but right now . . ."

Jill shrugged. He leaned over, and they kissed.

"One thing . . ." Jill said. Her eyes looked away from him and then flicked back. "It's probably too much to ask . . ."

"Nothing's too much for you to ask of me," Jacob said. "I know that I've been distracted with a variety of . . . *things*, but there's nothing in my life that's more important to me than you."

Jill's lips turned up in a kind of smile, but her eyes held her doubt.

"Ask away," Jacob said.

"I wonder if you could say 'No' to your father and his new company and . . ." Jill said. "I . . ."

Jill swallowed hard.

"I just would really like it if we had some just *normal* life," Jill said. "9-to-5 living where I see you every day and . . . We sleep in the same bed and . . ."

"You don't have to worry about what mythical creature might kill me at any moment?" Jacob asked.

"Well, sure," Jill said. She smiled. "More than that . . ."

Her voice gained power, and, with it, she could speak her truth.

"I need time with you," Jill said. "Normal time. Morning time. Sneaking-in-some-lunches time. Dinner time. Talking. Laughing. Hanging-out-in-the-garden time. Working on houses. Just time to be you and me, and the kids."

In case she had more to say, he waited to respond.

"That's all," Jill said. "That's really what I need."

He opened his mouth to respond, but she rushed forward.

"But that's too much to ask, I know," Jill said. "We have people who need wells and your father, who needs whatever he needs, and Val is struggling and . . ."

Jill let out a defeated breath. Jacob opened his mouth to respond again.

"I am not saying that I wasn't a part of all of these decisions, including the decision to come here to dig some wells. I was a part of every decision. I *agreed* with everything. It's just that I realize that . . ." Jill said. Her hands went to her chest. "I need you. For me."

His hand cupped her face, and his thumb stroked her cheek.

"Of course," Jacob said. He nodded. "That sounds wonderful."

The clouds lifted from Jill's face. She gave him a bright smile.

"You want to know what I think you should do with the well-digging business?" Jill asked.

"Absolutely," Jacob said.

"I think Gando could run the drilling company. He hasn't really done anything since getting out of the military," Jill said. "We could use some from the payment of that hotel loan to help him get started. You, Blane, Aden, and Sam could mentor him. I bet Tres would help. We could come down as a family for a weekend every month or so."

Jacob smiled.

"That's the best plan I've heard yet," Jacob said. He bent down and kissed her lips. "You are brilliant."

"Thanks," Jill said.

"And it isn't what you need," Jacob said. "What do you need *now*?"

"I was thinking that I would read a book and maybe . . ." Jill said. "I mean if you want to make love we can but . . ."

"I brought my ebook reader," Jacob said. "I just started that mystery series you told me about."

"Oh, it's good," Jill said. "You'll like it."

"Then, I agree with your suggestion," Jacob said. "Let's read our books for a while. Of course, if the spirit moves . . ."

Jill laughed. He got up from the bed and took his ebook reader from his computer case. Jill lay down on the bed. He sat in the chair and put his feet up next to hers. She rested her elbow on his shin.

For a while, they were together, in the same location, resting in the silence and peace of each other.

It was absolutely perfect.

CHAPTER 538

SORRY, SORRY, SORRY

A break in the story for a PSA from the Girlfriends

"Hi," Sandy said. "Claudia asked the girlfriends and me to say a few words about . . ."

Sandy looked at Jill in such a way that it was clear a baton had been passed. Sandy was standing next to Jill, with Tanesha next to Jill. Heather was standing on the end, next to Sandy.

"The world is pretty rapey right now," Jill said. "Claudia asked us to talk to the violent-assault survivors in the crowd."

"And all those who love assault survivors," Heather said. "Because you're impacted, too."

Jill and Sandy nodded.

"Everywhere you go now, people are spouting their opinions on who committed violent sexual assault and how victims lie," Tanesha said. "News stations spend hours tearing down sexual-assault victim. Cruel commentators on social media spout disrespect. . ."

"There's plenty of gross old men, that's for sure," Sandy said.

"'She deserved it,'" Heather said, mimicking one of those men.

"'It was a long time ago,'" Sandy said. "'I don't see why it matters now.' 'Why can't she just get over it?'"

"Right," Tanesha said. "Like, who cares if he sexually assaulted someone? She doesn't matter."

"It's insanity," Sandy said.

"Dumb," Jill said.

The woman crossed their arms across their chests in silent agreement.

"They act like we don't matter," Jill said.

"Like all women don't matter," Sandy added.

"We're just here, like paper towels, to be used and discarded," Heather said. "We don't have feelings. We don't experience trauma."

"Worse yet, they act like we should be honored," Tanesha said. "That someone would find us attractive enough to violate us."

Sandy, Heather, and Jill looked at Tanesha for a moment. Then, they all nodded.

"Like we don't live under the shadow of what happened to us," Sandy's voice was quiet and small.

"Every day," Jill said.

For a moment, no one said anything. Jill cleared her throat.

"We're here to tell you — you don't have to listen to this nonsense," Jill said.

"These are evil words, designed to wound you," Sandy said. "They are designed to stop you and every other sexual-assault survivors from ever speaking your truth."

"And to tell our daughters and sons that they should expect to be raped," Tanesha said.

The other women nodded.

"As a society, we no longer shut our eyes to sexual violence," Heather said.

"We try to stop it," Tanesha said.

"Things have really changed," Heather said. "Some people are still living under these old rules, so they say stupid, callous things."

The girlfriends nodded in unison.

"You know what happened to you," Sandy said. "That's enough."

"We believe you," Tanesha said.

"Certainly if you want to tell someone . . ." Heather added.

"Find someone safe," Jill said. "Make sure they are ready to hear you, and tell them. You don't have to share your stories with anyone else, certainly not someone who's going to tell you that you did something to make your abuse happen."

"'Well you *were* drunk,'" Sandy said. "'And that dress . . .'"

The women scowled.

"We're really good at finding the wrong people to tell our traumas to," Tanesha said with a nod.

"That's the truth," Heather said.

"Don't do that," Jill said. "If you're ready to tell your story, find someone safe to tell it to."

"Exactly," Sandy said.

"As long as you vote," Jill said. "And call your representative."

"Or email," Sandy said. She looked at Jill. Jill nodded. "That's what I did."

"I texted," Heather said.

"Democracy requires that we all participate," Tanesha said. "But once you have spoken to your representative? Feel free to turn off the television, Internet . . ."

"Twitter," Jill said. "Facebook."

"Not being on Twitter or Facebook for a week will not kill you," Sandy said. "It won't reduce your brand or get you out of touch. Not even a little bit."

"Your job as an adult is to protect yourself from harm," Tanesha said.

"There's no way for you to not take the cruel, dismissive comments of these old men . . ." Heather said.

"Millionaires," Tanesha said. "Every one of them."

Heather scowled at Tanesha.

"What is your issue with the millionaire thing?" Heather asked.

"They are not like us," Tanesha said, with a shrug.

Jill put her arm around Tanesha's waist.

"You will hear their words as if they are being said about you, directly," Heather said. "Their words will enter your heart and mind and psyche. No matter what anyone tells you — it will feel like they are talking about you, right into your very soul."

"Period," Tanesha said.

"When you listen to words that justify sexual violence, you are harming yourself," Sandy said. "And trust me — you will turn that attitude on yourself. In no time at all, you'll treat yourself as cruelly as they are treating her."

"Your mind can't sort out the difference between this woman, this stranger, and you," Jill said. "After all, she was sexually violated. You were sexually violated. Of course, these old men are talking about you. Even if you know that's not true in your mind, it is going to *feel* true."

"That's just how our minds work," Heather said.

"You deserve more than that," Tanesha said.

"For the next week or so, you have our permission to ignore what's going on in the world," Tanesha said. "You can cocoon yourself in a book series or television show . . ."

"Take a break from the media. Find something to distract you," Jill said. "Rewatch the seasons of your favorite, non-violent show. Katy and I are working our way through *Gilmore Girls*."

Sandy and Heather nodded.

"I'm watching *Greenleaf* on my phone," Tanesha said. "So good."

"That is good," Heather said.

"That's too emotionally intense for me," Sandy said. "I've been watching old Disney movies with Rachel Ann and Noelle. *The Shaggy Dog*, stuff like that."

"Certainly, you can always read the *Denver Cereal* from the beginning," Jill said.

"You can even set it all down and get out into the world," Tanesha said.

"Volunteer at a charity," Sandy said.

"Bake up a storm," Jill said. "Like Sandy has."

"I have," Sandy said with a nod.

"The point is that you get to decide what comes into your head," Heather said. "Be careful. Don't let this B.S. . . . ."

"This old way of thinking, represented by these old men," Tanesha said. "Millionaires who are not like you or me or anyone you know . . ."

"Don't let it into your head," Heather said.

"We give you permission to take a break," Tanesha said.

"In the meantime, we'll be here," Sandy said. "Hanging out in the kickass town of Kayenta, Arizona."

"Do you think Blane and Nelson will ever get it together?" Jill asked.

"What about Tres Sierra?" Tanesha asked. "He's looking sexy as hell."

Heather blushed, and the women laughed.

"You do you," Sandy said. "We're in this together."

"Take care of precious you," Heather said. "You're worth it."

"No matter what you do, if you start to feel like you just can't take it anymore," Tanesha said, "ask for help. Don't let this ridiculous moment in history put an end to your life. Call the suicide support line. Talk to someone. Tie a knot to the end of that rope and hold on. These are not our values, at least, not anymore."

Sandy and Jill nodded. Heather looked at Tanesha before they both nodded.

"And if anyone asks why you're taking a media break, you can just tell them that your girlfriends told you to," Tanesha said.

"Damn straight," Heather said.

Jill and Sandy nodded.

"Now back to our story," Sandy said.

~~~~~~~~

Sunday night — 8:11 p.m.
Kayenta, Arizona, at the hotel on the Navajo Reservation

"Hi," Nelson said as he entered the spa area.

Blane looked up at Nelson. Heather had set up a dozen comfortable reclining chairs for people to sit on while Blane treated them in a more "community acupuncture" style. Blane's last patient had left, and Blane was cleaning up the room.

"Hi," Blane gestured to a chair. "I can treat you while I clean up."

"I . . . uh . . . I . . ." Nelson said.

Unsure of how to proceed, he sat down in the chair Blane had indicated. Blane picked up his wrist.

"Can I see your tongue?" Blane asked.

Nelson stuck his tongue out. Blane looked at his tongue and nodded.

"Listen," Nelson started.

Blane was walking away from him. Blane washed his hands, picked up a pack of needles, and walked back to where Nelson was sitting.

"I'm listening," Blane said in a wry voice.

Blane began sticking needles into Nelson in what seemed like a random order.

"We haven't had a chance to talk since . . ." Nelson said.

"Since you showed up uninvited in the SUV with a life-threatening illness?" Blane asked. "Refused to leave? And then proceeded to nearly *die* while we're on the road? You mean, we haven't talked since then?"

"Sure," Nelson said. "Yes."

Blane put in a few more needles.

"You need about a half hour," Blane said. "An hour, if you can spare it."

Blane walked away from Nelson and went back to tidying up the room.

"Can you just stop?" Nelson asked. "We need to talk."

"You've said that," Blane said. "But you're not talking."

Nelson groaned. Blane picked up an antiseptic spray. He began spraying surfaces of the clinic room and wiping them with a clean towel.

"I understand that you're mad," Nelson said.

"I'm not mad," Blane said.

"Fuck," Nelson said. "I went to see you because I had to talk to you, to make it work out. I didn't want you to come here and have this . . . this . . . *thing* that I had done between us. I didn't know that I was sick."

"How is it, then, that you had a number of newly filled prescriptions in your bag?" Blane asked.

Nelson didn't respond. Shaking his head, Blane kept spraying things and wiping them off.

"I don't have any idea of what to say," Blane said. "Honestly. How you could take such a risk with your health is unfathomable to me. Truly. How could you do that?"

"I . . ." Nelson said and then shook his head.

"Did you just *expect* me to save you?" Blane asked. "Cement our relationship with 'my *need* to save people'? Isn't that what Enrique used to say about me? 'Stupid Blane, always needs to save people. It's the only way he feels like he is worthy.' So you figured that you'd foist yourself on me and that would, what? Cement our relationship?"

"I forgot that he used to say that," Nelson said.

"You *forgot*?" Surprised at how angry he was, Blane shook his head. "I don't have time for this. I need to be at a meeting in ten minutes to decide what to do with these water wells. I can't show up there pissed off."

"Why not?" Nelson asked. "I thought you were all 'honesty is everything.' What could be more honest than what's going on here?"

"They read minds, asshole," Blane said. "Jacob will know in two seconds flat that I'm upset. Any emotion is a way into my head. It's only a matter of time before . . . I don't really want to express myself to the entire world. I mean, you want everyone to know — literally see in their minds — you coughing up a fist of mucus?"

Nelson looked a little green. He shook his head.

"I didn't think so," Blane said.

He looked away from Nelson to put the cleaning supplies back in the cabinet. He started straightening the room.

"I find myself in the position of having to apologize to you again," Nelson said. He winced. "I have taken advantage of your understanding."

"Again," Blane said.

"Yes, again," Nelson said. "I . . .I don't know even what to say. This — all of this — from seeing MJ to panicking to having Hedone's intervention and seeing Jax again and reconnecting with my father and . . . God, I felt so heard yesterday."

"Before you almost died," Blane said.

"Yes, before I almost died," Nelson said, his voice rising in irritation. "I didn't intend to get so sick. Yes, I knew that I might have a flare up. I've been working crazy hours, up all night, getting ready for the trial. I could feel my chest tightening, so I ordered refills and picked them up. When I realized you were leaving, I went to get in the SUV. That's it. That's all that happened. I didn't have some nefarious plan to get sick or nearly die. It just happened."

Blane didn't stop moving, but he also didn't respond. So Nelson pressed on.

"I couldn't leave things the way they were," Nelson said. "I had to make some effort to reconnect with you. I couldn't just let you go and . . ."

Nelson shook his head.

"I'm sorry, I guess," Nelson said.

"Everyone is sorry," Blane said, his voice hot with rage. "Everyone is always sorry. Sorry this happened. Sorry I hurt you. Sorry you were hurt. Sorry. Sorry. Sorry. Sorry. You were sorry yesterday. And today? You're sorry again. What's going to happen next that you'll be sorry about?"

The door opened, and Jacob peeked inside. He looked at Blane and then at Nelson.

"Jake's here to talk to me about this water-well stuff — you know, what we are here to *actually do*?" Blane said. "Nelson has another twenty minutes on his treatment."

Rather than respond to Blane, Jacob shut the door behind him. He looked at Nelson again and then at Blane.

"Did I walk in on a recital of the monologue on 'Sorry'?" Jacob asked.

"Fuck you," Blane said.

"Also known as the 'Sorry Soliloquy,'" Jacob said. "Personally, I like the latter name but the former also works."

"What?" Nelson asked.

"Blane does not like the words, 'I'm sorry,'" Jacob said.

"I thought that was how we do relationships!" Nelson said. "One person screws up, and the other person says that they are 'sorry.'"

Jacob put an arm over Blane's shoulder and patted his chest with his other hand.

"When someone has been truly harmed in their lives, they've heard a lot of the word 'sorry,'" Jacob said. "Abusers say that they are sorry but never change their behavior. Social workers are sorry that one thing or another happened but don't do anything to fix the problem."

"Like banning certain people from getting foster children," Blane said.

"Like putting monsters in prison rather than allowing them to be around vulnerable children," Jacob said. "Like boyfriends who cheat and don't care who knows. Like doctors who are sorry that you're addicted to medications but give you more medications to become addicted to."

"Everyone's fucking sorry," Blane said.

"Yes, yes." Jacob looked into Blane's face. They shared a look for a long moment before turning back to Nelson.

"You really *do* look alike," Nelson said.

"See!" Blane said. "He's not even listening."

Blane gave an angry grunt and tried to get away. Jacob held him in place.

"The key . . ." Jacob said, pointedly. Nelson nodded that he was listening. " . . .is not that you are sorry. Everyone is sorry. The key is to do something about it. In this situation, it occurs to me that you might actually be *thankful* rather than sorry."

"But I am sorry!" Nelson said.

"See what I mean?" Blane asked.

"This man saved your life," Jacob said. "And you're sorry?"

Nelson looked at Jacob for a moment and then looked at Blane.

"Come on," Blane said. "Let's just go. He doesn't get it."

"Give him a chance," Jacob said.

They turned to look at Nelson. He seemed lost in thought. Noticing that Jacob and Blane were looking at him, he shrugged.

"I don't always do the right thing," Nelson said. "I mean, everything is so new that . . . How can I be held to a standard where I don't fuck up?"

"The question is not whether or not you'll fuck up," Blane said. "Or even be sorry, but . . ."

"People who are genuinely sorry change their behaviors," Jacob said, cutting off Blane. "Rather than saying a blithe 'sorry' for foisting your deathly ill body on a near stranger, you could say, 'Thank you for helping me, staying with me, saving my life. I will do everything in my power to not be in that condition again.'"

"Ah," Nelson said. "That's what you mean. Me saying 'sorry' doesn't say what I'm going to do in order that it won't happen again. But . . . I was sick."

"You *knew* that you were sick!" Blane's anger exploded. "You got your prescriptions filled! What the fuck did you think would happen?"

"I didn't think," Nelson said. "That's probably not very satisfying, but it's the truth. I didn't think about how you would feel when I stormed out the other night. I didn't think about what would happen if I was sick on the drive to the middle of nowhere."

Jacob held Blane in place. When Blane didn't respond, Nelson continued.

"I should have," Nelson said. "I didn't. I wanted so badly to be with you, to be your lover, but I see that my desires have made me thoughtless, to you — the person I actually wanted in my life."

Nelson looked at Blane.

"For that, I am sorry," Nelson said. "I will try not to be so thoughtless."

Blane seemed to be thinking about what Nelson said, so Nelson continued.

"Thank you for giving me a chance," Nelson said. "Thank you for saving my life. Thank you for giving me a chance to be a part of all of this. I can only say that I will do everything in my power to not be thoughtless."

"And not so sick?" Blane asked. "I had the deadly version of that virus, and I found ways to stay healthy. It took time and effort, but I made the effort."

"And not become so ill," Nelson said. "To the best of my ability."

Blane still didn't respond. Jacob shook him.

"You are an only child," Blane said.

"I am that," Nelson said, with a laugh.

"Take his needles out. I'll wait for you outside." Jacob turned to Nelson and said, "We really have to go. Don't say anything."

Jacob left the treatment room and stood in the hallway. Blane took Nelson's acupuncture needles out. He picked up Nelson's wrist.

"You're stronger," Blane said. "But still on the edge. You could make a full recovery or get sick again. It's up to you."

Blane nodded and went to wash his hands at the sink. Nelson got up and stood next to him.

"You should try to get a treatment in tomorrow morning," Blane said. "We head out at 5:30 am but I can see you at 5 if you need it. There are a few other people who will be here. I can place the needles, and Heather will take them out."

Nelson held out his arms. Blane looked at his arms. Against his better judgment, Blane let Nelson hug him. Nelson kissed Blane's cheek.

"I will do better," Nelson said.

Blane nodded. He walked out of the clinic room. Jacob was waiting for him in the hallway.

"So you decided to mess in my life because . . .?" Blane asked.

"Just returning the favor," Jacob said.

"I never," Blane said.

"I seem to remember someone finding the zoo pass and hand-drawing a map to parking? Someone enrolling Katy at the Marlowe School under the name Katy Marlowe?" Jacob asked. "Telephones for Jill? Car? Health insurance for both of them? Gave me the credit for being 'so thoughtful.' Any of that sound familiar?"

"Me?" Blane put his hand on his chest in mock surprise.

"Very funny," Jacob said. "You told me that we meddle..."

"Because we can," they said together.

Aden met them in the hallway. Over Blane's head, he asked, "How'd it go?"

"Good," Jacob said.

"Did he get to the 'I'm sorry; you're sorry; everyone's sorry' speech?" Aden asked.

"You know he did," Jacob said.

Aden patted Blane's back.

"At least you're consistent," Aden said.

"Is there some reason I deserve this?" Blane asked.

"Reservation at 17th Avenue Café?" Aden asked. "6 o'clock was booked out for two months until you called."

Blane shot Aden an irritated look and then laughed.

"We meddle because we can," the men said together.

Laughing, they went into the meeting to make a plan to dig a few water wells.

~~~~~~~~

Sunday night — 8:21 p.m.
Kayenta, Arizona, at the hotel on the Navajo Reservation

Tres opened the door to his room the moment Heather knocked. He grinned at her and stepped back. She held up a pint-sized carton of vanilla ice cream.

"The brownies are almost done," Tres said.

He gestured toward the small microwave midway into the room. He waved for her to come inside. She hesitated for a moment and then stepped inside the room.

Her eyes instinctively flicked to the wall on her right. Tres's room was on the other side of her and Blane's room. Right now, Tink was next door with Wyn and Mack. She hoped they were all right.

Tres stepped in front of her gaze.

"Tink's taken the kids to Charlie's room," Tres said. "I checked on them on my way back to the room. They are watching kid movies with Noelle, Ivy, and Wanda. Charlie's ordered pizza and Cokes for everyone.

He has that credit card from Sandy. Nash and Teddy were on their way."

"Why don't I know that?" Heather asked. "Usually Tink . . .?"

"I told her that I would tell you," Tres said. "She knew that we were going to hang out this evening."

Blushing, Heather nodded. The microwave dinged, and Tres went to the microwave.

"You seem uncomfortable," Tres said, as he opened the microwave.

"I'm kind of stuck on the whole sleeping thing," Heather said. "I know it's just one dumb detail, but . . ."

"I sleep alone," Tres said with a grin.

"I know," Heather said. "I mean, Tanesha told me, you know, when you were together, and then last week. I just . . . why?"

"Tanesha didn't tell you?" Tres asked.

"She doesn't know," Heather said.

Tres smiled and nodded. He reached one long arm to grab a kitchen towel. He used the towel to carry the small pan of brownies to the table. She went to the table. He'd set out two bowls and spoons. There was an open bottle of wine and two glasses near the wall.

"Please," Tres said.

He gestured to the table like the *maître d'* at an expensive restaurant. Grinning at him, she sat down. He sat down next to her. He scooped out the hot, moist brownies into the bowls and she added the ice cream.

"When I was little, I shared a room with my *abuela*'s mother," Tres said.

"Your great-grandmother," Heather said.

Tres nodded and took a bite.

"She was old," Tres said. "Tough as nails. She'd lived this amazing life. She worked in the factories as a young child during World War I and then again in World War II. She hunted down bandits in the wilds of New Mexico. Her father was a cattle rustler just outside of Juarez. She spent her entire childhood on the run. At ninety-five, she could shoot and dress an elk. She kept our freezer full of duck. Year round."

"She sounds like a hoot," Heather said.

"A true feminist long before that was even a thing," Tres said. "She was my favorite person in the world. That's why we shared a room. Mom used to say that I would just be in with her, anyway."

"Was that true?" Heather asked.

"Probably," Tres said. "I don't know. For as long as I remember, she and I shared a room. So . . ."

Tres shrugged.

"She used to tell me stories," Tres said. "She was a *great* storyteller."

"Any of it true?" Heather asked.

"Who knows?" Tres asked.

"You probably didn't care," Heather said.

"Not in the least," Tres said. "We'd lie down at night. And she'd tell me stories. I'd dream about her adventures all night. She'd asked me about them every morning."

Tres smiled.

"My favorite stories were about her father," Tres said.

"The bandito?" Heather asked.

"Exactly," Tres said. "And you know about *banditos* — right?"

"They sleep alone?" Heather asked.

"Precisely," Tres said. "You don't want to be encumbered by having someone else there when you have to make a quick getaway. Your life and the life of your gang could be in danger if you do."

Tres shrugged.

"It just stuck," Tres said. "I never really had someone to sleep with, so I didn't. Now it's just a thing."

"And you won't care . . .?" Heather asked.

"I don't know," Tres said. "What I do know is that we can stand on the side of this thing and ask 'what if?' forever. Or we can jump in and try it. The kids like me. Nelson and I get along well. I love Blane, as you know. Have long before we met. You and I — well, so far, so good."

Heather gave him a sly smile. When Blane was in the hospital, Tres had done everything in his power to help Heather. They'd spent nearly every afternoon together. Most days, they folded laundry or changed diapers or even went to the market. Once or twice, they fell into each other's arms.

"Nelson likes to sleep alone as well, in case you didn't know," Tres said.

"I did," Heather said.

"He didn't know about the *bandito* thing," Tres said, with a nod. "Turns out, that's not common knowledge."

His bowl nearly empty, he took a last bite and looked up at her.

"What do you want?" Tres asked.

Heather reached out her hand to him. He held it.

"I . . ." Heather said.

Rather than hear her out, he leaned forward and kissed her.

"I have only one short life," Tres said. "I want to spend what's left of it with you by my side."

Heather blushed. He held his hand out to her. Smiling, she let him lead her to bed.

CHAPTER 539

STEP FORWARD?

Sunday night — 10:21 p.m.
Kayenta, Arizona, at the hotel on the Navajo Reservation

Aden pressed the door open and waited.

"See you tomorrow, Dad," Jacob said.

Sam nodded. Blane gave Sam a hug.

"I'll see you at 7?" Blane asked Gando Peaches, Margaret Peaches' uncle. "We'll get breakfast and figure out what we need to do."

"See you then," Gando said.

Smiling, Blane nodded. He knew that Navajo people avoided being touched, including something like a hand shake. Gando was no exception. He nodded to Blane and went to talk to Alex Hargreaves, who was sitting on the other side of the room with her feet on the table.

Blane touched Sam's shoulder. Sam grinned at Blane. With a nod, Blane followed Jacob to the door. When Jacob was behind him, Aden moved out of the room. Jacob followed Aden. Blane jogged to catch the door after Jacob.

"Well that was long," Aden said, stifling a yawn. "Why was it so hard?"

"No idea," Jacob said. "One man wants to start a company. Another man wants to run the company. We have the money. Blah. Blah. Blah."

Blane yawned. The men looked at Blane, and he shrugged.

"There's a lot of drama in my life right now," Blane said.

Aden and Jacob laughed. They turned the corner in the hallway to see that Candy, Jill's older sister, was leaning against a wall.

"Hey," Candy said. "I wondered if I could talk . . ."

The men stopped moving.

"Whoa," Candy said. "That's a little intimidating."

"Do you need me?" Aden asked, putting his hand on his chest. "Because I'm beat."

"Blane," Candy said.

Aden nodded and started down the hallway. Jacob didn't move. Candy gave him a classic annoyed-sister look. He gave her a classic younger brother "What?" look in response. Blane watched them both with amusement.

"Candy?" Blane asked.

"We're here for the week," Candy said. "Jill suggested we come and bring the girls. But . . ."

Candy shot a worried look down the hallway.

"How can I help?" Blane asked.

"It's Kimber," Candy said. "You know that she can be . . . well, there's no beating around the bush: she can be a real mean girl."

Blane and Jacob nodded in near unison.

"Oh, you know about it," Candy said, looking relieved. "I thought I might have to explain everything and . . ."

"Noelle is pretty good at letting everyone in her orbit know what is going on with her at all times," Jacob said. "I think . . . Blane, did you treat her?"

"I might have," Blane said, vaguely. "What can I help Kimber with?"

"She's afraid," Candy said. "Kimber, that is — that she'll fall in with the mean girls and . . . Well, I know what it sounds like, but Kimber finds that kind of behavior to be highly addictive. For her, that is. She doesn't want to go back to being a mean girl."

Naturally thin, Candy's light hair and thin face made her look near skeletal when she was worried.

"Is there something in particular going on?" Jacob asked.

Candy gave him an irritated look and then shook her head.

"I'm supposed to tell you to not read me," Candy said with a nod. "But actually, I'm kind of relieved. I know this 'who's addicted to being mean' is kind of weird — and *a lot* of people just think she's a bad girl — but . . ."

"She and Noelle worked it out," Jacob said. "Noelle couldn't be friends with someone mean or bad. She just doesn't have it in her."

"We're trying to say that we understand," Blane said. "Would you like my help?"

Candy nodded.

"There's something going on with these girls and Nash?" Candy asked. "Do you know about it?"

Blane and Jake shook their heads.

"You know, that look-alike thing is really kind of cute," Candy said. Seeing their exhaustion, she pressed on. "I couldn't get it out of Kimber, you know? That's why I didn't want Aden to be here, because . . ."

The men looked at Candy. Her face flushed, and she looked like she was going to cry.

"I'm happy to help," Blane said. He touched Candy's arm in support. "Are you up in the morning? Can you get there by 6 tomorrow morning? That should give me a chance to talk to Kimber and see what she feels like she needs."

"We're up," Candy said, looking relieved. "We'll be there."

"You know where?" Jacob asked.

Candy nodded.

"See you then," Blane said.

Relieved, Candy rushed away from them. She stopped midway and turned around.

"Thank you," Candy said. "This is a big help and . . ."

Blane and Jacob nodded. Candy blushed again and ran back to her hotel room. Blane looked at Jacob and then shrugged.

"You're a popular guy," Jacob said. He nodded forward. "Steady on."

Jacob pushed Blane forward. By the time Blane could catch his footing, Jacob was gone. He shot a dark look in the direction Jacob had gone and only then noticed that Nelson was sitting on the couch. Nelson had a headset on. He was looking forward into his laptop and talking as if he were on a video call. Feeling Blane nearby, he looked up.

He gave Blane a beautiful smile. Blane felt a brief burst of joy and then remembered that he was angry with Nelson. Blane looked down as Nelson said his goodbyes into the computer. Unsure of what else to do, Blane continued walking toward Nelson.

"That was Ava," Nelson said. "She wants me to stay by the phone in case I'm recalled for that trial."

"No clinic time?" Blane asked.

"I don't think so," Nelson said. "I told Nadia today that I was still a little sick. She's fine with it. I might go in later in the week, if I don't have to return to Denver."

"Nadia seems really great," Blane said.

"She is," Nelson said. "One of the best people I've ever known. Oh, Ian is here, too. Do you know him?"

"I treated him, his partner, and their daughter this afternoon," Blane said. "Don't ask me the partner's name. I don't think I ever got it. The daughter is called..."

Blane closed one eye and thought for a moment.

"Madison," Nelson said. "His husband is Jeff."

"Husband," Blane said. "I never really get used to that."

"Me, neither," Nelson said. "It sounds good though."

Blane nodded.

"Nice of you to treat them," Nelson said.

"It's what I do," Blane said with a shrug. "I need to check on the kids."

"They're with Tink and Charlie and the other kids," Nelson said. He gestured down the hallway. "Mack said he wanted you not to forget to say 'good-night.' So cute."

"He's like that every night," Blane said. "Something about going to sleep freaks him out. He feels better, safer, only if he says good night to me and his mom. It was crazy when I was in the hospital, but somehow Heather managed it. You mind?"

"I just need to..." Nelson said.

Nelson closed his laptop computer and shoved it into a backpack. He pulled off his head phones and shoved them into the backpack. He was almost done when Alex Hargreaves and Gando came out of the room.

"Hey, Blane," Alex yelled. "You mind if I go with you?"

Blane shook his head. Alex gave him a broad smile. She looked at Blane and then at Nelson.

"Tomorrow," Alex said. "To the Navajo Nation Business Development offices?"

She looked at Nelson and then at Blane again.

"Not tonight," Alex said, with a grin. "Since you might have plans."

"Funny," Blane said.

"Grumpy, grumpy," Alex said. "Nice to see you, Nelson. You're looking nice tonight."

"I shaved," Nelson said.

"Glasses, too," Alex said, gesturing to her face. "Handsome man."

With that, she and Gando walked down the hallway. Blane scowled after them.

"I don't think she meant anything by that," Nelson said. "They tease each other a lot."

"Yes," Blane said. "I know."

He let out a big sigh.

"You're still angry with me," Nelson said. He got to his feet. Before Blane could protest, he gave Blane a hug and a kiss on the cheek. "How was your meeting?"

"Good," Blane said. He gestured to where Gando and Alex had disappeared. "We're going to the Nations Business Development Center to get Gando set up. Alex wants to come because she's going to put in money. She thinks they'll want to know where the money comes from and why."

"Alex and Gando?" Nelson asked.

"Military thing," Blane said. He opened his mouth to explain and then wondered if it was classified. He shrugged. "I don't really know the details."

Nelson nodded. They started walking toward Charlie and Tink's room.

"I ran into Tres," Nelson said.

"Oh?" Blane asked.

"Heather was 'recalled to Olympia,' whatever that means," Nelson said.

"Something must have happened," Blane said. "She can bend time now, so she's never gone very long. Did she lay her body down?"

"That's what Tres said," Nelson said. "Do we know what that means?"

"It looks like she's sleeping but she's not breathing," Blane said. "Her human body stays in a kind of stasis. It's warm to the touch, but she's not there."

"Like a coma?" Nelson said.

"But not breathing," Blane said. "Did Tres say how their dessert date was?"

"Good," Nelson said. "He felt like they are moving forward. He's excited. Happy. It's . . . nice to see."

Blane nodded. For a few minutes, they walked in silence.

"I don't know how to get us back on track," Nelson said. "I . . . We've just had so much trouble . . ."

Blane took a breath to respond.

"And I know that I'm at fault for most of it," Nelson said with a nod. "But I think that some of it is that we don't know each other very well, trust each other . . . maybe at all. We're just starting that process, and I can't help wondering if . . ."

Blane stopped walking and turned to look at Nelson.

"Just ask," Blane said.

"Is it too late?" Nelson asked.

"*There's no time for us . . .*" Blane sang.

"Oh, God — you are not singing Queen, are you?" Nelson spit out laughing.

"*There's no place for us . . .*" Blane sang. "*What is this thing that builds our dreams for us, yet slips away from us . . .*"

Nelson was laughing so hard that he started to cough. They stopped walking. Blane patted Nelson's back until Nelson caught his breath. When Nelson stood up, he pointed at Blane.

"No," Nelson said. "No Queen."

"If you say so," Blane said.

They both laughed and started walking again.

"We're just getting to know each other," Blane said. "Jake reminded me that you've never really been in a relationship, and I . . . Well, I have been in other relationships besides Enrique, but . . ."

Blane sighed.

"Let's just say that I'm trying something new, as well," Blane said. "I was a fool with Enrique, a complete fool. I don't want to do that ever again. I have way too much to lose to throw it all away like I did with Enrique. On the other hand, I don't want this . . . friction, either. I don't like it. It's not natural for me."

Nelson nodded. When Blane didn't say more, Nelson turned to look at him.

"I don't want it, either," Nelson said. "I really . . ."

Nelson sighed and shook his head.

"That's a good way to look at it," Nelson said. "We're both learning."

"About each other," Blane said.

"I thought a lot about what Jake said," Nelson said. "And what you said. And . . ."

Blane stopped walking and turned to look at Nelson.

"Thank you for saving my life," Nelson said. "I wouldn't have expected it. I'm so grateful you did. I . . . Honestly, I never remembered that Enrique used to say that about you. He . . . well, I just didn't want to lose my chance with you."

Rather than get into the argument again, Blane simply nodded.

"You're welcome," Blane said.

"Me, my people, my father — love, for us, is rare," Nelson said. "Something to do with the whole 'immunity to magic.' It doesn't come easily and is found only once a lifetime. I learned that my father and Maresol were lovers for a number of years. They are still very close. But they are only sexual partners — not even lovers. I may find another sexual partner, but I will only have one love. You're really it for me."

Nelson took Blane's hand.

"I didn't want to lose my chance at having love in my life," Nelson said. "Having you in my life."

They walked hand in hand.

"So you want to . . ." Nelson said.

Blane shrugged.

"Probably not tonight," Blane said with a saucy grin.

Nelson blushed and wouldn't look at him. Blane chuckled.

"Seems like it's late, and we have early mornings," Blane said. "You are still recovering. Maybe tonight's not the best night."

"Maybe?" Nelson asked.

"You sleep alone," Blane said.

"That's true, but . . ." Nelson said.

Blane grinned and didn't say anything. They kept walking down the hallway. They got to a turn, and Blane spun into Nelson. He gave him a hard kiss on the lips and pressed Nelson's hips toward him. Blane stepped away and continued walking down the hallway. It took Nelson a moment to catch up.

Nelson cleared his throat.

"Well," Nelson said with an intentional croak.

Blane laughed. Nelson fanned himself with his hand. Grinning, Blane softly knocked on Charlie and Tink's door.

~~~~~~~~~

Monday early morning — 3:34 a.m.
Kayenta, Arizona, at the hotel on the Navajo Reservation

"Blane?"

Nelson jerked up to sitting on the queen sized bed. His hand automatically went to where Blane had been when Nelson had fallen asleep. He glanced at the adjoining door.

The adjoining door was firmly closed and the lock turned.

He noticed that he was naked. He started to fall back to the bed.

"Don't." A woman's accented voice — English? Irish? — came from the middle of the room.

Fully awake, he sat up and turned on the lamp on the bedside table. Standing in front of him was a woman. No, an elf. He blinked in the dim light.

She was a fairy warrior.

She wore a suit of modern military armor. She had a thick sword in a scabbard on her belt. Unlike any fairy he'd ever seen, she also had a handgun in her waistband. The top of a compound bow stuck out an inch above her head.

Her hair was long, curly, and vibrant red. Her hair was held in place by a thin, but not insignificant, precious-jewel-encrusted tiara. Her eyes were larger than normal, auburn in color, with fairy long lashes. Her face was easy to look at — beautiful, in a kind of precious or rare way. Her mouth was set in a strong line.

He squinted. He had met her before, but . . .

She pulled a sword from its scabbard. His eyes focused on the sword. The blade was unevenly shaped. One side of the blade was thin, like a Japanese sword fighting sword and designed to be razor sharp. The other side of the blade was brutishly thick, like a broad sword or a falchion.

Blunter, this side of the blade was for hacking. It could easily take off a limb in one blow and a head in two. The blade came together in an uneven foible that ended in a viciously sharp point.

"Where'd you get that?" Nelson asked.

"I took the head of the human who possessed it," the fairy said.

Princess? Fairy princess? Fairy warrior princess? Was there such a thing as a fairy warrior princess?

"Okay," Nelson said. "It hasn't been sharpened in . . ."

The fairy warrior princess looked at the blade.

"I keep it sharp with magic," the fairy warrior princess said.

"You must be very strong," Nelson said.

The fairy warrior princess grunted.

"The edge will never hold," Nelson said. "You need it properly sharpened. How long has it been?"

"Few thousand human years," the fairy warrior princess said. "It still works pretty well."

"Not really," Nelson said. "It wasn't designed to hold magic, so the magic will start to dissipate almost as soon as the spell is cast."

"How could you possibly know that?" the fairy warrior princess said.

"See the notch on the pommel?" Nelson asked.

The fairy warrior princess blinked at him.

"The nob on the end of the handle?" Nelson said.

The fairy warrior princess looked for the notch at the end of the pommel. She nodded when she found it.

"It matches a notch on the guard," Nelson said.

She looked on the piece of metal that separated the handle from the blade.

"Looks like a scratch," the fairy warrior princess said. "The sword has had quite a lot of use."

"Odd that the two random scratches line up," Nelson said.

The fairy warrior princess nodded.

"It says '*Semaines*'" Nelson said. "'*Semaines*' on the guard and repeated on the pommel. If it's the blade that I think it is, the pummel should read '*W. Semaines*,' for its maker."

The fairy warrior princess looked at her sword.

"Well, I'll be," the fairy warrior princess said. "How would you know that?"

"That is a missing blade," Nelson said. "It is a real prize. My father has been looking for it all of his life. His father, too."

Shaking his head, he moved to get up.

"Do you mind?" Nelson asked.

"I don't," the fairy warrior princess said.

"I'm naked," Nelson said.

The fairy warrior princess appeared to laugh at him before her face turned to stone.

"Get dressed and packed," the fairy warrior princess said.

"Why?" Nelson asked.

"You've been found," the fairy warrior princess said. "There are forces coming for you. They mean you no good will. They will bring destruction to every human in this place and feel justified in doing so."

Nelson gawked at the fairy warrior princess.

"Go," the fairy warrior princess said, pointing to the bathroom with the sword. "Now."

His shy embarrassment for being naked in front of this stranger evaporated. Nelson jumped up and started toward the bathroom. He stopped midway.

"What about the people here?" Nelson asked. "I cannot just leave them to fend for themselves."

"There is nothing you can do here," the fairy warrior princess said.

"I can fight!" Nelson said. "My problem. My fight. I will not run away."

"Not this time," the fairy warrior princess said. "You love these people?"

Nelson nodded.

"You need to flee this place," the fairy warrior princess said. "Disappear."

"But I . . ." Nelson started.

"Just until this threat is neutralized," the fairy warrior princess said. "Go. Get packed or I will take you, naked and all!"

"Who will save them?" Nelson asked.

"Your pursuers will meet a power they have only imagined," the fairy warrior princess said. "How do you fight the wind? The rain? The sheer power of the Earth herself?"

"Abi," Nelson whispered.

"You're not as stupid as you look," the fairy warrior princess said.

The fairy opened her left hand, and a ball of light appeared. She tossed it at Nelson. It smacked him on the rear, and he ran to the bathroom. He grabbed his medications and used the toilet.

"Take everything," the fairy warrior princess said. "Anything left of you will be destroyed down to the DNA level."

He grabbed his toothbrush and ran into the room. He pulled on his jeans as he walked and yanked a shirt over his head. He shoved everything else into his backpack. When he turned, a bundle of his gear was floating in the air. He held open his backpack, and his gear floated inside.

"Are you ready?" the fairy warrior princess asked.

CHAPTER 540

ENTER THE TEMPLARS

"What are we . . .?" Nelson asked.

Before he could finish his statement, the fairy warrior princess grabbed him around the waist. Time seemed to both stand still and flash by. He opened his mouth to scream and then found himself in the middle of his own apartment. He blinked and then blinked again.

He felt fine.

"You feel okay?" the fairy warrior princess asked.

"Blane said I should feel nauseous," Nelson said.

"The magic sticks to Blane and Jacob," the fairy warrior princess said. "It throws off their equilibrium. Magic does not appear to stick to you."

"It's in my father's line," Nelson said. "Why am I here?"

"We have determined this was the safest place for you," the fairy warrior princess said.

"Because I am on my own?" Nelson asked. His voice rose in panic.

"Because powerful beings have already fortified this dwelling," the fairy warrior princess said. "You are a consort to a goddess, step-father to her children. The work was done a year or more ago."

"A year ago? But . . .?"

The fairy warrior princess sighed.

"Those of Olympia live outside of time," the fairy warrior princess said as if she were speaking to a child. "They came here a year or more ago because of something that is happening now or will happen. Their efforts will shield you, now."

"What about the trial?" Nelson asked. "Ava thought I might be called in to testify. I would have to leave here!"

"We've induced the defendant to settle," the fairy said.

"What?" Nelson asked. "Who *are* you?"

"I am Edith," the fairy warrior princess said. "Second daughter of Queen Fand. Sister to the Blue Fairy and Prince Finegal."

"And my sister," said another fairy who appeared next to her.

The sisters hugged. This fairy was gorgeous — full-breasted, narrow-waisted, and wide-hipped. She looked like every heterosexual male's dream. Her eyes were big and just a touch too wide. Her hair was full and fell in perfectly maintained auburn curves down her back to her round, high rear. Her make-up was perfect. Was she wearing make up? She was wearing an expensive, hand-sewn dress, and five-inch high heels in matching burgundy.

"Princess Mari," Edie said. "You know me as Edie."

"I knew there was something going on with your hair," Nelson said.

"Yes," Edie said. "The braid is a cover for all of this. Before you ask, James knows that this is what my hair actually looks like; what I actually look like."

"What will happen to everyone in Arizona?" Nelson asked. "Blane? Heather? The children?"

"They are safe," Edie said. "Mari will stay with you. If, for any reason, you need to leave this location, she will go with you."

"But . . .?" Nelson started.

"She's looks a little soft, but if someone gets through the protection, she will defend you," Edie said. "I've never known her to lose at anything. Except maybe to our mother."

"Not anymore," Mari said.

"Yes, not anymore," Edie said. "You can trust that Mari will defend you."

Nelson turned to give Mari an assessing look.

"She is a magnificent cook," Edie said. "Truly the only one of us that can make anything worth eating. Mari is great fun to be around. You'll enjoy your time."

"But . . .?" Nelson started.

"We have told your friends — Ava in particular — that you have taken ill," Edie said. "That won't stop O'Malley from sniffing around — he can smell magic and knows a lie — but Mari and O'Malley are great friends. You will stay here for a while until an accord is made or those who threaten you are no longer living."

Mari nodded.

"Rest now," Edie said. "We'll be in touch."

"Would you like me to sharpen your sword?" Nelson asked. "In return for taking care of me and Blane and the rest?"

Edie gave Nelson a long look.

"Can he really do that?" Mari asked.

"He is a weapons master by birth," Edie said.

"I was sharpening blades when I was a child," Nelson said. "Your sword needs real attention from someone who knows how to care for it."

With a nod, Edie gave the sword to Nelson. She smiled at Mari and then disappeared.

"Can you really do that?" Mari asked. "Make a sword sharp again?"

"Do you have one?" Nelson asked.

"Your family made a blade for me," Mari said. "A thousand or so human years ago. It's a named blade . . ."

"The Fairy Princess," Nelson said. His voice held a touch of awe. "The blade is only myth. Legend. It's not on my father's list because he doesn't believe it exists."

"It was a bride's gift from someone," Mari said. "He died after giving it to me. Killed by Shiva. And rightly so, I might add, although it infuriated my mother."

"It would be my honor to work on that blade," Nelson said.

Nelson dropped his head in real reverence. Mari shrugged and looked at him.

"You look exhausted," Mari said. He looked up at her. "Why don't you sleep for a while? All we have to do now is wait."

Nelson looked at Mari for a long moment.

"How is it that you cook?" Nelson asked. "Your brother told us that no fairy can make food."

"We can't make it with magic, that's for sure," Mari said.

"But you can?" Nelson asked.

"I've been going to Chef's school," Mari said. "My best friend is Sissy Delgado. I was complaining that I love food but couldn't can't make it. She told me that if I wanted to know how to do something I should go and learn how. So I did."

Mari shrugged.

"It's actually pretty fun," Mari said. "So while it's true that we fairies cannot make food with magic, it is also true that no one ever bothered to teach us how to cook."

"Will you teach the others?" Nelson asked.

"Maybe," Mari said with a shrug. "I managed to get myself banished."

"I'm sorry to hear that," Nelson said.

"I'm not," Mari said. "I spent many hundreds of years stuck in the Queendom waiting for my mother to trade me to someone for something she wanted. Now, I'm on my own. I have a good man. He had plenty of money, so I have lots of clothes and shoes and . . . I'm learning a trade. I have real friends. It's pretty great, really. I'm happier than I've been in all of my long life."

Nodding, Nelson stifled a yawn.

"Go on," Mari said. "When you wake, I'll make you some breakfast."

Nodding to Mari, he went into his bedroom. Taking off his clothing, he realized that he still smelled like sex. He took a shower. More than a little intimidated by the fairies, he got in bed, if only to hide. He fell into a deep sleep.

~~~~~~~~

Monday early morning — 5:00 a.m.
Denver, Colorado

When Nelson's alarm went off at 4:10 am, he groaned and turned it off. He woke up at five and got dressed in his workout gear. He came out of his bedroom and went to the kitchen to make coffee.

Mari was leaning against the kitchen bar. She held out a cup of coffee. He took a sip and then looked at her.

"Perfect," Nelson said. "How did you . . .?"

"Hedone," Mari said.

"Hedone has been here?" Nelson asked.

"Of course," Mari said. "She wanted to make sure you were safe."

Nelson blinked at Mari for a moment before grinning.

"So it's going to work?" Nelson asked.

Mari just smiled at Nelson.

"What?" Nelson asked.

"Dear boy," Mari said. "You are simply such a sweet human. That's all."

"Why?" Nelson asked with a scowl.

"You care about this family so very much," Mari said. "It's sweet."

Mari opened her mouth to say something else.

"Whatever," Nelson said. "I'm going to work out."

"I shall go with you," Mari said.

She pointed a finger at herself, and she was wearing workout gear. Her hair was pulled back into a simple ponytail, and she was wearing workout shoes. He was slightly surprised that she was small, not more than five feet.

"I can make myself taller," Mari said, reading his mind. "Fin does that. He didn't like that Jacob is taller than he, the Royal *Prince*. So he stretched himself. It's simple magic."

Nelson nodded.

"Sissy says that I need to get used to just being me," Mari said. "She says that I'm really great but I don't know it because my brain is clouded with ridiculous magic."

Mari nodded.

"It's true. My brain is clouded with magic," Mari said. "The more I am myself, the more I like myself. Mostly, I'm short because it's pleasing to the misogynist. You know, I'm the one for sale to the highest bidder."

"Gross," Nelson said.

"But factual," Mari said.

"Was factual," Nelson said.

"Ah, yes," Mari said. She grinned at him. "I am my own woman now."

Nelson smiled at her, and she blessed him with a genuine, non-magic smile.

"Does your boyfriend care?" Nelson asked.

"About my height?" Mari asked. She thought for a moment. "I've never asked him. He's a healer, so my magic isn't that interesting to him. He's much more interested in the fact that I am ruthless, not that I'm short."

"I guess that's good," Nelson said.

Mari laughed, and Nelson smiled. They started toward the stairs to the basement when Mari stopped walking. Nelson had this odd sense that the world around him flickered like an old film movie stuck between the scenes. He spun around to face Mari.

"What has happened?" Nelson asked.

"You could feel that?" Mari asked.

"It felt like the world, I don't know — *stuttered*?" Nelson asked.

Mari gave him a bright and beautiful smile. He pointed at her.

"No," Nelson said. "No trickery."

"Actually." Mari took such a deep breath that her shoulders rose and dropped. "You're right."

"What has happened?" Nelson asked again.

"Your beloved is a badass," Mari said.

"My . . ." Nelson raised an eyebrow. "Blane? A badass?"

Nelson shook his head. Mari nodded.

"I don't think so," Nelson said.

"You want to see?" Mari asked.

"See what?" Nelson asked.

"Blane staked his claim on you and repeled the forces that wanted to destroy everyone else," Mari said.

"What are you talking about?" Nelson asked.

Mari nodded.

"I'd have to see this to believe it," Nelson said with a sniff.

"We can watch," Mari said.

"Why did the world stutter?" Nelson asked.

"We had a delegation here to check that you were well," Mari said. "They left before you could take in that they had been here."

"Who . . . ?" Nelson asked. "What . . . ?"

Mari just smiled at Nelson. He glared at her.

"My father warned me about fairies," Nelson said.

Mari pointed at herself.

"Fairy," Mari said, brightly. "Your father warned you about me?"

Nelson shook his head.

"I'm going to work out," Nelson said.

"Okay," Mari said. "Do you want to watch what happened when we're done?"

"We can watch what happened?" Nelson said.

"Your father didn't warn you about the fairy gift of broadcasting events?" Mari asked.

"I don't know what that means," Nelson said. "But if you can show me this event that included Blane, then I want to see it."

"Okay, then," Mari said. "When are we going to fix my sword?"

"After we work out and have breakfast?" Nelson asked.

"Deal," Mari said.

She held out her hand, and Nelson shook it. She wandered into Nelson's living room and took a seat on his couch.

"We may as well be comfortable," Mari said.

Nelson shuffled to the couch and sat next to her. She pointed at his oversized flat-screen television. The screen flashed on. It was blurry at first, and then the image resolved.

"I put the time in the corner so you can see when it happened," Mari said.

"Thanks," Nelson said.

He leaned back into the couch.

"Oh, my God — that's the hotel!" Nelson said.

Mari shot him a dark look.

"No gods were involved in this," Mari said. "I did it myself!"

"What?" Nelson asked. "Oh. Uh. Sorry?"

"You should be," Mari said with a sniff.

"How am I to know that you were telling the truth? About . . ." Nelson gestured to the screen My father says that fairies lie."

"It's true," Mari said. "Most do. It's not something known in the royal family. Have you known Fin or Edie to lie?"

Nelson thought for a moment before shaking his head.

"Exactly," Mari said.

She pointed to the screen. Nelson squinted at first, and then his mouth dropped open in surprise.

"Oh, my God," Nelson whispered.

~~~

They struck at 4 o'clock on the dot. Moving toward the sleepy motel, the team of fifty men from the modern Templars ran into an unseen barrier. Laughing, the eldest member of the group took a long sword from his scabbard.

As the patriarch and official weapons master of the Templars, he could not be affected by magic.

The sword had the power to deplete godly and fairy influences. One touch should destroy the protective bubble. In their rage, they were prepared to lay waste to the entire hotel even if it meant killing everyone in the building. The team of Templars had not had a good bloodletting in more than a decade. They were ripe with their lust for blood.

As the blade approached the bubble, a man stepped out of the building.

This weapons-master patriarch hesitated. He looked to the leader before turning to squint at the door to the hotel. The leader of the modern Templars was well into his eighties. He and this patriarch of the weapons masters had gone through school together.

At the front door of the hotel, the man slowly pulled on leather work gloves, before tucking his hands into his khaki pants, and walked toward the edge of the bubble. The man had black hair and hazel eyes. He wasn't particularly tall by modern standards, but he had at least two inches on these French Templars. The man seemed fit. His face was pleasant and his expression unworried. He walked up to the other side of the bubble.

This patriarch of the weapons masters of the modern Templars gave this human a devious grin and stuck the blade into the protective bubble.

The man yawned.

In a flash, the man reached out and grabbed the sword. The man rotated and yanked the sword from this patriarch's hand. The sword shot through the protective bubble. While the man looked at the sword, the slice in the protective bubble healed.

"Who are you?" the patriarch of the weapons masters asked.

The man lifted a corner of his mouth in a grin.

~~~~~~~~~

"No!" Nelson yelled at the screen. "Blane!"

Mari cackled a laugh. She paused the scene so that they wouldn't miss anything.

"What did he do?" Nelson asked.

"He took the sword from the man," Mari said, laughing. "Badass Blane."

"But . . ." Nelson started. "He . . ."

"That your grandfather?" Mari asked.

Nelson walked up to the screen to take a better look.

"I . . . well . . ." Nelson said.

"The man standing next to him looks just like you," Mari said.

"I . . ." Nelson said. Shaking his head, he walked back to the couch. "I don't know who they are."

Mari gave him an exaggerated sigh. He blinked. She disappeared and reappeared with Nelson's father, Pierre. Pierre was wearing flannel pajama bottoms and a fleece sweater. He had a crutch under his arm.

Pierre arrived with a kind of thud. He looked at Mari and nodded as if to say, "Nice."

"Father?" Nelson asked. He automatically spoke in French.

Pierre turned to see his son. He held out an arm, and Nelson hugged his father.

"Up bright and early, I see." Pierre responded in French. "He didn't keep the pride from his voice. "Mari said that you needed me?"

"You know each other?" Nelson asked.

His voice reflected his surprise that Pierre was familiar with any fairy, since Pierre hated fairies.

"First time making her acquaintance," Pierre said. "I was having coffee with O'Malley. He told me that if Mari said you needed me, then you needed me. Here I am."

Nelson's hand went to his chest. He and his father had been estranged since he ran away at the end of high school. Nelson's eyes welled with tears.

"Now, none of that," Pierre said, patting Nelson on the upper arm. "I thought you were in Arizona with Blane and the kids. But Mari said that you were watching some assault by the Templars? Something about your . . ."

Nelson pointed to the television screen.

"Oh," Pierre said.

Pierre walked to the television screen. It was so similar to what Nelson had done that Mari grinned at the man.

"Uh," Pierre said. He turned to look at Nelson. "Well … Uh …"

Like a drowning man, Pierre looked at Mari.

"Where is this?" Pierre asked.

"That's the hotel in Arizona," Mari said in perfect French. She'd obviously followed the entire conversation. "The one where Blane and his family are staying. Everyone is there, including the Oracle. Abi. My sister's there, too. Do you think they knew that the Oracle was inside? They do know the consequence of killing an Oracle, right?"

"I know the consequence of killing an Oracle," Pierre mumbled.

He turned to look at his son. His mouth moved, but nothing came out.

"Well," Pierre said. "Son …"

He pointed to the screen and looked at Nelson again.

"Uh …" Pierre swallowed hard. "I mean …"

Pierre went completely still. So still that Nelson got up from the couch and went to his father.

"What is it?" Nelson asked.

Pierre gave Nelson a desperate look.

"Remember how I told you that your grandparents were dead?" Pierre asked.

Mari started to laugh. Pierre's eyes flicked to her.

"I think we're long past that, Papa," Nelson said. "You told me things to keep me safe. Some of them were true. Some of them were not true."

"Sounds like good parenting to me,' Mari said.

"Exactly," Nelson said.

Pierre nodded and looked at the screen again. He pointed to the patriarch of the weapons masters of the Templars.

"Meet my father," Pierre said. "Your grandfather."

"And his lover?" Nelson asked pointing to the head of the Templars.

Pierre's head jerked to look at Nelson. For a moment, Pierre just blinked. Nelson nodded.

"These men are lovers," Nelson said. "Look at their body language."

Pierre gawked at Nelson for a long moment. Nelson pointed from one man to the other. Pierre started to laugh.

"Why is that funny?" Nelson asked.

"Because in all of this time — my entire life — I have never thought of it," Pierre said. "Not even once. But . . ."

"Who is he?" Nelson asked. "This lover."

"He is your mother's father," Pierre said.

CHAPTER 541

HUMAN

Sunday night — 12:01 a.m.
Kayenta, Arizona, at the hotel on the Navajo Reservation

"I'll tell you what," Blane said, "why don't you see if you can fall asleep with me here? If you can't sleep, I'll go next door."

"I don't know," Nelson said.

"What are you afraid of?" Blane asked.

He gave Nelson a cocky smile in challenge. Nelson shook his head.

"I sleep alone," Nelson said.

"Let's see," Blane said. "Just close your eyes."

Nelson closed his eyes. In spite of his whole "I sleep alone" thing, he was out in a second. Chuckling to himself, Blane rested against the pillow.

He'd thought all of this would be too weird. And, when he stepped back and thought about his life, it all seemed pretty weird. Yet in the actual day-to-day living of this life, everything was pretty good.

He found himself becoming fond of Nelson. Not love. Not yet. But he could feel it growing inside him. It was a terrifying and wonderful thought. He closed his eyes to rest for a moment.

"They are coming."

The words echoed in his head. Blane sat up. He got out bed, pulled on his clothing, and went into the adjoining room. Heather's body was still lying on the bed. In all of her finery, Hedone was standing next to the bathroom. Abi was sitting in the chair.

"Have fun?" Abi gave Blane a bright smile.

Scowling, Blane gave her a curt nod.

"What's happened?" Blane asked.

"The Templars are on their way," Hedone said. "They plan to kill everyone in this hotel and possibly in this entire town."

"Why?" Blane asked.

"Because they like to kill," Abi said. "It's been a while since they let loose. The hotel is isolated in the middle of a whole lot of nothing. They can kill everyone and be gone before anyone notices."

"They believe that they can leave the country without raising any red flags," Hedone said. "This 'action' will get their teams ready for what they see as the inevitable defending of France."

"'Defending of France'?" Blane asked.

"From the Muslim horde," Abi said.

"What 'Muslim horde'?" Blane asked.

"Refugees," Hedone said.

Blane shook his head in disgust.

"Their understanding of the world is a little archaic," Abi said.

"Obviously," Blane said. "When will they be here?"

"They will attack at four," Abi said.

"What's the news from Olympia?" Blane asked.

"Olympia cannot stand in the way of this event," Hedone said. "Ares refuses to sanction this action, but he cannot block it from happening."

"Just out of curiosity," Blane said, "why?"

"There is an old agreement that Olympia will not interfere in the Templars' business," Abi said. "I cannot get involved, either."

"You mean, *more* involved," Blane said.

"Yes, well, no one said that I couldn't get you ready for this," Abi said, with a smile.

Blane looked at her and blinked.

"You are ready, right?" Abi asked.

"I suppose so," Blane said.

"You need to sleep now," Hedone said. "We'll wake you in time."

Nodding, Blane went into the bathroom. He took a shower. When he came out, Abi was gone.

"When will you come back?" Blane asked.

"When it's over," Hedone said. "I won't leave you powerless in the middle of all of their family mess."

"Thanks," Blane said.

Hedone gave him a soft smile.

"Sleep now," Hedone said.

Nodding, Blane got into the second bed. Hedone touched his forehead. He fell into a deep, restorative sleep.

~~~~~~~~

28 days after Blane's bone-marrow transplant
1:23 a.m.
St. Joseph's Hospital, Denver, Colorado

"Hey," Abi said as she entered the visiting chamber attached to Blane's hospital room.

Blane was lying on his hospital bed reading a novel. He looked up when she came in.

"What do you want?" Blane asked.

"Now, now," Abi said. "Where *are* your manners?"

"You forget that I know you," Blane said.

Abi laughed. She sat down in a chair near the glass. He watched her sit and went back to his book. He hoped that if he ignored her, she would go away. After a few minutes, he lowered the book to look.

She was still sitting there.

"Why are you here?" Blane asked.

"Can't a girl come to visit a friend?" Abi asked.

"'Girl'?" Blane asked.

Abi laughed.

Scowling, Blane went back to his book.

"You know, I could take this darkness from your mental field," Abi said. "Heal your heart and mind."

He dropped the book and stared at the ceiling. She waited.

"I don't want it gone," Blane said finally. "I don't ever want to forget what can happen if you are a fool."

"Never forgive yourself?" Abi asked.

"Never let my guard down again," Blane said.

"But you love Hedone completely," Abi said, mildly.

"Heather is different," Blane said. "Safer. Our love for each other . . . It will never end. We have children, and . . . I don't need to remember that she can gut me at will."

"Why is that?" Abi asked.

"She won't do it," Blane said.

Abi was silent for a moment.

"You know that's a fact," Blane said.

"Yes," Abi said. "You are correct. You and your bitterness are safe with Hedone. Her love is not human, so it does not waver, manipulate, or be used to bludgeon. This Enrique? He is so important that you should carry his darkness for the rest of your short life?"

Sighing, he set down his book and went to the glass.

"How can I be of service to you, First Woman?" Blane asked.

"I actually came to be of service to you," Abi said.

Blane didn't respond at first. After a moment, he squinted.

"How did you know that I would be awake?" Blane asked.

"Hedone," Abi said. "She said that you have trouble sleeping through the night. I figured that since you were awake, you may as well do something."

"What did you have in mind?" Blane asked.

"Well . . ." Abi said.

She gave him a sly smile.

"Just spit it out," Blane said.

"Your body has recently been infused with . . . mmm . . . I guess the easiest way to say it . . ."

"Yes — go for easy, not complete," Blane said. "The boy is a moron."

As if she were reassessing him, Abi squinted at him.

"I feel you are saying something that I am not understanding," Abi said.

"Sorry, I just really hate being here," Blane said. "I'm grateful for the miraculous nature of this healing, but I have a newborn, a wife, and a family that could really use me. I feel useless here. Frustrated."

Abi nodded.

"I would, as well," Abi said. "I understand."

"Would you like to play poker?" Blane asked. He pointed to the cards. "Chess?"

"I had a better idea," Abi said.

"Okay," Blane said.

"You have had the building blocks of humanity introduced into your system," Abi said. "This material . . ."

"Stem cells?" Blane asked.

Realizing that she might have something interesting to say, he sat down in the chair on the other side of the glass.

"Yes, that is what they are named," Abi said. "They are like tiny pieces of, for lack of a better understanding, me."

"I'd never thought of it like that," Blane said. "But that makes sense."

"I thought that together — you and I — we could harness the potential power of this gift," Abi said.

"Why?" Blane asked.

"That is a good question," Abi said. "However, I don't think there is an answer to 'why.'"

Blane nodded.

"You see, for most of human life, humans have struggled for basic survival," Abi said. "Even a few decades ago, food was questionable. Shelter was only for the very rich. Now, most people have food and shelter and . . ."

Abi shrugged.

"You are well fed," Abi said. "Your basic needs are taken care of. You're an adult — a fit adult, I might add. You have a family that loves you. You have work you enjoy. Your life is stable in a safe city in the middle of the country."

"And now I have the building blocks of humanity," Blane said. "What does that mean?"

"I have no idea," Abi said.

Blane gave her a long look.

"Okay," Abi said. "I have *some* idea."

"Go on," Blane said.

"I am made of the components which made the world," Abi said. "You are as well. It's just that I am . . . purer, I guess, so would be the world. More elemental."

"Loki told Heather that you were dropped here," Blane said.

"Loki is full of shit," Abi said.

Blane laughed.

"That is the proper expression, isn't it?" Abi asked.

Blane nodded.

"I am made of this place," Abi said. "Gilfand, as well. One male. One female. Forged out of the very dirt and air at the moment of creation. Life."

Abi nodded.

"More like caretakers," Abi said.

"Guardians," Blane said.

"Yes," Abi said. "We are guardians."

"Librarians?" Blane asked. "Of the creatures who live here."

"That, too," Abi laughed.

"What do you want to do?" Blane asked.

"I want to see if this new 'stuff of life' can give you, a normal human adult, more of the earth's power," Abi said. "Can we train it into you? By all measure, you are an adult. And yet there is this part of you that is from the very beginning of human life. What if we use your developed brain and body to capture the raw human power and . . . Well, honestly, I don't know."

"Aren't you doing that with Katy?" Blane asked.

"Not that you know of," Abi said.

Blane grinned, and Abi laughed at his grin.

"What kind of powers can I have?" Blane asked. "I mean, I thought I might just move things around, like Jacob does. That seems pretty cool."

"Oh," Abi said. "Not really, and certainly it is not a power you'd want to get as an adult. Have you seen Jill's twins? Their ability to use their skill is just forming. If you became psychokinetic — Jacob said that was the term for it . . ."

Blane nodded.

"There is a reason it begins in children," Abi said. "It takes a lot of years of practice to be able to use the power with any skill. It would take the rest of your life to gain real acumen. Psychokinesis *is* powerful, but surely you must know that pales to the magnificent power of this earth."

Abi grinned at him. When she smiled, Blane realized that he really liked Abi. He liked how hard she worked and how much she gave to those around her without being a martyr. He gave her a fond look and then scowled.

"What is it?" Abi asked.

"Will it hurt?" Blane asked.

"Why do you ask?" Abi asked.

"Hurting is generally bad," Blane said. "To modern humans, that is."

"Oh?" Abi asked. "Hmm . . ."

She was silent so long that Blane realized she was joking. He grinned.

"Pain?" Blane asked.

"I don't know," Abi said. "I can say that I doubt it, but that would be just a guess. I am not human, so I don't know human frailties. I will say that it's something we will do together. It's not something I can do *to* you."

Blane nodded that he understood.

"Let me say that I would never do something that would cause you distress or harm," Abi said. "Not in the least."

"Because you don't do that to humans?" Blane asked.

"Because Hedone would be very angry with me," Abi said. "It's probably hard to imagine, but she and I are good friends. It's hard to find a real friend who has been around as long as we have. Most of them are psychopaths or hermits."

Blane nodded. They looked at each other for a long moment.

"I am at your command," Blane said, finally making a decision.

"Good," Abi said. "I spoke with Hedone. She said she could easily spare you a few hours a day. Are you well enough to start now?"

"Why not?" Blane asked. "What could happen?"

Abi gave him a beautiful smile, and Blane laughed.

~~~~~~~~~

Monday early morning — 3:30 a.m.
Kayenta, Arizona, at the hotel on the Navajo Reservation

Hedone touched Blane's shoulder.

"It's time," Hedone said, softly.

Blane got out of bed and went to the bathroom.

"I do *not* feel ready," Blane said when he came out of the bathroom.

She kissed his cheek. He started to dress.

"You can do this," Hedone said.

"There's so much on the line," Blane said.

"Of course," Hedone said.

"Is Jake awake?" Blane asked.

"He will be waiting for you in the lobby," Hedone said. "Aden, too. Even Sam. Of course, Delphie. Edie. My grandfather and I will be there."

"Abi?" Blane asked.

"Of course," Hedone said. "Gilfand, too."

"Quite a crowd," Blane said.

"This is your fight," Hedone said. "They cannot intervene unless the Templars get past you."

"I'm more than a little intimidated," Blane said.

"Don't be," Hedone said. "You should know that Abi is well known for breaking her promises."

"Good to know," Blane said. "What will happen to her if she breaks her promise?"

"This is her world," Hedone said. "She can do what she likes. She has a particular distaste for injustice. "

"This is her world, and we're just living in it?" Blane asked.

"Exactly," Hedone said.

They heard Nelson call Blane's name. He opened his mouth to respond, but Hedone shook her head.

"Where will he go?" Blane asked.

"Edie will take him home," Hedone said. "He is safe there."

Blane nodded.

"It's nice that you're allowing yourself to care," Hedone said.

Blane looked at her for a long moment and nodded.

"Surprises me," Blane said.

"Not me," Hedone said.

"He is such a sweet man," Blane said.

"Sexy, brilliant, kind, honest," Hedone said. She looked at him and asked what she wouldn't when she was Heather. "And in bed?"

"Good," Blane said. "We are compatible in all kinds of ways. And he .. . Well, he seems to think I am ... adequate, as well."

"Surely more than adequate," Hedone teased.

"Hmm," Blane said with a scowl.

Hedone nudged him, and he grinned. He finished dressing in silence.

"How?" Blane asked.

"How what?" Hedone asked.

"How did they find him?" Blane asked.

"Those girls? The mean girls that Candy's daughter Kimber is upset about?" Hedone asked. "The ones that Noelle is steering clear of?"

Blane grunted.

"They posted his photo on Instagram," Hedone said. "The Templars were on a plane within the hour."

"With their swords? Gear?" Blane asked.

"Packed away in luggage," Hedone said. "Told customs that they were a Templar reenactment group on tour here. I guess they even have badges."

"Well, if they have *badges*," Blane grunted.

"Exactly," Hedone said. "You should know that they have had this planned for a long, long time. It would have happened at some point. They feel like God led them to the photo and to this resolution of their problems."

"Which is what?" Blane asked.

"They want control over Nelson so that they can get at this famous Templar fortune," Hedone said.

"So Nelson *is* the fortune that will lead them to a fortune," Blane said. "Just moronic."

Hedone nodded.

"And Nelson?" Blane asked.

"He's not here anymore," Hedone said. "They will not get their prize tonight."

Blane looked at the clock by the bed.

"Time to go," Blane said.

"I love you, Blane," Hedone said.

"I love you, too, Hedone and Heather," Blane said.

They kissed and held each other close.

"Now, go fight some Templars," Hedone said.

Blane went through the door to their room. He didn't go very far before he picked up Aden and Jacob. Neither man said anything. They just started walking by his side. Dressed in her warrior wear, Abi joined them when they turned the corner. Decked out in armor, Gilfand walked behind them. When they reached the lobby, Blane stopped walking.

The lobby was full of people.

Sam came up and shook Blane's hand. Delphie grinned at him from a seat at the couch. He heard a whistle and turned to see Alex Hargreaves, her husband, John Drayson, and her brother, Colin, walking down the hallway.

Alex pointed at him with her microbow.

"Before you ask," she said. "We're human."

"I'm human," Sandy said as she jumped to her feet. "I'm not going to let those bastards kill my family and friends."

"Fuck that," Tanesha said, at her side.

"I thought . . ." Blane started.

"*My* grandfather hasn't made any contracts with Templars," Tanesha said with a sniff.

"The archangels don't ever make covenants with humans," Abi said in a low voice. "They find the practice to be ridiculous."

"Dare I ask why?" Jacob asked.

"'We made no covenants with the beasts or the dinosaurs,'" Abi said, mimicking someone's voice. "Why would we make them with these creatures?"

Aden snorted a laugh. Blane grinned.

"Plus, Heather can't be here," Jill said. With a flick of her wrist, she opened a retractable telescopic baton. "We're here to stand in her place."

"You are not human," Blane said.

"If those bastards think they will come for our families . . ." Mike's voice came from down the hallway. Valerie was by his side. "They have another think coming."

He nodded to Sam and said, "Sorry, we're late. We had to get the kids to Charlie."

Perses appeared next to Mike.

"I am a Titan," Perses said. "Their mother is human. We are not of Olympus. We have made no agreement with these. . . creatures."

Overwhelmed, Blane could only nod. Valerie put her hand on Blane's arm.

"Abi says it has to be you," Valerie said. "We're here to support you."

"And to kick ass," Alex Hargreaves said.

Valerie kissed Blane's cheek and went to stand next to Jill. Blane looked from face to face.

"What is your plan?" Alex asked when he got to her.

"I was just going to go out there," Blane said. "I . . . well . . ."

"Here's what we know," Alex said. "There are fifty men coming toward the hotel. They are armed with archaic weapons. It seems that a few have picked up some form of gun, but they have limited ammunition. It's also likely that they are inexperienced with their weapons."

"How do you have this intel?" Blane asked.

Abi looked at Alex and nodded.

"Ganny's on horseback with twenty ex-military guys," Alex said. "They've been tracking this party since it came onto the reservation. The reservation police are on their way."

Blane nodded.

"Abi tells me that you can do this," Alex said. "We are also here to support you. Be assured. We will not let them hurt you or anyone at this hotel."

Blane's eyes flicked to Alex's husband, John. His eyes gleamed with an eerie glow. John gave Blane an assuring nod.

"Thanks," Blane said.

He looked out the window and saw the men approach.

"Looks like they are here," Blane said.

He nodded to his friends and family. With a snap of his fingers, he created a force field around the hotel.

"Show time," he said to himself and stepped out the door.

CHAPTER 542

WHO IS TO BLAME?

Monday early morning — 4:00 a.m.
Kayenta, Arizona, at the hotel on the Navajo Reservation

Blane stepped out of the hotel. From where he stood, he could see men wearing archaic armor lined up along the force field he had created.

They were intimidating in some deep, ancestral way. Their costumes, and even their beards, were innately familiar. They were the "good guys" in every movie and book. They are the Templars. As a Catholic, he had heard his fair share of stories about their power and brilliance. Even the red cross on the men's chests stirred something inexpressible inside Blane.

They believed that they were doing the Lord's work.

He wasn't a lapsed-enough Catholic not to have that mean something to him.

Abi always said that his best defense was his averageness. No one was going to suspect that he was something to be reckoned with.

Remembering her words, he yawned as if he were bored.

He pulled on the leather gloves, stuck in his hands in his pockets, and walked forward.

He stood there for what seemed like forever.

An elderly man in front of him shared the same look as Pierre Semaines, Nelson's father. He was about the same height and build. His face bore the deep wrinkles, almost scars, of a life of self-righteousness. And still, the man was familiar enough to make Blane smile.

Another man stepped up to the one with the sword. This man, clearly the leader, looked so much like Nelson that he could have been Nelson's twin. Although Nelson was taller and bigger than this man, they had nearly identical faces and similar intelligent eyes. This man moved close to the other in a way that indicated, at least to Blane, that they were lovers.

The man who looked like Pierre Semaines stuck a sword through the force field.

Blane grabbed the blade of the sword and yanked. The sword easily came out of the elderly man's hand. The force field healed.

Blane looked at the sword for a moment. He set the point of the blade on the ground and twirled it by the handle.

The Templars were screaming and pounding on the force field.

Behind Blane, he heard a kind of scrambling. Wearing jeans and a T-shirt, Tres Sierra ran to his side. Tres swung a baseball bat into his other hand in threat to the Templars. Blane gave Tres a questioning look.

"I couldn't let you face them alone," Tres said. "Came out my window."

Blane grinned at Tres before turning back to the Templars.

"We can take them," Tres said.

Blane shot him a look.

"We want the traitor," said the man who looked like Pierre Semaines. "Bring him to us, and we will leave!"

"Who are they talking about?" Tres asked.

"Nelson," Blane said, in a low tone. "He is their prize."

"Fuck you!" Tres said and pointed the end of the bat at the men. "You cannot have him."

Raising his eyebrows, Blane turned to look at Tres.

"Well, they can't," Tres said.

Blane grinned. Hearing the door to the hotel open, Blane turned to see the people, his family, moving out of the hotel.

The Templars pounded on the shield.

His family behind him waited for him to do something.

"What are you going to do?" Tres asked.

Blane looked at him again.

"No pressure, man," Tres said, with a laugh.

Blane took a step forward. Holding the sword by the handle, he pointed the sword at the man he'd taken the sword from.

"This is a day of reckoning," Blane said. "Behind me stand humans able and willing to fight you hand to hand."

Blane pointed to the people behind him.

The head of the Templars pointed behind Blane at Hedone and Ares.

"They cannot be involved," the head of the Templars said.

"No, but I can." Perses appeared right behind the heads of the Templars.

Perses swung his sword, indicating that it would be nothing to take their heads. The elderly men stepped away from the Titan and ran into the protective shield.

Blane took a step forward.

"On your command." Perses winked at Blane from the other side of the protective shield.

"There is also an army, a human army, less than a mile from here," Blane said. "They come to protect their people. They come to stand up to the invaders — you."

"You can't have him!" Tres said.

Blane looked at Tres.

"Sorry, man," Tres said. "It just came out of me."

Blane gave him a nod before turning back. He pointed the sword at the Templars again.

"You have a choice," Blane said. "Attack us and die. As sure as I'm standing here, you will die here."

"He lies!" the head of the Templars said.

The Templars roared with life.

"The old ways have faded like leaves on a very old tree," Blane said. "You can set down your weapons and join us. Bring your God given mission into the present and future. Or cling to archaic ideas of your own superiority and watch it fall away before your eyes."

"We want only the boy," the head of the Templars said.

"At the cost of everyone here," Blane said. "That is indefensible. You will not get him."

Rage coursed through Blane, and he felt a sense of power rise inside him.

"You killed his mother," Blane said. He pointed the sword at the head of the Templars. "You tried to kill his father and him! They barely survived!"

Blane gasped a few breaths to keep his rage in check.

"You've lost the right to him," Blane said. He stuck the sword into the ground. "We lay claim to him."

"Yay!" Tres said. "He's ours!"

Tres mimicked Blane's actions with the baseball bat. The baseball bat fell over. Tres picked it up and leaned it against the sword. Blane looked down to keep from laughing.

"You have a choice — come at us, and you will die," Blane said. "Set down your weapons, come inside. We will greet you like the family that you are. We'll give you a little time to make this decision. Don't wait too long, or the Navajo warriors will be upon you soon enough."

Blane turned around and started walking back to the hotel. Tres jogged to catch up. They went through the door, and the rest of the group shuffled inside.

Delphie hugged Blane and kissed his cheek.

"What happens now?" Tres asked.

"Now, we wait," Abi said.

"And hope that they make the right choice," Hedone said.

"You sure I can't just kill them and be done with it?" Perses asked. "Easier."

"*Dad!*" Candy said with a shake of her head. "*No!*"

Everyone laughed.

~~~~~~~~

Monday early morning — 4:00 a.m.
Kayenta, Arizona, at the hotel on the Navajo Reservation

There was a knock at the door of Tink and Charlie's room. Charlie was holding Wyn so Tink got up to answer it.

She opened the door a crack.

A woman, about Tink's size, was standing outside the room. The woman was wearing a blue, green, and aqua cape made out of what looked like parrot feathers. The cape covered a gown that rivaled any Tink had ever seen.

"Hello?" Tink asked.

"My father asked me to come to help protect you," the woman said.

"Who are you?" Tink asked.

The woman looked at Tink and blinked.

"You smell of Olympia," the woman said.

"So?" Tink asked.

She started to close the door, and the woman stopped her.

"I apologize," the woman said. "I was taken off guard by . . ."

"What?" Tink asked.

"We could be twins," the woman said.

"I'm human," Tink said. "You're something . . . I'm not sure. You feel like Perses, but you don't look like Mike or Jill or . . ."

The door wrenched open, and Edie stepped out. Still wearing her armor, she stepped through the door to assess the threat. Edie took one look at the woman and dropped to a knee. She grabbed Tink's hand, but Tink shook her off.

The woman grinned at Tink.

"Hecate," Edie said. "To what do we owe this honor?"

"My father asked me to help watch over the children," Hecate said. "He has had many dealings with these Templars. They are not the most straight-forward of folk. The fairies have an accord not get to, involved as does Olympia. There is no such agreement with Titans. He thought the children could use some serious fire-power. Plus . . ."

Hecate shrugged.

"I heard Hedone was here," Hecate said.

"She's my mom," Tink said.

Hecate squinted at the girl.

"Not by birth," Hecate said.

"Well, duh," Tink said.

"She is my best friend," Hecate said. "Father said my siblings are here as well. I have met them only once when they were infants."

"Your father is . . ." Tink said, in an irritated voice.

"Lord Perses," Edie said.

"You're Jill's sister?" Tink asked. "Candy? Mike?"

"Different mothers," Hecate nodded. "Oh, do get up, Edith. We need to talk about the fairy Queendoms."

"As you wish," Edie said and stood.

"She can't go in there wearing that!" Tink said.

Hecate grinned at the girl.

"If you're a friend of my mom's, then I need to help you the best I can," Tink said. "Can you change what you wear?"

"It's not a Titan gift," Hecate said. "We cannot make something out of nothing."

"Edie?" Tink asked.

"What would you like her to wear?" Edie asked.

"Just give her something of mine," Tink said. "You know, jeans, shirt, bra . . . maybe add that blue and green to her hair?"

Hecate transformed into an outfit similar to Tink's. There was a swipe of blue and green running through one side of the Titan's dark' curly hair. Tink gawked at Hecate. She looked enough like Tink to be her mother. Hecate grinned at the girl.

"We need to get out of the hallway," Edie said.

Tink shifted back.

Had Heather known that Tink looked like her friend? Is that why they'd adopted her? What would Mack say? Was this woman her real mother?

It had never occurred to her that the woman who'd raised her had not given birth to her. She tried to remember if her mother had been pregnant with Chet. She shook her head to bring herself back to the present.

Hecate moved into the room. She checked the window and the door before sitting down in a chair Edie had cleared of sleeping babies. Hecate took the babies into her lap.

Tink couldn't take her eyes off this Hecate. She was about to say something when Mack came up to her. She picked up the boy. Finding a place near where Noelle was lying on the bed, she sat down with Mack.

They waited.

~~~~~~~~
Monday early morning — 4:17 a.m.
Denver, Colorado

"This was just a bit ago," Pierre said in French. He pointed to the time in the corner of the video. "Can we see what's going on now?"

Pierre and Nelson looked at Mari. She gave them an impassive look.

"If you can do this, then you can do . . .?" Pierre reasoned.

"It's not a question of whether I *can* do it," Mari replied in French.

"Then what is it?" Nelson asked.

"I have a feeling that . . ." Mari looked from Pierre to Nelson. "This will not end well."

"You mean if we watch, we may see the death of these Templars?" Nelson asked.

"The death of your family," Mari said in a soft, kind voice. She nodded. "That feels like it will come to pass."

"Because you have seen it?" Nelson asked.

"That is not a fairy skill," Mari said.

"Because you've walked time?" Nelson asked.

"That is also not a fairy skill," Mari said, irritably.

"Then why?" Nelson asked.

"If you live by the sword, you will die by the sword," Pierre said.

Mari nodded.

"I believe the same thing," Pierre said.

Mari watched him for a moment.

"That's awfully hard for . . ." Mari said.

"They killed my wife," Pierre said. "Nearly killed me and my son. They've been chasing us all of our lives. I . . ."

Mari jumped up and walked to the screen.

"You will let me know when you've had enough," Mari said. "You may have prepared for this Pierre, but Nelson . . ."

"I was an ER doctor," Nelson said. "I have seen every form of violence one human can do upon another."

Mari gave a slight shrug. She snapped her fingers, and the screen changed.

"When you've had enough, just say so," Mari said.

The door to the hotel was closing. Everyone had gone inside. The Templars stood at the barrier. Pierre and Nelson stared at the television. Slowly, they backed up until they were sitting on the couch. Mari sat down between them.

The scene began to unfold.

~~~~~~~~

"To me!" the head of the Templars yelled. "Come to me!"

The men surrounding the hotel ran as fast as their heavy, antiquated armor would allow. The younger men jogged easily to the head of the Templars, while it took the older members a few minutes.

"What say you?" the head of the Templars asked.

"Fight to the death!" Pierre's father yelled.

His words were met with a roar of approval, especially from the younger members of their party.

"We must . . ." the head of the Templars started. At the sound of a police siren, he yelled, "Retreat! Retreat!"

The fifty members of the Templars ran away from the hotel. They passed two or three buildings before turning into the vacant garage where they had gotten dressed.

"We will fight another day!" the head of the Templars said as he opened the door.

The door swung open, and the first of the Templars ran inside. They were just inside when Gando Peaches arrived with his team of ex-military on horseback. One of his men flagged down the Bureau of Land Management police cruiser and the two cars from the Navajo Nation Police. The police were just getting out of their vehicles when four FBI vehicles came squealing into the parking lot around the garage.

The police closed off the road. Gando and his team guarded the door until they were replaced by police officers. Gando and his team dismounted from their horses and led the animals away from danger. Once the horses were secured, they returned to join the police on their line.

"You inside!" the FBI yelled on a bullhorn. "You are surrounded! Come out with your hands up!"

There was no response from inside. The police settled in for what was likely to be a long morning.

~~~~~~~~~

"What's going on in there?" Pierre asked.

Mari looked at him. Her large eyes opened and closed in some imitation of a blink.

"Do you know?" Pierre asked. "Can you show me?"

"You are sure?" Mari asked.

Pierre nodded. She looked at Nelson, and he nodded.

The scene on the screen changed. They were inside a darkened room. There was an odd sound, almost a ticking, but . . .

"They're dead," Nelson said.

Pierre looked at him.

"That's the sound blood makes when it hits concrete," Nelson said.

The men looked at Mari.

"How?" Nelson asked.

"I do not know," Mari said. "That sounds like a lie, but it is not."

"Show me," Pierre commanded. "I want to see this room."

Sighing, Mari snapped her fingers. The lights turned on inside the garage.

The men visibly recoiled from the sight.

~~~~~~~~~

Monday early morning — 4:47 a.m.
Kayenta, Arizona, at the hotel on the Navajo Reservation

While Blane encouraged them to head back to bed, these friends and family refused to leave. They were there for the duration. Jeraine took over the hotel's breakfast kitchen. Using basic ingredients, they were soon eating a variety of yummy things. Soon, they were quietly talking, laughing. Alex Hargreaves took over the coffee making. Soon, the hotel ground coffee transformed into something wonderful. They drank cup after cup of coffee and ate in this quiet communion.

Blane was getting ready to check on the Templars when a cell phone rang. He looked over to see Alex Hargreaves answer her phone. The room fell silent.

"Ganny?" Alex said.

She listened for a long moment. Her only expression of emotion was the blinking of her eyes.

"Wow," Alex said. She looked at Blane. "I'll tell him. Tell them we're all hanging out in the lobby."

Gando Peaches must have said something funny because she laughed.

"Of course," Alex said. "Come on over. There's plenty."

She realized everyone was watching her when she hung up her phone. She flushed at the attention and then gestured to Blane.

"We're all in this," Sandy said. "You need to tell us what you know."

Alex gave Sandy a long look. Her husband put his hand on her leg. She looked at him, and he gave her a soft, loving smile. She looked back at Sandy.

"Okay," Alex said. "You're right. It's just . . . Uh . . ."

Her eyes flicked around the room, touching everyone in attendance.

"Well . . ." Alex said. "It's . . .how do you say it now? Not safe for work?"

"Sensitive material," John, her husband, said.

"What is it?" Blane asked.

"Okay, if you're sensitive, you should leave now," Alex said.

When no one moved, Alex squinted and tipped her head in disbelief.

"We killed the St. Jude murderer," Tanesha said.

"We've seen some grisly shit," Jacob said.

"Okay," Alex said with a nod. "Ganny and his men were about a mile from here when they heard police sirens. They picked up their pace. They were near enough to see the Templars jogging down the street toward an old, abandoned garage."

"The one at the end of the street?" Blane asked.

"I guess so," Alex said with a shrug. "Ganny said that they figured they had to change out of their gear. So he and his guys chased them to the garage. No sooner than they'd surrounded the building and the Navajo Nation police, the BLM police, and the FBI showed up."

"All three are responsible for crime on the reservation," Blane said with a nod.

"He said they waited for . . . well, all this time," Alex said. "Half hour or so. The FBI used their bullhorn, to try to raise them but . . ."

"What happened?" Blane asked.

"They forced the door open and went into the garage," Alex said with a shake of her head. "Everyone inside was dead. Ganny said 'cut down,' as if they'd been attacked with swords, possibly the swords they were carrying."

She looked around the room from horrified face to horrified face.

"Here's the thing — they didn't see anyone go in and no one came out," Alex said. She looked at Perses, and he shook his head. "They have no idea who or what could have done this thing or if they attacked each other."

Alex nodded.

"It happened while the police and Ganny were standing outside," Alex said.

A kind of shocked hush came over the crowd. No one knew what to say. After a moment, Alex sat down.

"Now what?" Blane asked Hedone in a low tone.

She shook her head. She had no idea.

Denver Cereal continues...

Aaron Alvin:
Father of Ava; also called "The spider" by Yvonne Smith.

Abi the Fairy:
General in Fairy Corps; great-grandmother of Tanesha; Fin's partner; First mother

Aden Norsen:
CEO at Lipson construction; single father of Nash and Noelle; husband of Sandy.

Alma Fontaine:
Mother of Heather Lipson; Psyche.

Alexandra Hargreaves:
Identical twin to Max Hargreaves; 'The Fey;' the leader of the Fey Team; wife of Dr. John Drayson; sister to Colin and Samantha Hargreaves.

Anjelika:
Megan, Mike, Steve, Candy and Jill's mother; grandmother to Katy; wife of Perses.

Andrea Menendez or Andy Mendy:
Mother of Sandy; Seth's love & lover from the time he was 14 until he lost her when he was 30.

Annette:
Reality television star; mother to Jabari; Jeraine Wilson's ex.

Arthur "Raz" Rasmussen:
Member of the Fey team; boyfriend of Samantha Hargreaves.

Ava — Amelie Vivian Alvin:
Denver Police Crime Lab Technician; fiancé of Seth O'Malley; daughter of Aaron Alvin.

Ben Red Bear, Detective:
Denver Police Detective in charge of investigation of rapes; possibly involved in the distribution chain.

Bestat Behur:
Partner to Zack Jakkman; stepmother to Teddy; dragon.

Beth Baker:
Ava's best friend; Child Psychologist; murdered by Saint Jude.

Blane Lipson:
Jacob's 'cousin;' assistant to Jacob Marlowe at Lipson Construction; Chinese Medicine doctor; husband of Heather; father of Mack; getting bone marrow transplant for HIV infection.

Bob aka 'Blood spatter Bob': Former expert forensics instructor with the FBI; currently a laboratory technician in Ava's Denver Police Department lab.

Bumpy Wilson:
Good friend of Seth's; medical doctor; father of Jeraine Wilson, husband of Dionne, born Leroy Wilson.

Candace or Candy Roper:
Daughter of Anjelika; sister to Jill.

Charlie Delgado:
Stepbrother of Sandy; street kid; drug addict; moved in with Sandy in *Cimarron*.

Chesterfield or Mr. Chesterfield:
Rodney Smith's large black dog, which he was given in prison from the Puppies for Prisoners program; best friend of Jabari.

Jabari Wilson: Young son of Jeraine Wilson and Annette; biological child of Tanesha Smith and Jeraine Wilson

Jacob Marlowe:
Son of Sam Lipson and Celia Marlowe; husband of Jillian Roper; brother of Valerie Lipson; president of Lipson Construction; owns his own rehabilitation business; carpenter; hockey player, teller of Denver Cereal.

Jeraine Wilson:
R&B sensation; husband of Tanesha Smith; son of Bumpy; drug and sex addict.

Jeraine Wilson, Junior: Young son of Jeraine Wilson.

Jillian or Jill Roper:
Daughter of Anjelika and Perses; mother of Katy Roper; wife of Jacob Marlowe; ex-wife of Trevor Mc Guinsey; pregnant with twin boys.

John Drayson, MD:
Vascular surgeons; husband of Alex Hargreaves.

Julie Hargreaves:
Mother of Paddie Hargreaves; wife of Colin Hargreaves.

"Ivy" Anna Marie McDonald:
Street child; friend of Tink and Charlie's; youngest assaulted in rape case with worst injuries; Delphie's niece.

Katy or Katherine Anjelika Roper Marlowe:
Daughter of Jillian Roper and Jacob Marlowe.

Leslie: A laboratory tech in Ava's Denver Police Department lab.

Leslie Roper:
Wife of Steve Roper; mother of infant Elisa Roper.

Levi Johanssen:
Won Delphie in a card game when she was 5-6; held her as a slave/The Oracle Tabor; attempted to kill Delphie; deceased.

Liban:
Queen Fand's twin sister; looks like Cleopatra.

Lizzie O'Malley:
Daughter of Seth O'Malley; Biological mother to Conner Hargreaves. Girlfriend of James Schmidt.

Mack Lipson: Infant son of Heather and Blane Lipson.

Margaret Peaches or Sergeant Margaret Peaches:
Fey team member; partner of Sergeant MJ Scully.

Manannán:
A Celtic sea deity; possibly first ruler of the Isle of Man; husband of Queen Fand, ancestor of Jacob Lipson

Maresol Tafoya:
Seth O'Malley's housekeeper; mother of Bonita's Seth's second wife; friend of Delphie.

Max Hargreaves:
Identical twin to Alex Hargreaves; brother to Colin and Samantha Hargreaves.

Megan Roper:
Daughter of Anjelika and Perses; partner of Tim; mother to Ryan and two other boys.

Mike Roper:
Son of Anjelika and Perses; husband of Valerie Lipson; art mentor to Noelle Norsen; hockey goalie; painter.

Michael Bladen Roper Marlowe:
Infant son of Jill and Jacob Roper-Marlowe; identical twin of Tanner.

Mitch Delgado:
Sandy's stepfather who she called 'Dad'; father of Charlie and Sissy; Seth O'Malley's best friend; died of lung cancer 8 or 9 years ago.

MJ or Sergeant Michael Scully Jr.:
Fey team member; partner of Sergeant Margaret Peaches; husband of Honey Lipson.

Molly:
Bookkeeper for Jacob Marlowe's rehabilitation business; wife of Pete.

Nadia Kerminoff, MD
ER doctor, ex-lover of Ivan, Russian mother, wealthy American father; "dark arrow" soulmate of Nash Norsen.

Nash Norsen:
Son of Aden and Nuala Norsen; brother of Noelle Norsen; "dark arrow" soulmate of Nadia Kerminoff.

Nelson Weeks, MD: A technical analyst in Ava's Denver Police Department lab; ex ER doctor; love interest of Blane Lipson.

Noelle Norsen:
Daughter of Aden and Nuala Norsen; sister of Nash Norsen; artist.

Nuala Norsen:
Ex-wife of Aden Norsen; biological mother of Nash and Noelle Norsen.

Paddie Hargreaves:
Best friend of Katy Roper; nephew of Alex and Max Hargreaves; son of Colin Hargreaves.

Patty Delgado:
Mother of Sissy and Charlie; mother to Sandy; wife of Mitch Delgado.

Pete:
Husband of Molly; father of her children; friend of Aden Norsen.

Perses:
Paid assassin; rescuer, Titan, and biological father of Jillian Roper.

Rodney Smith:
Father of Tanesha; imprisoned for 26 years for a murder he didn't commit; husband of Yvonne Smith; site manager at Lipson Construction.

Ryan:
Oldest son of Megan Roper and Tim.

Sam Lipson:
Husband to Celia Marlowe; married to Tiffanie Lipson; boyfriend of Delphie; father to Valerie and Jacob Marlowe-Lipson; step-father to Brianna, Becky, Honey and the 'step-whore.'

Samantha Hargreaves:
Sister to Alex, Max and Colin Hargreaves; girlfriend of Art Rasmussen; best friend of Valerie Lipson; criminal defense attorney.

Sandy Delgado Norsen:
Best friend of Jillian Roper; one of Jill's group of best friends; wife of Aden Norsen; hairdresser.

Sarah:
Yellow Labrador belonging to Jacob Marlowe.

Seth O'Malley:
Godfather and biological father of Sandy; best friend of Sandy's step father; Denver Police Detective; gifted composer and prodigy pianist

Stepsister or Stepwhore:
Eldest daughter of Tiffanie Lipson; sister to Honey, Briana, and Becky Lipson; step-daughter of Sam Lipson; second wife of Trevor McGuinsey.

Steve or Stephen Roper:
Son of Anjelika; middle child of Roper family; medical nurse to Honey Lipson; husband of Leslie.

Sissy Delgado:
Stepsister of Sandy; anorexic; talented ballet dancer; lives with Sandy and Aden.

Tanesha Smith:
One of Jillian Roper's best friends; wife of Jeraine Wilson; medical student.

Tanner Handy Roper Marlowe:
Infant son of Jill and Jacob Roper Marlowe; identical twin of Michael.

Teddy Jakkman
Son of Fey Team member Captain Zack 'the Jakker' Jakkman; best friend of Nash Norsen; dates Noelle Norsen.

Tink or Tiffanie:
Street kid; friend of Charlie Delgado's; attacked and beaten by gang of rapists, Heather and Blane Lipson's adopted daughter.

Tim:
Partner to Megan Roper; father of Ryan and two other children.

Trevor Mc Guinsey:
Ex-husband of Jillian Roper; assumed father of Katy Roper; fiancé to the step-whore.

Valerie Lipson:
Daughter of Sam and Celia Marlowe; wife to Mike Roper; soap opera and movie actress.

Wanda (Wade) Le Monde:
Met Sissy at Eating Disorder Inpatient Treatment; transgender child; daughter/son of Erik and Edith; girlfriend of Frankie Aziz.

Wes or Wesley Kapanski:
Hollywood producer; Was engaged to Valerie Lipson at the beginning of Denver Cereal.

Yvonne Smith:
Mother of Tanesha Smith; forced into prostitution after her husband was imprisoned.

Zack 'The Jakker' Jakkman
Father of Teddy, Britanie, and Samuel Jakkman; 'The pilot' to Sissy & Charlie; Sandy's childhood pen pal; friend of Sandy's.

THE STORY CONTINUES AT
DENVER CEREAL.COM

FIND US ON FACEBOOK:
FACEBOOK.COM/DENVERCEREAL

**If you like *Denver Cereal*,
please take a moment and leave a review. Your
review helps *Denver Cereal* continue.**

MORE ABOUT CLAUDIA AT:
CLAUDIAHALLCHRISTIAN.COM